BEYOND *the* RED
MOUNTAINS

BEYOND
the
RED
MOUNTAINS

GREG JOHNSON

New York

BEYOND—*the* RED MOUNTAINS

Published in New York, New York, by Morgan James Publishing. Morgan James and The Entrepreneurial Publisher are trademarks of Morgan James, LLC.
www.MorganJamesPublishing.com

The Morgan James Speakers Group can bring authors to your live event. For more information or to book an event visit The Morgan James Speakers Group at
www.TheMorganJamesSpeakersGroup.com.

A **free** eBook edition is available
with the purchase of this print book.

CLEARLY PRINT YOUR NAME ABOVE IN UPPER CASE

Instructions to claim your free eBook edition:
1. Download the BitLit app for Android or iOS
2. Write your name in **UPPER CASE** on the line
3. Use the BitLit app to submit a photo
4. Download your eBook to any device

ISBN 978-1-63047-434-8 paperback
ISBN 978-1-63047-435-5 eBook
Library of Congress Control Number:
2014916511

Cover Design by:
Rachel Lopez
www.r2cdesign.com

Interior Design by:
Bonnie Bushman
bonnie@caboodlegraphics.com

In an effort to support local communities, raise awareness and funds, Morgan James Publishing donates a percentage of all book sales for the life of each book to Habitat for Humanity Peninsula and Greater Williamsbu⁻⁻

Get involved today, visit
www.MorganJamesBuilds.com

Habitat
for Humanity®
Peninsula and
Greater Williamsburg
Building Partner

To Jean,
without whom this book
would not have been possible

Prologue

A cloud of dust exploded from the stack of books as Kelvin set them down with a bit more force than necessary.

Kelvin Drake was a strong young man of average height with brown hair. Within the past year, he had finished his formal education, and it was time for him to learn the trade that would become his career.

Backing away, he coughed as the dust entered his lungs. "I can't take this anymore," he said under his breath. "I can't stay here and work for my father."

Kelvin's father, Carl, presided over the ruling assembly in Triopolis, and Kelvin had been an apprentice under him for the last couple of months.

In the beginning, he was excited and thought he might be able to make a difference working in government, but it turned out his father only gave him meaningless jobs like this one. He was tasked to clean the archives in the basement of Town Hall. Kelvin often wondered if his father really wanted him working there or if he simply felt obligated to employ him because they were family.

Kelvin and his father had a distant relationship. With Carl's successful career in politics, he rarely had time to spend with his son. Even if Carl was home, his time was usually spent in his office addressing the seemingly unending issues of the day.

Kelvin loved and respected his father, and he very much enjoyed the times they spent together, though they were few. He just wished he had more of them.

The sight and sounds of his father hard at work behind the desk in his study were some of the most common memories from his childhood. The door was regularly left cracked open to give the impression of an invitation to enter, but he knew his father had more important things to do than listen to his questions.

Kelvin's mother had died in childbirth, which meant he was raised primarily by their housemaid, Ms. Parkinson. Carl stayed out of her way and let her run the household, which also meant taking care of Kelvin.

The basement was dark and smelled like musty old books. The only window was at the far end of the room. It was near the top of the wall, which was at ground level, on the exterior of the building. The placement of it was why Kelvin began his undertaking on this end of the room.

The small amount of light that penetrated the dirty window, combined with the light from the oil lamp, gave him an acceptable work environment.

Relics of Triopolis's past were stacked in front of shelves filled with books lining all four walls. Over the years, pathways had developed between and around the piles of historical items. Eventually the stacks had grown too high and fallen over, creating mountains in the basement. Everything Kelvin touched was thick with the dust of hundreds of years of storage.

As the day went on, he grew more and more bored, and it was very warm in the confined space. His sweaty body was coated in dust, and he was miserable.

Walking over to the small window, he stood on the wooden bench just beneath it. Looking out, he watched the crowds of people walking by and wondered about the interesting conversations they were having. Everyone's life seemed so much more interesting than his was.

"I bet their jobs aren't as boring as mine is," he muttered.

Most of the people working around Town Hall were involved in the governing of the city. In his younger years, he had often thought, *What could be more interesting than affecting the laws of Triopolis?*

His interest, no doubt, had come from overhearing his father's conversations.

Parents teaching their children history were also intermingled in the crowds of professional men and women. They were easily spotted because of their casual dress and by the way they pointed at the buildings and sculptures of the government center.

Looking at the position of the sun in the sky and feeling the pangs of hunger, Kelvin determined that it must be lunchtime. Jumping down from the bench and sitting on it, he opened the brown canvas sack that held his midday meal.

Bread, beef jerky, and an apple were what he had packed today. He preferred to eat jerky for lunch as opposed to fresher meat. The only other way to preserve it was to cover it in salt, which made it last, but all that salt also made it unbearable to eat.

As he finished eating, he heard footsteps descending the stairs. There was only one person who knew he was in this miserable place. As he suspected, it was his father, who now stood in the entryway.

Carl Drake was a short man, mostly bald, with a wisp of gray hair on his head. In his younger years, he was well built and strong like his son, but the years in government had taken their toll on his physique.

In his youth, he had been an accomplished boxer, winning many bouts, but it had been years since he had seen the inside of a gym.

"How's it going?" he asked, looking around the room at his son's progress.

"Not bad, I suppose. Look at what I have done so far." Kelvin pointed toward the small clean corner to the right of the window.

A nod was all he received from his father. Even though Carl was not a man to show his son appreciation or tell him he did a good job, the ever-optimistic Kelvin always tried to make him proud.

"I have been dusting the shelves all morning," continued Kelvin. "This place is a mess!" The dirt on his clothes was proof.

"No one comes down here very much anymore," commented Carl. "It's sad, really, because this is our history."

Kelvin listened without a word, but he wondered why his father couldn't just have a servant do this menial job.

"Did you have enough to eat?" Carl asked, receiving a positive answer from Kelvin.

"Oh, I almost forgot," said Carl, handing him the cup in his hand. "I brought you some water."

"Thanks, it's getting pretty warm down here," replied Kelvin, taking a big, refreshing drink of the ice-cold water.

Before Carl turned to leave, he reminded Kelvin to arrange and organize the items by date. Carl was always particular about having things in order. Kelvin remembered how angry his father would become when, as a child, he put a book in the wrong place on the bookshelf.

Kelvin nodded in compliance, but he wanted to scream, "Why are you torturing me with this horrible job?"

The awkward exchange was normal between the two. Carl was not a bad person; he just never took the time to develop a relationship with his son.

After his father closed the door behind him, Kelvin wasn't quite ready to get back to work. Standing up, he looked at the clean corner that had taken him all morning to complete. A sense of accomplishment filled his mind as he stared at the bare wood-planked floor.

Something interesting caught his eye. "What is that?" he asked aloud.

He noticed a small object wedged between the wall and the shelf. Slowly inching his way toward it, his eyes grew larger as he tried to get a better look. With the light not completely reaching the corner, it was covered in shadows. He continued his slow advance as if the thing was going to jump out at him.

"What am I doing?" he asked, laughing at himself. Straightening from his crouched position, he finished his walk to the corner in a normal fashion.

Six inches separated the shelf from the wall, and it was clear that the resident spiders ruled this area. The thick cobwebs would have deterred most people, but Kelvin was determined to reach the hidden object.

On his knees, he swiped a path through the web with his hand. "Ugh!" he groaned.

The pieces of silken web clung to him as he tried to shake them off. The spider's adhesive was surprisingly strong, and he had to wipe his hand against the wall to free it from the disgusting, sticky string.

With the obstruction to his sight cleared, the hidden object came into view. It was the corner of a small book wedged between the wall and the wooden shelf support.

Reaching under the web and around the end of the shelf, he grabbed the corner and pulled, but it wouldn't budge. Trying to force it out was not working. He stopped when he noticed the frame of the shelf was digging into the cover, so he backed up to assess the situation.

"I will have to clear the shelf," he concluded.

Kelvin removed everything from the corner of the bottom shelf, and then he was able to dislodge the book.

The dirty leather-bound book looked very old. Interestingly, it had no title. Kelvin thought this was strange because, even though this was only his third day, he had noticed how detailed the librarians of Triopolis had always been. Every book he had seen in the archives was meticulously labeled.

Kelvin could hardly control his excitement as he flipped the cover open. Inscribed on the first page was a note.

It is the fifth year of light, but it still feels dark.

    Luther has gone too far. In case we are wrong, find the tablet, and you will learn the truth.

—Donovan

"Could that be the Donovan who helped found Triopolis?" he murmured.

Chapter 1

Kelvin was torn from his memory of the day he found the old book in the basement of Town Hall by the shouting of his friend, Henry. "I've got one, I've got one! It's big too!"

He was fighting the fish with all his might. First Henry had the advantage, taking in some line, then the fish gained the advantage and he had to let out the same line he had just brought in.

This went on for at least twenty minutes before the fish's head finally broke the surface of the water. Kelvin was waiting with the net, and he scooped it up.

"This thing is a monster!" he exclaimed, and he grunted with effort as he lifted the heavy fish into the boat.

Henry Walker was in his early forties with brown, thinning hair, and had been fishing these waters his whole life. He had learned the trade from his father, James, who had also been a leading producer of fish for the market.

Henry admired his catch lying on the bottom of the boat between the two seats. "I think that is the biggest tuna I have ever caught!" he exclaimed.

"It must weigh two hundred pounds," replied Kelvin. "Olaf's going to love this one."

Olaf owned a fish preparation shop just beyond the pier where they moored the boat. He specialized in whole fresh fish, which he cleaned and made presentable for market.

"Yeah, he will love this one, but it's not enough," said Henry, pessimistically. "We used to bring in ten times as many fish."

Kelvin knew he was right. He just stared out into the water as they headed home, wondering when they would return to the success of previous years.

They had been fishing in their usual spot, about halfway out on the eastern side of the bay. Henry had discovered the inlet early last season when he ventured out past the old stone watchtower.

The watchtower had been constructed hundreds of years ago, and an identical one stood directly across from it on the other side of the bay. No fisherman ever went any farther out into the bay than the watchtowers because it was considered too dangerous to do so.

Kelvin looked up and saw Triopolis, set perfectly in the center of the bay. The Red Mountains lined both sides of the water and extended ten miles inland before joining, making an almost perfect arch around the city. It was said that the gods raised the mountains to protect their people from the beasts that lay on the other side.

Parents scared their children with stories of ten-foot-tall hawks and fifty-foot snakes beyond the mountains that would snatch them from their beds if they disobeyed. Ms. Parkinson even named them Justice and Wrath. Kelvin didn't know if the stories were true, but they sure scared him straight when he was little.

Henry gently placed the boat up against the pier as Kelvin reached for the closest support post. After tying the front mooring line around the nearest dock post, he jumped out onto the wooden planks.

Walking to the back of the boat, he wrapped the rear mooring line around the post near the back of the boat and tied it, securing the boat. Even in the roughest water, two lines were enough to keep the boat fastened to the pier.

Henry's vessel was made of cedar ribbing and a white birch skin, which was the newest technology. He was the first commercial fisherman to use the new lightweight design he and his friend and boat maker, Jacob, had created.

It was first put to sea at the beginning of last season and was a great success. Because of the decreased weight, the boat was easier and faster to maneuver through the water, meaning they could go farther out into the bay than anyone else.

The boat he replaced was no more than a hollowed-out log, which was the style of all the other boats in Triopolis. These simple canoes were made by carving out the center of a log. They were bulky and slow, and because of this, it was very dangerous to stray too far from shore in them.

Many people laughed when Henry's new boat was unveiled. They said it would never float, and if it did, it would sink within an hour. They didn't know about Henry's secret ingredient.

Jacob had been tinkering with the design for years, but he couldn't find a substance that would keep the water from entering the boat where the sections of the bark skin met.

It was Henry who found the answer. He had stumbled upon a resin that seemed to hold very well underwater. It was used by crab men to mend their crab pots. Finding this resin was the final step for Jacob to complete his new boat.

"Maybe we need to go farther out and find new fishing holes," suggested Henry as he lifted their supplies out of the boat and onto the dock.

He had obviously been dwelling on their meager catch all the way in. Kelvin understood the pressure Henry was under because he had overheard his father complaining about the lack of fish in the market.

"Yeah, other than your big one, we didn't catch much," replied Kelvin. "Eric is going to be mad at us again."

Eric Feldstein owned the market where their catch would be sold, so it was very important to keep him supplied. Since he owned the only market in town, he controlled all of the food coming in. That meant the leaders listened to him if he thought there was a problem.

"Ah, I really don't care what Eric thinks!" spat Henry. "That guy is as corrupt as they come. If he keeps lowering his price, there won't be any fisherman left because it will be impossible for us to make a profit!"

Almost a year ago, Eric and Henry crossed each other, and a huge battle erupted between them. Eric was a shrewd businessman who had effectively bankrupted each and every one of his competitors, leaving his as the only place to sell food in town.

Having this much power and control, Eric was unrelenting, lowering what he would pay and forcing the fishermen into accepting lower profits. Henry and his fellow fishermen were outraged. Henry, being the leader and assembly member representing all fishermen, was responsible for going to battle against Eric within the governing assembly.

Both sides argued passionately in front of the Assembly, but it sided with Eric. The decision, which was backed by Kelvin's father, who was also the assembly chief, was that anyone could open a shop and compete with any existing business, but the market would not be manipulated by the Assembly. This meant that the Assembly would not step in and support a failing business.

It was a devastating decision for the other fish merchants in Triopolis because they didn't stand a chance against Eric's market. Within a month, all competition was wiped out.

This angered Henry to the point that he tried opening his own shop. His plan was to sell his own catch, taking out the middleman instead of selling to Eric. Eric treated Henry just like anyone else who dared to compete with him. Henry lost money from the first day and only lasted two months before he was broke.

Eric didn't stop there. Even though every competitor was gone and Henry had no choice but to sell to him, Eric would only buy Henry's fish at a lower price than he paid for everyone else's catch. Specifically, he paid ten percent less for Henry's fish than the fish caught by any other fishermen.

Henry was infuriated by Eric's spitefulness, but there was nothing he could do about it. Eric was the only person who could sell his fish, and his connections within the Assembly were too strong.

Ricky, one of the boys who worked on the docks, arrived with a wheeled cart to bring their catch up to the processing sheds.

"Hey, Ricky," greeted Kelvin.

"Another light catch, huh guys," replied the boy.

Ricky was thirteen years old and had been working here for about three years. He was one of a handful of boys hired to do odd jobs like hauling fish.

Three sheds stood a few hundred feet up a small hill from the docks for processing the fish. The buildings were identical in size, with stone walls and wood-plank roofs. The walls were lined with several windows, all open, to fumigate the intense fish smell.

Henry walked with Ricky to the first shed, which was for whole fish.

"Henry!" called Olaf Brown, the owner of this particular business.

"How ya doing, Olaf?" replied Henry, always happy to see his old friend.

Olaf must have been in his sixties and had been preparing fish for market for almost fifty years. Like many families in Triopolis, multiple generations of Browns had been in this business. In fact, Olaf's great-great-grandfather constructed this building when he first started in the trade.

It was very common for fathers to pass on knowledge to their sons and for the sons to make a living the same way, usually in the same shop.

A large boisterous man, Olaf wore a soiled white shirt that never seemed to cover his ample belly. In his shop, fish were rinsed and made presentable for the market. This is where the highest quality fish from the day's catch were prepared.

"Wow, you have a beautiful tuna here, Henry," Olaf exclaimed excitedly as he flipped it over to look at the other side.

The fishmonger was very animated and passionate when talking about seafood.

"This one will make you more money than the others combined!" He was referring to the four other tuna he had selected from Henry's catch.

"I knew you would like that one, Olaf," replied Henry. "It took me at least an hour just to bring it in! I just wish we could have caught more of them. Our best spots are drying up, it seems."

"I have noticed the decrease in numbers," Olaf sympathized. "With that special boat of yours, you could probably make it past the watchtowers. Hell, you could probably go all the way out of the bay!"

"I can't say that I haven't thought of that with the way the last couple weeks have gone," Henry admitted with a heavy sigh. Turning to Ricky, he asked, "Would you split the rest of these fish between Jules and Bart?"

"Yes sir," replied the boy.

Both Jules and Bart were in the preservation business. Jules was the master of the smokehouse. It was amazing how many different flavors he could add to the fish.

In Bart's shed, fish were dry-salted and preserved in salty brine. In both cases, the fish needed to be rinsed before eating to avoid being overwhelmed by salt.

Henry said goodbye to Olaf and walked back toward the dock to meet up with Kelvin. By this time, Kelvin had cleaned the boat and neatly returned their supplies to the storage closet and locked it.

Each docking location had a six-foot by three-foot storage closet so fishermen didn't have to lug their equipment back and forth from home each day.

"Well, he liked five of your tuna," said Henry.

Kelvin knew he was talking about Olaf since the most money was made from fresh fish.

"That's better than yesterday!" exclaimed Kelvin.

"Yes, but we need more," replied Henry. "Do you want to grab an ale before calling it a day?"

"Sure," answered Kelvin.

Fisherman's Pub was the place Henry liked to relax after a long day on the water. It was close to the docks, and many of his friends and peers hung out there. This was where he often held meetings with the men he spoke on behalf of in the Assembly since most of them were here at the end of the day anyway.

The pub was a dark place, having only one window right next to the door. The building was old and had not been kept up well at all. Stains on the floor and walls and the smell of stale beer in the air reminded visitors of the many years this watering hole had existed.

Candles flickered on each table, but dark corners remained for people who didn't want to be seen.

Henry chose one of those dark corners on this night. He returned many hand waves and greetings from his fellow fishermen on the way to a table near the back. His friends knew not to bother him when he was headed to one of the dark corners.

I would rather not speak to anyone I know tonight, thought Henry. *I don't want to have to explain another bad day on the water.*

All Kelvin had to do was gesture and their drinks were on the way to the table. Jake, the barkeep, knew exactly what Kelvin wanted before he ordered. He looked as old and tired as the building itself but remembered without a flaw what each of his regular customers drank.

As Jake put a tall glass of cold ale in front of each of them, Henry exclaimed excitedly, "That's what I need!"

Both men took long drinks from their mugs and set them down with smiles on their faces.

Henry broke the silence. "So, did you read that book you found in the basement of Town Hall?"

"I did," said Kelvin. "It was just a history of the three founders. There weren't any other references to Luther; only that strange notation on the front page."

The mention of the name *Luther* got the attention of an old man sitting in the dark corner nearest them, but they didn't notice.

"That's disappointing," said Henry, taking another drink of his ale.

"I know," replied Kelvin. "I was hoping it would tell me more about the Dark Days."

"Dangerous to be talking like that in public, isn't it?" asked the old man as he leaned forward into the light so Henry and Kelvin could see him.

"What do you really know about the Dark Days, and how do you know the name *Luther*?" asked the unknown man. "You could be locked up, or worse, if the wrong person heard you say that name."

"Who are you?" asked Henry, intrigued by his knowledge.

"My name is Borin," he replied, producing a gap-toothed smile.

He was an older man with stringy gray hair and a deep, coarse voice, and he looked too rugged to have lived in Triopolis for very long. His skin was wrinkled and showed the signs of many hard years.

"Do you know who Luther was?" asked Kelvin.

"I know who he was, all right," mumbled Borin.

Their excitement grew at his response.

Before answering, the uncivilized-looking man glanced around to see if anyone was listening. "Luther is someone who didn't see eye to eye with your gods," he said in a low voice.

"Are they not your gods as well?" asked Henry skeptically.

"They are not," he responded.

"What gods do you have then?" asked Kelvin.

"We have different beliefs," was his short response, accompanied by a smirk.

Henry was growing impatient with Borin's lack of answers.

"We?" he asked curiously.

"You see, he was one of my people," said Borin, dodging Henry's last question.

Kelvin looked at Henry, bewildered. Neither of them was quite sure what to make of the strange man sitting next to them.

Henry looked around to see if anyone was watching. The other patrons were enjoying their drink of choice, some having a merry time and some looking dogged.

"My people live freely in the forest," said the old man.

"Did you run away from Triopolis?" asked Henry, not understanding the stranger's meaning.

"No," he answered. "There are other people in the world—people who did not come from here."

Borin knew that the people of Triopolis were taught that they were the only ones to survive the Dark Days. The blank looks on his new friends' faces showed him they didn't understand.

"But we were the only people to survive," said Henry, confused.

Kelvin had remained quiet throughout the exchange but finally spoke to his boss and mentor.

"He's saying we weren't the only people to survive," he whispered, nudging Henry.

"That is correct," answered the gruff voice, taking a long draw of a cigarette he had rolled and lit while Kelvin was explaining his meaning to Henry.

"If other people existed, then why wouldn't we have seen you until now?" pondered Henry.

"Have you ever been in the forest and known that something had its eyes on you, but you could see nothing?" asked Borin. "We, like the animals of the forest, aren't seen unless we want to be. You have large bones in your museum of oversized animals, but you have never seen them. You think they are extinct, but they are still out there just like we are."

Henry and Kelvin both had a feeling of ignorance and anger because of the deceit they had endured for all these years.

"We were taught all through school that we were the only ones," said Henry, trying to find answers.

"They either lied to us or didn't know," replied Kelvin.

"Only one man knows," said Borin.

"The bishop!" blurted Henry.

The old man's head nodded confirming his suspicion.

"So, Luther was one of you?" asked Kelvin.

"Yes. When he was banished from our lands, he settled here."

"Why was he banished?" asked Kelvin.

"I don't know why, only that he was," Borin answered. "It is said that he traveled as far as Triopolis. His story went silent then picked up again a couple of years later when a man from Triopolis named Donovan came to our elders asking how to contain him."

"How to contain him?" repeated Henry eerily.

"Why would they want to contain him?" asked Kelvin.

"I don't know," Borin lied. "That's all I know of Luther."

Henry and Kelvin looked at each other, both excited about the thickening mystery.

"I think there is more to our history than we know," stated Henry.

"How can you walk around town without anyone asking questions?" Kelvin asked Borin.

"That's easy," he replied. "I just act like I live here, and because of the way I look, most people would rather ignore me. No one ever asks. Now, the bishop would probably not like it if he knew I was walking out in the open."

"He does like to control everything here," exclaimed Henry.

"Be careful," cautioned Borin. "He has spies everywhere."

As the warning came from his mouth, he glanced around the room for anyone who looked suspicious. Kelvin and Borin followed his lead, interrogating everyone in the bar with their eyes.

A chair fell backward, crashing to the floor, getting their attention.

"You've had too much!" yelled Jake to the stumbling man. "Go home!"

Feeling better knowing the man was drunk and not someone who had noticed Borin, they came back to their conversation.

"The bishop is a bad person," said Borin, remembering what happened all those years ago.

For the first time, Henry noticed the four empty mugs in front of the old man. The slight slur in Borin's voice confirmed the downed ale. *Does Borin mean to be talking this much, or is it the ale?* Henry decided to let the old man ramble while he listened.

"It was to the bishop that the farmer brought me after I was spotted," recalled Borin. "He interrogated me for hours until he finally believed my story. The farmer was not so fortunate. I found out some days later that he went missing. It's amazing what your leaders will do to keep you people ignorant of the outside world."

Henry and Kelvin stared at Borin, dumbfounded by what they were hearing.

"We were always taught that we were the only people who survived the Dark Days," said Kelvin, shaking his head in dismay.

"Yeah, I am on the Assembly, and I have never heard about you or Luther or any of this," said Henry, upset at the bishop for keeping secrets from him. "I wonder if the rest of the Assembly knows."

Henry was beginning to question if he had been deceived by everyone or just the bishop. It was easier for him to believe it was the bishop alone.

"The sacred writings tell us that the three gods Nelson, Donovan, and Rowen fought back the fire demon," recalled Kelvin. "With this victory, they stopped the spread of the liquid fire that flowed from the peaks of the surrounding mountains. The liquid fire destroyed everything and everyone on the planet except the land where Triopolis is now."

"Well, you know your religion," replied Borin with a smirk.

"I guess it's a good thing I have never been a believer," said Kelvin with a laugh, relieving the tension.

"I have seen much of the world, but I have never seen a fire demon," said Borin, and they all had another laugh.

"Do you think the bishop had the farmer who first saw you killed?" asked Henry.

"There is no doubt," replied Borin. "Your leaders will do anything to keep you in the dark about the rest of the world. I have heard of them executing people for knowing less than that farmer knew."

"Why would they do that?" asked Kelvin, perplexed.

"Think about it," answered Borin. "If the people of Triopolis knew they weren't the only people on the earth, there would be anarchy. Your whole religion would fall apart. Everything you have believed for hundreds of years would be gone.

"The prospect of other people discovering your city was not something the leaders of Triopolis had to worry about until recently. When the Red Mountains calmed and the lava flowing from their peaks hardened, we were able to cross them.

That is how my people found you, and others have come too. They have either been turned away or killed to protect the lie."

Looking toward the lone window in the pub, Borin could see that the sun had completely descended from the sky, and night had come.

"Well, gentlemen, it is time for me to go," he said.

"Stay," pleaded Kelvin. "I will get you another mug."

"Oh no!" exclaimed Borin, looking like he had seen a ghost. "I have seen that man with the bishop! I have to get out of here!"

He jumped from his seat and headed toward the kitchen, looking for another exit to escape unseen.

Opening the back door of the pub, Borin looked both ways to make sure it was clear before he exited the building. Not seeing anyone, he slunk along the shadow of the building until he got to the corner, and then he headed toward the road that went from the docks to the city.

As Borin disappeared around the corner, the bishop's man appeared from the opposite corner. It was the same man Borin had seen pass by the window earlier. He moved to the corner his prey had just gone around to see him walking down the dirt road toward the city. He continued his pursuit.

"The man in the window was Baldwin," said Henry. "He is the bishop's muscle."

"I have seen him with my father too," replied Kelvin.

"He's not someone you want after you," warned Henry.

Chapter 2

Meeting Borin the previous night had awoken the adventurer in Kelvin. His adventurous side had been dormant for years, but now it was free and controlling his every thought. Sleep evaded him as he contemplated his renewed search for more truths about the past and their people's history.

As a child, he practically lived in the forest, sneaking out on one dangerous adventure after another. By nine years of age, he had slain his first deer. It took a second arrow at close range to finish the large doe, but it was his first kill.

It took every bit of Ms. Parkinson's energy to keep track of where the boy was each day. He fished in the river, climbed the largest trees he could find, and explored all the way up to the mountain's ridge. It all ended one afternoon in his eleventh year, after the boating accident that took his brother's life.

After the accident, Kelvin became much more cautious and rarely did anything that might cause physical harm. The most dangerous activity he participated in was football. The occasional collision between players at the goal, or a kick on the shin, was the only danger he willingly faced.

In the seven years following the accident, Kelvin focused his attention on his studies, always finishing top in his class. When formal education ended at seventeen, he became interested in the history and politics of Triopolis. His free time was spent immersed in any book he could find on those subjects.

It was a book titled *The Peaceful Conquest*, about how the early leaders laid the foundation of what Triopolis would become, that initially piqued his interest. The book was recommended by his father, who also liked to read about the people who came before them.

It was probably a desire to be like his father that led Kelvin to read the book, but he really enjoyed it. Realizing that he had an interest in the subject, he started on a journey to gain as much knowledge as he could find.

His thirst for knowledge led him to ask his father for an apprenticeship in government. Begrudgingly, Carl agreed and put him to work in the basement of Town Hall.

After only a month of work in the archives, Kelvin couldn't take it any longer, and he went to work with Henry. Carl was just as happy to see him go as Kelvin was, but he never told his son this.

Jumping out of bed and getting dressed, Kelvin couldn't wait to get started with his day. He was still amazed and excited about the astonishing tales told by Borin. He had read and studied so much about Nelson, Donovan, and Rowen, the founders of Triopolis, but this man told a completely different story.

Was Borin's story true? If so, then how could the writers of so many history books be wrong? Did his father know the truth?

Many questions spun around Kelvin's head, but one thing he knew for sure was that he wanted to find the truth.

His sleepless night did not affect him at all as he rushed out of the house grabbing a piece of Ms. Parkinson's freshly baked brown bread. Happily, he devoured his warm breakfast as he walked down the street toward Town Hall.

Passersby in front of Town Hall went about their business as if he didn't exist. This was exactly what Kelvin wanted. He leaned against the stone base of one of the many light poles that lined the square in front of the government building.

Knowing the Assembly would be tied up in meetings for most of the day, Kelvin thought it would be the perfect time to sneak into the archives. Even though the assembly meetings were open to the public, no one ever attended.

Not wanting to be asked to join the meetings, most people stayed as far away from Town Hall as possible. This meant today would be the only day this month that the government office would not be bustling with activity.

The receptionist, Mrs. Thatcher, used to say those were her favorite days of work because nobody bothered her. Kelvin even remembered catching her reading romance novels with her feet up on the desk a few times.

From his vantage point, he could see through the window to the left of the door. Keeping his back toward the window, he occasionally turned his head just enough to survey the situation inside. It was crucial that he not linger long enough to be noticed by Mrs. Thatcher.

She knew him well, and if she noticed, she would certainly have yelled out to him causing a scene. Her loud intrusive nature and penchant for gossip would wreak havoc on his need for stealth. She must be avoided at all costs.

It wasn't long before it was time for the receptionist to refill her cup of tea. This is what Kelvin was counting on. Remembering that Mrs. Thatcher usually started her day with at least three cups of mint tea, he sprang into action.

He cracked the door open as she disappeared into the small kitchen behind the stairway. The wooden staircase was the focal point of the lobby, and it led up to the second floor. The top floor of the two-story building was where the city's officials kept their offices.

Facing an empty lobby, Kelvin made his move toward the basement door. Nervously, but quickly, he crossed the thirty feet from the door, passed Mrs. Thatcher's desk, and made it to the relative safety of the hallway. Ten feet and then a turn to the left and Kelvin was out of sight.

The large room where the meeting was taking place was on the opposite side of the ground floor to the right of the doorway. Having rounded the corner, he was hidden from anyone in the lobby walking past the hallway.

There was nothing at this end of the corridor. It ended abruptly at a window that was nearly covered by a young tree that grew just outside, near the corner of the building. To the left was the entrance to the archives.

Not wanting to waste any time, Kelvin pulled the door open and walked into the basement. The musty smell brought back memories of long days spent in this place. Letting the door shut behind him, darkness encircled him.

Looking to his left, he saw the outline of two small oil lamps on a shelf built into the wall. They were kept there so that anyone entering the basement could light them and banish the darkness.

Feeling the weight of both lamps, he determined that each was about half full. He put them down on the floor in order to maximize his vision with the thin sliver of light from underneath the door. Working quickly, he poured the oil from one lamp into the other, leaving the empty one on the step.

Cradling the small lamp, he cautiously descended into the growing darkness. Very little light from the small gap under the door reached the bottom of the unusually long staircase. The small window on the far side of the room wasn't much help either.

Luckily, because he had used his tinderbox many times, he was confident of his ability to light the lamp in the darkness. Setting the kiln-fired clay lamp on the floor, he reached into his pocket and retrieved the fire-starting kit. He had grabbed it on his way out of the house, knowing it would be dark in the archives. Taking out a piece of char paper, he laid it out on the floor near the lamp.

Fascinating stuff, char paper, thought Kelvin.

Derived from organic material that had already been burned, char paper ignited quickly and burned slowly. It was perfect for lighting fires such as the one needed for the lamp. The material was first discovered in Triopolis from the lava that flowed out of the volcanoes in the Red Mountains. Now, however, it was produced intentionally in the char shops near the market.

Fumbling through the small leather pouch that held his fire kit, Kelvin took out the steel and flint. He rubbed both together generating sparks, which lit the char paper. Not taking long, he joined the smoldering paper and the linen wick protruding from the lamp.

The modest flame combined with the small amount of light penetrating the dirty window on the far wall produced a surprisingly clear view of the room. Disappointment immediately overtook Kelvin when he noted the clutter that had built up since he was last there.

It looked as if he had never organized a thing. Much like that first day he entered the basement, shelves were overflowing, and accumulated relics cluttered the floor in front of them.

The basement walls were constructed of stones with a lime- and sand-based mortar to fill the cracks. This could only be seen on the back wall containing the window, because shelves covered the other three.

As the years passed, the building had shifted, causing cracks to form in the mortar. This allowed water to seep through, creating an unseen and unnerving drip. Kelvin inhaled the thick musty air. It was a smell he had hoped never to experience again.

"Where to start?" he asked himself.

Remembering that as you walked toward the far wall you went back in history, he took his first steps. Kelvin didn't think it was planned this way; he just figured people didn't want to spend any more time than was necessary in this eerie place. They probably walked straight back from the stairs, dropped their item, and quickly left.

After spending a month in here while working for his father, Kelvin became tolerant of the basement. Many of the people working upstairs thought it was scary, and only came down if it was absolutely necessary. It was for this reason Kelvin felt comfortable that his search would be uninterrupted.

Walking around the stacks of books, papers, and other artifacts, Kelvin reached the back wall. He began his search by sifting through books on the nearby shelf. With so many, he had to decide whether any particular book was worth investigating further simply by the title.

Most of the documents on this shelf were government related. "Every law ever written in the whole history of Triopolis must be in here," he murmured.

He scoured through the books stacked in front and on the shelves. He chose to search this side first because it was the same half of the room that he had spent a month cleaning and organizing.

After searching for what seemed like hours, Kelvin was becoming discouraged. He retreated to the old wooden bench beneath the window and sat down.

"Maybe this wasn't a good idea," he muttered. "I had forgotten how many books and writings are actually here."

He looked at the untouched second half of the room, situated to the left of the window. A large mound of books filled the back corner. He remembered the pile well as it was the sole reason he had started organizing on the opposite side.

Chewing on a piece of dried fruit he pulled from his pocket, Kelvin contemplated the room. A ray of sunlight somehow made it through the grime on the windowpane and pooled on the basement floor in front of him.

The dust from his rummaging could be seen in the lone ray of light. The particles were dancing playfully in the air, swirling in the light before being whisked away into the darkness. He sat watching the dust for another couple of minutes before it hit him.

How can the dust be swirling? The air in here is stagnant, and there is no access to the outside, so how is the dust moving?

Rising from the bench, he stepped toward the beam of light. As he did so, the slightest draft tickled his left arm. Turning toward the light breeze, he held out his lamp. It appeared to be coming from the mound of books.

With the excitement of his mission returning, Kelvin studied the mountain. The mass almost reached his head and was five feet wide at its base. It filled the space between the shelf and the wall and then some.

At first glance, it looked to be made up solely of books, but upon further inspection, Kelvin could see other objects intermingled. He saw half of a metal pot, the point of an iron stake, a metal-framed mirror, and a wooden hammer.

It seemed as if this section of wooden shelves had disintegrated, dumping the artifacts onto the floor. He didn't believe that was the only cause of such a large mound, however. Based on his experience with how much each shelf could hold, there had to be another contributing factor.

Studying the mound, his suspicion grew. Someone must have moved the artifacts. If the shelf had fallen, the pieces would be much more scattered. The pile only covered half of the bookcase with the broken shelves. If nothing had been moved, the mountain would be centered on the ruined bookshelf.

Setting the lamp on the floor to cast a pool of light, his suspicion was confirmed. To the left of the pile, gouges and scratches scarred the wood floor. The marks looked like they had been made when the shelves had fallen.

"Who would have done this?" he wondered.

The draft seemed to be coming from the top of the heap. Investigating the side nearest the wall, he was surprised to see a tiny path winding its way against the wall and around the mound.

Following the short path, he found the draft was actually coming from between the stone wall and the bookshelf. There he found a tiny space, less than the width of his body. Without thinking, he turned sideways and shuffled into the tight passageway.

It was only a little longer than the bookshelf, and after a couple of steps, he saw a hole. A section of what Kelvin thought was the exterior wall was broken away, revealing another small corridor.

A second stone wall was constructed three feet in front of the actual exterior wall. His adrenaline pumping, and again without thinking, Kelvin stepped through the breach into the second passageway.

The hole was almost large enough to walk through without ducking. It looked as if it had been made some time ago because there wasn't much debris left.

Kelvin again asked the question, "Who did this?"

Looking to the right, he saw the corridor end at the edge of the building. It continued to the left. With excitement, anxiety, and fear overtaking his body, Kelvin continued his journey.

This corridor was a little wider than the last, so he was able to walk normally without sidestepping. With the lamp leading the way, he inched forward. Suddenly, another opening appeared. This time it was on the primary wall.

Reaching the opening, he peeked in holding the lamp in front. "Another chamber?" He gasped at the thought of what might have taken place here.

A doorway was cut into the wall. This was no mere crack in the wall that had grown over time. It was meant to be here, with its elaborately carved support columns and perfectly formed arch.

He saw nothing but darkness beyond the few feet of minimal light from the lamp. The coppery-brown marble floor tiles were the only thing that came into view when he moved the lamp from side to side.

Finally summoning enough courage, Kelvin stepped through the threshold. His shoes echoed, hauntingly, as they hit the stone floor. "This room must be large," he surmised from the sound of the echo.

Still, nothing appeared as he cautiously moved into the hall. One slow step after another, he continued to swing the lamp back and forth to light his way. As he progressed into what seemed to be the center of the room, fear eroded his confidence.

His heart pounded faster and faster, his palms moistened with sweat, and his breathing grew louder and louder. Visions of bats attacking his head or a snake silently swallowing him whole plagued his mind, but worst of all, fears of being devoured by a massive spider consumed him.

"Don't think like that!" he said to himself with contempt. "You will never survive if you give in to fear. Think of a bright sunny day at the beach."

After a moment's pause, he smirked and answered himself. "Easier said than done," he said with a snort, jumping at a strange noise he thought he heard.

Walking straight ahead seemed like the most logical idea. This way he would know where the exit was in case a quick escape was necessary. A way out was becoming even more important as the oil in the lamp diminished.

Slowly inching forward to restrain the nervous energy that consumed his body, he studied the new territory after each step. He was so fixated on each inch he conquered that he didn't even realize he was moving so slowly.

Being in this room made him very uneasy, but he wasn't sure exactly why. Maybe it was the usual fear of the unknown, or was it something else?

Seeing something emerging from the darkness, he held out the lamp to make out what it was. Not seeing any obstacles on the floor between him and the object, he quickened his pace.

A stone pedestal on which sat the largest oil lamp he had ever seen came into view—but it wasn't an oil lamp at all. The liquid was almost gel-like and did not smell like oil. Two iron stands with candles four feet off the ground stood on either side of the large stone bowl.

With his almost empty lamp, Kelvin touched the withering flame to each candle causing them to light. The room opened up before him. It was like nothing he had seen before. The bronze marble floor looked as if it had just been polished yesterday, and the breathtaking vaulted ceiling was supported by massive crisscrossing arches.

Looking past the stone bowl, he couldn't help but be drawn to a huge portrait of an ominous-looking man. In front of the painting stood a large, square wooden table that looked like it was used as a desk. Walking up to it, Kelvin recognized the dark reddish hue of cherry wood.

The tall, thin man stood at attention in the painting. His hair was as black as the oil in Kelvin's lamp, accompanied by a thin and meticulously groomed mustache and beard. An elegant red robe enveloped the man with the stern look on his face.

Luther was inscribed at the bottom of the portrait. Kelvin couldn't believe he was looking at the unknown founder of Triopolis.

So you're Luther, he thought. *You do look dangerous, don't you?*

Kelvin wondered what Donovan meant when he wrote that Luther had gone too far. Was this Luther's chamber? Is that why a second wall was built to hide it?

Kelvin stood, paralyzed, staring at the painting. It was as if he was being held in place by some unseen force. He tried but couldn't turn away. It felt as if he was not in control of his body.

He wanted to move, but nothing happened. Then a light breeze brushed his arm, and control returned to him.

Did that just happen, or was I imagining it?

He couldn't tell because it all seemed to have happened inside his head. Looking back at the portrait, he tried to recreate the feeling of being mesmerized and paralyzed at the same time, but nothing happened.

"It had to be in my head," he murmured, hoping he was right.

Kelvin wanted to believe the strange feeling was just paranoia caused by the constant state of anxiety he was in, but something told him it wasn't.

The light from the candles flickered, causing shadows to move about the room, making the situation even more unnerving.

The large wooden table was piled high with books and papers. Rifling through them, nothing caught his attention. It wasn't until he moved past the stacks on the corner that he found something that looked interesting.

Walking behind the table, he noticed the most peculiar book lying flat in the center. It had no title and looked much older than the others. Fear shot through him as he picked it up.

There wasn't any dust on this book, he noticed. In fact, nothing on the table was dusty. Someone had been there recently!

Kelvin tried to calm himself by focusing on the book.

The cover was old and worn, and felt like it was made of leather. Opening it, the pages felt like they were sealed in a smooth clear substance.

That must be how it has lasted this long.

The first page read, "My findings . . ." The following pages were filled with mathematical equations, elemental charts, and astronomical diagrams. Looking up from the book, Kelvin noticed the entire room for the first time.

The walls were lined with tables, cabinets, and other objects unknown to Kelvin. On the left side, the tables were filled with stills, crucibles, glass tubes, and earthenware pots. The first cabinet contained jars labeled *Purified Water*, *The Stone that Burns*, and *Iron Flakes*.

Moving along the wall, he saw a chart hanging above a second cabinet. It was a diagram of a man's body with each part labeled.

This cabinet was much more grotesque and sat next to a table with different sized knives, sawing instruments, and small metal forceps. Some of the jars in this cupboard were labeled *Goat's Blood*, *Boar Intestine*, and *Ground Hawk's Bone*.

Feeling his stomach turn, Kelvin walked to the other side of the room. This part of the laboratory seemed to focus on celestial bodies. Charts of star positions in the sky and their meanings hung from the wall.

A metal model of a constellation stood on one table, which Kelvin immediately recognized as the Great Northern Bear. He was also intrigued by a strange contraption resting on the other table, a tube made of leather with a round piece of glass at each end. On one of the ends, the glass piece was about half the size of the one on the other end. This leather tube was fastened to a wooden tripod. Like a new toy, he had to try it out.

Looking through the tube using the small eyepiece, he was amazed at how big everything became. Tiny specks of dirt could be seen on the wall.

Fascinating!

Spinning the telescope around, he looked at various objects in the room. On the other side, he could see the red spot on the back of a tiny spider dangling from the ceiling. He could even read some of the papers on the table that stood beneath the portrait of Luther.

The sudden sound of something tumbling down the stairs separated Kelvin from his fun.

"The oil lamp!" he said, angry with himself for leaving it out. *Why didn't I put that back on the shelf?*

Panic gripped him as the echo of footsteps followed the clanking lamp down the staircase. With a quick glance around the room, he searched for a place to hide.

A long rectangular metal box, not far from the doorway, sat near the opposite wall. The lid was pulled back with one end on the floor and the other leaning on the top of the box. The space between the box and the lid was just large enough to squeeze into, but it left no room to move.

From this vantage point, he had a perfect view of the doorway. He didn't know if the person in the basement even knew this room existed, but he hid just to be safe.

What's that smell? He crinkled his burning nostrils.

The smell was like a mixture of the chemicals Olaf used to clean his fillet knives and a dead animal.

Curious, Kelvin crawled forward enough to look over the edge of the box. What he saw made him gag. The sight of the dead man submerged in preservation liquid almost made him retch. He could taste the mixture of his lunch and the acid from his stomach in his throat.

Inching back into his hiding place, his heart was racing, and he couldn't control his nerves. He couldn't stop his hands from trembling against the cold stone floor.

You have to relax, he said to himself inwardly. *You will surely get caught if you continue like this!* As he tried to control his thoughts, he also tried to slow his breathing. It was the only way he could think to slow his racing heart.

The old floorboards in the basement creaked as what sounded like two men walked about the space.

They know about this room, he thought, hearing the two men enter the narrow corridor.

"You left the candles burning again," one man said to the other.

"I am sorry, sir," replied the other man.

Kelvin breathed a silent sigh of relief at having escaped that potentially fatal mistake, but as soon as he heard their voices, he knew who it was. He watched from the shadows as the bishop and his man, Baldwin, entered the room.

The bishop was a middle-aged man with a bald head, beady black eyes, and a shadowy personality. Kelvin thought it was interesting that he was wearing a red robe. After seeing the portrait of Luther in a red robe, he wondered if there was a correlation.

Baldwin was a big strong man with long, blond hair. He seemed to talk only when the bishop asked a question, and he obeyed every command.

"I am becoming disappointed with your lack of progress," said the bishop.

"Sir, I have looked everywhere," pleaded Baldwin.

"The inscription clearly states that the tablet can be found in the House of the Founders!" spat the bishop.

"I have searched everywhere in the church," responded Baldwin. "There are no passageways, and there is no nook or crevice that I haven't investigated."

The bishop turned and took a step toward the coffin sheltering Kelvin.

Uh oh, he thought, frozen.

He didn't move a muscle save for his involuntary breathing. To him, each breath sounded like stampeding wild boar. He did everything he could to keep his rhythmic breathing regular and quiet.

The bishop stood near the coffin with his arms folded across his chest and one hand on his chin. Kelvin could see his beady eyes through a small gap between the lid and the box, caused by the slightly warped metal lid.

"Could it be in another building?" he asked Baldwin. "The other old structures in town, like the library and the museum, aren't old enough, and I have already searched this building."

"No, it has to be the church!" he exclaimed, answering himself. "The inscription was clear. I want you to search again, Baldwin. There has to be a secret passage somewhere."

"Yes, sir," replied Baldwin, discouraged that he was being made to investigate something that he knew didn't exist.

As they moved toward the doorway, Kelvin heard the bishop say, "Remember to search the building in terms of the fire in the year 321. The church was rebuilt after the fire nearly destroyed it."

Watching the two men leave the room, Kelvin allowed himself to exhale in relief. He could finally shift his body to release the tension and cramping in his muscles. His nerves calmed enough for him to inch his way backward out of his hole, but when he heard footsteps returning to the room, he froze.

Luckily, the coffin was in a corner of the room where very little light reached. The bishop walked through the doorway and to his desk without seeing Kelvin's exposed feet.

Kelvin watched as the bishop opened the old book on the table and read something with deliberate intent. He turned toward one of the chemistry tables and arranged some instruments.

Realizing it was now or never, Kelvin slowly crawled out of his hiding spot and crouched in the dark corner. He would wait until the right moment to sneak out the door. It was only ten feet away, but his timing would have to be perfect.

The bishop was mixing chemicals together, causing a smell worse than the dead man in the coffin to permeate the room.

As if I didn't already want to get out of here . . . , thought Kelvin, scrunching his nose.

The bishop was likewise affected by the smell, as evidenced by his frequent coughing.

Get out now! Kelvin shrieked inwardly.

One of the instruments contained a dark liquid that had reached a boil, and the beaker was whistling like a teapot. Combined with the bishop's frequent coughing, there was plenty of noise for Kelvin to slip out unheard.

And he did.

Chapter 3

Elizabeth looked into Prince Richard's eyes and obediently replied "I will" as he slid the silver ring onto her finger. She fought with all her might to hold back the tears, unable to tell if they were tears of joy or pain.

It was every girl's dream to marry a prince, but that is where the fairy tale ended for Elizabeth. Richard had his father's handsome face, but everything else about him physically and mentally was ugly indeed.

He stood slightly less than six feet tall with a weak frame and a slight build. His stature drove him to periods of feeling inferior to other men at court, but his free spirit helped him overcome those dark moments. His blond, scruffy hair looked as though it had never seen a comb, and at twenty-one, he was three years older than his bride, a beautiful young woman with flowing brown hair and irresistible blue eyes.

A spectator looking on would have thought them the perfect royal couple.

If they only knew the truth, thought Elizabeth. *Have I sold my soul to be a princess? Will I ever be happy in this arrangement?*

Her wedding was supposed to be a bride's happiest day, but she felt none of that now. For most of the afternoon, Elizabeth was lost in her thoughts. She responded when necessary and gave the occasional smile, but her head was elsewhere.

She remembered that day almost a month ago when she happened upon Richard and Albert in the Great Hall. Albert was Richard's friend and the head of his personal guard.

He was a couple inches taller and had a much more solid build. His hair was short almost to the point of being shaved to fit his more conservative appearance.

She entered the hall at dusk, with the last few remaining rays of light from the setting sun peering through the windows on the western wall. Halfway through the large room, she heard voices behind one of the stone pillars to her left.

Curious, she slid up against one of the massive columns to have a look. The sounds were of two lovers speaking softly. Peeking around the corner, she saw them locked in an embrace.

How sweet, she thought, turning to walk away.

Not careful enough, her bracelet scraped the stone, echoing throughout the cavernous room. The kiss abruptly ended as the two frightened men glared at Elizabeth.

"Richard!" she gasped.

There was her future husband standing with his lover. In that moment, all of her illusions of a fairy-tale life with her prince vanished. It seemed like hours, but was only a matter of seconds before he spoke.

"Elizabeth, I . . . I can explain," he sputtered.

Before he could finish the statement, she was running back the way she had come. Richard's instinct was to chase her so that he could explain. He caught up to her as she reached the stairs that led to her apartments.

The time since then had been spent working on a deal that they could both live with. Richard refused to leave Albert, so she had no choice but to accept his offer. Calling off the wedding would be scandalous, so that was not an option.

Both of their fathers had too much invested in this marriage for them to cause trouble. Elizabeth couldn't bear the thought of her father's disgrace from such an action. Richard would not let the marriage fail because doing so would bring his father's wrath down upon him.

In public, they would put on the face of a happy couple in love, but privately, they would live separate lives. Elizabeth was free to see whomever she liked, as long as it remained a secret. Of course, the formalities of producing an heir would be honored in time.

Throughout the wedding, she was fixated on her situation, wondering if she was destined to be unhappy for the rest of her life. Another moment requiring a smile broke her from her trance.

The court erupted in a chorus of clapping and cheering as the ceremony came to an end. Smiling dutifully, Elizabeth thanked those near her as she made her way to her seat at the king's table.

The king stood and excitedly clapped his hands together, cheering, and then announced, "We shall have the largest feast the city has ever seen!"

King William Westville was a well-built man with thick arms and legs complemented by a barrel chest. He looked every inch the ideal knight, the exception being his once brown hair and full beard were now showing signs of age.

Still looking good for his forty-five years, he didn't quite have the strength he once had. His many battle scars were coming back to haunt him, acting as another reminder of his mortality.

The king's excitement was twofold. Not only was he happy that his son was now married, but also because the marriage had linked the royal Westvilles with the only other family in the realm that had a legitimate claim to the throne.

The Granvilles were an ancient family that traced their roots back almost as far as the Westvilles. There had been many marriages between the two families over the years resulting in Westville blood running in the veins of the Granvilles.

Unfortunately, Lord and Lady Granville never had a son survive childbirth, making Elizabeth their only child. Without a son, they would have a difficult time establishing their claim to the throne if anything happened to Lord Granville.

The crafty old man, Lord Granville, knew the game well having spent so many years in the service of kings. He had held many offices while serving not only William, but also during the short reign of William's father.

The people would not support their claim without a son, so the Granvilles did the next best thing: they married their daughter Elizabeth to Richard Westville, which meant that their family name would now be entwined in the story of the future King Richard.

Both fathers were proud of themselves for making this marriage work. The king was secure in the knowledge that future sovereigns would have the name Westville, and Lord Granville was now linked to the throne.

The banquet hall was lavishly decorated with many paintings depicting great feats of the Westville kings. The largest was a massive depiction of King William's greatest victory at the Battle of Midalo fifteen years earlier. It hung directly behind his chair at the royal table.

The banners of all the prominent families in Westville were suspended from the ceiling, adding an array of color. Flowers of every type and fragrance were placed throughout the room, giving the hall a most refreshing aroma.

The food was like nothing anyone had ever seen. The first course consisted of every vegetable imaginable and greens prepared for any appetite.

Then came the parade of meats. Beef, venison, chicken, duck, pig, rabbit, eel, and cod were brought in and placed on the royal table. After the nobles chose their cuts, the rest was laid out on a table for the other guests.

If that wasn't enough food, the third course consisted of bananas, strawberries, raspberries, and small cakes. To wash it all down, the wine flowed like water.

"Can you believe this feast?" Richard yelled excitedly, walking up to Albert.

He was forced to scream because Albert was standing close to the musicians. His friend loved the stringed instruments, with the lute being his favorite. Richard often joked that if they hadn't met, Albert would have been a professional musician.

As they walked away from the dance floor, Albert asked sarcastically, "So, how do you like your wife?"

Richard looked at him with a smirk on his face, and playfully nudged him in the shoulder with his forearm. They giggled together as they reached the table of meat and each picked up a plate.

Richard moved past the venison and chicken, and stopped at the pork. He motioned for the servant to slice a piece for him. As the servant was putting a rather large piece of tender pork loin on his plate, Richard's eyes met his father's from across the room.

The king seemed to be irritated and was scowling at his son.

"Uh-oh," said Albert, not looking up from his plate as he was being served the chicken. "It seems your father is not happy with you."

"When is he ever happy with me?" scoffed Richard, looking down at his full plate.

They both turned away from the king's glare, snickering as they went off to find a quiet place to eat their dinner.

Elizabeth watched this scene from her seat at the end of the king's table nearest the buffet of meat. Her hand, hidden under the table, clenched in anger. She felt betrayed by her husband.

Why would he put me through this? He has already ruined my life, so why does he taunt me by giggling with Albert in front of everyone?

Lynessa, her newly appointed attendant, sat to her right. Only a few years older than Elizabeth, she had shoulder-length auburn hair and a small frame.

One of the benefits of joining the royal family was having attendants take care of your every need. At first, Elizabeth was uneasy about having a constant shadow, but now she was becoming more comfortable with Lynessa's comforting presence.

Only knowing each other a little more than a month, Elizabeth enjoyed her company. This did not mean she trusted Lynessa with all her secrets, though. Taking her father's advice, she did not gossip about the king or his son. For this reason, Lynessa did not know about the understanding Elizabeth had with Richard.

"I am sorry," said Lynessa, despairingly. "He hasn't said a word to you since the ceremony, has he?"

"Not one," agreed Elizabeth. "What do you know about Albert?"

The only time she had met him was that evening in the Great Hall, and that was hardly the time for an introduction. Although she wanted to know more about the man who stole her husband, she was glad that Richard did not bring him when visiting her.

"I don't know much," replied her attendant. "I have only been at court a little while, so I have not had a chance to get to know him."

Lynessa was not telling the complete truth. Everyone in the hall had opinions about the relationship between Richard and Albert, but she wasn't about to mention that to Elizabeth.

"I want you to find out what kind of man he is," commanded the princess. "But be discreet. I don't want anyone to know what you are doing."

"Yes, My Lady," she responded obediently.

Lynessa was young, but she was also experienced in dealing with matters of intrigue. She had learned how to navigate court politics from her sister.

The next morning, Elizabeth woke a little later than usual. She slipped out of bed and walked over to a set of doors made mostly of glass. They opened out onto a balcony overlooking the gardens.

"What a beautiful morning," she murmured. Then, as if Lynessa knew when Elizabeth would wake, she entered the chamber, filling the room with the aroma of the princess's favorite herbal tea. Seeing Elizabeth standing on the balcony, she set the tray on a small table set in the morning sun and pulled out two chairs invitingly. Pouring two cups, she handed one to Elizabeth.

"You do such a good job," complimented Elizabeth. "You are too good to me."

Lynessa nodded, thanking her, and took a sip of her tea. This was one of Elizabeth's favorite daily rituals. She had tea every morning with Lynessa as they discussed the day's agenda.

"I had a strange dream last night," commented Elizabeth. "I leaned in to kiss my husband, but when I opened my eyes, another man was there, someone I have never seen before."

"I hear it's normal for wives to dream of other men," comforted her attendant.

"Sir, wake up," said Jacob, shaking Richard lightly on the shoulder. "Sir, please wake up."

Jacob was a short man with long, thin brown hair and a slight frame. He had been in the king's service for many years, earning his current position when the prince came of age.

"What!" screamed Richard, rolling onto his back. "What do you want?"

"Sir, the king is on his way," answered his attendant in a trembling voice.

This isn't like Jacob, Richard mused. *It must be serious.*

He jumped out of bed, grabbed his trousers from the previous night, and stepped into them. His shirt was also on the floor next to the bed. He snatched it up and in one motion pulled it over his head. As if on cue, his father burst through the door.

"Why did you not spend time with your wife last night?" bellowed the king. "I don't think you said one word to her! What is wrong with you? That is your royal duty! The whole affair was to show off the next king and queen of Westville!"

The king was now standing directly in front of Richard. His hands were gesticulating and his face was red with anger.

"Did you spend all of your time with Albert?" he demanded to know.

The look in Richard's eyes betrayed him, and his father knew the answer.

"This is unacceptable!" yelled the king, storming out of the room.

Furious, Richard skipped breakfast and went straight to the training ring. He needed to blow off steam, and what better way than swinging a large piece of steel.

The ring was a wooden enclosure used for training in hand-to-hand combat. The roof was solid, but the walls were open to allow fresh air to filter through the structure. It was rather small, but the yard surrounding it was also used for training. The protected area inside was reserved for nobility, and that was where Richard found Albert.

Silence ruled as they donned their armor. Thick quilted padding was worn underneath a metal plate skin. No helmets were worn because, much to the dismay of Albert, Richard didn't like wearing them to practice. By the look on his friend's face, Albert knew today was not the day to argue that point.

Albert, being much larger, could easily best his prince if he wanted to, but his goal was to make Richard a better fighter. He waited for the prince to begin.

From the start, Richard was imposing his will. He violently swung his blade, driving Albert backward. He was actually giving his larger sparring partner a good run around the ring.

Might he finally be coming into his own? Albert wondered.

He had been waiting many years for his prince to know his own strength and stand up for himself. Richard's father had pushed him around and belittled him his whole life. Richard always shrank back into his shell until he was dismissed. Albert had witnessed many of these occasions. He was determined to empower Richard to make a stand.

On this day, Albert recovered from each of Richard's jousts, only to be sent right back out of the enclosure. He got in the occasional blow, but he was mostly on the defensive. Finally, after nearly half an hour, Richard began to tire.

Stopping, he said, "I'm sorry. I'm just so frustrated with my father. He's always telling me what to do, and he never asks what I want. He burst into my bedchamber this morning, screaming at me for not spending time with Elizabeth last night."

"I told you, it's okay," replied Albert. "I understand it is your duty, and you have to at least act like you love her."

"I know." Richard sighed. "It's just so awkward being with her. I know what I am putting her through is wrong, so the easiest way for me to deal with it is to avoid her."

It always frustrated Albert when Richard avoided dealing with tough situations, especially when they had to do with the king. He tried to explain to his prince that it only made him look weak. The king would never respect his son unless he stood up to him.

***

Elizabeth and Lynessa walked through the main gate in the castle wall, leading their horses. Made of thick, ancient stone, the wall completely encircled the castle. It stood over fifteen feet tall, but it hadn't been needed for protection in many years.

The castle was more of a magnificent palace now than a defensive fortress. It had been more than three hundred years since the castle was besieged.

Elizabeth liked to get out and enjoy the fresh air on sunny days. She enjoyed physical activity and was much more athletic than she looked. Riding, archery, and even the occasional round of swordplay were sports she enjoyed, even though her father thought they were unbecoming of a princess.

Elizabeth didn't want anything to do with riding sidesaddle or trotting her horse at a dainty pace. She had the strongest and fastest horse available, and she ran it hard at every opportunity.

"Come on Lynessa," she called. "Let's give these animals some exercise!"

They both nudged their horses with the heel of their boots and leaned forward in their saddles, sending their steeds forward.

Elizabeth rode a strong hot-blooded white stallion she named Wind. Lynessa followed on Wind's brother, Almond, named for the light brown color of his coat.

After riding for almost an hour, they slowly pulled on the reins and shifted their weight back in their saddles. The horses slowed to a steady walk. Spotting a grassy area under a large oak tree Elizabeth motioned to stop.

"This looks like a good place to rest and have lunch," she said, "and there's plenty of grass so the horses can graze."

"All this riding has made me hungry," said Lynessa.

Jumping down from her horse, she grabbed the basket carrying their food. On top of it was a blanket she laid out on the grass. Setting the basket in the middle, she opened it and began setting up their lunch.

"What did you bring to eat?" asked Elizabeth, not waiting for each item to be revealed.

"Strawberries, bread, goat cheese, and of course wine," answered Lynessa, as she reached for the bottle and pulled out the cork.

As Lynessa poured the wine, Elizabeth retrieved the rest of their lunch from the wicker basket. "Mmm, I love the sweetness of strawberries when they are in season," she exclaimed, taking a big bite of a large juicy berry.

"Here, try this bread," offered Lynessa. "It was baked this morning."

They were laughing, telling stories, and enjoying the beautiful sunny day. A pair of songbirds perched in the tree provided a soothing melody as they finished their midday meal.

"What have you found out about Albert?" asked Elizabeth, finally.

Lynessa knew that she would want to know, but she wasn't going to bring it up until asked. She didn't want to be the cause of distress to her mistress.

"He is the son of Albert Karlson, a wealthy cloth merchant in the western part of town" she began. "He does not seem to have any noble blood, but he has been educated as a noble. Albert Senior was smart enough to know that intelligence and noble connections were the most important gifts he could give his son.

"He paid a handsome sum of money to Lord Francis Gildon to take young Albert as his squire. I heard from Francis's son Henry that he gave the lord twenty percent of his profits for ten years to land the position for his son.

"This is how Albert Junior came to know Prince Richard. They had the same tutor until age ten, at which point Richard went on to be educated as a future king and Albert continued his education with the other noble boys.

"Albert and Richard became very good friends during those years, and they have continued that friendship until this day. On your wedding night, they left the Great Hall soon after we saw them eating together and were not seen by anyone after that."

Elizabeth was amazed at how easily Lynessa could gather information. *I wonder how she does it?*

As the sun made its descent in the sky, the princess and her servant rode at a much slower pace than earlier in the day.

They approached the castle just as the sun was setting in the western sky. The sky glowed orange as the sun's rays clung to the last few remaining clouds, a struggle the sun would inevitably lose as it slipped lower and lower on the horizon.

The king sat at the head of the table in the chamber where the Private Council met. The council consisted of four of his closest and most trusted advisors. It was in this chamber that the Kingdom of Westville was ruled.

The council was made up of Lords Arthur Morel, Francis Gildon, Julius Talon, and Edward Rosser. These men served at the pleasure of the king, which meant their time on the council lasted as long as he wished it to.

Lord Morel and Lord Rosser had occupied their seats for many years and were indispensable to His Highness. The other two seats, however, changed often, due to the inconsistent nature of the king's temper.

"Gentlemen, what do we have on the agenda today?" the king began.

"Sir, may we begin with the levy on wine?" asked Lord Morel.

Lord Arthur Morel, a short, bald man, was the self-appointed leader of the councilors. He assumed the post based solely on the fact that he was the most tenured member of the Private Council, just passing his twentieth anniversary.

The king allowed it because Lord Morel had proven to be a very useful man. Devious, cunning, and accomplished in the art of manipulation, he was known as "the Fox."

"We may," replied the king.

"Thank you, sir. I would like to propose that the tax on wine should pass to me."

Everyone in the room knew that Arthur deserved the tax because he was the reason it had come up for bid.

James Handley was the previous owner of the wine tax. He was a wealthy self-made man who had climbed as high as the Private Council. The owner of the tax for a number of years, he became upset when the king wanted to lower his cut.

In all situations of tax collection, the Crown took a portion, and some was passed on to a fortunate beneficiary. Of course, the king decided what percentage was kept by the Crown and what was passed on.

It was in this very room, three months ago, that James belligerently disagreed with the king's decision to drop his revenue to one percent. The king was furious with his disobedience.

"Sir, I must protest," argued James. "Cutting my income in half is simply unacceptable! Who can live on a one-percent tax on anything?"

"Calm down!" yelled the king, raising his voice to drown out James's complaints.

"I cannot calm down when I am being cheated out of my financial well-being!" cried James.

With that, he threw his chair back and stormed out of the council chamber. The other council members looked at each other understanding that they would probably never see Lord Handley again.

The king could not hide his anger. The scowl on his face made everyone in the room tremble with fear. Knowing the temper of their sovereign, not one council member disagreed with him for the rest of the meeting.

Later that evening, a conversation supposedly took place between the king and Lord Morel. The next day, Lord Handley's body was found in the sewer. It had multiple stab wounds in the torso, and the head was almost completely severed. There was no doubt that Lord Morel had one of his unsavory acquaintances handle the deed.

The king looked at each man seated at the table. "Does anyone here disagree with Lord Morel receiving the tax on wine?"

"No, My Lord," responded each man, obediently.

"Good," said the king. "Lord Morel, the one-percent tax on wine is yours."

A slight sneer of joy appeared on his face at winning this victory.

The meeting continued with the council discussing various problems that needed resolution. Most were mundane issues such as insufficient sanitation in the northern sections and the housing shortage in the west. These routine tasks bored the king.

His mind wandered through the rest of the meeting, knowing his men could handle these issues without his help. The only reason he stayed was because of his need to speak to Lord Rosser privately afterward.

As they adjourned, everyone cleaned and organized their individual workspaces at the table. They said their goodbyes and exited the room.

Only the king and Lord Rosser remained at the table. Lord Rosser was a tall, husky man with brown, wavy hair and a full beard. He came up through the ranks in the army and was ever obedient to his king.

He had known His Majesty for some time, and could tell something had been disturbing his thoughts throughout the meeting. For this reason, he stayed behind to listen to his king.

"What is it, My Lord?" he asked.

"It's my son," answered the king. "He doesn't seem to like his wife, and I can't understand why."

"These things happen," consoled Lord Rosser. "She has been the talk of the town ever since she came of age. I don't believe you could have chosen a better wife for the prince."

"I am sure you are right." The king hesitated. "I just can't help but think there is something wrong with my son. He spends all of his time with Albert and none with his wife. I had hoped it would change after the wedding, but he ignored her all night."

"Something wrong, sir?" asked Lord Rosser, trying to clarify.

"I am worried he likes Albert too much."

Lord Rosser was not surprised by this comment. In fact, he had been waiting for the king to come to that conclusion. He had known such rumors were floating around court.

"It had to be his mother that did this to him," spat the king. He was now getting agitated as he always did when speaking of Richard's mother. "I swear she had the devil in her!" he yelled.

Richard's mother was William's second wife. His first wife, Lisa, was his one and only true love. In his younger days, the king was a kind and generous husband.

Many people said it was because Lisa kept his emotions balanced. She was from the noble House of Gildon, of which his councilor Francis was now the head.

He and Lisa knew each other for many years before being married. Their relationship began when they were children. Since they were noble children of the same age, they were tutored together and often played together.

It was customary for a prince's schooling to prepare him for kingship beginning at age ten. Even though William and Lisa no longer had the same tutors after that age, they still saw each other often. As they got older, their relationship grew as well.

Lisa's father was aware of their relationship and did all he could to nurture it. He made sure that she was properly prepared to be a queen. His ambition always included becoming part of the royal family by way of his daughter's marriage to Prince William.

William and Lisa had a wonderful and loving marriage. When she died giving birth to a stillborn son, he was devastated. With Lisa no longer in his life to keep him balanced, his temper took over.

Within a month, he was married again. Those closest to him advised him to take another wife as quickly as possible. He wasn't ready but agreed that it was necessary for the future of his kingdom. He had no children and needed a male heir to secure his house.

A member of the Private Council at the time, Henry Kerrich, had a daughter, Angie, who he was pushing toward the king. She was a young girl of seventeen and had no interest in marrying anyone, let alone the king.

A social butterfly and free-spirited girl, she liked drinking, dancing, and enjoying life. She did not act as a queen should, but she was not brought up to be one. It didn't take the king long to realize his mistake.

She too died in childbirth. Luckily for him, she gave him a son who grew into manhood. The Westville line would continue with Prince Richard.

The king soon found out that it was the best possible outcome. After her death, he heard whispers of her inappropriate behavior. Continuing her free-spirited ways, she never settled down into her role as queen.

When the king heard the stories and accusations, it was impossible for him to believe she had been faithful to him. This sent him into a rage.

He was heard many times saying that if she hadn't died, he would have killed her himself. His rage lasted for days, and he could not be consoled. He did not mourn her death, instead he wished she had lived so he could exact his retribution.

Henry Kerrich was the person who would pay for his daughter's indiscretions. The king charged him with treason. He claimed that Henry intentionally set out to embarrass and make a mockery of him and his title. Henry was swiftly tried, convicted, and hanged.

Speaking of his son to Lord Rosser, he spat, "Richard got his self-indulgence from his mother. That woman had dark spirits in her. She knew nothing of how a queen should carry herself. Her free-spirited ways brought down her whole family. Oh, I wish she had lived to see what her actions caused."

Lord Rosser sat and listened to the king's rant. He knew there was nothing he could say to stop him. The rant simply had to run its course, and it now seemed to be over.

"What do you mean Richard likes Albert too much?" asked Lord Rosser treading lightly.

"You know what I mean," the king answered through clenched teeth. "I think he would rather lie with a man than a woman!"

"I have heard those rumors at court, My Lord," confessed Lord Rosser.

"Oh great, now there are rumors!" he yelled. "They are already making a joke of this family!"

Calming down, but still fuming, the king stared out the window. In a low, determined voice he commanded, "I want you to find out the truth."

"Yes sir," replied Lord Rosser, leaving his sovereign to his thoughts.

Chapter 4

The next morning, after tea with Elizabeth, Lynessa hurried down to the stables. At the wedding banquet, she had overheard Richard and Albert talking about going for a ride this morning. Finding a perfect hiding spot, she waited for them to arrive.

This was the royal stable, so only members of the royal household had the privilege of keeping their horses here. The stalls were twice as large with wooden shutters covering the windows. They could be opened or closed to maximize temperature control.

Cleanliness was of the utmost importance. The walls were scrubbed daily and the straw bedding was changed twice a day. The king considered his horses to be part of his family. If one were to become ill from neglect by a caretaker, it would have been disastrous for that person.

Lynessa found a spot a few feet from the back door. It gave her full view of the stable and easy access to her horse. She was crouching below a window on the outside of the building. The slightly opened shutters allowed her to see in.

She wasn't concerned about Richard or Albert coming through the back door, because everyone used the front door at the opposite end of the building.

This door was rarely used by anyone except the stable boys, and she didn't see any of them around.

It wasn't a long wait before voices could be heard. Even at this distance, she was easily able to determine that the voices were those of her two targets. One of them must have told a joke by the way they were laughing when they entered the room.

"Where should we go today?" asked Albert.

"How about to the lake?" offered the prince.

"Okay, sounds good—we haven't been there in weeks," agreed Albert.

Lynessa peered through the small crack between the two wooden shutters, listening to their conversation. As they were talking, they walked down the row of stalls. About halfway on the left, they reached their horses.

This put Lynessa far enough from them not to be seen but close enough to hear what was being said. Because of the secret nature of their ride, they prepared their own horses. This job would normally be done by grooms.

Richard and Albert were aware of the rumors about them and wanted to be as discreet as possible. Richard surmised that it would probably not be good to be seen riding off to the lake together. It would only perpetuate the rumors.

"Are you ready?" asked Richard, turning to see if his companion was finished saddling his horse.

Both Richard and Albert chose to ride a dark brown Palfrey as opposed to the Destrier that most noblemen rode. Richard said he preferred the Palfrey because of its smooth gait.

"Let's go," said Albert, trotting toward the back door.

Oh, my god! thought Lynessa. *They are coming toward me! I thought no one used this door!*

She quickly stepped backward and remained crouched so they wouldn't see her. Her movement was so quick that she didn't see the rock directly behind her. Her left foot landed on the side of it, throwing her whole body off balance.

"Oof!" she yelled, as her body hit the ground.

Luckily, the noise from the approaching horses covered up her muffled exclamation. She quickly got to her knees, knowing there wasn't much time before she would be seen. All she could think about was how angry Richard would be with Elizabeth if he saw her maid spying on him.

Still crouching, she scampered toward the corner of the building and dove around it. Just as her feet flew out of sight, Albert came through the door with Richard close behind. They were completely unaware of the scene that had just preceded their arrival.

Who is that? Lord Rosser wondered. *What is she doing here?*

He was standing on the wall surrounding the castle, where he had been watching Richard and Albert as the king had instructed him to do. He had followed the prince through the city gate, and then he had decided the best vantage point would be from the ramparts.

Lord Rosser did indeed have a good view high up on the wall. Observing the prince, he soon saw Albert appear from around the first row of houses on the western wall.

Over time, the city had converged on the castle as if it was besieging it. As the city grew, the king allowed houses to be built closer and closer to the castle. He felt it was much cheaper than expanding the city walls to account for the growth.

"Is that Lynessa?" Lord Rosser wondered this aloud, an expression of surprise on his face. "It looks like Lynessa."

He pondered the developing situation, his chin resting against his balled-up fist as he leaned against the battlement. The vantage point where he stood had been built for archers long ago when Westville still needed to defend herself against enemies.

He was surprised at what he was witnessing, and various scenarios played out in his head.

"That must mean Elizabeth is also questioning Richard and Albert's relationship," he concluded. "I wonder what Lynessa knows? I must speak to her."

Lynessa listened as the horses' hooves thundered off, but she still peeked around the corner to see if they were gone. Standing up, she could see they were already a good distance away. Luckily for her, they had already cleared the livestock enclosures and were cresting a hill in the distance.

The livestock pens were enclosed with stone walls no taller than three feet high. These walls not only kept the animals in, but also protected them from predators. Each type of animal had its own enclosure. There were pigs, sheep, cattle, and a much smaller area for chickens.

Footpaths wound their way around each stone enclosure. This allowed the workers to navigate their way through the enclosures without having to walk all the way around them.

Lynessa quickly made for her horse. As planned, Almond wasn't far away. His stall was just inside the back door, opposite of where she had been hiding.

I have to catch up with them, she thought, hurrying.

Disappointed by her clumsiness, she was now scrambling to gain back wasted time. Quickly unlatching the gate to the stall, she hopped into the saddle, which she had prepared earlier. Then she heard a voice from the other end of the stable.

"I wouldn't follow them if I were you."

She froze, and didn't have to turn around to know who it was. She felt that sinking feeling in the pit of her stomach that always accompanies dread. The voice of Lord Rosser was unmistakable. People in Westville knew his reputation, and they trembled in fear just being in his presence.

"Lord Rosser," Lynessa said in a shaky voice.

"They will see you," he continued, now standing in front of her. "Based on the direction they are heading, I would say they are going to the lake. There isn't a place for you to hide between here and the lake."

She was nearly in a state of panic now, having heard of the captain's ability to question. Her palms were sweating and her heart was pounding. Wanting to draw in breath, she couldn't.

What should I tell him? He will want to know why I am here and who sent me.

Seeing the panic on her face, he gave assurance that he meant no harm. He knew she would never talk until she calmed down. They spoke about the wedding and the exceptional musicians that had performed that night. It only took a few minutes before she seemed to relax enough for him to continue.

"What is your interest in Richard and Albert?"

Her first thought was to deny everything, but she knew it was obvious that she meant to follow them. "What do you mean?" asked Lynessa coyly.

"Don't play games with me. I have been watching you spy on them ever since they arrived at the stables."

Is he watching Richard or Albert? Why else would he have been monitoring the stables?

"My interest is in Albert, not the prince, My Lord," she said.

"What do you want with him? Or is this something you were commanded to do?"

He would have been very surprised if Lynessa was doing this of her own volition. A lady's maid would not dare follow the prince without being asked to do so.

"My Lord?" she asked, unable to come up with a reason.

"Did the princess ask you to do this? What does she want with Albert?"

Knowing he was on to her, she fumbled with her thoughts. Her head was spinning with fear. *The most terrifying man in Westville is standing in front of me. He will know if I am lying.*

"Yes," was her meek reply.

By the pliable tone and submissive body language, Lord Rosser knew he had her right where he wanted. She would tell him everything he needed to know.

"What information does she seek?" he asked.

Lynessa could hold back no longer. She told Lord Rosser everything. All of the concerns the princess had about Albert were revealed.

"I think we are both looking to answer the same question," said Lord Rosser confidently. "Does the princess want to know if Richard and Albert are unusually close?"

She hesitated then said, "I believe so. She never said it, but I too have heard the rumors, and I believe that is what she really wants to know."

He thinks I am weak. My plan worked perfectly.

Lord Rosser seemed excited to hear this information, so Lynessa decided to press her advantage.

"There is more, My Lord," she continued in her submissive tone. "I have heard rumors that it is not just Albert the prince favors."

"There are others?"

"Yes, My Lord. I do not know names, but it is said that the prince is close with other men at court too."

"Where did you hear this?"

"There was talk at the wedding feast—men I did not know, being so new at court, My Lord."

Lord Rosser was astounded by the news. His first thought was that she was lying. *What reason does she have to lie? It is true; she is a young girl new to court.*

Lord Rosser's arrogance caused him to fall into her trap. Normally, he had more information than the person he was interrogating, but this time he did not. He had not looked into her background prior to this conversation and wasn't aware that this was not her first time at court. He considered the girl naïve and thought she couldn't possibly best him in a battle of wits.

Pondering this new knowledge he said, "Since we are both looking to answer the same question, we should help each other. I wish for you to bring me any new information you should find on the matter."

"Yes, My Lord," she replied sheepishly and with a sly grin.

Galloping up the Northern Road, Lynessa's excitement overtook her anxiety from the interaction with Lord Rosser. Adrenaline coursed through her veins, having bested the great captain.

She lied to Elizabeth instead of telling her about the conversation with Lord Rosser. Her mistress could see that she was distraught returning from the stables, but Lynessa told her a sad story about a dying dog. Believing the untruth, Elizabeth told her to take some time to recover.

Needing to release some tension from the day's deceits, she rode Almond hard. His strides were long and fast as they made their way to the meeting place. Her hair blew in the wind as the powerful animal dashed through field and forest.

Reaching the small pond fed by the bubbling natural spring, she saw Terryn waiting for her there. Barely giving her horse time to stop, Lynessa leaped from Almond's back and ran toward her true love. She squeezed him hard as they embraced.

"I've missed you," he said, enjoying the hug.

"I wish we didn't have to hide," she replied. "I wish we could be together for everyone to see."

"In time, my love," comforted Terryn, kissing her on the forehead.

Terryn Rosser was nephew and heir to Lord Rosser. Lord Rosser's twin brother was killed at the Battle of Midalo when Terryn was just five. He took the boy under his wing, teaching him how to fight and, more importantly, how to lead an army.

Terryn stood a little past six feet tall and had short brown hair. The light stubble on his face looked as though he was trying to grow a beard, but this was the length he always kept it. He had the same muscular build as his father and uncle.

Sitting on a stump watching the bubbles from the spring, Lynessa told Terryn her news. Word for word, she described the interrogation by his uncle.

"Not many trained men would be able to handle him as you did," he commented, impressed.

She clutched his hand lovingly, blushing, as if to say thank you.

"So, the king has my uncle investigating Richard and Albert's relationship," said Terryn, thinking out loud. "You were wise to feed him both true and false information. You will earn his trust when he confirms the truths."

Terryn was now contemplating his plan. He was an ambitious young man, and although he loved his uncle, he felt it was time for him to elevate his station.

He knew Lord Rosser's fortune would pass to him upon his death. He had also been groomed to follow in his uncle's footsteps as captain of the army of Westville. Fame, fortune, and power awaited Terryn as soon as Lord Rosser was out of the way.

"My uncle cannot be disgraced because I am his blood," shared Terryn. "That means I would also be disgraced and wouldn't inherit anything."

"If only he would die," suggested Lynessa.

"I couldn't do that," he insisted.

"It could be an accident," she said cleverly.

Terryn put his arm around her as they sat. He stared up into the sky wondering what he was more afraid of, his ambition or Lynessa's.

Chapter 5

The Temple of Apollo was where Elizabeth went to think, not because she was a particularly religious person, but because it was always quiet. She prayed to Apollo when necessary, but she was not a true believer.

The temple was an octagonal building constructed with reddish brown brick. A large stained glass window was set in each of the eight walls, adding to the majesty of the building. The slightly domed roof was capped with a modest statue of Apollo.

Apollo was the first king of Westville and worshipped as a god. Every king since could trace his lineage directly to the great man.

Over five hundred years ago, Apollo began uniting the clans east of the Dragon Mountains, named thus because, when angry, they spat fire so high the clouds burned, or so they believed.

Most clans willingly submitted to Apollo's will, and those who didn't were forced to by the sword. This unification became the Kingdom of Westville, named after the surname of the great man. Some clans did not come easily. Some fought for hundreds of years. King William's defeat of Midalo saw the last fall.

As Elizabeth pulled on the heavy wooden door, the sweet smell of burning incense met her nostrils. *The soothing smell of the temple*, she thought, taking a deep breath and entering.

The interior of the building was full of paintings and sculptures devoted to Apollo's many accomplishments. The temple had a high ceiling to accommodate a very large statue of Apollo crushing his enemies.

This statue was the focal point of the worship hall, standing behind the high priest's podium. In front of the podium, chairs and benches were arranged in rows to accommodate worshippers. The first two rows on either side of the aisle were designated for the royal family and other members of the nobility.

Looking around, she saw that she was alone. Not really having a purpose, Elizabeth meandered aimlessly. Her path took her past many great paintings displayed on the walls. Lost in her thoughts, she made her way all the way around the hall. Not knowing why, her stroll ended in front of a case at the back of the room.

The wooden case had a glass top and was not far from the door through which she had entered. The case contained Apollo's Codex.

Apollo's Codex was a collection of writings left by the first king. This book was what the people of Westville lived by.

There were writings on how to raise a proper family, how to support your family, and how to act toward your neighbors. Everything you needed to live a proper Westvillian life could be found in the book. Of course, people followed the writings to varying degrees, but every family had a copy of the Codex in their home.

Closing her eyes, Elizabeth contemplated her life. She didn't know what to do about Richard. "How can I be the wife of a man who doesn't love me?" she whispered. "Will it always be this way? Am I destined to be unhappy for the rest of my life?"

The voice of the high priest brought her out of her pity.

"Well, hello, Princess," he greeted his guest. "I'm sorry, I didn't mean to surprise you," he said, noticing her jump from being startled.

It was not uncommon for her to be surprised by the high priest. When she and the other children came to the temple for their lessons on Apollo, many jokes were made about how quietly the high priest moved. Some children said he moved as silently as a snake, while others said he had the feet of a mouse.

"Hello, High Priest," she replied with a bow.

He was of average height, with thin white hair, and slightly overweight. He had been high priest in Westville for as long as she could remember. In fact, his age was another thing children joked about. Some said he had been here longer than Westville itself.

"You look like you have a lot on your mind, my dear," he said.

"More than you know."

Elizabeth and the high priest had always had a good relationship. He was someone she could always talk to, and she often came to him for advice.

"The original Apollo's Codex, written in his own hand," he commented.

"I know I should feel more looking at it, but I don't," she replied. "I have never felt a connection to Apollo."

The high priest had a contemplative look on his face, but it was not one of surprise.

"There is something I want to ask you," she said and then hesitated. "I have heard a rumor that is most disturbing."

"What rumor?" he asked, trying to help her get it out.

"I have heard that Lord Granville might not be my real father," she finally said.

"Ah, I was wondering when this would come up," replied the high priest, understandingly. "He is your father, but your biological father he is not."

She looked at the high priest astonished, not expecting this answer. She had fully expected him to confirm that he was indeed her father.

The high priest knew that this was not a rumor that she had heard, but an insight. He had taught and counseled her nearly her whole life. When she was younger, he noticed that she possessed an inner strength and intuition that he had not seen in many years.

"I have heard that I am Midaloan," said Elizabeth.

"You are not Midaloan," he responded. "What do you know of the outside world?"

"After the king defeated Midalo, we are the only people left," she recited.

"That is what everyone thinks," said the high priest. "It isn't true. There are other people out in the world beyond our borders."

"As the darkness descended upon the earth, the people who survived were scattered across the land," began the high priest. "They gathered together in small groups in order to survive. Our god, Apollo, united many of these groups in this area, and it became Westville. The groups in the area who did not agree with Apollo would soon be destroyed by him.

"He began taking them by force and incorporating them into Westville. Soon the remaining groups knew they would have to band together in order to fend off the king."

"They became Midalo," added Elizabeth, remembering her history.

"Yes," replied the high priest.

"Now for the part you weren't taught in school. We assume, with a great deal of naiveté, that everyone came together in small groups and either joined Westville or Midalo. That isn't completely true.

"Certain people reside beyond our borders who did not join groups in this area. They are travelers mostly, keeping an eye on the world as it changes. They watch in the forest but are not seen. They are a race with much wisdom.

"Some years ago while gathering berries in the forest, I ran into a traveler named Borin. He told me a tale of an ambush by wild men that he witnessed to the west of Midalo.

"Wild men are people you do not want to stumble upon. They run in small packs and only serve themselves. Some, like the group he saw, can be quite brutal.

"What was surprising to Borin was that the group of travelers they attacked included a woman with a baby. This was most unusual. The woman didn't look like a member of their group, and no one ever traveled through the forest with an infant.

"The attacking party killed everyone in the group, including the woman, but they didn't notice the child. The woman wisely hid the baby's basket behind a tree, just before the attack began. Miraculously, the baby did not make a sound through the short battle.

"After the raiding party left the scene, Borin gathered up the child to take her to a safe place. As he was walking toward Midalo, where he intended to leave the baby, he ran into the king's army marching toward the doomed city. He changed his plan and put the baby down, hoping that one of the soldiers would see it and take it somewhere safe.

"A much younger Lord Granville was the first to spot the basket. Approaching it with his squire, he saw the baby girl. Giving it to the young man, he told him to ride directly to his wife, Elena. He warned the boy not to be seen by anyone.

"The Granvilles had been unsuccessful in having children, you see. They knew this was considered a sign of weakness, so Lord Granville saw this as an opportunity. It was perfect timing because Elena had been pregnant and recently miscarried, and they hadn't announced her pregnancy.

"This baby was only a few months old, so it would be close enough in age to pass as their own. That baby was you, Elizabeth."

Elizabeth's eyes widened. "Am I . . . ?" she croaked, but the high priest interrupted her before she could say another word.

"To answer your question, no, you are not Midaloan. I don't know where you are from, but you are not Midaloan."

Elizabeth was only moderately surprised. "I think I have always known," she replied solemnly. "I could not give justification, but I have always had a feeling they weren't my real parents."

"I tell you this because I believe you should know the truth," he explained. "I beg you not to mention to anyone that I told you, though. Lord Granville would have my head!"

"Of course not," replied Elizabeth. "Thank you for telling me the truth."

She pondered the ramifications if anyone were to find out. She and her whole adopted family would be disgraced. She would not let that happen.

The large wooden door opened with a creak, and an old man entered the temple. He quietly took a seat on a bench in the back row. With their privacy compromised, Elizabeth rose from her chair and again thanked the high priest.

Leaving the temple at a quick pace, many thoughts ran through her head. *Lord and Lady Granville are good people. They saved me from certain death in the forest, took me in, and treated me as if I were their own. Not once did they ever treat me like I wasn't their own blood.*

She felt a mixture of excitement and sadness. The excitement came from learning the truth, but she was sad to hear how her mother had died.

⤛⤜

Knowing Richard would probably be at the lake for most of the day, Lord Rosser decided it was time to speak to his attendant, Jacob. Opening the door to the servants' dining hall, he entered. Jacob was sitting by himself at the table in the far corner. It looked as though he had just finished his breakfast.

"Hello, Jacob," greeted Lord Rosser.

"Hello, My Lord," replied Jacob, wondering what the head of the King's Guard wanted with him.

This dining hall was plain and serviceable, being in the servants' quarters. Its walls were bare stone, and its tables and benches were made of rough-hewn wood. It was joined to the kitchen. Today the atmosphere was loud with many of the tables full, but Lord Rosser's presence was noticed the moment he entered.

"Would you take a walk with me?" he asked Jacob in a manner that didn't give Jacob a choice. "I have a few questions to ask you."

"Yes sir," answered Jacob, swallowing the lump in his throat along with his last bite of food.

Quickly rising from his chair, he followed. He left his dirty plate and cup on the table, not wanting to keep Lord Rosser waiting.

As they exited the room and turned down the corridor, Lord Rosser explained the reason for his visit. "Jacob, I want to ask you a few questions about your master, Prince Richard. Does he spend a lot of time with Albert?"

With the first question, Jacob knew he was in a difficult situation. He knew where Lord Rosser was going with this line of questioning, as it was a question many people wanted to ask but didn't dare to.

"Yes sir, he does," he replied.

"Have you noticed anything odd when they are together?"

"No, nothing out of the ordinary, sir."

Jacob had been at court for many years, and he knew his longevity was due to the ability to stay out of these kinds of situations. He would not survive being put in the middle of a battle between Lord Rosser and his prince.

"Where are they now?" asked Lord Rosser.

"They're at the lake," he answered quickly.

Jacob didn't realize it, but he had just given Lord Rosser a valuable piece of information. It was now known to Lord Rosser that Jacob did know about Richard and Albert's secret rendezvous. At the stable, he saw that there were no stable boys preparing their horses. This told him that it was a secret ride, because no member of the royal family would willingly prepare his own horse.

"How often do they leave the palace secretly?" continued Lord Rosser.

"Secretly, sir?" asked Jacob, stalling for time, not realizing he had already said too much.

"Do you think I'm a fool?" yelled Lord Rosser, grabbing Jacob by the shirt and pushing him against the corridor wall. "I could destroy you and your family! Tell me the truth!"

Jacob opened his mouth, but no words came out. Lord Rosser let him down releasing the pressure on his lungs. Gasping for air, he responded, "They leave the palace together quite often, sir."

"Where do they go?"

"They go to the lake, the beach, and sometimes all the way up to the Midaloan ruins," replied Jacob stammering and shaking in fear.

Lord Rosser decided to press his advantage and go for the kill. "Do they love each other in an unusual manner?"

Jacob didn't know what to say. He was beginning to panic on the inside. He knew the answer was yes, but he couldn't betray his master.

Summoning one last bit of strength, he said, "No, My Lord. I have never witnessed anything resembling unusual behavior."

Lord Rosser wasn't completely convinced of Jacob's lie, but he had gotten the information that would help his investigation. He handed Jacob a small bag of coins and said, "This conversation never took place."

Chapter 6

Henry stepped out the door of his house and turned down the dirt road toward Town Hall. He had been dreading this meeting for days. With the shortage of fish, he knew he would have to endure much criticism.

The Assembly was the group of men who governed Triopolis. They usually met once a month, but could meet more often if the need arose.

The walk was much more difficult this morning, dodging the puddles that had formed in the road from the overnight rain. This was the kind of day that made him regret living on the outskirts of town.

Henry often wished the Assembly would agree on covering the roads with paver stones like they had done around Town Hall. They would be a little bumpy, but at least you wouldn't have to deal with the mud. A long shot, he knew, because of the expense of stone, but sometimes he just liked to complain.

Complaining came easily on the mornings of assembly meetings. It always seemed like someone caused him irritation in that group. The inability of politicians to get along was tedious at times.

He learned long ago to expect the worst, and he was never surprised. The only problem was this negativity put him in a foul mood all day long.

Wood-plank homes with roofs covered in either wood or hardened clay shingles lined the streets. Some were very narrow with two stories, while others were wider and only one level. The houses on this street had very little space between them, which is why a law was passed nearly fifty years ago requiring shingles on the roofs.

It was once commonplace for fire to burn through large sections of the city each year. Houses used to have thatched roofs, allowing fire to spread at alarming rates. The slightest cinder or spark immediately ignited the dried-out straw. Shingles still burned, but not nearly as fast as thatch.

The colors varied on each house, depending on the type of wood used. Some liked the lighter color of maple or the darker color of oak, while others preferred the reddish tint of cherry.

As Henry turned the corner onto Government Street, he got his first glimpse of Town Hall. It was one of the most beautiful buildings in all of Triopolis. Red brick covered the exterior and the windows were framed in bright white. An imposing building, it had two stories with six windows across the front on the second story and two on either side of the front door on the first.

A large fountain was the focal point of the square leading up to the building. It was of a deer jumping over a fish with its eye on a stalk of corn, which symbolized the three founders of Triopolis. They were Nelson, who led a clan that lived off the bounty of the sea; Donovan, whose people hunted wild game in the forest; and Rowen, whose followers cultivated the land and grew crops. The three founders of Triopolis were revered as gods.

Triopolis had grown during a time of constant upheaval. The instability of the ground beneath their feet kept every living creature on edge. Without notice, a mountain would erupt into a massive explosion, sending dirt and debris into the atmosphere.

The constant spewing of what people called liquid fire from the gaping mountaintops flowed down to the valley, destroying everything it touched. These explosions were so common that the mountains glowed red from the amount of liquid fire coating their slopes. This is how they became known as the Red Mountains.

In conjunction with the constant volcanic activity, earthquakes struck with devastating efficiency. People were known to disappear, having fallen into crevices in the earth's crust. They opened rapidly only to slam shut minutes later.

The people had little hope for the future. Anything they built nature soon took away. Those days were known as the Dark Days.

"What an awful time to live," muttered Henry, contemplating the stone sculpture.

He often reminisced about the stories of the history of his people when walking to Town Hall. Thinking about how tough it was for the founders made all of his problems seem petty.

Nelson, Donovan, and Rowen led the three groups of people that survived the Dark Days. During those trying times, the ash and debris from the bursting mountaintops allowed very little sunlight through. Food was scarce, and the leaders knew that if they didn't band together, they would all perish.

Many dangers existed in the dark world in which they lived. Marauders, desperate for food, attacked day and night, stealing whatever they could consume. They were unrelenting and lived by no moral code. If a person was between them and a meal, death was the only answer. It didn't matter if that person was a man, a woman, or a child.

The unified groups were ruled by the founders, and decisions had to be unanimous in order to become law. The first written rule of government was that Triopolis would always be ruled by an assembly and not a king.

The Founders' Code was a group of laws written by the gods binding the three societies together. The code began with four simple rules. They were:

Triopolis will always be ruled by the Assembly.
No one shall inflict physical harm on a neighbor.
No one shall steal from a neighbor.
No one shall damage the property of a neighbor.

As is the nature of man, the number of laws increased as time passed. Over the years, each member of the Assembly put his mark on the code. Many addendums had been added and new laws written as needed to govern the populace.

Henry smirked as he thought about how Carl Drake had taken control of the Assembly. In doing so, he had made himself the de facto king. It went against everything the founders wanted.

He had always known that Carl wanted and pushed for more power. Henry had recently noticed the bishop getting involved in Carl's schemes. This was something he would have to keep a close eye on.

As Henry reached the impressive stone sculpture in front of the city building, he saw William approaching from his left. "Hello, William," he greeted his long-time friend.

"Henry, how have you been?" reciprocated the slightly overweight middle-aged man.

"I am doing all right."

William Ward, in charge of defense, was Henry's biggest ally in the Assembly. With the people of Triopolis being alone in the world, they didn't really have a need for defense. William's team mostly handled law enforcement among the populace and dealt with the occasional wild animal that wandered into town.

"I am not looking forward to this meeting," commented Henry. "Our catch has not been meeting demand lately."

"Ah, well, Carl has to understand that sometimes the fish just don't bite," said William.

"I wish that were true," said Henry, following his old friend through the large wooden door of Town Hall.

They were the last to arrive and took their seats at the far end of the table. The Assembly room was on the first floor of the building after a right turn from the door.

The room had a very large window on each of the two exterior walls, flooding it with sunlight. The assembly chief, Carl Drake, was positioned at the head of the rectangular wooden table. He sat in a large oak chair, oddly resembling a throne. This gave Henry another laugh to himself at Carl Drake's expense.

To the right of Carl sat Walter Browne representing the wild game trade, and William next to him. The bishop sat at the foot of the table with Henry and Kevin Fletcher, the representative of agriculture, to the left. These six men governed Triopolis.

The structure of the Assembly had stayed intact, just as the founders had designed it, for the most part. There had always been a member representing fishing, hunting, and agriculture. The positions of defense minister, religious leader, and assembly chief had all been added in the past hundred years.

"All right, everyone is present," began Carl from his throne. "Let's begin. I would like to start by discussing our meat supplies. I have a report from Eric Feldstein. In it, he details the situation at the market."

"He says wild game, produce, and grain levels have been at all-time highs. In some cases, he has even been able to decrease prices. His concern is with our fishermen. The report states that the amount of fish he has to sell has steadily decreased over the past three months. Henry, what is your response to this?"

Henry turned and met Eric's glare. The merchant had an arrogant smirk that really got on Henry's nerves. It was always on his face when he knew he had the upper hand.

Eric looked every bit the part of a man who would stop at nothing to get his way. Eric was burly, with a thin layer of brown stubble on the top of his head. He had the looks of a man who would just as soon break your legs to win an argument as take his case to the Assembly. Because Henry was a member of the Assembly, he didn't have to worry about receiving physical harm at the hands of Eric, despite the fact that Eric was a known thug who got his way by any means necessary.

The focal point of the assembly room was the large, rectangular, oak table where the members sat. A short dark wooden wall with matching dark cherry spindles separated them from the painted white chairs set out for the citizens who attended the meetings.

It had always been important to the founders that everyone was allowed to join the assembly meetings and submit topics for discussion. These days, however, very few people attended. In fact, in today's gathering only four citizens sat watching.

"Our primary fishing spots are depleted," responded Henry. "My guys and I have been searching for new locations for nearly three months. We have found a couple good ones, but not enough to meet the market's demand."

"In three months, you couldn't find a few good fishing holes?" said the bishop with an accusing sneer on his pug-like face.

The bishop was not to be taken lightly. Many men who had crossed him had either come up missing or had their careers ended by one of his made-up scandals.

Being the bishop of Triopolis meant he controlled everything to do with the well-being and beliefs of the people. The powers of his office were as vague as they sounded, and he used this to spread his influence as far and wide as possible.

In the time of the founders, the position was that of a healer, and the occupant was responsible for physical and spiritual healing. Over the years, it had evolved into what it was today. The current bishop was responsible for turning it into a position of power and influence. His predecessors focused more on the religious aspect of the position and usually stayed out of the political power struggles in assembly meetings.

Henry's temperature was now rising as the anger built inside him. "You have to understand this is no easy task," he rebutted. "It is impossible to see below the waves and know where the fish are!"

"Well that is precisely your job, oh great man of the sea!" jabbed the bishop. "You are the leader of the fishing trade, so we expect you to be able to find fish!"

"Carl, this is ridiculous," exclaimed Henry, addressing the assembly chief. "For twenty years, I have been supplying this city with fish, and now I am accused of not being able to find them!"

Henry was irate as he sat back down because he suspected that the bishop and Carl were working together against him. This was so often the case lately. It was almost as if the bishop had some kind of control over Carl.

"I am sorry, Henry, but I have to agree with the bishop," said Carl. "We have seen a dramatic decrease in fish, which is vital to our people's diet. We have to look at it from the perspective of the greater good of the people we govern."

Henry now knew he was in trouble. Carl usually didn't give his opinion until the rest of the Assembly had a chance to speak. Upset, he knew the fight was lost.

Eric had given the bishop a crate of fresh tuna for his dinner party last week as a bribe to get Henry replaced. What no one knew was that the bishop didn't need bribes to bring Henry down. He had plenty of desire and muscle to do it himself.

"Maybe it is time to find someone new to represent the seafood industry," proposed Carl.

Henry jumped to his feet. Now it was confirmed that he was indeed fighting against the bishop, Eric, and Carl. They all wanted him out, and it would only be a matter of time before the bishop found a way to manipulate William, Kevin, and Walter for their votes.

"My forefather was a founder of this city and is worshipped as a god!" he yelled. "A Walker has had a seat at this table since the beginning!"

"Maybe your comfort in that fact has brought about your complacency," goaded the bishop.

"Or maybe the blood of the great man is running thin in his line," added Eric from the audience.

Henry was ready to explode after that comment. His face was red, and a vein pulsated on his right temple as if it were going to burst through his skin.

"Gentlemen!" yelled Carl, knowing he had to step in before Henry strangled the bishop. "Let's all calm down! We have to move on. We will end this discussion for now and continue it at a later date."

Carl knew the point was made to Henry when that defeated man fell back into his chair, seething with anger.

The rest of the meeting was a blur to Henry as he replayed the events in his mind. He couldn't even remember what else was discussed. All he could think about was how he was ambushed by the bishop and Carl.

As the meeting broke, Henry rushed out of the room, not wanting to speak to anyone. William followed and caught up with him just outside of the building.

"You're in trouble, friend," said William as they walked through the square. "It seems that the bishop and Carl are united against you."

"I don't know how I didn't see this coming," said Henry, upset with himself for not being prepared for what had happened.

"Well, I just wanted to tell you that I am here to help if you need anything," offered William.

"Thanks," said Henry as they parted and went in opposite directions on Settler's Street. Henry was heading to his boat for the rest of the day.

"Hello, Ms. Parkinson," Kelvin announced himself, walking into the foyer. He had lived in this home his whole life. It was not the luxurious mansion you would expect for the assembly chief, but it was by no means a small shack either.

"Ms. Parkinson?" he said again, walking into the kitchen.

"She must not be home," he concluded.

On the butcher-block island in the center of the room sat a plate of freshly baked cookies. Taking one, he bit into it. *Mmm, ginger,* he thought happily. *My favorite.*

He was startled by the sound of raised voices coming from the direction of his father's office. He followed the voices, slowly making his way down the hall. Stepping as quietly as possible, he approached the door, which was open a few inches.

His stealthy walk brought him behind the door. Peeking through the crack at the hinges, he saw the most astonishing scene. His father was taking orders from the bishop.

Kelvin slumped back against the wall in disbelief, but he didn't have time to consider what he had just witnessed.

The front door of the house slammed open and shut with a loud crash.

The conversation stopped, and both men turned toward the door that Kelvin was hiding behind. His heart raced, but his legs were frozen. He couldn't move.

Get out of here! he ordered himself.

He wanted to run away, but it was too late. His father was at the door. Reaching his hand out, Carl grabbed the door handle.

When Kelvin knew he was caught, he closed his eyes, grimacing in fear. He could already hear his father yelling at him. Thoughts of imprisonment or worse were running through his head. Touching his neck, he could feel the hangman's rope.

Kelvin was surprised when the door was forcefully pushed shut by his father. He exhaled in relief. He slid down the wall and crumpled onto the floor, exhausted.

After sitting in disbelief for what seemed like hours but was only a minute, he wiped the sweat off his brow. *Whew, that was close!*

Getting back to his feet in a crouched position, he looked through the keyhole. He could hear Ms. Parkinson putting groceries away in the kitchen. She must have had her hands full went she came into the house, and slammed the door by shoving it with her foot.

He assumed he only had a couple minutes before she discovered him. The adrenaline was pumping through his veins. He was fearful of the consequences if he were caught, but the excitement was too much. He had to continue listening.

His father and the bishop were now speaking in quiet voices. Kelvin was upset because he thought he had missed the most important part of the conversation.

"All right, this is what has to be done," directed the bishop.

Hearing his father agree obediently, his mouth fell open in shock. *No!*

His brow and palms became sweaty again. He was shaking from what he had just heard his father say. He couldn't believe what they were planning. *I have to tell Henry!*

Kelvin quietly walked back down the corridor away from the office door. Upon reaching the corner, he turned toward the front door of the house and began to run.

Sprinting past the kitchen, he said hello to Ms. Parkinson. She returned the greeting, but he was already opening the door and didn't hear her.

"He is always in such a hurry," she said, shaking her head.

"I have to tell Henry!" said Kelvin, rushing down the street.

<hr/>

It was dusk as Henry walked home. The sun slowly descended behind the tree line of the mountains to the west. The thick layer of clouds that had prevented the sun's rays from reaching the ground during the day was now breaking apart. A yellowish orange glow filled the western sky as the last few rays broke through a little too late to warm the day.

He had gone to the docks to be alone and process what had taken place at the assembly meeting. This was where Henry often went when he needed to blow off steam. He didn't want to go home or to the pub to discuss it with anyone. He had to figure it out himself first.

It always frustrated his wife, Mary, when she tried to get him to talk through his emotional distress and he just sat in silence. She didn't understand that he did his best thinking while engrossed in his work. Working relaxed his mind and allowed his thoughts to flow freely.

It took a couple of hours for Henry to inspect and organize their equipment because of his leisurely pace. He looked into the large wooden trunk that housed his fishing gear, admiring his work.

One day, years ago, Henry grew tired of lugging his gear all the way to the storage shed and back each day. His idea was to fasten the trunk to the dock itself. It was a brilliant idea that quickly caught on with the other fishermen. It wasn't long before every boat had a large box attached to the dock.

With the dock being built of wood, it was under constant attack from the elements. This constant bombardment meant that regular maintenance was necessary, and about every twenty seasons, the whole structure had to be rebuilt.

This dock, which had just been rebuilt the previous year, was T-shaped and extended thirty feet into the bay. All the fishermen were thankful to Henry for pushing the Assembly to tear down the old dilapidated landing pier. Even to this day, the occasional fisherman honored his work with a gift of a cup of ale at the pub.

Henry admired the way everything in the trunk fit perfectly. The rods were organized by size and the line and hooks arranged by strength.

Perfect, he thought, closing the lid on the box and fastening the lock.

His mind was clear from the day's trials, and the pains in his stomach told him it was almost dinnertime. It was time to head home.

At the top of the gradual slope in the road, Henry could see Fisherman's Pub. It was tempting, but Kelvin was coming over for dinner, so there wasn't time to stop.

The pub looked little better on the outside than the stained floors and walls of the interior of the building. Two lights on either side of the entrance door were the only welcoming signs on the building.

It looks a lot better in the dark, he mused wryly.

The sun had now completely set, but he could still see the well-worn boards making up the skin of the building. The cover of darkness hid many of the defects in the old, worn structure, but even the darkest night couldn't hide all of them.

A rustling in the bushes suddenly got his attention. Turning to look, he saw the light from the closing back door of the pub quickly diminish.

A narrow strip of overgrown grass lay between the pub and an old vacant building whose dilapidated condition matched that of the pub. Convinced someone from the pub had thrown out some meat scraps that a rabid dog was probably tearing into, he continued his journey home.

It was only a couple of steps later that he again heard more noises. This time they were voices that sounded very anxious, coming from the darkness. They were hushed but frantic. Henry had an uneasy feeling about the situation, but felt he needed to investigate further.

Walking as lightly and slowly as possible, he tried not to crunch the gravel beneath his feet. He walked straight toward the abandoned building. Luckily, it wasn't far off the road.

Grass grew between the building and the road allowing him to pick up his pace. Reaching the relative safety of the building, he crept forward in the darkness.

Peeking around the corner, he couldn't make out who the men were. The shadows looked as if they were in the field behind the pub. The waist-high grass hid the bottom half of their bodies, but Henry could see the outline of the men.

There were two male voices, but he only saw dark shadows moving against the backdrop of the moonless night.

Squinting, he tried to see what the two men were doing. With his sense of sight all but gone, his attention naturally turned to his heightened sense of hearing. The men's voices weren't recognizable, but Henry, closing his eyes to concentrate, thought he heard what sounded like digging.

Opening his eyes again with the hope they had adjusted to the darkness, Henry tried to make out the faces of the two men.

The door of the pub was suddenly thrown open, and a third man came barreling through, propping the door open with a bucket.

Having hidden completely when the pub door opened, Henry again slipped his head around the corner. Horror overtook him when he saw what they were doing. The man who opened the door was joined by a fourth, and they were pulling on the feet of a dead man.

Who is it? Henry wondered.

He would soon have his answer. As the body came down the stairs, the poor man's head turned toward Henry.

That's Borin! He wanted to yell this, but he kept it in his thoughts.

He barely held back another gasp when he saw what had killed his new friend. A gash in the side of his neck showed that someone was skilled with a blade. The fourth man quickly grabbed Borin's arms to lessen the noise of the body being dragged. They turned away from Henry and headed toward the field.

Henry slid his head back around the corner and leaned against the wall to catch his breath.

"I think we deserve twice the pay for this," said one of the murderers. "He didn't go as easily as we were told he would."

They were paid? Who would want to kill Borin?

"You, there!" yelled one of the assassins.

Panicking, Henry wondered how they had seen him. His legs were moving faster than he thought possible as he fled the scene. He knew that if he were caught, he would surely join his friend.

Once back on the road, he turned to look for his pursuer. He hadn't come around the corner yet. Henry's legs didn't stop until he reached the busier streets of the town center. Again, he turned and saw no one.

For just a second, he allowed the elation of not getting caught to consume him. To be safe, he didn't walk straight home. A few intentional wrong turns and a couple circles around buildings that were not on his way made him feel more comfortable. Still, no one was on his trail.

Fear propelling him forward, he walked the rest of the way home in record time. His eyes darted back and forth, scanning the scene for anything out of place. He only began to relax when the light that hung next to the front door of his house came into view. He had never been so relieved to see that door.

Standing outside his house, he tried to calm his nerves before entering. The last thing he wanted was to worry Mary or the children. Before opening the door, he took one last look to see if anyone had followed him. Alone, he turned the doorknob and entered.

The first face he saw was Kelvin's, who had arrived earlier. He was sitting in the wooden rocking chair near the fireplace sipping a cup of wine.

The room was cozy with the crackling fire spreading its warmth throughout. A green curtain covered the large front window while the art hanging on the walls added more color. Mrs. Walker's love of flowers was evident with vases filled with colorful blooms placed around the room.

A rush of heat and the smell of roasting chicken hit Henry as soon as he opened the door. He smiled because his wife had prepared his favorite meal, knowing that he had probably had a rough day at the assembly meeting.

"You're late," said Kelvin.

"I have good reason," replied Henry. "You will not believe what I just saw."

"Hello, Father," greeted his daughter Stephanie, who was thirteen but wished she were older.

She blushed, looking at Kelvin, her crush on the handsome young man evident to everyone in the room. Henry looked at Kelvin, and they both chuckled.

His twelve-year-old son Jeremy had followed his sister into the living room and repeated the greeting.

"Hey, guys," responded Henry. "How was your day?"

"Good," they both responded, walking past their father and into the kitchen where their mother was finishing dinner preparations.

"What did you see?" asked Kelvin when they were gone.

"Borin is dead!" whispered Henry, still amazed at what he had witnessed.

"That was fast," Kelvin said.

"I saw his dead body being dragged out of the pub by four men I didn't recognize," whispered Henry, the panic increasing in his voice. "His throat was slit!"

Henry then realized what Kelvin had said. "What do you mean, that was fast?" he asked.

"Oh, I have quite a story to tell you, too!" exclaimed Kelvin. "On my way over here, I stopped at home and overheard my father and the bishop talking about Borin. I have been here for almost an hour waiting to tell you, but it sounds like I'm too late."

"Dinner's ready," called Mary from the kitchen.

"Let's finish this after dinner," said Henry, getting up. They went to the table and took their seats, their pleasant expressions hiding the portent of their discovery.

"Mmm, that chicken smells great!" exclaimed Henry from his place at the head of the table.

Both he and Kelvin tried to act normal so they didn't alarm Mary and the children. No one talked as everyone filled their plates and enjoyed the delicious meal Mary had prepared.

Mary was the same age as her husband. She had shoulder-length brown hair and a motherly figure. They had been married for nineteen years.

Mary served chicken, roasted potatoes bathed in butter, and a roasted vegetable mixture. Kelvin often wondered how her chicken was always so juicy and tender. It was so easy to dry out the meat, but she never did.

"Thank you for inviting me over for this amazing meal, Mary," said Kelvin breaking the silence. "It isn't very often that I get to eat with family. With my father being so busy, it's usually just Ms. Parkinson and me."

"Well, you are welcome to join our family anytime," offered Mary.

"How was the assembly meeting?" asked Kelvin, taking another slice of chicken and a couple more potatoes.

"It went about as well as expected," answered Henry. "The bishop is up to something again."

"That's not surprising," commented Mary.

"Yeah, he always has his spies digging for dirt," replied Kelvin, knowing a whole lot more about the bishop after today's discovery.

"I remember the stories my father used to tell me about him," recalled Henry. "He warned me to never cross that man. It's kind of ironic, isn't it? The religious man is also in charge of espionage!" All three adults at the table laughed.

Jeremy was listening to the fascinating conversation, but not involving himself in it. Unlike Stephanie, Jeremy loved to listen to his father talk about politics. His sister was easily bored with political intrigue and would rather be out with her friends.

"What's more concerning this time is that he has your father on his side," said Henry. "The bishop came after me in the meeting armed with a letter from Feldstein. They are really putting pressure on us to catch more fish."

Henry was becoming agitated, remembering the frustration of the meeting. "I don't know who they think they are," he said. "The Walkers have been leading the fishing industry since the days of the founders!"

"I think that is exactly why the bishop wants you out," replied Kelvin. "He knows how popular you are."

"That's true," added Mary. "He needs a good reason to get rid of you; otherwise, the people wouldn't stand for it. Even the all-powerful bishop answers to the people!"

"Why has the amount of fish decreased, Father?" asked Jeremy, breaking his silence. Jeremy had always wanted to follow in his father's footsteps.

"I mean, the ocean is huge, so how could fish really decrease?" the boy continued.

"Fish follow a pattern, son," responded Henry. "A school of fish will usually frequent the same places each year and then continue the cycle. When we say the number of fish is decreasing, we just mean that the areas we have been fishing are decreasing."

"Oh," was his son's only response.

Stephanie continued to eat her dinner in silence, still not very interested in the conversation, but stealing glances at Kelvin whenever he wasn't looking.

"I guess we are going to have to find some new areas to fish tomorrow so that we don't give the bishop any reasons to come after us," suggested Kelvin.

"I have been finding fish for twenty years," boasted Henry. "I am not too concerned about being able to find more. We will find more fish. We just have to go a little farther out in the bay."

Mary gave Henry a worried look. It always concerned her when her husband talked about going farther out into the bay. She knew too well the stories of fishermen getting caught in storms or strong currents that pulled them out to sea, never to be seen again.

Everyone had now finished their meal. Stephanie was the first to get up, bringing her dishes to the washing bucket.

The large wooden bucket was filled with soapy water. This is where cooking utensils and dinner dishes were cleaned. This task fell to Stephanie as one of her after-dinner chores. Returning to the table, she grabbed another handful of dishes.

"Jeremy, I believe you still have schoolwork to finish," said his mother.

"Yes," grumbled the boy, heading to his bedroom.

"You will appreciate how we push you in school later in life, son," said his father. As was usually the case, Henry's comment received no response.

Henry topped off his and Kelvin's cups with red wine, and they went to sit by the fire.

"I love this chair," said Kelvin, returning to the rocking chair. "I wish I had one."

Henry stoked the fire then sat in his favorite chair next to the fireplace opposite the rocking chair.

"What did you overhear your father and the bishop talking about?" he asked.

"They killed Borin!" exclaimed Kelvin. "I heard them talking about him, calling him the wild man. They thought he was spending too much time talking to our people. Their concern was that people would start asking questions. They agreed that they could not allow anyone to find out where Borin came from."

Kelvin grew angrier as he spoke. His fist was clenched so tightly that his knuckles turned white.

"They agreed that the only way to protect the people was to eliminate him," recounted Kelvin. "What bothered me the most was the way my father stood there and took orders from the bishop. He didn't disagree with him or anything. He just listened and obeyed. How could the bishop have that much influence over the assembly chief?"

Henry was not surprised. He had seen the bishop wield his power earlier that day.

"He seemed like a good person," said Henry, moving the conversation back to Borin.

"He did, and that's why I don't understand why he was murdered," answered Kelvin.

"I think we have stumbled onto something very interesting," said Henry, "with the inscription you found in the book and now the understanding of who is running Triopolis. We have been blind to the truth. Carl and the bishop have been hiding a lot from us."

"There's more," added Kelvin. "I snuck into the archives during your meeting today. I was looking for more information on Luther."

"Did you find anything?" asked Henry, surprised.

"Oh, did I!" replied Kelvin. "I found a hidden chamber in the basement, and the bishop was there with his man Baldwin!"

Henry's eyes widened as he listened with anticipation.

"The bishop is into a lot more than we know," said Kelvin. "The room was a laboratory. It was filled with chemicals, herbs, animal parts, and even a human skeleton."

"The bishop is a healer," replied Henry. "He would need those things to develop his tonics and remedies."

"Yes, but it wasn't always his laboratory," Kelvin said excitedly. "It was Luther's! The room was ancient with inscriptions in the old language carved into the walls. Remembering some of what I learned in school, I was able to translate a few phrases:

I am Luther. All shall kneel to me. With the power of my mind, I will conquer. Through the shedding of blood, I shall create a new world."

"The more I hear about Luther, the happier I am that someone got rid of him," responded Henry. "If the bishop found this chamber, does that mean he is learning the same powers Luther had?"

"I think it does," replied Kelvin in a scared tone. "Luther talks about the power of his mind, and look what the bishop has done to my father."

"He does seem to have some sort of control over him," agreed Henry. "How deep does this go? It would be too dangerous to mention this to anyone because we don't know who we can trust."

"This is all starting to make sense," said Kelvin. "My father would never murder anyone. I heard the bishop telling him what must be done."

"I agree," replied Henry. "I have never known your father to be a cruel man."

"The bishop knows about the tablet," added Kelvin. "The job he was giving to Baldwin was to find the tablet for him. I heard the bishop tell him that the tablet was placed in the House of the Founders."

"The church," replied Henry.

"That is where Baldwin has been looking, but he hasn't found it yet," answered Kelvin.

"Hah!" laughed Henry, after a moment to think. "They're looking in the wrong place! That church was built almost two hundred years after the Dark Days.

"My father told me a story once that had the original meeting house of the founders where the school currently sits."

"I wonder if it's true," replied Kelvin.

"Let's take tomorrow off and look," suggested Henry, taking a large gulp of wine. "We can't trust anyone with this knowledge, so we must find the truth ourselves."

Henry's sense of duty was taking over. He was summoning all of his adventuring courage from his ancestor, Nelson Walker.

This part of the conversation ended with Mary joining them. Carrying a cup of wine for herself, she sat in a comfortable armchair positioned directly in front of the fire with the men on either side of her.

"I ran into Ms. Parkinson at the market today," she said. "She seemed down and commented on how the house just hasn't been the same since Robert died."

"That's true," replied Kelvin. "After my brother died, my father has not been the same. I think he blames me for the accident."

Robert was two years younger than Kelvin. He had the same confident and adventurous nature. They always tried new things that often pushed the boundaries of safety. If their father had been aware of the risks they often took, he would not have allowed them on the river that day.

"I don't think I ever heard the story about what happened to him," said Mary.

Kelvin stared into the fire with a look of sadness. "We were fishing on the river. The water was rough that day. We probably shouldn't have been out there, but we were arrogant kids who thought we were invincible.

"We came around a corner in a patch of fierce rapids and slammed into a rocky outcrop. The boat flipped over, throwing both of us overboard. Luckily for me, I was thrown over the side of the boat opposite the rocks. Robert wasn't so fortunate.

"The rocks were loosened by the collision and crumbled into the river. Just as his foot hit the sand, a large stone landed on top of it pinning him to the bottom. I tried to free him but the rock was too heavy. He drowned—right before my eyes. There was nothing I could do to save him. I tried . . ." Kelvin's voice broke with emotion.

"Oh my God, I am so sorry!" exclaimed Mary. "I'm sorry for bringing it up."

"I think my father blames me for the accident," Kelvin said in a quiet voice. "He has become a sad man at home. He doesn't say much to me or Ms. Parkinson, and I think he tries to avoid us. Working all the time allows him to forget everything else."

"We are always here if you want to talk," consoled Mary.

"Thank you," replied Kelvin, finishing his wine and getting up to leave. "And thank you for dinner."

Chapter 7

G ood morning," said Henry, as Kelvin walked out of the grove of trees that grew near the back of the school.

They came early so they would have time to inspect the building before the kids arrived for classes.

"I'm glad we aren't on the water today," said Kelvin, looking up at the gray sky and feeling the strong breeze.

"Yeah, it definitely smells like rain," replied Henry.

The only thing Kelvin hated about his job as a fisherman was working in bad weather. He was already a little nauseated just thinking about how this wind would be churning the ocean.

Henry's tolerance was much higher having grown up on the water. His father regularly took him out on the boat to acclimate his son to the sea. He had always expected Henry to follow in his footsteps as he had done.

Feeling the first sprinkles of rain, Kelvin looked up and thought, *Yup, a good day to stay on land.*

For the moment, he had to focus on why he had met Henry behind the school. "I remember there being a large crack in the foundation over here," said Kelvin, pointing toward the opposite end of the back wall of the building.

"There it is," replied Henry, reaching it first.

A jagged crack snaked its way around a large stone in the old foundation. It looked as if it had probably formed from the shifting of the structure or the weather.

The schoolhouse was built at a time when stone was used for the foundation. This was long before the manufacture of concrete was perfected in Triopolis. Stone was very strong and sturdy, but the mortar used to fill in the gaps was susceptible to the elements. Because of this, cracks often appeared.

"I bet if we could take one of these out, the hole would be big enough for us to fit through," said Henry, looking at the large embedded stone.

"I would fit, but I am not sure about you, old man!" replied Kelvin jokingly.

He was referring to Henry's growing mid-section that accompanied most middle-aged men, and he took every opportunity to send a jab Henry's way.

"You are so funny!" Henry exclaimed. "I can't wait until you are in your forties, and it happens to you!"

Henry was very easygoing when it came to jokes, and they both laughed.

Getting back to the task at hand, Henry reached into the canvas sack he had brought and pulled out a hammer.

"Well, you came prepared," commented Kelvin.

"And it's a good thing," said Henry, taking a whack.

Chips of mortar flew in every direction as Henry repeated his act of violence on the only thing stopping him from entering the building. The mortar disintegrated almost immediately after contact with the hammer.

"Thanks to the builders for mixing this bad batch of mortar," said Henry, jokingly.

After working his way around the stone, it began to loosen.

Henry put the hammer down and wiggled the large rock out of its home. It hit the ground with a thud, and Kelvin helped him roll it to the side.

Kelvin, never feeling comfortable without his trusty tinderbox, pulled it out and lit a piece of cloth. He had wrapped the cloth around a stick, and it resembled a torch.

When he was younger, he and Robert had been stranded overnight in a cave. They had no way to light a fire. It was dark and scary, and Kelvin vowed he would never again be without his flint and steel.

Reaching the torch into the hole, the underbelly of the old school building appeared before their eyes.

"I don't see anything," said Henry.

"Just an empty space," replied Kelvin, disappointed.

He swung the torch from one side to the other, but the whole space looked empty. "Let's go in," said Henry, crawling into the hole he had carved out of the foundation.

Kelvin followed nervously and was surprised at the drop to the floor upon entering. The surprise continued when he stood up. He could stand upright without hitting his head on the floor beams above.

The stale, moldy air beneath the school welcomed the light breeze that entered through the breach in its wall. For the first time in hundreds of years, fresh air was allowed to infiltrate the chamber.

Moving forward, they soon realized that even the breeze could not penetrate very deeply in such a confined space. It was still difficult to breathe.

The cobwebs were so thick they had to brush them aside like tree branches in a forest as they moved deeper into the basement.

"I hate spiders and the nasty webs they weave," commented Henry, picking the sticky remnants off his clothes.

"So, do I," replied Kelvin, showing his friend his arm, which had just taken down a very thick web.

Henry laughed. "That's disgusting!" Kelvin's arm was so thickly coated with cobwebs that it looked like it was in a plaster cast.

When they first shed light on the space, it looked as though cobwebs completely filled the room. After hacking their way through the dense netting of sticky fibers, they discovered that the back half of the room was clear.

"Strange that the spiders don't build webs on this side of the room," commented Kelvin, curiously.

"Look," said Henry, pointing at an open shaft in the back corner of the room.

Hurrying to it, Henry said, "I think this is what we are looking for."

"It has to be the entrance to the House of the Founders," replied Kelvin. "Why else would there be a wooden shaft in a dirt floor?"

They both peered into the hole, but everything was dark. Even when Kelvin reached the torch down, he saw nothing but the first few rungs of a ladder attached to the wall.

"Why won't the light penetrate any further?" Henry pondered.

Kelvin tore a small piece of char paper from his tinderbox, lit it, and dropped it in the hole. Almost immediately into its flight, it was extinguished.

"How could that be?" he wondered aloud.

They both knew char paper smoldered instead of burning quickly, which is what made it so effective for lighting fires. It should have continued to smolder all the way to the bottom.

"I don't like this at all," said Kelvin, apprehensive. "Why did they hide the House of the Founders instead of just tearing it down?"

"It seems like it would have been a whole lot easier," agreed Henry.

"Luther must have done some pretty bad things for the founders to go through all this trouble to hide any evidence," said Kelvin.

"It is exciting, though," commented Henry. "We could be rewriting our history. Let's go down and take a look."

"This ladder doesn't look safe," worried Kelvin, reluctantly following his friend.

The ladder looked as old as the building, and they were surprised it could still hold its own weight, let alone theirs. The dry, old wood creaked with every step as they descended into the cavern.

Kelvin felt much better when his feet were again on solid ground. Henry was already there holding the torch so that Kelvin could see where he was stepping.

They were in a hallway that only went in one direction. "I have a strange feeling down here," said Henry.

"You too?" asked Kelvin, trying to figure out what the feeling was.

The walls were surprisingly clean, and the air was much more bearable than it was in the spider-infested room above.

As they walked down the corridor, they heard a click, and the hallway was filled with light. Every torch hanging in its wall sconce ignited at the same time.

"Who's there?" yelled Henry.

"Hello!" yelled Kelvin.

"You dare to enter my domain uninvited!" boomed a terrorizing voice.

"Who are you?" yelled Henry.

Both men were frantically looking in every direction, trying to figure out where the voice was coming from, but no one was there. They were panting like they had just run a marathon.

Everything they knew about life—what was possible and what was not—changed in an instant.

"Bodiless voices, torches lighting on their own," said Kelvin. "This stuff only happens in books. Maybe this is why the founders tried so hard to wipe Luther from history."

"What kind of powers did this man have?" wondered Henry out loud. "We had better be extra careful in here."

As they walked down the corridor, Henry had a bad feeling that the stone walls would become their tomb. Reaching the first intersection, they stopped to decide which way to go.

"Right or left?" asked Kelvin.

"Let's try left," chose Henry, turning and proceeding down the hallway in that direction.

Henry's eyes were fixed straight forward. He walked cautiously, looking for anything out of the ordinary. *Nothing will sneak up on us*, he thought to himself, more in reassurance than in fact.

"Aaaah!" he yelled, falling forward.

His foot was caught on something, and he couldn't get it out. Looking down, he saw the still armored skeleton of the last adventurer to walk these halls. His foot was caught on a piece of the armor. He summoned all his strength and kicked his foot forward, causing the skeleton to roll over and freeing his foot in the process.

Click reverberated throughout the corridor.

"Watch out!" yelled Kelvin.

A huge boulder, half the size of the hallway, crashed onto the floor from above. Henry was blown backward by the concussion from the falling rock. Lying on the ground staring at the ceiling he said, "I don't like this place!"

"That dead man saved your life," said Kelvin. "It would have been you under the rock if you hadn't kicked him forward."

Henry just lay there for a moment appreciating his life before getting back to his feet.

"This seems to be some sort of maze," said Kelvin.

"Yeah, and not for fun, either," replied Henry. "It's designed to kill people who aren't supposed to be here."

They walked back through the intersection and down the hallway to the right. Both men were on edge as they moved forward. They listened for the dreaded click, which they now knew meant danger was imminent.

Coming upon another intersection, they had three different choices.

"Left," suggested Kelvin.

Cautiously, they advanced. Inching their way forward, they waited for the click, but none came. This corridor was long, but they could not relax. Tension filled every muscle in their bodies as they strode forward.

Coming to the next intersection, they again had a decision to make. Indecision and fear made it difficult to choose which direction to take.

"I don't know," said Kelvin, sighing in frustration. "The first time we turned left, we quickly discovered that was the wrong choice. At the second intersection we turned left, and it was correct. Does that mean we should turn right this time?"

"Right, left, right," repeated Henry. "Right it is." Deciding for them, Henry took the lead, slowly advancing.

At the same time, they both noticed an opening in the floor ahead. "Be careful," urged Kelvin.

They slowly shuffled their feet closer to the opening. They were both standing at the edge when the terrorizing *click* echoed through the corridor.

"No!" yelled Henry, jumping back.

Kelvin didn't react quickly enough, and the section of floor he was standing on jerked, knocking him over. It tilted as if it was trying to dump him into the pit below. *Click, click, click*—the mechanism sounded like a chain lowering him to his doom.

The section of floor was hinged with one end declining into the pit. He scraped and clawed at the floor, trying to save himself, but the floor was smooth as if it had just been polished. There was nothing for him to grab on to.

Will this be the end? he wondered, as his body slid further down the ramp.

He continued grasping for anything, but the smooth surface didn't give any help. His last attempt was in desperation as he tried to dig his fingernails into the stone floor.

Just when he was about to give up, he caught sight of Henry's hand reaching toward him from the top of the ledge. He grabbed it just as the floor fell away. There he was dangling over the edge with only one arm being held by his friend and mentor.

The section of floor that once supported him was now hanging in the same vertical position offering no support. Determined to get the best of the smooth surface and save his life, he repeatedly swung his feet against it. Groping it, he tried to find some small crack or indentation that would support his weight.

"Stop!" said Henry. "I can't hold you!"

The sweat building on Kelvin's arm acted as a lubricant, and Henry's hand slipped.

"You have to give me your other hand!" yelled Henry.

He couldn't. The exhausting, frenzied attempt to save his life had drained Kelvin of all his energy and was beginning to sap his will to live.

"Oh my god," said Henry, realizing what was in the pit. "Don't look down!"

Kelvin instinctively snuck a glance into the pit. Hundreds of rats were awaiting the arrival of their next meal.

"Look at me!" yelled Henry, trying to take Kelvin's mind off of the pit teeming with ravenous rodents.

Immediately, visions of that terrifying day twelve years ago filled Kelvin's head.

The sensation of little feet crawling on his body brought the young boy from his slumber. The last thing he remembered was lying on top of the large mountain of hay. He had fallen asleep after hours of playing in his uncle's barn.

Screaming and shaking his body like he was crazed, he realized what was actually crawling on him. It must have been twenty rats covering his body, scurrying about as if everything was normal.

He jumped to his feet slapping and swiping at his body, trying to free himself of the oversized furry creatures. The boy would endure many bites from the rats that day. The trauma from that experience was something he had never forgotten. Those rats haunted him in his nightmares.

"I hate rats!" yelled Kelvin, thinking about the agony of being devoured by them.

With his newfound will to live, Kelvin swung his free hand up just enough for Henry to grab it. "I am not going to be eaten by rats!" he screamed.

With Henry pulling on both arms, he again swung his legs toward the wall, and this time he was able to get just enough traction to help Henry pull him to safety. Both men lay on the floor, crippled by their exhaustion.

"I thought I was dead," panted Kelvin. "Why did you tell me not to look? Of course I am going to look when you say that!"

"I knew you hated rats," explained Henry. "You looked like you were giving up, and I knew that would re-energize you. It worked!"

"Well, I guess I can forgive you since you did save me from falling," Kelvin said with a laugh.

Walking back the way they had come, Henry wondered aloud, "Did we make a mistake coming in here? Are we in over our heads? Some of the things we have experienced seem so unreal."

"We have to continue," answered Kelvin, with rare confidence. "We have to find the tablet before the bishop does."

Hearing the bishop's name brought Henry back around, and Kelvin could see the hate building in his eyes.

"You're right," he said. "We have to find the truth about him. I wonder how much of this sorcery he knows. He could be much more dangerous than we think."

They both pondered that thought and bristled with fear. "We have to get to the tablet first," said Kelvin. "It could be the death of us if we don't."

Continuing straight through the intersection, their journey progressed. Neither said a word. Ears were perked, listening for anything that might bring them danger, but their thoughts were focused on the bishop. They knew what would happen if he found the tablet before they did.

A long straight stretch passed before their next decision. Left or right were their options.

"I am sick of all of these possibly deadly decisions," said Kelvin, mentally exhausted.

"How much longer can this maze be?" asked Henry rhetorically. "This guy has a really sick sense of humor."

"Left or right?" asked Kelvin.

"I think it's left again," replied Henry, leading the way.

The anticipation grew along with increased anxiety. The two adventurers were waiting for the next attempt on their lives. What direction would it come from? Would something fall from the ceiling? Would they be attacked from the walls? Step by step, they advanced at a snail's pace.

With no attempt on their lives, they came to the next corner. This time they had but one choice. The corridor turned left only.

"This is new," commented Kelvin.

"Yeah, but is it good or bad?" said Henry in a droll tone.

The moment they turned the corner, they saw an emerald green glow emanating from a chamber ahead.

"This must be the end," said Kelvin apprehensively.

"Let's hope it is the end of the maze and not the end of us," said Henry.

They stopped and stared at the light, pondering what to do.

"Well, there's only one way to find out," said Henry, stepping around his more cautious friend.

Kelvin followed as Henry walked toward the light. Standing in the entryway, they looked in awe at the room before them. The green glow seemed to be emanating from the bricks in the wall.

The room was neither small nor large, and the walls were bare except for the green glow. The only adornment was a stone pedestal about four feet high standing in the center of the room.

"That's it!" said Kelvin breathlessly.

Slowly they approached it, looking in all directions, anticipating the dreaded *click*. To their relief and surprise, the unwanted sound did not come.

Reaching the center of the room, Henry said, "I can't believe there wasn't another trap!"

"I was expecting one too," replied Kelvin in amazement.

On top of the pedestal was the prize they had been searching for. "A map!" exclaimed Kelvin.

"Yes, but where does it lead?" asked Henry.

Befuddled, they looked at each other realizing that their journey was only just beginning.

The stone tablet was displayed on the pedestal as if it was meant to be read where it lay. It wasn't thick, and didn't look all that heavy. Curiously, there were pockmarks and scrapes on the sides as if it had seen much use over the years.

"The way this tablet looks, I would say whoever put it here was in a hurry," speculated Henry. "There was no time to polish a stone of such importance?"

"It says it begins at the Black Lake," read Kelvin. "Where is that?"

"I have never heard of it," replied Henry. "I have never heard of any of these landmarks."

"The Giant's Legs, the Snake River, and the Lone Soldier," read Kelvin. "I am going to need more time to study this."

He took a folded piece of paper and a small wood block from his pocket and placed them on the tablet. Unfolding the paper, he spread it over the stone tablet and rubbed the block over it to create an impression on the paper.

This would allow him to take the directions with him without having to carry a cumbersome stone. As he started the make the rubbing, they both froze when they heard another click. They looked at each other as if to say, "What now!"

A green mist appeared from the back of the room followed by the voice again. "Only the Enlightened will be accepted in my presence. Find it or die!"

Kelvin frantically finished the rubbing and shoved the paper back into his pocket, leaving the block.

When the voice finished speaking, the green mist formed into the most horrifying, ghoulish creature imaginable. Large fangs dripping with blood hung from its upper jaw. Slowly rising to the ceiling, the winged gargoyle-like monster stretched its short arms and flexed the massive claws attached at the ends. Letting out a blood-curdling scream, the creature swooped down at the two intruders.

"Run!" screamed Henry, as they took off back down the hallway.

"Do you remember the way out?" yelled Kelvin.

"Yes, follow me," Henry screamed, sprinting forward.

They made turn after turn correctly, retreating through the maze. At each corner, they saw the green phantom on their tail.

Suddenly, Henry slowed. "I can't remember which turn we made here," he said.

They looked back and saw the demon gaining ground during their moment of indecision. Drool was oozing from its lips as it anticipated its catch.

"Right!" screamed Kelvin, and they quickened their pace. "That was close!"

"Just keep running!" replied Henry. "There's the ladder!"

Henry grabbed it and climbed as fast as he could.

Kelvin, a few steps behind, leaped for it. In midstride, his hand landed just below Henry's feet. Reaching the top, Kelvin pulled his feet through the threshold. The specter disintegrated, slamming into the wall below.

Sprawling out on the dirt, they basked in the glow of their survival. Not able to get a word out because of their accelerated panting, they stared at the underside of the floor of the schoolhouse.

The dirt stuck to their sweat-soaked clothes from the long run through the maze. It didn't bother them at all. They were just happy to be alive.

"I have never been so happy to be at school," said Kelvin, jokingly. Henry let out a loud howl of laughter.

"Well, now we know what we are up against," said Henry. "But are we equal to the task."

Exiting the hole in the foundation of the school, they placed the stone back into its place hoping no one would notice that it had been broken loose.

"I will come back tonight after dark and replace the mortar to cover our trail," said Henry.

"We must have been in there all day because school is just letting out," said Kelvin, as they walked into the forest behind the school and out of sight.

Chapter 8

Henry stretched his arms over his head and let out a long, fulfilling yawn. Turning toward the middle of the bed, he was surprised Mary wasn't there. This was unusual because she normally slept later than he did. As he was trying to figure out why she was awake so early, the intoxicating aroma of bacon caught his nose. *Mmm*, he murmured.

Quickly jumping out of bed, he dressed and headed into the kitchen.

"What's the occasion?" Henry asked, alluding to the fact that she rarely made a full breakfast on a weekday. Walking directly to his wife, he kissed her on the cheek.

"No reason," she replied, smiling from the kiss. "I just thought you might like breakfast this morning. I know how much you like bacon and eggs."

Henry sat down to eat, and Mary joined him with a cup of tea. "This is a new flavor," she commented, holding a dried tea leaf.

Mary smelled it as her husband devoured a slice of the salted pork. He took a long, slow sip of the leaf-flavored water. "Oh, you're right," he said. "It is a little sweeter than usual."

"The merchant said it is a new plant he found in the mountains on the western side of the bay," she said.

He took a much larger drink this time. "I hope a lot of these plants grow there because I really like this tea," he replied.

Looking out the window, Henry noticed that it was already light out, which meant he was behind schedule. He quickly scarfed down the rest of his breakfast. "I am sorry to eat so fast," he said. "I am late already."

"I know, and it's all right," replied Mary. "Just leave your dishes and I'll take care of them."

"Thank you, and I love you," said Henry, as he opened the door.

"I love you, too," replied Mary, latching the door behind him.

Walking down the street toward the dock, Henry had a glow about him and a smile on his face. He loved his wife. He could always count on her support, and she gave him the push he sometimes needed.

I should do something to surprise her tonight, he thought. *I don't do that enough. I will get her flowers on the way home.*

Having settled on his plan, he enjoyed the warm morning sun that f ollowed him.

Approaching the docks, he saw Kelvin packing the gear into the boat, readying it for another day on the water. "Good morning, Kelvin," said Henry, slightly embarrassed for being late.

"I was wondering if you were coming to work today," Kelvin replied jokingly, and they both laughed.

Henry helped Kelvin put the last of the supplies into the boat, shut the storage closet door, and hopped into his normal seat in the back. While Henry was doing this, Kelvin untied the mooring lines and climbed into the front seat.

"You ready?" Henry asked.

"Let's go," Kelvin answered, grabbing the cedar oar and pushing the boat away from the dock.

As they floated into the bay, Henry was on one side in the back and Kelvin on the other side in the front. Dipping their oars into the water, they pulled backward, propelling the boat forward.

"We really need to have a good day," said Henry in a very serious tone. "The way Carl and the bishop are complaining, I would love to come back with a boatload of fish. Are you all right with going farther out today?"

"Yeah, whatever it takes to keep them quiet," replied his partner. Kelvin was not excited about going farther out into the bay, but he knew it had to be done.

Their strokes were powerful and efficient. The boat glided through the water with the grace of a dolphin. Henry loved the feel of the salty mist on his face as they crashed through the small ocean swells. The gulls flying above seemed to think they had something of interest, occasionally swooping down near them to investigate.

The adrenaline from the excitement of yesterday's adventure must have taken over, because they reached their old fishing spot nearly ten minutes faster than normal. By the look of the position of the sun in the sky, it was another thirty minutes of rowing when Henry finally stopped.

"Let's try here," he said.

They had gone a little more than halfway out in the bay, hugging the coastline on the east side. Being the experienced fishing boat captain that he was, Henry knew they would be safe as long as they stayed close to shore.

The water was perfect today. The small gently rolling swells were calming and posed no threat. Clouds were beginning to come in from the west, but the wind was almost non-existent.

"We really couldn't have asked for better weather," said Kelvin, looking up at the sky.

Agreeing, Henry brought in his oar and picked up a fishing rod.

Their poles were made of wood from the ash tree and were about three feet long. The wooden stick had a metal bracket near the base and a wooden pulley at the other end. The string ran from the bracket down the length of the pole over the pulley and into the water.

They held the poles in one hand and pulled on the string with the other, wrapping it around the bracket to pull the line in. The addition of the wooden pulley at the end was the newest technology and helped with the weight and tension when a fish was hooked. It also helped keep the string from fraying.

They typically used bits of chopped-up fish as bait, but sometimes they also used worms and leeches. Henry and Kelvin baited their hooks and threw their lines overboard.

With the work done until someone hooked a fish, they finally had an opportunity to discuss yesterday's adventure.

"Did you have a look at that map again?" asked Henry.

"I spent all night trying to figure it out," replied Kelvin. "It depicts places I have never been to and never heard of."

"I looked at some old maps I had at home and couldn't find those cities either," added Henry. "I wonder if they have different names now."

"I hadn't thought of that," replied Kelvin. "If that's the case, I think we are even more lost." They both laughed.

"I did go back and replace that stone we removed," said Henry. "By now the mortar is probably dry, so it should look like it was never touched. I even covered up the mortar dust and stone shavings on the ground to completely cover our tracks. All that remains is a not-unusual foundation crack."

"Thanks," replied Kelvin.

"The last thing we need is for the bishop to find the tablet," commented Henry, with a look of distaste.

"What happened between you and the bishop?" asked Kelvin.

"The bishop and I go way back," answered Henry, remembering that day. "I was young, and Mary and I had only recently been married."

"It was the day my father passed away, and the Assembly didn't want any interruption in their proceedings. The bishop saw his opportunity, and he pounced. I was so ignorant then." Henry had a look of contemplation, lost in his memories.

"The bishop was close with my father, so he knew I would trust him. The night of my father's death, he came to my house. Mary was out visiting her mother, who was sick, so I was home alone.

"He gave me a proposal that no one so young would pass up. He offered me my father's seat in the Assembly in exchange for loyalty, and I agreed. He made sure the fishermen's vote was unanimous, as was the Assembly's. I think he already had the fishermen's votes before he even came to see me.

"I did everything he asked of me. Every vote he wanted, I gave to him." Henry was disgusted with himself as he told the story.

"You're not the bishop's man now," said Kelvin.

"No, I am not!" spat Henry.

"The night he made me the offer I had mixed emotions. I was grieving for my father, but I was also excited about the seat in the Assembly, so I went to the pub for a few drinks."

"Of course you were excited, you were just given an Assembly seat," said Kelvin, understandingly.

"Everyone who had voted for me was there," continued Henry. "They kept buying me drinks. We had a great time joking and laughing. There was this woman, Natalie, who watched me from across the room. At that age, I admit, I was not the most faithful husband."

"Does Mary know?" asked Kelvin.

"No, I never told her," replied Henry. "I figured the best thing for our family was for me to take it to my grave."

"About a month later, Natalie met me at the dock as I was coming in for the day. She told me that she was with child. As you can imagine, it was quite a shock. She was realistic about our situation and didn't want anything other than support. I took care of her until the child was born."

"You really lucked out," said Kelvin. "She could have caused a lot of problems for you."

"That's exactly what the bishop thought when he found out," replied Henry. "Even then, he had his spies everywhere." Henry paused, remembering. "He was so angry, yelling at me and screaming, and he asked if I was trying to ruin him. He said, 'I brought you under my wing, and this is how you repay me? Your father would be so disappointed in you!'

"His solution was that Natalie and the baby had to leave Triopolis. I was in shock. I couldn't believe what I was hearing. Sending someone away from Triopolis was equal to a death sentence. There was nowhere else to go. They would have to find a way to live in the wild, alone, he said. Of course, the bishop knew this all too well, having sent many people away in his time. I was too cowardly to oppose him. I said nothing."

Henry sighed with deep remorse at the painful memory.

"I was such a stupid, selfish boy," he lamented. "All I cared about was my career."

"I can't imagine having to make a decision like that at my age," consoled Kelvin.

"The bishop made me watch as Natalie and my daughter Louisa were left in the forest. They were told to never return. I wanted to run after them, but my legs wouldn't move. I just stood there. My heart was torn apart as I watched tears fill Natalie's eyes.

"I searched for them for weeks, starting at the river, figuring they would want to stay near water. Upon reaching the base of the mountain, I turned to the west and searched every possible inch of the forest. After my exhaustive search in that forest, I crossed the river and searched to the east, but they were gone. It was no use. I knew I had sent them to their deaths."

Not waiting for Kelvin to comment, Henry justified his decision and tried to make himself feel better by adding, "He took advantage of an immature young man."

"I wonder if Borin knew anything about Natalie and Louisa," said Kelvin.

"That's one question I had wanted to ask him," replied Henry. "Now I will never know."

"Should we move to another spot? We haven't had a bite yet," said Henry, pulling his line all the way in and setting the pole in the bottom of the boat. He wanted to change the subject. It shamed him to think about that dark time in his life.

"Let's go farther out," he added.

"How far are you thinking?" asked Kelvin, trying to hide his nervousness.

"Let's go out to the edge of the bay."

"Has anyone gone that far before?" asked Kelvin, anxiously bringing in his line.

"Not that I know of," replied Henry arrogantly.

"All right, let's go," agreed Kelvin.

Looking up at the sky and seeing the sun gave Kelvin some measure of comfort. Straight above them, the sun beat down, framed by a few wispy clouds.

They grabbed their oars and pulled on them, moving the boat toward their goal. For the next few minutes, there was silence. Both men were anxiously contemplating the danger in their journey.

"I have to feed my family, right?" asked Henry, needing reinforcement for his decision.

"Yes, you do," answered Kelvin.

"The weather's perfect for the risk we're taking," justified Kelvin, trying to keep himself calm. "The sun is shining, the water is calm, and there're only a few wispy clouds and a light breeze."

They continued to row, staying close to the shore on the east side of the bay.

"Wow!" exclaimed Kelvin. "I never knew Rock Island was so big. It looks much smaller from Triopolis."

They both took in the magnitude of the large, rocky island that stretched half the width of the mouth of the bay. It was centrally located, with waterways on both its right and left sides.

Old legends said that the gods placed this rock at the entrance of the bay to keep the sea monsters out. In a way, that made sense to the ever-practical Kelvin. Everyone in Triopolis believed that sea monsters were usually responsible for foul weather. Besides, the island did keep the large ocean waves from pounding the shores of their fair city.

Reaching the edge of the bay, the awe-inspiring sight of the open vastness of the ocean was impressive. Dark blue water stretched as far as the eye could see. They both took a moment to ponder the immensity of the great body of water.

"This is truly amazing," marveled Henry, breaking the silence. "There is nothing but water. I don't see land of any sort. Is this the end of the world?"

"Seeing this really makes you wonder how big the world is," replied Kelvin.

"Come on!" encouraged Henry. "This water has never been fished. It should be easy!"

Turning the boat to the east, they rowed toward a sheer rock cliff jutting out into the ocean.

"The waves are much bigger out here," commented Kelvin as they rose and sank with the deeper ocean swells.

"We should be all right as long as we stay close to the shore," said Henry reassuringly.

"How does this spot look?" asked Henry when they neared the cliff.

"Let's try it," responded Kelvin.

"I have a good feeling about this place," said Henry excitedly. They brought their oars into the boat and readied their equipment for a good day of fishing.

Kelvin was the first to get his line in the water. "I got one!" he yelled immediately.

"Already!" replied Henry, surprised. "I haven't even gotten my line in the water yet!"

Kelvin quickly pulled in a nice size sea bass measuring approximately two feet. Just as the fish flopped on the floor of the boat, Henry announced that he also had one. They hit the jackpot. Every time their line entered the water, it came back up with a fish dangling on the end.

Three hours later, their catch consisted of thirty-three fish of varying types. The box in which their catch was stored, which sat between the two seats in the boat, was overflowing. They could've caught more, the fish were so plentiful, but their boat couldn't handle the weight of a single fish more.

"We needed a day like this," remarked Kelvin.

"Yeah, this should keep Feldstein and the bishop quiet," answered Henry, defiantly.

They were both wrapping up their gear when Kelvin noticed where the current had taken them. "Henry, look how far we've drifted from shore!" he exclaimed, unable to hide the panic in his voice.

"This is not good," replied Henry, and then he looked to the sky with a sense of foreboding. They had been so busy reeling in the fish that they hadn't noticed the stiff breeze and the darkening sky.

A storm was brewing, and it was almost on top of them and moving quickly.

"Quick, row!" yelled Henry.

They furiously worked their oars, trying to outrun the storm, but it was no use. They were moving farther away from the bay. The strong current was taking them east. The waves were rising higher and higher as the wind whipped them into a fury.

They brought their oars into the boat at the same time, realizing that their attempts to paddle were futile. There was no hope of overpowering the turbulent water. They were now at the storm's mercy.

Henry yelled, "Use the fishing line to tie the oars to the seats!" He knew the last thing they wanted was to be without oars when the storm subsided.

The storm's fury was unbearable. Waves crashed down on the boat and the sound was deafening. They were now lying on their sides facing each other, their arms wrapped around one seat, their legs wrapped around the other as they held on for their lives.

The ocean would decide whether they lived through the storm. Waves tossed the little boat from side to side at will. Henry looked at Kelvin as if to say, "This was a mistake."

Looking at each other, they wondered when death would come. A huge wave twenty feet higher than the boat came crashing down on top of them. It hit with the force of a twenty-foot oak tree. Then everything was black.

Kelvin was almost out of breath, stretching for the ball with his left foot. Just able to save it from crossing the line, the momentum of his body sent him flying off the field of play. Before he landed over the sideline, his outstretched foot landed squarely on the round brown ball. It was propelled back into play as his body landed out of bounds.

The ball was sailing across the middle of the field. Out of nowhere, his teammate David jumped making contact with his head in mid-air. The force from his head changed the direction of the ball, and it headed toward the goal.

It sailed over the goaltender's outstretched arms, and the fans went wild with excitement. Just as the ball slammed into the back of the net, Kelvin's eyes opened, and he came back to reality.

He panicked. *I can't feel my legs! Where am I? What happened?* These were the thoughts racing through his head.

Lying on his stomach, his hands were still wrapped around the back seat and his feet around the front seat of the boat. As he tried to answer those questions with his head still groggy, he stared at the bottom of the boat.

Everything was silent. He could see, but he heard nothing. *Am I dead? Would my head hurt this bad if I was?*

Finally catching up with his surroundings, he turned toward Henry whose arms were also still clenching the boat seats.

Feeling returned to Kelvin's arms and legs when he released the death like grip he had on the boat. As he did this, blood rushed back into his extremities causing a tingling sensation. Sitting up, he looked over at Henry and noticed that his eyes were also open.

"Kelvin, are you alive?" asked Henry.

"Yeah, I'm okay," he replied. "How about you?"

"My legs are a little numb, but other than that, I think I'm okay," responded Henry.

They had run ashore somewhere to the east. That was about all they could remember from the previous night. They weren't quite sure where they had landed, but they knew it wasn't Triopolis.

They were on a white, sandy beach, and beyond that, they could see thick, lush vegetation. The sky had completely cleared, and the sun was shining down on them. The storm must have passed a while ago because their clothes were completely dry.

Chapter 9

It was late at night, and the king was distraught with questions about his son. Stumbling down the hallway in a drunken stupor, he mumbled, "What is wrong with him? How could William, the conqueror of Midalo, have produced a son who would rather be with a man than a beautiful woman? It couldn't have been me! It had to be his mother's fault. What a mistake I made marrying that woman. It haunts me to this day!"

A mixture of guilt, confusion, and rage melded together inside his head. It was not a good combination for a man who had already consumed more than his share of wine.

The corridor in this part of the castle was not well lit. Oil lamps hung from the stone walls in sconces, but there were too few to completely illuminate the hallway.

The king was on his way to find a bite to eat. When he drank, it was common for him to eventually make his way to the kitchen. A little food after a night full of wine was probably good for a man known for the vast amounts of drink he consumed.

Reaching his destination, the king found the room was completely dark, so he took a nearby oil lamp from its sconce in the hall. Bringing the light around to the doorway, the kitchen opened up before him.

It contained two large open hearths against the back wall where most of the meats and soups were prepared.

The fireplace on the left had four large chains dangling from the ceiling. Three of them had large iron pots attached at the end used for boiling liquids. The fourth was missing its pot and hung aimlessly.

On the right, a large spit hung over the fire pit. It could hold one very large animal or many small ones at the same time. Various smaller spits, pots, and pans lined the walls around the cooking stalls.

Two stone ovens sat against the wall on the right. These were used to bake the pastries and pies that the king loved so much.

To the left of the entrance to the kitchen was where the meat was cleaned, trimmed, and prepared for the flames. There was one very large wooden table that stretched almost the full width of the room.

Everything was precisely where it should be. Water buckets were stacked against the wall, with bread and pastry pans on shelves next to them. All of the dishes, utensils, and cups were neatly stacked. Leo, the master of this space, ran a very tight ship.

Entering the room, the king noticed a loaf of bread sitting out as if someone was about to eat. Even in his drunken state, he thought it curious that something was out of place. He didn't ponder it long before the delectable aroma overtook him and he made for his midnight snack.

The loaf of bread sat on a wooden table in the center of the room with a knife lying next to it. The thought of tearing into bread baked by Leo made his mouth water.

The king loved his master chef's abilities in the kitchen. He once said that Leo was the most important person in his court. His counselors and noblemen were a little embarrassed by the comment, but they couldn't deny Leo's ability either.

"Oh, no butter," lamented the king, staring at the bread.

The sight of the enticing perfectly browned loaf of bread made the king completely forget his earlier anger. These quick mood swings had become common as he aged. One minute he was the nicest, calmest, most gracious ruler, and the next he was a vengeful tyrant with a penchant for conspiracy theories.

Knowing right where he could find the butter he so desperately wanted, the king walked toward the cupboard that held it. He opened the door and removed a small crock. The wine glasses were perched on a shelf directly above the cupboard, and he grabbed one with his free hand.

Returning to the table and setting the savory spread next to the bread, he headed to the wine casks. They were stacked to the right of the doorway just beyond the cupboards containing the plates and bowls.

The first glass of wine never made it back to the table. The king gulped it down without moving away from the sturdy oak casks. He again filled the cup and returned to his bread.

Dipping the same knife he had used to cut the bread into the butter, he spread it onto his slice. Taking his first bite, he knew he had made the right decision to come to the kitchen. He didn't know what Leo used to sweeten the bread, but if he could have only this bread for a meal, he would be the happiest man alive.

Finishing the slice, he started working on that second glass of wine. With food in his stomach, his thoughts returned to Richard, and the confusion set in once again.

"Why is this happening to me?" he murmured, his eyes watering from feelings of shame and guilt. "Will my line end with Richard? How will history judge me?"

Sitting at the table, hovering over the loaf of bread, he continued to drink the wine. It was no doubt helping to intensify his emotions.

"Aaah!" he screamed, violently throwing the now empty wine glass against the wall. It shattered, sending small pieces across the room. Rage had again taken over.

Getting up, he sent his chair flying backward with his powerful foot. Not concerned with the mess, he headed for the exit.

The king's head was spinning and his sight was blurry, causing him to sway back and forth through the corridor. He had frequent encounters with the walls on each side as he stumbled forward.

If his son would not lie with his wife, how could he be king? If the king passed his realm to Richard, would he be throwing away his good name? If Richard didn't succeed him on the throne, who would be the next king?

His conspiring was interrupted when a servant girl came barreling around the corner ahead. Not far around the corner she stopped dead in her tracks, realizing it was the king standing in her path.

"Well, what have we here?" he asked, deviously.

"I am sorry, My Lord," she stammered nervously, not used to being in the presence of His Majesty.

The young girl, in her white and brown uniform, had heard of the king's late night excursions to the kitchen, but she had never before witnessed one. In her haste, she had forgotten to put on her white cap. The jet-black hair on her head was balled up neatly as if the cap still covered it.

"I left some bread out in the kitchen, and I wanted to put it away before Master Leo found it," she explained, nearly hyperventilating.

"I don't care about the bread," replied the king, contemplating the girl lustfully.

The torches in the hallway flickered from the occasional draft as he stared at her with wicked desire. Sensing danger, she slowly backpedaled, moving away from him. This only made her situation worse. She had backed into a dark space out of reach of the two nearest sources of light.

The king advanced with a hungry outstretched hand. Having her was his all-consuming desire. The fear in her eyes was unseen in the darkness. She wanted to scream but couldn't because this was the king. He could do whatever he pleased without consequence.

The next morning he didn't remember the incident in the hallway. This was common for him after a night of heavy drinking. Even if he had remembered what happened, he had the ability to justify his wrongdoings and absolve himself of blame.

This was one of his strengths. With his uncontrollable and inconsistent temper, the king became very good at justifying his actions in times of rage.

"My head is killing me," he muttered to himself, tossing to and fro in bed for relief from the pain. "I must have had more wine than I remember."

"James!" he yelled.

James was his loyal bedchamber attendant who had served him since he was a child. "Bring me some water," he demanded.

"Certainly, sir," replied James, leaving the room to get a jug of water.

The king was in obvious discomfort as he shuffled over to the window and pulled back the curtains. Opening the shutters, he felt the cool morning breeze on his face. "Ah, that feels good," he said.

He was still standing in front of the window when James returned with a jug of water. He placed it and a cup on a small table in the sitting area.

"Is there anything else you need, sir?" asked James.

"No, that is all," responded the king.

Henry and Kelvin were both now sitting upright in the boat trying to comprehend what had happened to them. "I can't believe we are still alive," commented Kelvin.

"The gods were on our side last night," replied Henry.

Kelvin nodded in agreement. "I'm really thirsty. I wonder if we can find any fresh water."

"Yeah, and some food," responded Henry, feeling the pain of hunger in his stomach.

They both got up and stepped out of the boat onto the first dry land they had touched since the previous morning. "Ah, it feels good to stretch the legs," said Kelvin, feeling the blood circulating through them again.

Henry surveyed the area. They were on a desolate white, sandy beach. The tide was at its peak, leaving only twenty feet of beach before an abrupt transition to a heavily wooded forest. The beach seemed to go on for miles in each direction. The width of the sandy shore varied but the distinct line between sand and forest continued as far as the eye could see.

Turning back to his boat, its condition brought about feelings of doubt in Henry. "This doesn't look good," he said, eyeing the large gash in the side of the hull. "I guess we found the weakness in this style of boat building."

"It didn't sink, so I don't think it's a weakness at all," replied Kelvin. "We were pounded by some massive waves last night, and we're still here!"

"Good point," pondered Henry. "A dugout would have become water-logged from the inside and sunk."

Inspecting the large hole in the side of the boat, Henry discovered that a seam in the skin had pulled apart. He tried to pull the two sections together, but there was still air between them.

"Oh, I see the problem," he said. "A piece is missing."

"It looks like it was torn off this edge," replied Kelvin, looking at one side of the open seam.

"We could try to find what we need to fix it in the forest," suggested Henry, pointing to the nearby trees. "I would need the bark of a birch tree and sap from a pine for the adhesive. Then we might be able to patch the hole long enough to get us home."

Kelvin wondered if he would ever see home again as they walked toward the forest. He could almost smell Ms. Parkinson's freshly baked biscuits as he thought of the two hummingbirds that fluttered past his bedroom window each morning.

Reaching the vegetation, they saw a nearly impassable forest floor. Thick, bushy plants of various types combined with heavy grass filled in the undergrowth. Hiding underneath, broken branches and fallen trees made traversing the forest nearly impossible.

"Look at the size of those thorns!" exclaimed Kelvin, pointing at a bristly plant with long sharp barbs for its defense.

"Let's walk up the beach and see if it thins out at all," answered Henry, bristling at the thought of brushing up against the frightening shrub.

Walking what seemed to be east, based on the position of the sun, they studied the new land. The sand on the beach was not soft but not hard either. Their trail was washed away by the incoming waves, but the sand gave enough support for them to advance at a normal pace.

After walking for nearly three quarters of an hour, they finally found success.

"Look," said Henry, pointing at the break in the foliage.

"This path looks manmade," replied Kelvin, nervously. "It must be the wild men Borin spoke of."

"Let's hope we can go unnoticed," said Henry, looking back at Kelvin apprehensively.

They were surrounded by tall trees with thick foliage high above their heads that blocked out the sunlight. The forest floor just off the path was dense with bushes, grasses, fallen trees, and broken branches.

The light breeze rustling the leaves gave them an unnerving feeling as they walked down the trail. Cautiously looking back and forth, they were startled by the sound of a woodpecker beating its beak into an oak tree.

Their senses were on edge as they searched for the needed building materials. Listening for footsteps or voices, the two explorers were ready to jump into the bushes and hide at the sound of any unknown noise.

The trail, being so well worn, had to be travelled often, so they fully expected to encounter someone or something along the way. Kelvin, having spent so much time in the forest as a youth, knew that a path like this could not have been made by anything other than humans. That, however, didn't mean that animals wouldn't also use it.

After walking for about a mile, Kelvin remarked, "I can't believe we haven't found food or water yet."

"How can a forest this size not contain any birch or pine trees, either?" complained Henry.

"Do you believe Borin—about the wild men?" asked Kelvin. "Do you really think there are other people out here?"

He was just trying to find a way to calm his nerves. His heart seemed like it would beat out of his chest from the nervous energy, and he thought conversation would calm him.

"He seemed like he knew what he was talking about," replied Henry. "He didn't seem like the kind of guy who jokes around."

"You're right about that," Kelvin replied with a laugh.

"Water!" yelled Henry excitedly.

Henry was pointing ahead and to his left. A small stream was trickling through the forest. This section of the stream was where it came nearest to the trail. From here, it meandered away from the path on both ends.

Their mouths were bone dry, and the weariness of dehydration was beginning to set in. Kelvin knew his mouth would be watering right now at the sight of the stream if he were able to produce any saliva.

Both men, forgetting the need for silence, bolted toward the fresh water. Voraciously, they cupped their hands together and brought handful after handful to their lips, slaking their thirst.

Splashing water over their faces and clothes, they didn't care as they drank. The feeling of water filling their mouths and wetting their throats as it made its way to the stomach was invigorating.

Having their fill, they stepped back and basked in the glow of hydration. "That felt great!" exclaimed Kelvin. "I didn't know how much longer I could go without water."

"I was thinking the same thing," agreed Henry. "Now we need to find food."

Knowing the potential danger of staying in one place too long, they made their way back to the trail. Not far past the creek, they came to a sharp corner in a particularly dense section of the forest. The thick stand of trees hindered their ability to see what lay ahead.

"By the gods!" exclaimed Henry, as they finished the turn.

Kelvin didn't have to ask what Henry meant because he saw it too. They both gazed in awe at the outskirts of a city.

The city had no walls. Roads and rows of houses populated the city all the way to the forest edge. The houses were made mostly of whitewashed stone. Sturdy construction was necessary to withstand the strong winds that often blew unhindered from the sea.

Henry was amazed at the amount of stone used in construction. His experienced eye knew this just from looking at the solid structures. "This is not Triopolis," he said, still in amazement.

"Only a few days ago, we learned of wild men, and now we are looking at a city greater than Triopolis," Kelvin said, breathless with admiration at what lay before him. "I feel like we don't know anything about the world we live in." He paused for a moment and added, "Do you think they know about us?"

"I can't imagine they do; otherwise, we would surely have heard of them," replied Henry.

"Yes, but we didn't know about Borin's people until recently, even though they knew about us," Kelvin countered.

"You're right," admitted Henry. "I just hope they're friendly."

In the confusion of their discovery, they completely lost track of their surroundings. An old man coming from the city turned onto the path. "He sees us!" whispered Henry. "Act normal," he said under his breath so the old man wouldn't hear.

The approaching stranger looked surprisingly similar to them. He wore a round-brimmed hat with a khaki-colored shirt and pants. His clothes looked to be made of cotton, as were theirs.

It looked like he was going fishing with a rod over his shoulder and a bucket in his other hand. "Hello," said the old man, as he passed the two bewildered foreigners.

"Hello, sir," they both replied, surprised that he didn't suspect them.

"We didn't seem out of place to him," Henry said under his breath when the old man had passed. He was feeling better about their situation. "His clothes looked like ours, so I think we can blend in."

"Should we go into the city?" asked Kelvin.

"I think we should," replied Henry. "We desperately need food, and I think that's the best place to find some."

Henry and Kelvin both composed themselves, looking down at their clothing to make sure they looked as presentable as possible. They were mostly clean from the soaking they had received the night before, but the rough night had also done some damage. Kelvin's shirt had suffered a large tear across the chest, and Henry had a hole in the right knee of his pants.

The forest trail ended where the city street began. They were still walking on dirt, but the street was a little wider than the trail. Each house had a stone-covered walkway leading from its doorway to the street.

The stone houses had wood-plank roofs, which Henry immediately noticed because most houses in Triopolis were made of wood.

The street was empty as they made their way forward. Each house had subtle differences that distinguished it from its neighbor. The color of the shutters seemed to be a personal preference, as there was a profusion of browns, grays, greens, and blues. Some had flowers planted in window boxes, and some had flowers in the front lawn.

When they reached the first intersection of two streets, they noticed a sign pole reading Forest Lane and Market Street. "This place doesn't seem to be all that different from home," commented Henry. "Houses and streets are similarly arranged."

"It makes you wonder how two cities that don't even know the other exists can look so similar," mentioned Kelvin, curious.

The two lost adventurers stood at the corner looking down Market Street. "Look at all of those people," said Henry nervously.

Where they stood, they were alone, but a crowd gathered at the far end of the block.

"I guess we will find out if we can blend in with them," replied Kelvin.

This was their biggest concern. An inability to blend in with the locals could be disastrous for them if the inhabitants were hostile to foreigners.

Still standing on the corner, they watched as people went in and out of shops. The far end of the street was bustling with activity. Couples walked hand in hand, shop owners stood at their doors encouraging customers to enter, and kids splashed in the puddles left by the overnight rain.

Realizing that by standing on the corner and looking uncomfortable they were creating a scene that might draw unwanted attention, they began walking down the street. Hesitantly, they moved toward the congregation of people, trying to act as if everything were normal. Their apprehension and fear of being recognized as outsiders caused their motions to be awkward and unnatural.

Getting closer to the busy end of the street, their uncertainty disappeared. "No one is looking at us," noticed Kelvin.

"No, they aren't," Henry replied. "I think we'll be all right."

They were surrounded by shops, cafés, and merchants. Looking at the various shops, they saw clothiers, a shoemaker, and a hat maker. "Everything you would ever need is right here," commented Henry.

"This is much bigger than the market at home," observed Kelvin, as two small boys accidentally bumped into him while playing.

"Pardon me, sir," said their mother, trying to catch up to them.

"Clothes are much more colorful here," noticed Kelvin.

Observing the people walking past, he noticed that men dressed mostly in pants and shirts that were similar in design to theirs. The brown and black spectrums were most common with the men. The women dressed with more variety and color.

The women working in the shops and those who looked somewhat poor wore clothes with the same brown and black colors as the men. Women who were obviously wealthy liked to experiment with color.

Many bright green, orange, and yellow dresses could be seen throughout the crowd. These women were also adorned with hats and jewelry in a show of their wealth and position in society.

The street emptied into a large square that was filled with even more shops and merchants. Permanent shops encircled the public square and the center was open for anyone who had something to sell. Anything you would need for daily life could be purchased here.

The east end of the market was completely devoted to food. If it was grown, farmed, hunted, or caught, you could find it here.

Clothes, linens, utensils, tools, toys, medical equipment, and anything else one might need for the house, work, or play could be found in one of the many shops. The bustling market had a pleasant and exciting atmosphere. It was fast-paced with merchants shouting advertisements for their products and various musicians playing around every corner.

"Food!" yelled Kelvin, lunging toward the food vendors to his right. His progress was halted when Henry grabbed him by the shirt.

"Wait!" he exclaimed. "How are we going to buy food?"

"You're right, I hadn't thought of that," replied Kelvin.

"We have to find out what they use as money," said Henry. "Let's walk around and watch these people to see how they conduct themselves."

They set out exploring this fascinating place. Walking past stalls fully stocked with fruits, vegetables, bread, eggs, cheese, and meats made their mouths water, but they had to figure out how to buy some. They each watched as transactions were made.

"They use silver coins," said Henry, after watching a few transactions at a nearby stall.

"I think the number written on the small piece of white paper is how many coins each item costs," replied Kelvin. The small piece of paper was consistently located just in front of the item for sale.

"That woman gave one coin for a scoop of peanuts. The woman over there gave three coins for a loaf of bread."

"Look," said Henry, now standing in front of the meat shop. "That man gave a whole handful of coins for that enormous salmon."

"So, how do we get these coins?" asked Kelvin.

"Good question," replied Henry.

They were now walking away from the food shops toward the center of the market. "Who do you suppose that is?" asked Kelvin, pointing at the very large statue in the center of the market.

The statue was of a man in full battle armor. He was holding his helmet under one arm and his sword in the other. A shallow pool encircled the statue with benches surrounding it.

"Apollo Westville," read Kelvin from a small plaque. "He must be somebody important."

They took up a spot on one of the empty benches and tried to find a solution to their dilemma. How could they acquire coins in order to buy food?

"We could beg," offered Kelvin.

"I am starving and would do just about anything at this point," replied Henry.

They got up from the bench, swallowed their pride, and began asking the passersby for food or money. They were both ashamed of the level they had stooped to, but these were desperate times.

Elizabeth and Lynessa walked out of the hat shop and headed toward the center of the market. They were looking for something to stave off their growing hunger. A morning full of shopping made them work up quite an appetite by midday.

"Look at those two ruffians," laughed Lynessa, pointing at two men on the other side of Market Street. "Couldn't they find better clothes to wear to the market?"

"Oh, Lynessa, you are always so mean to poor people," commented Elizabeth.

"And you are too nice to them, My Lady," she responded, respectfully.

She was right. Elizabeth did have a soft spot for people less fortunate than herself. After her conversation with the high priest, she wondered if it was because of her roots as a commoner.

Taking a second look, Elizabeth went as pale as a ghost. She had seen the younger man before. He was the one she was kissing in her dream.

She had told Lynessa about the dream when it happened, but she could not tell her this now. A dream is one thing, but telling people that characters in dreams are standing before you in real life is another thing entirely.

I would be labeled crazy, she thought. *They would lock me up as insane.*

"Are you all right, My Lady?" asked Lynessa, seeing the look on her face.

"Yes, yes, I am fine," she replied. "Just famished, I think."

"I don't care if he is poor or not, the brown-haired one is handsome," said Elizabeth, sounding like any young woman who's attracted to a good-looking young man.

Lynessa turned and gave them a closer look. "You're right, he is handsome," she replied, and they both giggled.

But when they looked back across the street, the two men were gone. They had disappeared into the crowd.

"Well, that's disappointing," pouted Elizabeth. "I was looking forward to some harmless flirting while doing my good deed for the day feeding the poor!"

Lynessa giggled at her mistress's daring sense of humor.

With the appealing scenery across the street now gone, they headed out into the market in search of food.

The two ladies had to walk past the stalls with fruit, vegetables, and fresh meat in order to reach the café they had decided on for their meal.

The crowd was thick today, but they quickly parted to let the princess pass. It was as the crowd moved out of her way in front of a stall filled with apples that Elizabeth saw him again.

The man from her dreams looked in shock as his cover quickly evaporated. She saw the luscious green apple in his hand before the merchant did. It was when he shoved the stolen apple into his pocket that the seller noticed.

"You there!" yelled the clean-shaven middle-aged man from behind the fruit counter. "Put that apple back!"

As he was yelling, the fruit merchant squeezed between the apples and a crate of bananas. He jumped on the thief's back as he was trying to flee. Kelvin was surprised by the force of the skinny man, and they both collapsed to the ground.

"What is going on over there?" asked Lynessa.

"I am not sure," lied Elizabeth.

Getting involved in a street fight was not something a lady would normally do, but Elizabeth was different from most ladies. She was also intrigued by this man from her dream.

"What is the meaning of this?" she yelled in a commanding voice, hovering over the two men on the ground.

The merchant looked up and immediately jumped off the thief's back. "I am sorry, My Lady," he said, standing at attention.

"What has this man done?" she asked.

"He stole an apple, My Lady," replied the shopkeeper.

Kelvin slowly rolled over to see who this woman was. An involuntary smile came to his face as he looked up at her and took in her beauty.

"What is your name?" she asked.

"Kelvin," he answered, still unable to suppress his smile.

Lynessa, knowing what the princess would want, approached the merchant. "For your trouble," she said, handing him five silver coins, which was enough to buy five apples.

"Thank you, My Lady," replied the merchant, appreciative of the kind gesture, and he returned to his position behind the fruit counter.

Kelvin was still lying on his back looking lustfully at Elizabeth in her flowing purple dress. Henry was frozen, wondering how he was going to get them out of this situation.

"Please get up off the ground," Elizabeth finally said, breaking the silent attraction.

Henry came to his friend's aid and offered a hand. Kelvin grabbed it, pulled himself up, and brushed off the dirt.

"Thank you for helping us, ma'am," said Henry.

"Ma'am!" exclaimed Lynessa. "Do you know who this is? Elizabeth is a princess of Westville!"

"I am sorry," he replied, embarrassed. "I didn't know."

Henry and Kelvin didn't know how to act in the presence of royalty, but they tried by bowing their heads. "I am very sorry, but we are not from here," said Henry, trying to help the situation.

Not from here? Elizabeth remembered her conversation with the high priest about travelers and wild men. *Where are they from? They don't look like either.*

She held her hand up motioning to Lynessa to stop. Her interest was now piqued knowing they were from a different land.

Elizabeth, noticing the crowd was also becoming interested in the conversation, asked Kelvin and Henry to walk with them. If these two men were indeed foreigners, the last thing she wanted was for the people of Westville to know. It would draw unwanted attention to them, and that could be dangerous.

Elizabeth took them out of the market and down the street leading to the castle. They were heading in the opposite direction from which they had come. Soon the castle came into view.

Henry nudged Kelvin and murmured, "Look at that!"

The structure looked more and more awe-inspiring as they advanced. They were slightly disappointed when Lynessa turned to the right and took them under a white lattice arch. They were in the largest garden they had ever seen.

Flowers were blooming. Perfectly manicured shrubs and trees dotted the landscape. Henry was most interested in the many pools and fountains that adorned the garden. The castle was still a ways off in the distance, but it still struck an intimidating pose.

Elizabeth was headed to the place she went when she needed to be alone. It was a secluded little nook in the back corner of the garden. Two white benches were framed by what had been a brick wall about seven feet high.

The brick was no longer visible with the successful onslaught of the lush green ivy. Elizabeth had been coming here for years, and each year the ivy claimed more and more of the wall, just as she hoped it would. It was only last year that it completely conquered the wall by slithering over the top.

When they had all entered the alcove and taken their places on the benches, Elizabeth said, "We will have privacy here. No one ever comes to this part of the garden."

"I apologize if we startled you," she continued, "but I didn't want to make a scene in front of all of those people."

"We thank you for that," replied Henry. "A scene is exactly what we don't want."

"So you say you aren't from here?" she asked.

"Yes, that is correct," replied Henry.

She looks familiar, he thought. *Do I know this woman? Where have I seen that face before?*

"Well, where are you from?" asked Lynessa, impatiently.

Henry and Kelvin looked at each other as if to say, "Should we tell them?"

Kelvin shrugged his shoulders as if to answer, "They seem like they want to help us."

"Well, Princess, we think we came from the west," said Henry.

Lynessa, sensing his confusion as to how to address the princess, helped by explaining, "You may call her 'My Lady.'"

"Thank you." Relief and embarrassment swept over Henry's face. "My Lady, we were caught in a storm last night and marooned on a beach not far from here."

This was the first time he had looked Elizabeth directly in the eyes, and he was perplexed by what he saw. *She is so familiar to me.*

"Are you wild men?" Elizabeth asked. Lynessa gave her a curious look, not knowing what she was talking about.

"No," replied Henry. "We come from Triopolis."

"I have never heard of Triopolis," exclaimed Elizabeth.

She remembered what the high priest told her and couldn't contain her excitement. He had mentioned travelers and wild men, but nothing about other towns. She wondered why not.

"Is your home like ours here in Westville?" she asked.

"Yes, but it is a little smaller," replied Henry.

"Is that the name of this city?" asked Kelvin.

"Yes, you are in the Kingdom of Westville," replied Lynessa.

"This is amazing!" said Kelvin, excitedly. "Up until a few days ago, we didn't know there were any people outside of Triopolis, and now we have found a whole new city!"

Elizabeth felt the same excitement, but she kept her emotions under control for now.

"We were fishing and got caught too far from shore," said Henry. "We saw the storm coming, but the current was too strong. We rowed and rowed, but it was no use. The storm was fierce and the waves were massive. I am surprised we lived through it. We were lucky that the storm left us on your beach this morning."

"I don't remember anything after that," added Kelvin. "We must have been knocked out, being tossed back and forth and hit by the force of the waves crashing down on us."

"It is truly miraculous that you are with us today," marveled Elizabeth. "You must be exhausted. I can give you a quiet place to stay as well as food and drink."

"We would be grateful, My Lady," replied Henry.

Elizabeth took them to the temple. She knew the high priest would keep her secret.

"This is an amazing city," said Kelvin as he gazed at the façade of the temple. Entering, Elizabeth stayed close to the back wall and headed toward the high priest's study.

"Elizabeth!" he said, greeting her with his usual good cheer.

"Hello, High Priest." She smiled warmly, not sure what to say next.

"What have we here?" he asked, referring to her guests.

"These two men are from the west," she responded. "Another city does exist!"

She had a hard time hiding her excitement. "Interesting," responded the high priest as he inspected them from across the room.

"They were shipwrecked on the beach this morning," Elizabeth continued, surprised by the lack of reaction from the high priest at the knowledge of another city. Why didn't he ask any questions about the existence of this city? Did he know more than he had told her?

He realized his mistake after noticing Elizabeth's change in expression. "Where is your city?" he asked Henry, keeping up the ruse.

Henry retold their harrowing story of survival on the storm-swept sea and their fortunate landing on the beach.

"So, I believe Triopolis is to the west of here," concluded Henry.

This time, the high priest made sure he reacted as if he were hearing this information for the first time. Elizabeth watched intently to see if she could learn anything from his reaction.

"What are your names?" asked the high priest.

"I am Henry Walker, and this is Kelvin Drake."

So, a Walker still fishes in Triopolis, thought the high priest. He was very interested in Henry's lineage. "Who is your father? What did he do for a living?"

Henry answered his questions with no hesitation.

Remarkable, thought the high priest. *He really is a descendant of Rowen Walker.*

So many thoughts were running through his head that it took all his effort to control his expression.

"Sir, will you feed them and give them a safe place to stay?" asked Elizabeth.

"Of course, My Lady," he replied willingly. "We mustn't tell anyone about them—not yet, anyway."

"I will be back in the morning," she said to Henry and Kelvin.

"Thank you, My Lady," they both responded graciously, and watched as the ladies left the room.

Chapter 10

Terryn followed closely behind Lynessa as they quickly moved through the hallway. She was leading him through the servants' quarters in search of an alternative exit to the castle. They could not risk their relationship being discovered by the wrong person.

Being a nobleman with a significant inheritance in his future, Terryn could not risk dishonor from having a relationship with a servant. Lynessa understood this and was willing to wait until Lord Rosser died. She knew all too well the power the mistress of a lord could wield.

Terryn had been in the castle on official business of the Private Council. It was only when he was leaving that he was pleasantly surprised to run into Lynessa. Wanting to tell him about the day's discoveries, she summoned him to follow.

Exiting through a small wooden door, they appeared outside the castle not far from the stables. It was now dark out, which helped conceal them. This was exactly what Lynessa was thinking when she led them outside. The lack of light in this part of the yard meant that anyone who saw them would only see shadows and not faces.

She snuck a quick kiss before telling him her news. That was what she had wanted to do when she saw him in the castle. At every turn in the hallway, all she wanted to do was push him against the wall and ravish him with kisses.

"I feel the same way," he said softly in her ear, seeing the look in her eye.

Feeling the love reciprocated in his arms wrapped around her, she savored the moment. It was Terryn who first moved to untangle their arms because he knew that she would stay there forever if he didn't.

"Now, what did you want to tell me?"

Now that it was time to say it, she didn't know how. Would he believe her? She fumbled with her thoughts, trying to find the right words.

"Elizabeth and I met two men in the market today who said they came from the west," she finally blurted.

"Yes, these men are called barbarians," he replied knowingly. "We encounter them often while marching the army through the forest. Sometimes they are helpful to us, and other times they can be horribly vicious."

"I know, you have told me about barbarians before, but these men said they were from a city called Triopolis," she said.

"Another city?" questioned Terryn. "That's impossible. They are no other civilized people out there."

"I thought that too, but they seemed to speak the truth," she replied, convinced.

"How did they come to be here?" he asked.

"They say they were tossed ashore on our beach by an ocean storm."

Terryn pondered this for a moment. "I suppose it's possible that some barbarians settled into cities. It makes more sense that they would settle rather than wander aimlessly through the forests."

Changing the subject, he said, "So, where are they now?"

"They're in the temple. The princess brought them there for the high priest to look after. She seems to want to keep them hidden."

"Hidden, why?" he asked, confused.

"I am not sure," she replied. "I will try and get more information."

"I have nothing against the princess," he said. "I would gain nothing from bringing her down. I will not tell Lord Rosser of this. He would only parade them in front of the king and take all the glory. I must be the one to tell the king, but the time has to be right."

"Why can't you do it now?" asked Lynessa.

"I have never had an audience with His Majesty alone," he answered. "My uncle has always been with me. If I were to ask for one, Mr. Blakely would certainly inform him, and he would want to know why."

Mr. Blakely was the steward of the royal household. This meant he was in charge of all affairs for the running of the household including access to the king. He was an older gentleman with a round face and a belly to match. He had been appointed in the first year of the king's reign and had served him faithfully ever since.

"You're right," she replied. "He would definitely tell your uncle. What will you do, then?"

"We must wait for now," he plotted. "We must wait until the time is right, and then I will strike."

The high priest let Henry and Kelvin eat alone. He had a whole turkey roasted for them accompanied by potatoes and carrots. They tore into the meat as if it was the last they would ever taste.

"It feels like it has been weeks since I ate," exclaimed Kelvin, chewing noisily on a large piece of tender breast meat.

"This is so good," replied Henry, spearing a small buttered potato with his fork.

Being alone, they forgot their table manners and greedily devoured the food. Utensils were optional as they grabbed chunks of meat with their hands and popped carrots into their mouths. This was the effect of not having eaten in over twenty-four hours.

Meanwhile, the high priest frantically rifled through an old, dusty, leather-bound book. He was in a small, stone-walled room beneath his study in the temple. It contained many old books and other personal items collected over the years.

He was sitting on a small wooden stool in the center of the room with only the light from his oil lamp to aid his search.

Mumbling to himself, he quickly flipped through the last pages in the book and returned it to the shelf. He spied another that looked more promising. The title of this one was *The Founders and Their Flock*.

The entire bookshelf was full of books about the history of Triopolis. A copy of every book written in the first hundred years of the city's existence resided on this shelf.

Every time he happened on a picture, he inspected it closely. "No resemblance," he would whisper and move on.

"If those two have seen a picture of me, I am doomed," he said aloud. "It was a good sign that they didn't seem to recognize me."

He flipped through book after book, page by page. The air was becoming thick with dust as he opened each volume. Most of these hadn't been touched in years. He kept them in his secret vault for times like this when he had to know if he was in danger.

Finishing the last one, he shut it and exhaled slowly, feeling relieved. Just then, he heard the door to his study open. His servant, Lewis, entered the room looking for his master. Not seeing him in the semi-darkness, he left to continue his search.

The high priest, satisfied with his investigation, ascended the stone stairs and entered his private room. The stairway to his secret room was hidden behind a door concealed in the wall. It would not be seen unless the person knew it was there, but just for precaution, a decorative wooden obelisk helped to hide it.

Lewis had a strange look on his face as he entered the office after hearing the bell used to summon him. Sometimes it seemed to him that the high priest was a ghost and could appear and disappear at will.

He was asked to bring their two guests in when they had eaten their fill. Knowing that the two guests had almost completely finished the turkey, he went to get them.

Returning to the study, Lewis showed Henry and Kelvin where to sit. They waited for the high priest to acknowledge them. They were seated in two chairs placed in front of his sturdy walnut desk. Their anxiety built as the high priest stared down at the papers he was reading.

Multiple candles lit the room now that darkness had overtaken the world outside. This room was half library and half workspace. The ceiling was not as high as it was in other parts of the temple, giving the room a cozy feeling.

It was filled with many reminders of Westville's past. A painting of what looked like the phases of construction of the temple hung on one wall. Another wall contained a picture of the king's coronation. Kelvin noticed a statue of a woman looking up at the sky labeled *The Queen of the Stars*.

Before taking his leave, Lewis gave each of them a cup of wine to help them digest the massive meal they had consumed.

"So, you say you are from a city called Triopolis," the high priest began.

"Yes," replied Henry, giving his partner a confused look. They both knew that no one had mentioned the name of the city in their previous conversation.

Elizabeth and Lynessa could not have told him because they left without mentioning it, thought Kelvin. *What is he up to? How does he know of Triopolis?*

The high priest took a long sip of wine from his glass. He held it up and watched the light glimmer off of it.

"Look at that sparkle," he said in admiration. "It's crystal."

He brought the glass down to the desk and looked directly at his guests. He wanted to see their reaction.

They didn't know it, but they were being tested. The high priest knew Triopolis well, and knew of the crystal mines to the east of the city. If these two men were who they said they were, they would know exactly what crystal was. He was pleased with their reaction.

He listened as Henry and Kelvin told the story of how they came to be in Westville. As he followed the events of the past day, he critiqued every detail in his head. Shipbuilding technology had not advanced to the point where open ocean boats were being built, so he had never taken that route. He did however know the Bay of Triopolis very well, and they seemed to describe it perfectly.

The story of their journey was accurate as far as the high priest could tell. Most importantly, the telling was exactly as it was before. None of the facts had changed. This was another test, unbeknownst to them.

"What is it like to live in Triopolis?" he asked the two friends, now believing that they did indeed come from there.

Henry and Kelvin replied by talking about the beautiful bay the city was set on and the lush fields where crops grew and animals grazed. The high priest's mind wandered while listening to their description.

He remembered how beautiful Triopolis was when he had last seen it. It had been so long. He imagined the trees in the forest were probably much taller now.

There was no comparison to the fruit grown in the nutrient-rich soil of the city on the bay. Eating the fruit grown here was as tasteless an experience as licking one of the many rocks in the soil.

So many years since I've eaten the luscious fruit of Triopolis, yet my taste buds still remember its flavor, he mused with longing.

With his two guests finishing their description of their homeland, the high priest felt his secret was safe. They did not seem to recognize his face, which made him feel confident that no pictures of him remained in their city.

"Well, gentlemen, it's getting late and the wine has run dry," said the high priest, getting up from his chair.

Henry and Kelvin also got up and thanked him for his hospitality. They were led away to their beds by Lewis, who had been summoned by the bell only minutes earlier.

Chapter 11

Elizabeth couldn't wait to get up the next morning. She had barely slept during the night because of her excitement to learn more about her guests and where they had come from. Her night of waiting finally ended when Lynessa rushed in with their usual morning tea service.

"No time for that today," she said, hopping out of bed.

"I thought you might say that," replied her servant, setting the tea tray on the nearest table. Elizabeth quickly dressed, and they prepared to leave the room. She was headed for the temple.

Opening the door, Lynessa screamed and nearly jumped out of her shoes. Prince Richard was standing in front of the door just about to knock.

"Forgive me, My Lord," she said, composing herself.

"No, you must forgive my intrusion," replied the prince, laughing. "I didn't mean to startle you."

Looking at Elizabeth standing behind her attendant, Richard greeted the princess with a slight bow of his head. "My Lady, I wonder if I might have a word."

She was surprised to see her husband here. He had never come to her apartment before. She wondered if he had ever been in this part of the castle. Still upset with him for the embarrassment he had made her suffer since their marriage, she was not overly happy to see him.

"I will take my leave, My Lady," said Lynessa, going back inside the apartment and closing the door.

Walking with Richard gave Elizabeth mixed feelings. He was her husband, and her duty as his wife was to love him unconditionally, but she could not forgive his selfishness. He had married her, but he preferred the company of Albert.

She knew that the marriage was arranged and neither of them had a say in it, but it saddened her nonetheless. Knowing she would live a lie for the rest of her life, she blamed the prince for her predicament.

Neither spoke as they walked through the corridor and down the stairs to the Great Hall. This was the exit she usually used when wanting to leave the castle quickly and inconspicuously. The majority of visitors congregated around the front gate leaving most people unaware of this rarely used exit.

The tension was thick, and the uneasiness between them obvious. Both Richard and Elizabeth were uncomfortable and unable to produce the first words.

Richard felt bad for what he was doing to her but could not betray his true feelings. He knew she must be miserable and understood if she never wanted to see him again.

It wasn't until they reached the Great Hall that Richard finally spoke. "I am sorry for what I have done to you."

Elizabeth looked at him in shock. She hadn't counted on this. An argument would have been much easier for her to deal with. Then she could stay angry with him, but an apology compelled her to make amends.

"I know it's not fair to you," continued Richard. "I didn't have another choice. My father wouldn't understand."

His admission was surprising and unexpected. He had hardly spoken to her since their pact was agreed upon. She fully expected to live completely separate lives, only speaking to him when the occasion dictated it.

What was the purpose of his apology? Did he want to be friends? Could she be friendly with a man who had treated her so unfairly?

On the other hand, a partnership would make this whole matter a little more bearable. Avoiding each other was not going to work out well in the long term.

Elizabeth knew Richard's father's reputation as an uncompromising man. She understood his impossible position. She had witnessed the king in one of his all-too-common fits of rage.

"No, it isn't fair at all," she replied. "I don't even know how I am supposed to act around you, let alone how to be a princess! You surprised me with this arrangement only days before our wedding day!"

"I understand," he answered, his head hanging low in disgrace. "I can't change the way I am. This is me, and it is how I was born."

"That doesn't bother me," she exclaimed. "It's fine if you want to be with Albert. I am upset that I am married with no husband."

"I can't change my clumsy handling of this in the past, but I would like to change how we go forward," said Richard, in a rare bout of confidence. "I would like for us to be friends."

Elizabeth walked in silence, pondering his proposal. This might be the best deal she was going to get. She understood his dilemma. Maybe the circumstance was to blame and not him.

"I would like that too," she finally responded.

Relieved, Richard could now relax a little more. He had been dreading this conversation for weeks before getting enough courage to have it. He knew he was stringing her along, but up until today, he had been too cowardly to make it right.

Looking up, he saw where their walk had taken them. Towering in front of them was the reddish-brown brick of the Temple of Apollo. Seeing where she had led them, he wondered if the rumor was true.

"I have heard talk of a strange man who came to the temple last night," he tested her.

Elizabeth's face went white with fear. How did he know about the foreigners, and so soon after their arrival? Who was his informant? Only a handful of people had seen them enter the temple.

She paused to plan her next move. She knew that her face had given her away. Richard undoubtedly knew that she knew about the foreigners, so she might as well tell him.

I guess I will find out if I can trust him, she resolved.

"There are two of them, and they are foreigners," she said. "I met them in the market yesterday. They say they're from a city over the western mountains called Triopolis."

Richard looked at Elizabeth unable to believe what he was hearing. He knew barbarians existed in the wild, but he had never heard of another city. He thought back to conversations of his father's that he had overheard through the years, and couldn't recall anything about other cities.

"A storm washed them up on the beach yesterday," she continued. "I found them scavenging for food in the market. Not wanting to create a scene in front of all those people, I brought them to the high priest."

"That was wise," he answered. "We don't want all of Westville to know that other civilizations exist beyond our borders. That would cause chaos. We should keep this between us for now."

"I agree," said Elizabeth.

"I would like to meet them," said Richard, excitedly.

Walking up to the large oak door, he opened it, allowing his wife to enter first. As usual, not much light from the outside made its way into the cavernous building. Candles were always burning in wall sconces to combat the darkness.

A servant carrying a large tray of what looked like food and water walked briskly through the center of the room. He was just passing the enormous statue of Apollo behind the altar when Richard hollered, "You there!"

When the servant turned to acknowledge them, Elizabeth realized it was Lewis. "My Lord, My Lady," he greeted the royal couple.

"Oh, Lewis," she said. "I am sorry, but we didn't recognize you. Where can we find the high priest?"

Interesting, thought Richard. *She treats even the lowest servant with the same respect she would a highborn person. This kindness is rarely seen in royalty.*

"He is with the guests, My Lady," responded the servant. "Follow me. I am headed there now."

Elizabeth and Richard quickly made their way up the center aisle to catch up with Lewis.

The door was already opened from when Lewis left the room to fetch the tray of food. He entered followed by Elizabeth and Richard.

The room they entered was the dining room, a moderately sized room with a large iron chandelier hanging above a thick wooden table that looked as if it would seat eight to ten people.

The chandelier was an iron circle with six pillar candles at even intervals. Surprisingly, it adequately illuminated the room with just those six flames. The walls were stone much like the rest of the building, but these were covered with tapestries of Apollo in divine poses.

On one wall between two stained glass windows hung a representation of Apollo with a yellow glow engulfing his body as he ascended to the stars. The others showed him giving food and water to the poor, healing the sick, and showing forgiveness to a thief.

The sight of Richard in the doorway surprised the high priest. Seeing this, Elizabeth calmingly said, "It's okay, I've told Richard everything."

Lewis put the tray of food on the table in front of Henry and Kelvin. He asked the high priest if anything else was needed, and his master thanked him and said that would be all. Intimidated by Prince Richard, Lewis quickly excused himself.

Elizabeth handled the introductions. "Henry and Kelvin, this is his Royal Highness Prince Richard. He is the son of the king and heir to the throne of the Kingdom of Westville."

"Hello," they responded with a bow.

"Welcome to our city," Richard greeted them.

Richard began by asking them about their terrible night at sea. He was particularly interested to learn how they had survived the harrowing ordeal. The two men from Triopolis began the story from when they had noticed the storm clouds forming.

Usually when a story was told over and over, the facts were embellished and the feat grew in its enormity, but this was not the case. The true story was much more fantastic than anyone could imagine.

Their emotions ran the gamut from the excitement of being in the open ocean to the primal fear of being tossed into the water by the untamed winds and ferocious waves.

Richard was amazed at what they had endured and the luck and fortitude they possessed to survive and land on his beach. He had doubted the story when

Elizabeth first told him, but seeing the expressions on their faces and the anxiety in their voices left no doubt of the truth.

"You say you are from the west?" asked Richard.

"We believe so," answered Henry. "We know the current and winds were taking us east at the time of the storm, but anything could have happened after we were consumed by it."

Henry and Kelvin continued to take bites of food in between questions. The high priest watched in amazement, surprised they could eat so soon after devouring a whole turkey the night before.

Elizabeth sat staring at Kelvin. *What is it about him? How could he have been in my dreams before we ever met?*

In her dream, she had a feeling that he had traveled a long way, but she did not know any details beyond that. It was too similar to be a coincidence.

The high priest watched Henry as the story was told. *This man shares something with Elizabeth*, he thought. *How could that be?*

He sensed a similarity between them, a bond of sorts. *There is a closeness there that only exists between a—no, that is impossible.*

His thought was interrupted by a knock on the door. "Apologies, My Lord," said Lewis, entering the room. "A message for His Highness, from the king."

"My father summons me," Richard announced, reading the note. "I must go for now, but you must not speak of Henry and Kelvin to anyone. If the wrong people were to discover them, it could be dangerous for us all."

He rushed out of the room with a feeling of exhilaration. He felt powerful having knowledge that his father didn't possess.

"I have been in a constant state of bewilderment since yesterday," commented Kelvin. "When I saw your city and met some of your people, I couldn't believe it. We had always been taught that we were the only people in the world. Then we met Borin, and now you."

Mentioning Borin's name, Kelvin looked at Henry for understanding. Henry nodded his acknowledgment and agreement.

The high priest perked up at the sound of Borin's name. "Did you say you met a man named Borin?"

"Yes," they answered, looking confused.

"Was he a tall man with long, thin gray hair?"

"With a full gray beard," added Henry.

"I think we know the same man," concluded the high priest.

He told them the same story he told Elizabeth about meeting Borin while gathering berries in the forest.

Henry and Kelvin looked at each other in amazement. Clearly, this Borin was the same person they talked to in the pub and the same person Henry saw being dragged out the back door with his throat cut. They couldn't believe that Borin had traveled all the way to Westville.

The high priest told them of Borin's occasional visits, and remarked how rare it was for his people to come here.

"They stay away because they are afraid of our army," he said. "The king has wrongly mandated that any barbarian encountered by the army should be killed. Unfortunately, he does not understand the difference between Borin's people and barbarians."

"We met Borin in a pub," said Kelvin.

"Ah, the man was always fond of a good mug of ale," said the high priest with a hearty laugh.

"We didn't know him well; only met him that one time," said Henry.

"He obviously knew a lot about Triopolis and its history," commented Kelvin. "He taught us more about our history in that one meeting than we had learned our whole lives."

He repeated the story he had heard so many times growing up about Nelson, Donovan, Rowen and the founding of Triopolis.

Listening to the story, the high priest began to reminisce. *So that's how the story goes now. It has changed so much over the years.*

Kelvin intentionally left out the newly discovered information about Luther and the founders because he and Henry weren't ready to share that with anyone yet.

"You see, our people have always been sheltered from the outside world," said Henry. "I would guess it is because we are surrounded by mountains on three sides and the ocean on the fourth. Those mountains can come alive at any moment and spew liquid fire at anyone who gets too close. They are impossible to cross, and we experienced what happens to people who venture too far out into the ocean."

"I don't know how Borin crossed them," added Kelvin.

If you only knew the truth, thought the high priest. *It was hidden from your people so long ago.*

"Is Borin still in Triopolis?" he asked.

"He is still there all right," replied Kelvin.

"He is dead," clarified Henry. "I saw his body being dragged out of the pub and into the bushes."

"Why was he killed?" asked the high priest, surprised.

"I am afraid our homeland has been overridden with corruption," declared Henry. "He was killed by our leaders. They wanted to keep the people in the dark about his existence."

"Not surprising," replied the high priest. What he didn't tell them was that the intentional suppression of the truth began with the founders.

Everyone in the room was surprised by this seemingly knowing response by the high priest.

How would he know what the politics in Triopolis are like? Henry wondered, and he slid a sideways glance at Kelvin, who returned it with a skeptical look of his own.

Kelvin glanced at Elizabeth to gauge her reaction. Their eyes met, and each of them knew they were thinking the same thing. The high priest knew much more than he was letting on.

"Borin was a good man," said the high priest, lost in reminiscence, unaware of the unspoken conversations going on around him. "I am sad to hear he is gone. I loved to hear about his journeys. Oh, the interesting stories he would tell."

Elizabeth noticed out of the corner of her eye that Kelvin was still looking at her. It was unlike earlier when their eyes had met in acknowledgment of what the high priest had said. This was different. It was a look of attraction. She felt her cheeks burning as she blushed. She turned to catch his gaze. They both smiled and he quickly looked away.

So he is interested in me, she thought. The excitement was nearly impossible to contain. She had not felt this way about a man in a long time.

The high priest wanted to find out more about Henry to better understand the connection he sensed between him and Elizabeth. *Maybe Borin is the link*, he thought.

To steer the conversation in that direction, he said, "There is more to the story of Borin," and he began telling the story of the raiding party of barbarians that killed her mother and how she was stranded in the forest only to be found by Lord Granville.

Henry immediately took notice as the story of the death of Elizabeth's mother was told. His jaw dropped as he listened. He looked back at Elizabeth.

Her features were so similar to Natalie's. Could it be? She had the same eyes and the same nose. She looked like she would be about the right age.

He finally answered his question. *She is my lost daughter, Louisa!*

As the high priest continued his story, Henry stared at Elizabeth, longing to reach out to her. Coming back to the tale, Henry couldn't believe what she had to endure. He felt ashamed at what he had done all those years ago.

The emotions inside were tearing him apart. Never in his wildest dreams had he thought this day would come. He had assumed his daughter was dead, but here she was sitting right in front of him. *How could I have sent them away?* The guilt he felt threatened to overwhelm him.

The high priest finished the story, and there was a lull in the conversation. Everyone felt awkward for their own personal reasons. Henry couldn't hold the truth in any longer. In a tone showing how ashamed and embarrassed he was, he said to Elizabeth, "I have something to tell you."

"What is it?" she asked.

"I think you might be my daughter," he replied, looking at her with sad eyes. "You look just like your mother."

Elizabeth didn't know what to say. Her confusion left her speechless.

"I am about to tell you a story that I never expected to speak of again," said Henry. "In fact, I had hoped to never have to tell it again, but that has changed now that my daughter is sitting here in front of me. Elizabeth, please do not judge me too harshly for what you are about to hear."

It is as I have foreseen, thought the high priest, happy that his abilities were still razor sharp after all these years.

The anticipation was overwhelming for Elizabeth as she listened to Henry telling the story. Kelvin, knowing the story, watched Elizabeth closely. He noticed a sparkle in her eyes from the excitement of meeting her father.

Tears came to Henry's eyes as he mentioned the scene in the forest when Elizabeth and her mother were sent away.

"I'm sorry, Elizabeth!" he cried. "I didn't want to abandon you and your mother. I searched the forest for weeks after, but you were gone."

Elizabeth reached her hand toward his, not knowing what to say. She was upset and happy at the same time. She held his hand tight.

"That bastard!" exclaimed Henry, referring to the bishop. "He manipulated me into making that decision. He took advantage of a naïve young man."

"He is still using people to suit his needs," interjected Kelvin.

Elizabeth, still holding Henry's hand, tried to console him. "It's all right, Father," she said, feeling strange calling him that. "I am happy we have finally found each other."

"I could never ask you for forgiveness, and I would understand if you never forgave me," said Henry, holding her hands and looking into her eyes.

This pushed Elizabeth to her emotional limit as tears slowly slid down her cheeks. Not liking to show this kind of emotion in front of others, she rushed out of the room. After waiting a few moments, the high priest followed.

"I can't decide if I should be happy to finally meet my father or if I should hate him for what he did," she sobbed to the high priest.

"I know, my dear," he consoled. "It is likely you will never be able to answer that question. You should just enjoy the time you have with him now."

"Of course, you're right," she answered, wiping the tears from her face. "You always make things so clear. I am acting like a child."

"It was so long ago, and he was so young," she continued. "Is it fate that brought him here?"

"Fate indeed," answered the high priest, his mind roaming.

His thoughts were now wandering toward her mother. *Who was she? Where did she come from?*

"A man having a child from an affair would be a serious scandal if it happened here, so we have to be understanding of the situation my father was in," reasoned Elizabeth.

"It would be very serious," agreed the high priest.

Elizabeth's mood started to lighten, and she composed herself. "What am I doing in here?" she said to the high priest, but more to herself. "My father is in the next room!"

She jumped up excitedly and ran back into the dining hall.

"Elizabeth," exclaimed Henry, getting up from his chair. "How are you feeling?"

"Much better," she replied, throwing her arms around her father.

"I am sorry for running out on you, Father," she said, finally loosening her grip.

"You have nothing to be sorry about," replied Henry, kissing her on the forehead. "It is I who am sorry for everything I have done, and I don't want us ever to be apart again."

Henry could only stare at Elizabeth in disbelief. This was his daughter, who he had thought to be dead, sitting next to him.

"Tell me about my mother," she said.

Henry, adjusting uncomfortably in his chair, said, "Your mother was a beautiful, caring woman. I regret that I didn't really get to know her until she was pregnant with you. Once we spent time together, we found that we had a lot in common.

"Of course this was a problem, because I was already married. Mary and I married way too young. Because of this, we had to learn to love each other during the first years of marriage."

Husbands having bastard children were not new to Elizabeth. It was very common at court with almost every nobleman having at least one. She smiled to herself thinking, *I will never have to worry about that with Richard.*

Elizabeth listened intently. It seemed that Henry had wanted to do the honorable thing with her mother. He was just caught in an impossible situation. Could she forgive him?

"Tell me about your family," said Elizabeth, not completely sure she wanted to hear about them, but she felt it was the right thing to ask.

"Mary and I have been married for many years," explained Henry. "We have a thirteen-year-old daughter named Stephanie and a twelve-year-old son named Jeremy."

"So, I have a brother and a sister?" Elizabeth added, happily thinking about what it would be like to have siblings.

"We have a modest house in the city, and I support the family by fishing," continued Henry. "Jeremy wants to be a fisherman like me when he gets older. He is very energetic and is always trying to talk me into letting him go to sea with me." *I am glad he wasn't on this trip*, Henry mused to himself.

"Stephanie is an obedient daughter and is very helpful with the household duties. She will make a good wife one day." Henry intentionally did not say much about Mary. He didn't want to chance upsetting Elizabeth again.

"Well, I am very happy to finally meet you," said Elizabeth, now standing. "I would really like us to build a relationship with each other."

"As would I," responded Henry, with a smile on his face. They hugged and Elizabeth left the room.

Her feelings were mixed, and she realized they might always be that way. She was on an emotional roller coaster, and she wondered how long it would last.

The thought of Henry abandoning them in the forest made her angry, but then she reminded herself that her biological father was now with her, and she was happy.

Another emotion playing a significant role was her feeling for Kelvin. She liked him and wanted to get to know him better.

Meeting the man who had left her to die in the forest was more than she wanted to deal with right now. Kelvin provided the perfect distraction.

As Elizabeth neared the exit to the temple, Lynessa opened the door and entered.

"My Lady," she greeted her.

"Hello Lynessa," responded Elizabeth. "Would you bring Kelvin to my favorite place in the garden? I wish to spend more time with him."

"Of course, My Lady," she replied, and went to find him.

"Thank you," said Elizabeth, with an excited smile on her face.

Stepping out of the temple, she saw Richard and Albert approaching through the courtyard.

"Lady Elizabeth," said Albert, with a slight bow.

She returned the greeting and asked why they were coming to the temple.

"We were wondering if the two foreigners would be interested in a shooting challenge," said Richard.

Archery was one of the many sports played by noblemen in Westville. The benefits were twofold. Not only was it a healthy and fun activity, but it also helped keep their battle skills sharp.

"That is a great idea," replied Elizabeth.

Everything has been so emotional today, she thought, but all she said was, "I think it would be good to have some fun and take our minds off of everything."

Of course, she was also talking about herself and the rendezvous she was about to have. On that thought, she added, "Kelvin and I are going to take a walk together, but I think Henry will join you."

"Perfect," replied Richard, with a slight sting of jealousy as they exchanged a knowing glance.

Lord Rosser waited until the king finished speaking to the man in front of his desk before he approached. The study was the place in the castle the king frequented the most. This is where he went to get away from his responsibilities. He often lost himself in the memories contained in the room.

It was an intimidating place for any man to enter. This room displayed artifacts pertaining to what His Majesty loved most—war.

The paintings on the walls depicted the many battles waged throughout the history of Westville, from the battles of unification fought by the king's ancestor, Apollo, through the final Battle of Midalo. Various suits of armor and ancient weapons were placed strategically throughout the room for maximum effect.

Once the door was closed behind him, Lord Rosser approached the king.

"Good to see you, Lord Rosser."

"Sire," he replied, "I have news of the question you instructed me to answer. My search has taken an intriguing turn. Elizabeth has Lynessa looking into the very same question."

"Interesting," replied the king. "Does she have an answer?"

"Not yet." Lord Rosser waited a beat before adding, "Richard and Albert do spend a lot of time together. They often leave the castle together in secret. I watched them saddle their own horses and ride to the lake."

"They're doing something they aren't supposed to be doing if they aren't using servants," reflected the king.

"My thoughts exactly," responded Lord Rosser. "I will dig up the proof you need, Sire."

"I know you will," said the king.

Lord Rosser had never failed His Majesty in any mission, and because of this, the king had the utmost confidence in him.

Leaving the castle, Lord Rosser didn't have to wait long before his next lead presented itself. Walking right past him were Richard and Albert, so he waited a few moments then followed them at a discreet distance until they entered the Temple of Apollo.

Lord Rosser stood behind one of the fountains in the courtyard of the temple. He had a view of the front door so that he would see when Richard and Albert left.

It was odd for Richard to come to the temple at all, much less twice in the same day, he mused. That led him to believe that something was going on inside the religious building. He made a mental note to speak to the high priest to see if he knew what Richard was up to.

That one piece of solid evidence still eluded him. It had to be irrefutable; otherwise, he would not tell the king, who would not be happy if he were embarrassed by using circumstantial evidence that turned out to be false. This was too important, and Lord Rosser would not risk his reputation and possibly his life by not giving the king solid evidence.

The door opened and Albert appeared followed by Richard and a third man whom Lord Rosser had never seen before.

Watching closely, he tried to figure out who it was. How was it possible that this friend of Richard's was unknown to him? He made it his business to know everything.

He continued his pursuit as the three men walked away from the house of worship.

Richard, Albert, and Henry arrived at the archery field not knowing that Lord Rosser was close behind. The king's archery attendant, Tommy, supplied them with the necessary equipment and helped them prepare.

Each man was given an arm guard and a leather glove for the drawing hand. Once those were properly fitted, they were each handed a bow.

Richard and Albert had their own specially designed bows while Henry used one of Tommy's, who figured this was a friend of the prince, so he should be given the best he had to offer.

The thing Henry didn't see were arrows. He didn't ask, not wanting to look like he didn't know what he was doing. He was the only member of the group to thank Tommy as they all headed out to the range.

Henry's question was soon answered. Approaching their shooting lanes, he saw a small square bundle of straw placed on the left edge of each lane. Stuck in the bundles were the arrows they were going to shoot.

Henry felt very comfortable with a bow in his hands because he had been hunting with a bow and arrow since he was a child. Surprising to him, the archery equipment was the same that he had used in Triopolis.

"All right, Henry, you first," offered Richard, wanting to see how good his competition was.

This was just for fun, but Richard was always very competitive. The only arguments that seemed to occur between him and Albert usually erupted due to a competitive situation.

Henry fitted the groove on the base of the arrow over the string. Holding the arrow between his fore and middle fingers, he slowly drew back the string. His eyes were fixed on the target, knowing that his audience waited patiently to see if he was any good. Being the new man here, he knew Tommy would also be watching from a distance.

As his heartbeat calmed, he released the arrow. Not more than a second later, the arrow stuck in the red center of the target thirty yards away.

"Nice shot," congratulated Richard, impressed with Henry's skill. Satisfied that Henry could shoot, Richard and Albert took their first shots.

"So, Henry, how do you like Westville?" asked Richard.

"It's different from Triopolis," he replied noncommittally.

They each pulled another arrow from their bundle. "You are more advanced in many areas than we are," he added. "Your buildings are much more elaborate and stronger, being made mostly of stone."

"Do you not have stone buildings?" asked Albert.

"We have some, but not as many as you, and we have nothing like the temple or your castle. Those are amazing structures!"

"Well, one thing we have a lot of here are rocks!" exclaimed Richard jokingly.

Each man took another shot with mixed results. Tommy stood about twenty feet behind them waiting to be called upon. Normally, he disliked waiting on the prince and Albert because they never discussed happenings at court, but today was different. He was interested in the third man, and he mentioned a place Tommy had never heard of.

It still amazed him that royalty looked right past him as if he didn't exist, carrying on with secret conversations as if he didn't have ears and a mouth for retelling their interesting tales. This both angered Tommy and pleased him. He didn't like being overlooked, but he loved hearing the details of court intrigue.

The three men spent the next hour shooting arrows and talking about the differences and similarities between Triopolis and Westville. Both were fascinated with Triopolis because a few days ago, they didn't know it existed. Henry felt the same fascination for Westville.

Richard wondered how much his father knew about Triopolis. It couldn't be much, he assumed. If the king knew, he surely would have conquered that city just like their ancestors had done with every other civilization they'd discovered.

Richard and Albert both set their bows on the ground next to the bail of straw that had held the arrows. Henry, not feeling comfortable leaving a mess for Tommy to clean, took his with him as they walked back toward the supply shed.

The servant noticed and quickly ran from the shed to Henry. He thanked him, relieving him of the bow. They exited the field through the gate to the left of the shed.

Lord Rosser peeked around the back corner of the supply shed, waiting until the three men were farther down the road and out of sight. Feeling comfortable that they would not be returning any time soon, he walked around the building and approached Tommy.

Seeing Lord Rosser appear from around the side of the shed surprised Tommy as he timidly welcomed him. "My Lord," he said, with a simple bow.

He was a little frightened to see the overbearing man approaching him. Like everyone else in Westville, Tommy knew and feared his reputation.

Lord Rosser walked directly to him using his physical assets to his advantage. Standing over the servant he subtly began his interrogation. "Hello, Tommy," he said. "How is your day?"

"Very well, My Lord," he replied, nervously.

Lord Rosser was trying to put Tommy at ease before asking the questions he really wanted answered. He had learned this technique over the course of his career. If people are comfortable, they will more easily give up the requested information.

He always preferred manipulation to torture because, in his experience, the information obtained was more reliable. While being tortured, a man would say anything to stop the pain. Lord Rosser would use any means necessary to get what he wanted, however, if it came to that.

"Have you had many visitors today?" he asked the servant.

"Not many," replied Tommy, becoming more at ease with the conversation. "The king was practicing earlier this morning, and Richard and Albert just left."

Sensing the moment was right, Lord Rosser asked, "Who was the other man I saw with Richard and Albert?"

"I don't know his name," replied Tommy. "I haven't seen him before, and it sounded like he was a foreigner."

"A foreigner?" asked Lord Rosser, interested. He knew of the barbarians, so he assumed the man was one of them.

"I can't say for sure, but it sounded like it, yes," responded Tommy. "I only heard pieces of the conversation, but I heard them mention a city named Triopolis. The man called it his home."

"I've never heard of Triopolis," replied Lord Rosser.

"Nor have I," said Tommy.

The king surely doesn't know of another civilization, Lord Rosser thought. *If he did, he would have confided in me, and we would already be marching an army there.*

Regrouping his thoughts, Lord Rosser moved to questions about Richard and Albert. He asked how often they came to the archery field and if it was at specific times of the day or if it was random. He also asked if Tommy noticed that their equipment ever looked out of place.

Tommy answered no to this question, but was confused by it. Lord Rosser was wondering if they ever came to the range alone, as with their secret rides to the lake.

"Well, thank you," said Lord Rosser. "You have been most helpful."

Tommy was again confused by Lord Rosser's comment about being helpful. Had he said too much?

Becoming more and more concerned, Tommy replayed the conversation in his head. *Does Lord Rosser know about the third man? Is that why he was here? Should I have mentioned the part about the man being foreign?*

Leaving the archery field, Lord Rosser was intrigued by the information he had just received. So there was a foreigner in Westville and a foreign city named Triopolis. His investigation had taken a very interesting turn.

How could he find out more about Triopolis? Who, if anyone, would know about a foreign city?

Pondering these questions to determine where his investigation would go from here, it hit him. "The high priest!" he said aloud.

Chapter 12

Elizabeth walked through the arched entrance to the garden, headed for her favorite nook. This was the same hidden corner where she had taken Henry and Kelvin after discovering them in the market.

"Hello," said Kelvin, as she came around the corner.

"Hi," she replied with a flirty smile. "Where is Lynessa?"

"She said she had work to do, and left a few minutes ago." He smiled, happy to see her again.

She sat next to him on the faded white bench that had been her seat on many warm afternoons. Sometimes it was with a book, and other times with only her thoughts to keep her company.

"So, how do you like Westville?" she asked.

"I like it a lot," he replied. "I have never seen anything like your castle. I would love to go inside."

"I would love to show you, but it's too dangerous," she responded. "The place is always crawling with people. Some of them are people who it would be best didn't know about you."

"Okay . . ." Kelvin replied, not sure what else to say.

"Come on," she said, jumping to her feet. "Let's go for a walk."

Kelvin smiled as he got up from the bench. "Great idea."

The attraction between them was apparent to both; they had been exchanging looks and smiles all morning. Their body language was unmistakable.

Elizabeth led them out of the garden and into the street that would take them to the market.

That morning, the high priest had given Henry and Kelvin clothes to replace their tattered rags. This helped Kelvin fit in as he was now walking among the people of Westville.

When he asked Elizabeth about the danger of them walking together in public, she told him there was nothing to worry about. She was the only royal who went to the market. The others simply sent their servants to fetch what was needed.

"It's unbelievable that you and Henry found each other after all these years," commented Kelvin.

"It really is," she responded. "I know I should hate him for what he did to me and my mother, but I can't. He is the father I never knew, and with him came many answers to questions I've struggled with my entire life."

"Despite what he did, Henry is a good man," said Kelvin. "He has been mentoring me for a while now, and he has been almost like a father to me. Not only do I work for him, but we are good friends. It's almost like I am part of his family."

Pausing a beat, Kelvin added, "I put much of the blame on the bishop. He's an evil man."

"Who is this bishop?" she asked.

"The bishop is the worst sort of man," he began. "He is a conniving, cruel man who cannot be trusted. He has built his following by taking advantage of men like Henry. As soon as they make a poor choice or run into a string of bad luck, he springs into action. He offers to help, but at a very high price. That price is usually in the form of political favors, which put them further in his debt.

"Our city is governed by an assembly, which the bishop is part of and which my father leads. The people don't know it, but we are really governed by the bishop. He has manipulated his way into almost everyone's life and taken control of the whole assembly. I was disappointed to find out that even my father was at his command."

"So, you are a prince?" she asked.

"No, we don't have princes," he answered. "When our founders formed Triopolis, the first law was that an assembly elected by the people would rule."

Elizabeth looked confused by this notion, so Kelvin explained in more detail how decisions were made.

"I understand what you are saying, but this is not so different from here," she stated. "You are still left with your father to make the final decision, or now the bishop. Our king has a council as well, but he makes the final decision."

Kelvin considered this for a moment. "I never thought about it that way, but you are right!"

Elizabeth smiled triumphantly. She always liked to be told she was right.

They continued walking down Market Street, enjoying the perfect spring day. The sun was shining, and there was very little wind.

On the outskirts of the market, a stage was being prepared for the actors who would later perform. The stage was raised a few feet above the ground with a canvas overhang to protect it from the weather.

"The theatre group has their first performance of the season tonight," explained Elizabeth.

"I love watching actors perform!" exclaimed Kelvin.

"They're performing *Eafa*," she answered. "It's about a prince who chooses to give up his right to the throne to be with the woman he loves."

"It looks like we have time before it begins," commented Kelvin, looking at the empty stage as they walked past.

"Yes, they usually begin just before sunset."

Seeing the cafés and food shops with the smell of fresh-baked bread in the air made Kelvin take notice of his rumbling stomach. He saw a small shop that had various cheeses and meats on display.

"Let's stop and get something to eat," he said, staring at the display.

"Great idea, I am hungry too," she agreed.

They shared a plate of cheeses, cured meats, and grapes, and each drank a cup of wine.

When Elizabeth tried to pay the man behind the counter, he said, "No, Princess, I couldn't possibly charge you."

"Thank you, kind sir," she replied.

"Do you ever have to pay for anything?" asked Kelvin, surprised by another free meal.

"It's one of the perks of royalty," she said. "Not to mention I am the only royal who spends time among the people, and they seem to love me for it. The king and the prince never venture out into the city unless they are surrounded by guards, so the people never have access to them."

"How is the cheese?" she asked, sitting down on the bench next to him.

"It's very good," he answered, taking another bite. "This one is very sharp."

People bustled about their business as Kelvin and Elizabeth enjoyed each other's company. The occasional dog would bark while a small group of squirrels frolicked in a nearby tree.

When the plate was picked clean, they rose and continued their stroll.

"How well do you know the high priest?" Kelvin asked.

"I have known him for years," she answered. "He is the person I talk to when I need guidance."

"I noticed a symbol on a book in his office that I recognize," he said. "I saw that same symbol on an ancient book I found in Triopolis. It's an eye encircled by a blazing golden ring."

"I think he knows more about Triopolis than he is telling," she speculated. "The way he reacted to you and Henry was surprising. He didn't seem surprised at all. Do you think he has been to Triopolis?"

"As we saw with Borin, someone could easily sneak into Triopolis without being noticed, but could he leave here undetected?" asked Kelvin.

"I can't recall when he was missing for any length of time, so if he ever traveled there, it would have been a long time ago," she said. She was quiet a moment before adding, "We have to talk to the high priest."

"Can we trust him?" asked Kelvin.

"Yes, I think we can," she answered. "I have always been able to trust him."

"But this is different," replied Kelvin, skeptically. "We are bringing up a topic that he obviously has wanted to keep hidden."

"This is true," she replied. "I think it will be fine. I sense that he wants to tell us more."

Kelvin was surprised that he already felt like he could trust Elizabeth. This was not something that usually came easily to him. It was now time to tell her about Luther and the maze beneath the school.

Hearing the story of Kelvin's adventures surprised Elizabeth. "You did all that?" she exclaimed.

She suddenly felt like she had achieved nothing in her life to this point. She was always adventurous and liked to do things that other royals wouldn't dream of doing, but she had never experienced something as exciting as Kelvin's experience in the maze.

"I'm jealous," she admitted. "I wish I could go on an adventure like that."

"It was terrifying!" he explained. "I wouldn't have gone if it weren't for Henry pushing me."

Reaching the temple, they entered. Crossing the main chamber of the temple and walking past the large stone tribute to Apollo, Kelvin shouted, "Wait! There it is again!"

He was pointing at the statue of a man trampling his foes. The statue was directly behind Apollo, and the symbol was plain to see on the man's chest: an eye inside a blazing golden circle.

Silently walking up behind them, the high priest heard the reference to the symbol. His pace quickened. He frantically grabbed Kelvin by the shoulders and looked into his eyes. "How do you know this symbol?" he demanded.

"I saw it in Triopolis," stuttered Kelvin, shaking in fear. He was staring into the eyes of a mad man.

He knew that Elizabeth trusted the high priest, but there was something about him that wasn't right. It wasn't a good or evil feeling that Kelvin got in his presence; it was just odd.

The high priest thought about the young man's answer for a moment. He hadn't prepared for this. Then his eyes calmed and he looked far away, as if he were no longer standing in front of them.

His thoughts take him elsewhere, mused Elizabeth, watching the scene.

The high priest was undecided as to how to proceed. For the last five hundred years, the topic of his past had not come up, and now with the sudden coming of this man, he was out of time.

Breaking his trance, he said, "I think we should go somewhere private to talk."

Elizabeth was startled by the high priest's tone. She had only known him to be a patient and helpful man, but in this moment, he was not at all patient. She and Kelvin followed him, unsure of the outcome of this meeting.

The high priest closed the door behind them and sat behind his desk. His two guests sat in the chairs facing him. They grew more and more nervous as the high priest stared at them in silence for several long moments.

"Where have you seen the symbol?" he finally asked.

"I saw it in a book," replied Kelvin.

"What book?"

"There was no title. I found it in the basement of Town Hall in Triopolis."

Kelvin's wracked nerves were quite visible. Elizabeth was shocked at the high priest's icy tone; she had never seen this side of him. She was starting to realize that he was much more involved in matters outside the temple than she knew.

Kelvin was mesmerized by the high priest's steady gaze. He couldn't turn away. The deep brown eyes held his head firm as they penetrated Kelvin's mind. He felt no pain, but he knew that this man was inside his head, reading his thoughts.

The high priest must have been satisfied with Kelvin's answers because in silence he got up and poured each of them a cup of tea. Kelvin was still stunned from the mesmerizing experience.

"I believe you," he finally said. "I thought I had removed all books referencing the Enlightened." He then decided that it was time to tell them the truth. "I was there in the beginning. I believe you know my name, Kelvin. I am Donovan."

Kelvin's mouth dropped open. He was stunned.

"But that would make you five hundred years old!" blurted Kelvin.

"Much older than that," responded Donovan in a reflective tone.

"You are Donovan, one of the founders and gods of Triopolis?" asked Kelvin, to clarify.

"I am the one you speak of."

"Long life is but one of the abilities of the Enlightened," said Donovan.

"The Enlightened?" asked Elizabeth.

"That is what it is called when you have the ability to control your mind as we do," said Donovan. "The symbol you saw on the statue is the sign of enlightenment."

"What do you mean by control your mind?" asked Kelvin.

"The gift of foresight is one ability we have," answered Donovan. "We can see things before they happen. Elizabeth, I believe you know what I mean."

Kelvin looked at her with confusion as if to say *how could you know?*

"You have had visions of things that would come to pass," continued Donovan. "The arrival of Kelvin, for example."

"But that was just a dream," she argued.

"No, it was much more than that," he said. "I first noticed your ability when you were very young. That is when I began to mentor you."

"You used to give me different exercises and tasks than the other children," she replied, remembering her religious studies classes as a youth.

"Yes, I had to find a way to teach you without anyone else knowing."

"Are there others?" she asked.

"There is one other," replied Donovan, in a foreboding tone. "His name is Luther. He is an evil man who was imprisoned behind thousands of feet of solid rock. He cannot hurt us now."

The name of his former nemesis reverberated in his head as he thought of things that happened long ago.

"Luther is still alive too," said Kelvin.

"You know who Luther is?" asked Donovan, concerned. "I had hoped that we had wiped his name from history."

"I first heard his name when I found the book," explained Kelvin. "Then I accidentally found a room under Town Hall that once belonged to him."

"You found his lab?" asked Donovan, surprised. "I thought we had hidden it forever."

"Unfortunately, someone else found it first," answered Kelvin. "The wall built to cover the entrance was breached before I got there. I saw the man who found the room first."

A look of horror suffused Donovan's face.

"He is called the bishop," said Kelvin.

"And he has been taught in the ways of the Enlightened?" asked Donovan.

"I believe so," replied Kelvin. "It appears that he is teaching himself."

"That is impossible. Our ways cannot be self-taught."

"Why was it necessary to imprison Luther?" asked Kelvin. "What did he do?"

"Luther wanted complete control of Triopolis," said Donovan. "He was corrupted by his thirst for power. We could not destroy him, so we did the next best thing. We locked him up.

"Luther tricked us all," continued Donovan. "You know the story of the founding of Triopolis, Kelvin. Well, Luther was the fourth founder. He came to us as a healer, knowledgeable in the art and science of medicine, and we agreed to let him be a member of our ruling assembly."

"You wrote the inscription in the book I found," said Kelvin.

"Ah, the book I left for Nelson," replied Donovan. "I left that for him just in case."

"In case what?" asked Kelvin.

"In case I was wrong about Luther. They needed to have a way to reverse my actions if necessary. Nelson agreed with me that Luther was the problem, but Rowen did not," explained Donovan. "Rowen was under Luther's spell, I later came to find out, and we had many bitter arguments. The air was so tense after I caged Luther that I agreed to leave and never return. I wasn't sure if I had done the right thing.

"You see, we could never prove that Luther was guilty," explained Donovan. "He had his henchmen do his bidding, but it was all covert. No one ever saw any murders taking place, but men disappeared regularly.

"Anyone who opposed him went missing, never to be seen again. Others were blackmailed or tortured at his pleasure. People were afraid to contradict him, so they fell in line with his wishes, just as he wanted.

"I never told them where Luther was held captive, but I left a trail of clues for someone to right the wrong, if it was necessary. Nelson was a true hero. He held Triopolis together when Rowen, Luther, and I tried to tear it apart. You are the descendant of a great man, Kelvin. Nelson was the best of all of us."

Kelvin felt a sense of pride for his ancient ancestor and family name.

"After that, I knew that no Enlightened could remain in Triopolis," continued Donovan. "I had to leave, never to return."

"How did you come to be in Westville?" asked Elizabeth.

"I thought you might ask that," he answered with a smile.

"I made a deal with the Grand Master, Jorin. He was leader of the people of Granite Lake. He passed on centuries ago and has been followed by his son

Meric. They were the master guides to enlightenment for those fortunate souls who possessed the abilities, like you," he said looking at Elizabeth.

"You said they were the guides to enlightenment," said Kelvin. "Does that mean they no longer are?"

"No, they are not," answered Donovan, sadly. "After things went so badly with Luther and so many lives were lost on his account, Jorin made their trade illegal. He commanded that no one would again be shown the path to enlightenment.

"The teachers became hunters. Jorin also commanded that all people who had been taught even the slightest amount must be destroyed. After a hundred years of slaughter, Luther, Jorin, and I were the last three living. Luther ended his days locked in the mountain. Jorin finished his time on earth in Granite Lake, and he allowed me to retire to Westville.

"Apollo was, by this point, deep into his wars of consolidation. His many successes over neighboring clans made him confident to the point of arrogance. Backed by this confidence, he would often walk alone in the forest to gather his thoughts and make plans.

"The forest was a very dangerous place to be alone at that time. He risked being ravaged by any manner of beast or being harassed by marauding wild men or even a man like me. He approached me as I sat by my fire cooking a mouthwatering juvenile rabbit."

The bishop paused to take a sip of tea. Kelvin and Elizabeth waited in silence, their minds a whirl of information, too much to take in at once.

"Apollo was a towering man, standing well over six feet. In one mighty swing of his long steel blade he could take a man's head clean off. His grip was so forceful that he could break all the bones in a man's hand with just a squeeze. His imposing size sent many an adversary running in the opposite direction.

"By the time we had finished our feast of rabbit, I had agreed to join him. A mutual respect grew between us as we witnessed each other's great feats in battle. Of course, my strengths were mysterious, and his were achieved by brute force.

"When the wars were over, he built this wondrous temple to himself and promised that I would always have a home in Westville. This was the greatest gift he could have given me, and I will always be thankful to him."

"Why does no one know this story?" asked Elizabeth.

"My powers were only known to Apollo, and he never revealed the secret to anyone," explained Donovan. "When some soldiers witnessed my powers in battle, he made them swear a vow of secrecy. Anytime a whisper of my abilities came out, Apollo publicly executed the accused as well as any friends in their circle, hoping to strike fear in the rest of the army. Eventually, the stories turned to rumors, and over time, they disappeared completely."

Finishing his tea, Donovan concluded the conversation, "I never thought the two great civilizations of my life would come together. Now that you have met, I feel a shifting force in the world that will be too strong for any of us to contain."

A knock on the door produced Lewis, peeking his head in. "Sir, Lord Rosser wishes to see you. I brought him to the bench by the fountain in the garden."

"Very good, thank you Lewis," replied his master.

Elizabeth looked at Kelvin with concern.

"Nothing to worry about," replied Donovan. "He will not hear about you." With that, he got up to leave.

"Lord Rosser, so good to see you again," was the high priest's greeting as he approached the bench.

Standing up to properly greet him, Lord Rosser replied, "It's been too long, old friend."

"I loved the stories you used to tell about your travels with the army," reminisced the high priest.

"Well, my adventures have almost ended now that old age is creeping in," answered Lord Rosser.

Looking at the aging warrior, the high priest could see some signs of aging, but he definitely would not say the man was old. Furthermore, he was indispensable to the king in running the realm.

"So what brings you here today?" asked the high priest.

"I have seen some strange things around here lately, and I was wondering if you might have some information," replied Lord Rosser.

The first set of questions was about Richard and Albert— their movements, actions, and anything else out of place about their relationship.

Realizing where Lord Rosser was headed with this line of questioning, the high priest praised Richard's virtues. "My Lord, Prince Richard has always been a staunch advocate of our programs in the temple. After all, I have helped tutor him since he was a child."

"I know," Lord Rosser replied. "I too have never had a quarrel with the prince, but the king has asked me to investigate, so I must."

"What does he plan to do if you should uncover the worst?" asked the high priest, knowing what the worst was.

Lord Rosser watched as two white birds circled the small fountain before gracefully touching down on the stone ledge. He never understood why, but he always seemed so at ease in these gardens. Maybe it was the high priest's calming presence.

The high priest could tell he was not going to like Lord Rosser's answer as he watched his friend contemplating the birds. "If the worst were to be discovered, I think the king would pass the succession of his crown to his brother, Charles, bypassing his eldest son."

"That is preposterous!" replied the high priest. "No such thing has ever been done in all of our history."

"That is why I hope it doesn't come to that," replied the old soldier.

"Is there even a precedent to support such an action?"

"You know as well as I that the king can create a precedent whenever he likes," answered Lord Rosser.

Thinking for a moment, the high priest said what his guest had hoped he wouldn't. "You can control what truth the king hears."

"I wouldn't dare think of doing that," was the quick response. "It would be treason, and that I cannot do."

"I know, friend, your loyalty has always been strong," complimented the high priest.

The conversation now changed to the other person Lord Rosser wanted to ask about. "Have you had any unusual guests lately? I saw a man I didn't recognize exiting the temple yesterday."

The high priest knew he was asking about Henry and Kelvin, but he took a moment to develop his ruse before answering. "When was this?" he asked, buying some time.

Lord Rosser wasn't made suspicious by his question because many people came through the temple each day, and he didn't expect his friend to know them all. Lord Rosser liked and respected the high priest, so this was a conversation rather than an interrogation.

"What did the man look like?" asked the high priest.

He was not surprised when Lord Rosser's description of the man matched Henry's perfectly.

"Oh, him!" exclaimed the high priest. "He was a peasant that the princess helped in the market. He had stolen an apple, and she felt sorry for him, so she brought him here for a hot meal."

"Sometimes I think the princess is too soft to be a queen," replied Lord Rosser.

They both laughed. Lord Rosser thanked his friend for his time and left.

Kelvin and Elizabeth sat in the main chamber of the temple looking at the giant statue of Apollo through different eyes. They now knew something that no one else in Westville knew about the statue. The man behind Apollo was Donovan.

"I don't know what just happened," said Kelvin, staring at the statue. "I have so many thoughts right now and so many ideas, but I don't know how to put them into words!"

"I know exactly how you're feeling," said Elizabeth. She too had been overwhelmed by the high priest's story.

"Who is Lord Rosser?" asked Kelvin.

"He is the captain of the king's army and head of his private guard."

Kelvin gave her a look of horror.

"It's okay," she consoled him. "After what we just found out about the high priest, I mean Donovan, I am sure he can handle Lord Rosser!"

Exiting the temple, they decided that a walk would be best to help them process their new view of the world. Heading toward the market, a slight breeze blew which was just enough to keep them cool while bathing in the sun's rays. Wanting to avoid the bustle of the market, they slipped past quickly.

Elizabeth was taking them down the same path that Kelvin had entered the city on a few days earlier. So much had happened since then. It seemed like a lifetime ago.

Upon discovering Westville, he could not have dreamed of how his worldview would change within a matter of days.

Why did this happen? Are the gods real? Did they bring the storm that carried us here?

"Wait a minute," blurted Kelvin.

"What is it?" she asked.

"I just put it together," he said. "I just met one of our gods!"

Elizabeth tried to understand by wondering how she would feel meeting Apollo, but it was impossible to contemplate.

"This knowledge must be kept from my people," he explained. "Our whole social structure would break down if they knew that everything they had believed in for so many generations was false."

"Well, I don't think Donovan will say anything," she replied. "He has kept the secret for a long time."

For the next few minutes, neither of them said a word. They just walked, consumed by their thoughts. People rushed by attending to their daily business. Children played loudly on the sidewalk, while the occasional horse trotted down the street ridden by its master or pulling a carriage. Kelvin and Elizabeth were oblivious to all of this commotion around them.

Finally, Kelvin broke the silence. "This has been a much more comfortable walk than the last time."

Happy with the subject change to a lighter topic, she replied, "I can imagine it was quite scary the first time. You probably didn't know if you would be met with friendship or danger."

"We did have all of those thoughts," he admitted. "We weren't sure if we should talk to people or avoid them."

"Well, I'm glad I'm the one who found you and not one of the king's guards," she said with a smile. "They probably would have locked you up!"

Kelvin, getting a little concerned, asked, "What about Richard? Now that he knows, will he tell his father?"

"No, I trust Richard," she said. "We have only been married for a couple of weeks, but we have developed a very trusting relationship. You see, he has a much bigger secret that he doesn't want to get out."

"I was wondering if he was your husband," Kelvin said, with obvious disappointment in his voice.

"He is my husband in title only," replied Elizabeth, noticing his disappointment.

She told him about the arrangement between them. It didn't get any easier as she listened to herself telling the story. She knew it wasn't right, and she couldn't imagine how bad it sounded to Kelvin.

"That's cruel of him," responded Kelvin. "How do you live that way?"

"I don't know," she responded. "I haven't figured that out yet. It's difficult because I really don't feel like I have another option. I am stuck."

Lost in their conversation, they hadn't plotted a course for their walk. Kelvin's legs took him the only way they knew. Coming through the forest, they stepped onto the white, sandy beach.

"Come on," said Elizabeth. "I want to see your boat."

Kelvin led her to the west, heading to the place they landed.

Walking leisurely along the water's edge, they were now carrying their shoes enjoying the warm sand on their feet. The occasional frothy, white wave flowed through their toes.

Each time one came close, Elizabeth playfully jumped out of its way, trying not to get wet. Kelvin watched her and smiled.

Elizabeth sensed her feelings for Kelvin building. It had only been a short time, but he was all she thought about. She knew that he felt the same way. She could tell by the way he looked at her.

"I am still amazed that you survived the storm and landed here," she commented.

"I ask myself how and why each day," he replied, remembering that horrible night. "It must have been fate that brought me here."

Kelvin was now looking directly into Elizabeth's beautiful, blue eyes. The extended gaze turned into smiles for both of them. She playfully leaned in and gave him a peck on the cheek followed by a long embrace.

Kelvin's surprise soon vanished, and he enjoyed the hug. He too had been anticipating this moment.

"I am sorry," Elizabeth said, composing herself.

"You don't ever have to apologize for that," he replied, with a smile on his face.

Elizabeth smiled back and kissed him again.

It wasn't much farther until they reached the place the boat landed.

"It was here!" he yelled. "Look, you can see the marks in the sand! This is where it was!"

The boat was gone.

Chapter 13

The sunlight faded as day became night. The setting of the sun made Kelvin forget about the storm clouds he had seen heading their way until he felt the first drops of rain on his arms.

Kelvin and Elizabeth were enjoying the outdoor play, standing under a large tree. The actors were protected from the light sprinkle, and they continued to perform. Between them and the stage, a grassy area was filled with people enjoying the first production of summer.

Their heads moved almost as one, scanning back and forth as the actors moved about the stage. Riveted to the story, no one seemed to notice that the rain had intensified.

Crack! Boom! exploded the loudest thunder Elizabeth had ever heard. Well, it was either the loudest or it just seemed like it because she wasn't expecting it.

Immediately after the electricity lit the sky, a torrential downpour erupted. The rain sent the crowd into a frenzy.

The tree branches had protected them from the light sprinkle, but now they were no help at all. The rain seemed to be coming at them from all directions.

"Follow me!" yelled Elizabeth to Kelvin.

She took off running as quickly as she could while holding her dress down with one hand to keep it from blowing in the strong wind. Kelvin could see that they were headed to the castle.

Running through the open gate, they made it to shelter. Shaking, wiping, and wringing their hair, they tried to get as much water as possible off of them. She had led them to the covered exterior doorway of the Great Hall, knowing it would be empty tonight.

Laughing, she said, "Wow, I didn't see that coming!"

"We are soaked!" exclaimed Kelvin.

"Let's go see if we can find some dry clothes," she suggested. The couple sloshed through the hall and up the stairs to her apartment.

Henry was walking as fast as his legs would take him, trying to get out of the castle without being seen. He had been with Richard and Albert ever since their time on the archery field earlier that day. Richard brought him to the castle to give him a tour and to join him for dinner. Then he gave Henry this route to exit the castle, knowing it would be deserted.

"This wasn't wise," worried Henry, as he navigated the lengthy corridors. "I should never have come here. It's too risky."

Richard had assured him that his father would be out hunting and not in the castle today, so it would be safe. He had also assured Henry that no one would question who he was when he was with Richard, but Henry wondered what would happen if someone saw him alone in the castle.

Rounding a corner, his foot landed on the stone floor but couldn't find traction. His arms flailed before finding the wall of the corridor just in time to catch his fall.

Why is the floor wet? he asked himself.

There was just enough water on the floor to make the stone slippery. His tension heightened, realizing that a puddle of water could mean someone was here.

As he walked at a much slower pace so as not to slip on the wet floor, he heard familiar voices that stopped him in his tracks. His curiosity conquered his fear of being seen, and he followed them.

Peeking around a corner, he saw where the water had come from. There stood Elizabeth and Kelvin, halfway down the corridor, dripping wet.

Henry felt slightly irritated at his friend's thoughtlessness. He was worried that Kelvin's irrational actions were going to be noticed by the wrong person. This could be dangerous because not everyone would be as accepting as Richard had been.

The protective feelings of a father were also starting to develop inside him, which made him even more upset with Elizabeth than he was with Kelvin. *She just met him*, he thought to himself. *He is a good person, but she hasn't had nearly enough time to find that out yet.*

He was beside himself when she flirtatiously touched his arm. He knew his recently found daughter would never give him a chance to redeem himself if he tried to stop the budding relationship. He wasn't sure if he should leave them, or if he should stay close by to make sure they were safe.

He tried to reassure himself with the thought that Elizabeth knew this place and the people in it better than he did. She knew what she was doing. He remembered the situations he had gotten himself into in the name of love.

He decided to stay where he was.

Pulling her hand away, Elizabeth reached toward the wall. Henry had not seen it before, but the two were standing by a door, and she was reaching for the knob to open it. The door opened and they stepped quietly into the room.

Henry crept down the corridor and reached the doorway just as the door closed behind Kelvin. He made up his mind. He would protect them by guarding the door.

Lord Rosser stumbled out of the alehouse, relieved to see that it was raining. He stood under the awning, planning his escape while trying to steady himself. He was swaying a little, and his knees were wobbly as a result of the amount of ale he had consumed with his supper.

Watching as people ran from the market to their homes or wherever they could find protection from the rain, he laughed and muttered, "It's just water, people! You are not going to melt."

He was not at all afraid of the rain. It was almost soothing to him, reminding him of how after a battle the field would be washed clean from a good downpour. It was as if Apollo was cleansing the dead in preparation for their arrival at his house in the heavens.

Is that Princess Elizabeth? he wondered, seeing a woman run past. "It is!" he said aloud. "But who is the man with her?"

Adrenaline took over, and his wobbly knees found their strength as he followed. Entering through the door to the Great Hall, Lord Rosser saw Elizabeth and the man disappear through the doorway on the opposite end of the room. He moved as quickly as his intoxicated body would take him across the smooth stone floor.

The quick sprint to the castle had made him queasy, but his determination kept him moving toward his goal. Almost reaching the end of the hall, he fell to his knees unable to take another step. His body betrayed him, and he collapsed to the floor.

He could feel the beer and salted pork that he had supped on gurgling in his stomach, causing a most uncomfortable feeling as acid moved up his throat. Then it was too late.

When the vomiting finally subsided, he crawled to a nearby bench and pulled himself onto it where he collapsed on his back. The pain and discomfort in his stomach up through his mouth overwhelmed him as he lay on the cold hard wood.

Lord Rosser knew that if he stayed on the bench, he would surely pass out, so he mustered all of his will and lifted himself to his feet. Stumbling again and moving slowly, he headed toward the torch-lit corridor ahead. He knew the way to Elizabeth's apartment, and that is where he figured they were headed.

Again, he asked himself, *Who is that man? Are there two foreigners here?*

He ascended the stairs in the hallway just off the end of the Great Hall and stepped into a corridor that ran perpendicular to another hallway. Slowly, he made his way to the intersection.

Even in his drunken state, Lord Rosser still had his wits about him, like any properly trained soldier. He slithered up against the wall in a dark area between two torches.

As soon as his back hit the wall, a man walked past down the adjoining hallway, almost throwing him off balance and taking him completely by surprise. *Whew, that was close*, he thought, relieved that he was standing in the shadows when the man passed by.

Lord Rosser quietly walked to the intersection of the two corridors. Peeking around the corner, he could see the unknown man doing the same at the next corner.

Is he watching Elizabeth? He obviously shouldn't be here; the way he is snooping around, he's up to no good. I am in charge of security for the king and his family, and this man is suspicious.

Suddenly, the man jumped back and threw himself against the wall, giving Lord Rosser a perfect view of his face.

He recognized the man as the one he had seen with Richard and Albert on the archery range, but that made no sense. If this man was friends with Richard, why was he spying on Elizabeth?

This confused Lord Rosser. He could understand why Elizabeth was investigating Richard, but why would Richard be watching her?

Judging that sufficient time had elapsed, he poked his head around the corner again. He was correct in his assumption that the man also continued to observe his section of the corridor. While he was watching, the man slipped around the corner and out of sight.

Lord Rosser followed and moved to the spot that the other man had previously occupied. Looking around the corner, he saw the man standing in front of the door to Elizabeth's rooms.

"Damn!" he whispered, pulling his head back around the corner. "He saw me!"

Lord Rosser looked around the corner again and saw the man coming toward him.

He stepped out into the open and presented himself to the man. They stood in the corridor facing each other, neither saying a word. Lord Rosser was a couple inches taller than the other man and much stronger looking. He posed, trying to use his size advantage to intimidate his foe.

Lord Rosser was the first to speak.

"Who are you?"

"My name is Henry."

"Why haven't I seen you before?" asked Lord Rosser. "I know all of Richard's friends."

Henry looked at the larger man with skepticism. "I am not from here."

"I know that!" spat Lord Rosser, his temper getting the best of him. The alcohol was preventing him from controlling his emotions as he usually did during an interrogation. "So, where are you from?"

"I am from the west," answered Henry. "I am stranded here with no way home."

"Liar!" yelled Lord Rosser. He had seen much of the west, and he knew that no one lived beyond the mountains. His intoxication had gotten the best of him, and he felt like he was being toyed with.

"It's true," replied Henry. "My boat washed ashore in a storm."

Lord Rosser grabbed Henry by the neck and slammed him against the wall. "Liar!" he yelled again, this time in Henry's face.

Henry almost passed out from the smell of alcohol and vomit on Lord Rosser's breath. It was horrendous, although it gave him hope. His adversary was much bigger, but he was also drunk. Henry believed he had a chance.

Pinned against the wall, Henry couldn't do much. He could only think of one movement that would free him from the stronger man's grip. His right leg swung up with as much force as he could gather. A loud groan escaped Lord Rosser's lips as Henry's foot landed squarely between his legs.

The overpowering hands holding Henry in place released their grip as the larger man fell to the floor writhing in pain.

Lord Rosser lay on the floor for no more than a minute, but it seemed like an hour as he waited for the pain to subside. Even with the large amount of ale in his system, the blow brought tears to his eyes.

Henry wasn't about to continue a fight with a man so much bigger than himself, especially because he was a foreigner with very few friends here. He backed away rubbing his neck to soothe the pain.

Lord Rosser's eyes finally cleared and he shot back to his feet full of rage. "You will pay for that!" he pronounced, pulling out a dagger strapped to his waist.

Henry knew he was in trouble now. If this man was willing to kill him to get into that room, what would he do to Kelvin and Elizabeth? His instincts and duty overtook him, and his only purpose in life became the protection of his daughter.

Lord Rosser lunged at Henry, who dodged the blade. Henry didn't have any weapon to defend himself with so he used his quickness, knowing the other man was drunk. Another slow, slightly off-balance lunge directed at Henry missed its target.

Henry danced around Lord Rosser to stay out of his line of fire. He dodged another lunge. This time, using the force from both of his arms along with Lord Rosser's forward momentum, Henry slammed his opponent into the wall. This stunned the intoxicated Lord Rosser for a moment.

Gaining his composure, he slurred to Henry, "Why are you protecting the princess and her deceit?"

"That man is a friend of mine," replied Henry. "We were stranded here together when our boat washed ashore in a storm."

"Oh, yes, you're from that other city!" exclaimed Lord Rosser, sarcastically slurring his words.

The armed man thrust his dagger at Henry. Before he could recoil from the attack, Henry grabbed the dagger hand with both of his and twisted as hard as he could. The blade fell to the floor just as Lord Rosser's opposite hand with its fist balled tight landed in Henry's stomach.

With a loud gasp, Henry released Lord Rosser's arm. Continuing to gasp for air, he tried to fill his lungs but it seemed impossible. He had no time to waste recovering. He couldn't let his enemy get to the dagger first.

Henry slammed his shoulder into Lord Rosser as he was bending over to pick up the blade, driving him past it. Both men flew to the floor from the force of the blow. Henry landed between Lord Rosser and the blade.

Lord Rosser was concerned for the first time that night. He knew he should not have started the fight in his inebriated state. If he had not been drinking, he would easily have had the advantage.

Lord Rosser was the first to get up. As Henry rose slowly to his knees, still affected by the blow to his stomach, Lord Rosser struck him in the head with his foot. The force of the kick sent Henry back to the floor.

Lord Rosser reached for the knife to finish off his adversary. Writhing in pain on the floor with blood flowing from his mouth, Henry saw a small piece of pointed metal near the base of the wall. He reached for it as he again got to his knees.

On his hands and knees, he felt his head spinning from the almost certain concussion he had suffered from the kick he'd just received. He hung his head low, waiting for his enemy's next move. Lord Rosser returned with the dagger in hand to deliver the final blow.

Standing over Henry and directly in front of him, he lifted the dagger and lowered his deathblow. Henry lifted from his knees and met Lord Rosser midthrust. Both weapons made contact at the same time. Henry's makeshift blade entered his enemy in the upper part of his abdomen. The blade did not stop until it found Lord Rosser's heart.

Lord Rosser's dagger sliced into Henry's back, headed for his heart. The force of Lord Rosser's body falling on top of Henry pushed the dagger completely through. It slipped between his ribs and pierced his heart from behind. The two dead men lay in a massive bloody heap on the hallway floor just outside the princess's apartment.

"My love, we have our weapon," said Lynessa, excitedly. "However, I cannot take credit. The princess has given us our tool to take down Lord Rosser."

Terryn looked at her, wondering what she was talking about. He could tell something was brewing inside her head, but up to this point, she hadn't given him a clue as to what it was.

They had stolen away to a small alcove in a seldom-used hallway in the castle. A single servant girl was the only other person in the corridor, but she was working on the other end, far enough away that she would not hear them talking.

"She is not Lord Granville's true born daughter!" Lynessa exclaimed.

Stunned, Terryn asked, "How is that possible?"

"She told me a story about Lord Granville finding her in the forest just before the Battle of Midalo," replied Lynessa. "Apparently, she is from a city called Triopolis, and Henry is her father!"

"Unbelievable!" shouted Terryn, loud enough for the maid at the end of the hall to look up. "This couldn't be any better."

"Lord Rosser is the one who pushed the king to consider the match for Richard," said Lynessa. "I was there that day in the Great Hall, and I remember it well. It was the feast of Apollo's passing on."

In the mythology of Westville, Apollo hadn't died. He had merely moved on to his place in the next life where he sat waiting for his future kin to join him. The day his life force left his mortal body was the day he passed on.

"Lord Rosser pleaded with His Majesty that this match was perfect for the realm," she continued. "The king was unsure because of the Granvilles' royal blood, but Lord Rosser was able to convince him.

"When the king hears that Elizabeth is not a true Granville, it will destroy your uncle. It will show that he did not research her background, and he will be in dishonor."

"Always stay out of politics," Terryn said, remembering what his uncle told him once. "It never ends well for those who get caught up in politics. You either end up dead or disgraced." He was silent before he added, "That was the warning my uncle left me with."

"He has a good point," replied Lynessa. "This time, however, the odds are in your favor. Do you want to replace your uncle and gain your inheritance?"

"Yes, I do," he answered excitedly.

"Okay, then this is how it must happen," she began. "You have to be the one to tell the king. If it's you, then you can save your family name and thus your inheritance. If someone else tells him, you and your whole family will take the fall."

"Yes," replied Terryn. "My uncle will be disgraced, but I will save the rest of the family and, more importantly, myself by being the one who discovers the falsehood."

"Exactly," she replied.

"I don't know how you come up with these deceptions, but I would never want you plotting against me," said Terryn.

Lynessa gave up her search and headed back to Elizabeth's apartment. She had looked everywhere the princess normally frequented throughout the day. Lynessa was very concerned as she moved quickly through the corridors of the castle.

Turning the corner, she entered the long corridor that led to the princess's rooms. Moving down the hallway, something on the floor came into view, but it was too far away for her to make out what it was.

"By Apollo!" she screamed, approaching the bloody heap.

Looking closely at the two men on the floor, a shriek escaped her lips. It was Lord Rosser and Henry. "How could this be?" she murmured. "Why were they even in the same place?"

Elizabeth's door opened and she appeared, having changed out of her wet clothes. "Lynessa, I heard you scream," she said, and then she saw the bodies. There she stood motionless in disbelief.

"My father!" she cried. "I only just met him, and now he's gone!"

"He must have been protecting you from Lord Rosser," said Lynessa. "We know he was watching Richard. I wonder if he saw them together and followed Henry."

Kelvin, who was watching from just behind the door, joined the ladies in the hallway. Looking at his friend lying on the floor, he wanted to cry out, but he knew that would not bring him back.

He looked at Elizabeth and said, "We have to get out of here, now! If we are here when the bodies are found, they will accuse us."

"He's right, My Lady," agreed Lynessa. "We must go."

"Quick," commanded Kelvin. "Put on warm, comfortable clothing."

He knew what the conditions would be like if they were to make it out of the city and into the forest. His clothes were still soggy, but he had no time to worry about that.

Elizabeth and Lynessa returned wearing trousers and long-sleeved shirts. Luckily, Elizabeth had kept the clothes she wore when Lord Granville allowed her to come along on a hunt. This was something she enjoyed even though it was not common among royal women.

"Where will we go?" asked Lynessa.

"We have to leave Westville!" exclaimed Kelvin.

"He's right," agreed Elizabeth. "We will never be safe here again. When the king finds out that a foreigner killed his captain and favorite advisor, everyone involved will be hanged. Our only option is to flee, and we must do it quickly. The smell of the bodies will soon attract attention."

Elizabeth looked in both directions down the hallway and whispered, "It's clear."

Lynessa followed her with Kelvin coming last. As Kelvin walked past the dead bodies, he ripped Lord Rosser's dagger out of his friend's back and wiped it on Henry's clothing. With all of the blood removed from the blade, he slid it through a loop in his belt and continued down the corridor.

It was a gruesome task, but Kelvin knew that a blade could prove useful in the wilderness. Hunting would be necessary if they hoped to survive. He was relieved that Lynessa and Elizabeth hadn't turned around and seen him take the blade. They might not have understood.

Elizabeth felt sadness as they walked away from her father. To leave him there in a bloody heap didn't seem right. He was her father, after all.

You must not think this way, she told herself. Of course, she knew that all these thoughts were normal and right, but she also knew that they would cloud her judgment. She needed to have a clear mind because her decisions in the next few hours would determine whether she lived or ended up like her father.

Quickly they moved through the corridors and down the stairs. They hesitated at the entrance to the Great Hall, looking in all directions to see if they were alone. Not seeing anyone in the large chamber, they moved against the back wall.

Staying close to the wall helped them remain in the dark, as only every third torch was lit. This was how rooms in the castle were kept if they were not being used frequently. That way the room wasn't completely dark if someone needed to come through.

"Be careful," whispered Elizabeth. "A servant is probably supposed to check on these torches occasionally."

"Yes, but they rarely actually do," replied Lynessa softly.

Am I doing the right thing? Lynessa wondered. *Should I stay with them, or should I turn them in? I could help Terryn by leading them to him. He would be praised by the king for capturing Lord Rosser's murderers. Yes, that is what I will do.*

Moving as quickly and quietly as possible, they were now halfway through the cavernous room. Seeing the large hearth directly across the Great Hall reminded Kelvin of another item they would need.

"Wait," he said as forcefully as he could in a whisper. "I want to get the fire kit from the fireplace."

"We don't have time," pleaded Elizabeth. "We have to get out of here."

He knew fire would be very important for them in the wild. Sure, it would be possible to start a fire without the proper tools, but having a flint would make the task so much easier.

"I will meet you by the exit," he said, heading directly across the room toward the fireplace.

Almost finishing his crossing, he heard a door open. In walked a young man wearing the white shirt and brown pants uniform of the castle's servants.

Kelvin dropped to his knees and slowly crawled to the base of the wall. He had already made it to the tables and benches lined in front of the fireplace by the time the servant entered the room.

Elizabeth and Lynessa were frozen with fear. They stood up against the opposite wall watching Kelvin scramble into the darkness.

Sitting in a dark corner where the fireplace met the wall, Kelvin watched the servant make his rounds.

Luckily for them, this servant didn't seem to care for his task. He walked right down the center of the room glancing in the general direction of each torch as he passed by. There was no chance of any of them being seen by this lazy boy.

After the boy left the room, Kelvin took the steel and flint from the firebox on the mantel and made for the exit door where he met his companions.

"That was close," said Elizabeth, waiting for Kelvin by the exit.

She hesitated before opening the door. "Where should we go?"

"What is the quickest way out of the city?" he asked.

"The quickest would be east, but that would not be the easiest," answered Lynessa. "We would have a better chance of not being seen if we went west."

"She's right," said Elizabeth. "Once we get past the temple, there are only the houses of common folk. None of them would recognize us dressed like this."

Right into my trap, thought Lynessa. She knew that Terryn was playing dice tonight at an alehouse on the western edge of town. If she could direct them to the vicinity of that house, she might be able to contact Terryn, and he could apprehend them.

They exited the Great Hall and turned west. The sky was overcast, which didn't allow much light from the stars or the moon, but at least the rain had ended. The lack of light would make navigating the forest more difficult, but it would also be harder for those following them.

Nervously, they crept away from the castle. The rain had kept people inside, leaving the streets almost completely vacant. The short walk from the castle to the temple was tense but uneventful. In fact, they didn't see one person on the way.

"I wonder what Donovan will think we should do?" asked Elizabeth, staring at the building, wondering if he was there.

"Donovan?" asked Lynessa.

"Yes, that is the high priest's real name," said Elizabeth.

"We don't want to do that, My Lady," pleaded Lynessa. "He would surely turn you in to the constable."

"I don't think he will," replied Elizabeth, firmly. "I want to talk to him."

The courtyard was empty so they walked directly to the temple door. Opening it just enough to slip through, they entered. Not wasting any time, they went directly to Donovan's study.

"Elizabeth," said Donovan, seeing them in the open doorway. "Come in, please."

"What happened?" he asked, looking at the bedraggled group. "Why are you dressed like that?"

Elizabeth stepped forward and told Donovan all that had happened that night. He took it in with a straight face, not revealing his thoughts on the matter. When she finished, he sat in his chair behind the desk and pondered the situation while the three fugitives waited for his response.

After many tense moments, he finally spoke. "You cannot stay in Westville," he said. "If you stay, you will be tied to Lord Rosser's murder. The king's punishment will be cruel and unforgiving."

"We thought the same," said Kelvin. "I think we should go to Triopolis."

"You would be safe there," Donovan agreed. "The road will be very difficult, but you must get as far away from here as quickly as you can. The king will send men after you. Come, follow me."

Donovan jumped from his chair and scampered out the door. They rushed to keep up wondering where he was taking them.

When their hurried walk ended, they were in the garden just behind the temple. He led them to the backside of the fountain that was the centerpiece of the garden.

Elizabeth was astonished at what she saw. There was a hole in the ground with wooden stairs leading down into the earth beneath the marble structure.

So this is how he comes and goes without anyone seeing him, she mused.

Donovan, watching as the three outlaws gathered at his getaway tunnel, pondered his current position. Elizabeth prepared to descend the stairs first, followed by Lynessa and Kelvin.

"Princess," beckoned Donovan. She turned toward him before entering the stairway.

"I regret that we did not get to finish your path to enlightenment," he said. "Listen to your mind. You have more knowledge than you know."

"If your path takes you to Granite Lake, seek out Aaron," said Donovan, before wishing her good luck.

Elizabeth gave him a hug as if to say "thank you." She then led Kelvin and Lynessa down the stairs and into the tunnel.

"Away!" said Donovan, in a commanding voice and the stairway disappeared.

"Keep up!" yelled Elizabeth, as she led them through the tunnel.

Fear pushed them to run as fast as they could. The tunnel was simple with earthen walls and floor, and with wooden beams in the ceiling, keeping it from collapsing in on them. The floor was flat and free of debris, aiding in their escape.

A light appeared in front of them. Getting closer, Kelvin could see the stars in the sky above. The tunnel came to an abrupt end, depositing them into a field to the west of the city. As Kelvin exited the tunnel, they turned to look at the hole they had just come through.

It was protruding from an earthen mound similar to the others in the rolling foothills. Not more than a moment later, the hole vanished, returning to grass matching the rest of the mound.

"What have we gotten ourselves into?" asked Kelvin, as he looked at the field ahead and the faint outline of the mountain peaks in the distance.

They hadn't noticed the cool breeze that had followed the earlier storm until now. It was either that or the cold shot of the reality of their situation that gave them each a shiver.

The torch that Donovan had given Kelvin as they were running out of the temple was dwindling. Moments later the last flame was extinguished by the wind, and he tossed the torch aside.

Standing on the edge of a grassy field, Elizabeth, Kelvin, and Lynessa wondered what direction they should go.

"Let's go; we don't have much time," urged Elizabeth, not feeling comfortable standing in one spot for too long. "We have to get as far away as we can before sunrise. They will come looking for us!" She couldn't imagine the horror of what would happen to them if they were caught.

Elizabeth's last statement sent chills down Kelvin's spine. He followed her without a word.

Chapter 14

The high priest sat behind his desk pondering his next move. He knew very well that the next decision he made would be one of life or death. A slight twinge of nervous energy pulsed through his body. Decisions like this were not new to him, although it had been many years since his last. Perhaps that was why he felt so nervous.

If he didn't notify the king of the evening's events and his involvement was uncovered, he would surely be executed. Lord Rosser was the king's friend and closest advisor.

He pondered who could have known that Henry and Kelvin were in Westville. Lewis had been his servant for a long time. Surely he hadn't told anyone. The princess wouldn't have told anyone, but what about Lynessa?

The high priest wondered who the princess's servant was associated with. *I don't think she spoke to anyone of importance,* he mused. *No, she would not have told anyone who mattered.*

Quickly he made his way to the castle. Through the front gate, into the grand foyer, and up the staircase he walked. Deep in the bowels of the old stone building, he entered the king's private chambers.

The high priest was one of the few people who had this kind of access to the king. It stemmed from the many years of loyal service he had provided the Westville family. He knew from much experience that the king would still be awake tending to the days' affairs even at this late hour.

Knocking on the door, he opened it to alert the king of his presence. His Highness was seated at a writing table with a small oil lamp burning. The mounds of papers gave witness to the amount of work he still had to finish.

"Sire," he greeted the king.

The news of Lord Rosser's death was a shock to him.

"Impossible!" he yelled. "Who could kill Lord Rosser, the greatest warrior in Westville?"

"I verified the story before coming to see you, Your Majesty.".

"I wish to see his body with my own eyes," said the king, skeptically.

He rose from his chair and the mountain of work to go see the unbelievable sight. The two men rushed through the hallways of the castle. At this late hour, only a few servants were scattered about. They kept to their tasks and willingly parted as the king and the high priest passed by.

As soon as they turned into the corridor that contained the site of the murder, the smell of death reached the king's nose. This made him increase his pace to see if it was true.

Reaching the dead bodies, he moved around so he could get a good look at the faces of the dead men.

The bodies had obviously been there for a few hours as evidenced by the bluish purple discoloration and the signs of bloating beginning to occur. He didn't recognize the other man, but there was no mistaking Lord Rosser.

The king did not show any emotion upon seeing the bodies. He had witnessed much death in many battles in his lifetime and was unmoved by the sight of a corpse.

"Who is the other man?" he asked.

"I don't know," lied the high priest. "I have never seen him."

"The more important question is why was he this close to the princess?" wondered the king. "She must have known him. People just don't walk into the castle unless they know where they are going. We must find her to learn the truth."

The king abruptly left the crime scene and the high priest. To take his mind off the shock of losing his friend, he focused on finding the princess and bringing her back for questioning.

The first rays of the morning sun could be seen over the horizon. The shivering refugees continued their journey away from Westville.

"I'm cold," complained Elizabeth.

"And hungry," added Kelvin.

He knew they would have to stop soon to eat, but he wanted to get beyond the thick foliage they were currently chopping their way through.

As Kelvin led the two ladies through the mixture of bushes, shrubs, vines, and saplings, he held the branches before moving forward so they didn't whip back into their faces.

I sure am glad they wore long sleeves, he mused as he rubbed against a thorny bush.

"Watch out for that bush," he warned.

Seeing the long sharp thorns, they both stepped aside to avoid the danger.

All three were miserable during this stretch of the journey. Not only were they cold and hungry, but this thick vegetation was very difficult to traverse, and it had been this way for nearly an hour.

"I can't take this anymore!" yelled Elizabeth. "There has to be an easier way."

Kelvin stopped next to a medium-sized oak tree, which offered a brief respite from the misery they had been enduring.

"This forest has to thin out soon," he assured them.

"I hope so, because this is impossible," replied Elizabeth.

All three of them sat at the base of the tree to rest.

"How are you doing?" Elizabeth asked Lynessa. "You have been very quiet since we left."

"I'm fine," she answered. "I'm just really nervous and scared."

"Oh, it's okay," comforted Elizabeth, putting her hand on Lynessa's shoulder. She was trying to be the strong one even though she was just as concerned about what lay ahead.

Her attendant took comfort from Elizabeth's words even though she was already betraying her. She had been tearing pieces of cloth from her undershirt, and every time they turned, she tied one to a tree. If they turned right, she tied it on the right side of the path, and on the left if they turned left. To signal that they had continued straight forward, a piece of cloth was left on the ground.

Lynessa remembered a story Terryn had told her about a soldier who was captured by a pack of barbarians. This man had done the exact same thing, and it led to the army finding him. She knew Terryn would remember and hoped he would find them.

"It has been tough going through these bushes, but not being able to see over them is worse," said Kelvin. Thinking for a couple more minutes under the oak tree, he said, "I got it! This tree is perfect for climbing."

The old scraggly oak tree they were sitting under had branches low enough to reach from the ground. Looking up into the canopy, Kelvin couldn't imagine a more perfect tree for climbing. The branches formed an almost ideal staircase.

"Be careful," cautioned Elizabeth, as Kelvin reached for the first branch and pulled himself onto it. He methodically moved from branch to branch until he had climbed about twenty feet.

"What do you see?" she asked.

"We are only about half a mile from a river!" yelled Kelvin.

This excited the two women and gave them hope. They were both relieved that the end of their slog through the dense vegetation was near.

Jumping from the lowest branch, Kelvin promised, "I will catch some fish when we get to the river."

"Ah, food!" Elizabeth exclaimed, and they took off in the direction of the river.

Noticing that Lynessa had fallen behind them, she called back, "Come on, Lynessa!" What Elizabeth wasn't aware of was why she was so far behind.

Lynessa had torn another piece of cloth from the area of her undershirt covering her stomach and tied it to a bush near the oak tree, signifying their right turn.

That one was close, she thought, with beads of sweat forming on her forehead from the suspense of her deception. *I will have to be more careful next time.*

While walking the distance to the river, Kelvin was looking for the right kind of tree branch to use as a fishing spear. Finding the perfect sapling, he cut it with the dagger he had drawn from Henry's body.

"My father taught me how to make fishing spears when I was younger," he said excitedly.

"You are going to fish with that stick?" asked Lynessa sarcastically.

"Yes," he replied, her doubt draining his excitement a little.

Kelvin went to work on the sapling. He started by slicing it at one end and continuing about a quarter of the way down. He then made another slice cutting across the first, creating four prongs on the end of the stick.

Wedging small stones at the base of the incisions firmly spread the prongs apart. A wrapping of string made from dead plant fiber held the stones in place. After sharpening the tips of the four prongs, the spear was ready.

"Well, I guess I was wrong," admitted Lynessa, watching Kelvin walk toward river with the spear clutched tightly in his fist.

With him out of earshot, Elizabeth again tried to comfort Lynessa. She felt bad about dragging her into this mess.

"I am sorry," Lynessa replied. "I just think the stress is getting to me."

"Well, I can certainly understand that," answered Elizabeth.

Lynessa was starting to wonder if she could keep up her charade.

Running through the trees, Albert rushed to find his prince. "He is not going to believe this!" he said, racing past trees and bushes. Smoke could be seen rising above the trees in the distance and the smell of burning wood reached him.

Finally, he broke through the undergrowth into a small glen surrounded by forest. They were not far from the beach but a good distance from the city so the smoke would not cause alarm.

"That was fast!" shouted Albert.

Richard stood alone next to the flames. Henry's boat, which was the fuel for the fire, was now just a small mound of smoldering ashes.

"This boat of Henry's was a brilliant design," commented Richard. "It had a very thin wooden skin attached to a sturdy frame. That must be the answer to traversing the open ocean."

He gazed at the campfire and added, "Well, now the evidence of their coming here is gone."

"My Prince, I have news," said Albert, still out of breath from his run.

After hearing Albert's story of the dual murder, Richard was in disbelief. *All this effort to destroy the boat so no one would find it was a waste*, he thought wryly.

"I don't even know why they would have been in the same place together," speculated Albert.

"I do," answered Richard, bitterly. "I overheard my father last night talking about a secret mission he had given to Lord Rosser. He was on to us and wanted to know the true nature of our relationship."

"Who was he telling?" asked Albert.

"I couldn't make out the other voice, and I wasn't in a position to see the man."

"What do you think the king will do if he finds out?" asked Albert.

"I don't know," replied Richard, consumed by his thoughts.

"Do you think he would try to take away your right to the crown?"

"I wouldn't be surprised if he did," was Richard's bitter response.

Terryn sat before the king, hardly able to contain the excitement of this moment. He had wanted it his entire adult life, but what he didn't expect was how it happened.

Relief spread through him every time he thought about how the foreigner killed his uncle, opening up the path to his inheritance. He would have followed through with Lynessa's plan if he needed to, but he was happy it hadn't come to disgracing his uncle.

"Well, my boy, are you ready to fulfill the destiny your uncle set before you?" asked the king. "Will you lead my army?"

Without a flinch of hesitation, the confident young man replied, "Yes, Your Majesty."

"Good," replied the king. "You have been trained by the best, and I know you will do well in my service."

The king had two thrones, the large oak chair that dated back to Apollo and the founding of Westville in the Great Hall, and the smaller blond walnut chair he was seated in.

He preferred this one because he had won it in battle. It was his prize for slaying the Midaloan king during his great victory. Every time he looked at it, he was filled with pride and had a great sense of satisfaction knowing it belonged to his greatest enemy.

Terryn followed the king to the window overlooking the parade grounds. Soldiers were gathering below. They all wore silver-plated armor with the red bear claw of the king emblazoned on their chests.

The Bear Legion was a mounted unit comprised of fifty elite fighters. Each member had to earn his red claw in battle. Once he had proven himself worthy, he was awarded the title of Bear Warrior.

The unit was named after the king. It was said that in battle he was as powerful as a bear. He was known for charging fearlessly into a fight and overpowering his opponents with his huge broadsword. The sight of it was like watching a massive brown bear overwhelming his prey.

Another story told throughout the ranks was that around the time the king had come into manhood he had had a confrontation with a black bear. The bear was feasting on a deer it had killed when the king stumbled upon it. A brawl ensued, leaving the bear dead and the king the victor, but the bear had marked the king with a bloody paw print on his chest. This forever became the symbol of the Bear Warrior.

Terryn had been a leader in the army for years, but he was still impressed by the awe-inspiring sight of the soldiers in their freshly buffed metal plate with swords at their hip, seated atop the finest battle horses in the realm.

He watched as Roland, the officer in charge and now his second in command, assembled the men into formation. Roland was a short stalky man with more years' service in the king's army than Terryn had been alive. As was his custom, he did not wear a helmet, preferring to let his thick gray hair blow freely in the wind.

The king told his new army commander the story of what happened to his uncle. He gave him all of the information he had gathered from the crime scene in the hopes that it would aid in his investigation.

Terryn already knew where they were headed from the conversations he'd had with Lynessa. She had told him about Henry, Kelvin, and Triopolis. Now that Henry was dead, Kelvin would surely try to return home.

He didn't tell the king this choice bit of intelligence, however. It was too dangerous to divulge information that would incriminate himself. Knowing this brought up too many other questions about Terryn and Lynessa's inappropriate relationship and deceptive activities.

"I want you to take the Bear Legion and hunt down those murderers," the king demanded sternly.

Terryn could see the anger in the king's eyes.

"Yes, Your Majesty," replied Terryn, brimming with confidence. "I won't let you down, sir!"

"I know you won't," answered the king.

The new captain saluted the king in the military custom by holding his right arm up, bent at the elbow in the shape of an L with his palm facing out. The king nodded his approval and Terryn turned to leave.

When Kelvin had filleted two large trout, he cooked them on the fire he had prepared. Not having proper cooking tools, he held the meat over the fire with the pronged stick he had used to catch the fish.

Turning the trout occasionally ensured even cooking. He only wished he had some salt for seasoning.

"That smells good!" said Elizabeth, as she and Lynessa appeared from around a tree.

"It's about the best I can do," he replied.

"It smells just as good as I have had from the palace kitchens," complimented Elizabeth, putting a smile on his face.

"Did you find anything?" he asked.

The ladies had been looking for berries or any other fruit to supplement the fish.

"We did!" exclaimed Elizabeth. "We have strawberries and blackberries, and we even found an apple tree. We picked some extra apples to take with us too."

"Good thinking," replied Kelvin.

He removed the four-pronged stick from the fire. Each prong held a perfectly cooked fillet of trout. Moving a few feet away from the fire, he pushed the end of the stick into the ground and left them to cool.

Elizabeth handed him an apple that he immediately bit into. The bittersweet juices from the fruit hit his tongue sending his taste buds into a frenzy.

Summer apples were his favorite. They were smaller than the apples that ripened in the fall and had a sweet-tart taste that he loved. Greedily, he tore through it as if he hadn't eaten in weeks.

"This is the best apple I have ever eaten!" he exclaimed between bites.

"We both ate one the moment we picked them off the tree!" replied Elizabeth.

All three were now sitting around the fire eating the fish and fruit that was their first meal since leaving Westville. "Does any of this terrain look familiar?" asked Elizabeth.

"No, but we are heading up into the mountains," answered Kelvin. "Based on what I remember of the landscape I saw from the ocean, I believe Triopolis is just over them."

Kelvin knew this was a guess based on information that may or may not be correct, but he didn't want them to know that he was just as lost as they were. For now, he felt it was best if they thought he knew how to get home.

"Well, it seems logical," said Elizabeth. "What is Triopolis like?"

This was the first time since they'd left the castle that she'd had time to consider their destination.

"That's a good question," replied Lynessa. "How do we know we will like it there?"

"I can understand your hesitation, but trust me, you will love it," replied Kelvin. "Triopolis is a peaceful place with very friendly people. The people of Triopolis would rather have fun and enjoy life than fight. We don't even have an army."

"I would hate to think what would happen if the king were to hear about your city," replied Elizabeth. "It would become another jewel in his crown."

"Well, we will just have to trust that Donovan will keep our secret," said Kelvin.

Lynessa jumped up from the fallen log they were sitting on. She had just realized it had been a while since she'd left her last marker.

"If you will excuse me, nature calls," she announced. *I wonder if Terryn's found my trail. He would remember the story. Did I remember it accurately? Am I placing the signs correctly?*

"Yes," Lynessa said under her breath, reassuring herself, tearing another piece of cloth from her shirt. "This is how the story went. My love will rescue me."

The traitor had just finished tying the piece of her undershirt to the tree branch just below eye level when she felt a searing pain shoot through her back. Fighting through the pain, she was able to turn her head just enough to see her attacker.

A large burly man dressed in animal skins stood behind her holding a bow. Just enough life remained in her to see the arrowhead that protruded from her chest. It entered through her back and sliced completely through her body.

A moment later she took her last breath as her limp body fell to the ground. The commotion alerted Kelvin and Elizabeth to the intruders.

They both jumped off the log and looked toward the noise. Before either could say a word, three ferocious-looking men came out of the bushes and encircled them. Two had swords at the ready while the third carried his bow with an arrow strung and drawn.

Panic consumed Elizabeth, while Kelvin's attention focused on one of the men in particular who looked very familiar. Studying the older man's face, Kelvin couldn't believe his eyes. It was Borin.

The other two men turned their attention to the sound of a fourth man in the distance walking toward them, while Borin and Kelvin looked at each other. Noticing that Kelvin recognized him, Borin slightly shook his head to tell him not to say anything.

Kelvin understood the message.

"Why did you kill her?" screamed Elizabeth, seeing the fourth wild man dragging Lynessa's corpse into view.

The large man stared at Elizabeth with contempt and did not answer.

"Algar, was killing her necessary?" asked Borin.

Borin commanded a certain amount of respect from the three younger men because of his age, but he was not their leader.

"She was a traitor," replied Algar. "She was the one leaving markers."

Borin looked at Kelvin and Elizabeth to explain what Lynessa was doing to mark their trail.

"She would never do that to me," exclaimed Elizabeth. "She was a loyal servant."

"Would one so loyal leave these?" asked Algar, producing three pieces of cloth. "Look," he continued, lifting up Lynessa's outer shirt with his blade to show the torn undershirt.

"Oh, my god!" exclaimed Elizabeth, realizing they were right.

"She had been acting strange," added Kelvin.

Elizabeth's feelings swung from sadness at losing her friend to anger that she had been betrayed by someone she had trusted.

"There is a large army from Westville only a couple of hours' march behind you," said Borin. "They are using these markers to track you. This is how we found you. We saw the army following the trail so we went ahead to see who was leaving the signals, and we came upon you."

"I saw her tying this piece of cloth to a tree when I killed her," grunted Algar, holding up the torn fabric.

"Treachery is not something we take lightly," said Borin. "Our people see it as the worst thing a person can do, and the only acceptable punishment is death. This particular situation is worse because we have a settlement near here, and she was leading the army toward it. This means she was also committing the offense toward us.

"You see, Algar had proof of her actions, so as is our custom when in the wild, he delivered the punishment."

The other three men stood quietly as Borin explained this to their captives because he was the only one with experience dealing with outsiders.

Elizabeth considered what would have happened if the army had caught them.

"So, the king has sent an army after us," commented Kelvin.

"Yes," replied Borin.

"We should go," said Algar, thinking how quickly those horses could reach them.

Chapter 15

Richard sat in front of the king's desk listening to his father explain why his wife had gone missing.

"I don't understand," said Richard. "Why would Lord Rosser be anywhere near the princess's rooms?"

The king paused before responding. He wanted to choose his words carefully so that he didn't let on that he'd had his son followed.

"I think we should focus on why this man killed Lord Rosser," he said.

Interesting, Richard mused with suspicion. *He chose not to answer my question.*

Richard knew his father to be a deceitful man, and the way he dodged his question made him think the king knew more than he was saying. Staring at him with contempt, he wondered how a father could so easily lie to his son.

They went back and forth answering each other's questions with more questions. Neither was willing to give more information he he they had to.

Richard finally asked, "So, what are you going to do about her disappearance and the murder?"

"I have dispatched Terryn with the Bear Legion to find her and bring her back," replied the king sternly.

A look of horror covered Richard's face. "The Bear Warriors are little better than animals themselves. They are merciless and unfeeling."

"Yes, that is their reputation," commented the king proudly. "Don't worry. No harm will come to your wife."

Knowing his father, these words did not calm Richard. He was more concerned for her life than he had been before this conversation.

Richard went to the archery range, where he met Albert. He was angry and needed to let off some steam. He hoped firing a few arrows at a target would do the trick.

Rarely did he leave a meeting with his father in high spirits, but today he was fuming mad. The king made it clear that he thought Elizabeth knew the unknown man. Dwelling on those thoughts since seeing Lord Rosser's body, he had developed a conspiracy theory that linked the princess to the murder.

Richard knew his father well. Elizabeth would never be allowed to live after what had happened. He was convinced that the king would execute her.

The exhilaration of adrenaline coursing through his body consumed him as he worked the powerful weapon. Three consecutive arrows were loosed before he paused to talk to Albert.

When Richard was upset, Albert knew that it was best to let him start the conversation. Many times he had tried to talk through a situation before Richard was ready, and it had always ended in an argument.

"My father is lying to me," Richard finally said. "He claims he doesn't know why Elizabeth fled the city, but I think he is part of the cause. Why would Lord Rosser be in the hallway at the door to her suite? It just doesn't make sense."

Now that Richard seemed to have moved past his silent anger, Albert felt it was safe to give his opinion. "What if Lord Rosser was following Elizabeth?"

"Could my father have known about Henry and Kelvin?" asked Richard.

"That might be why Lord Rosser was in that corridor," offered Albert.

"Why would Elizabeth bring them to the castle?" questioned Richard.

"She probably thought it was safe since that corridor is for her suite of apartments only," replied Albert. "What she couldn't have known is that she was being followed by Lord Rosser."

"I wonder where they are now," said Richard, with concern in his voice. "I hope they're safe."

Even though he had put her in an impossible position to begin their marriage, they were starting to form a good relationship. Richard admired her strength, and they were building a friendship. He now knew he would do whatever was in his power to save her from his father.

"I bet they will try and find Triopolis," concluded Albert.

"I hope Kelvin knows what he is doing," replied Richard worryingly. "Those mountains are treacherous, and they're filled with barbarians."

"It sounded like Kelvin had experience dealing with them," Albert said, trying to help Richard feel more confident in their survival.

"I hate the king," said Richard. "I have always been treated like he was ashamed of me. When I'm king, I will be much more just than he has been. I will not revert to the use of force to answer every difficult situation. Waging battles and sending out the army are not the answer to everything. I would rather the people love me than fear me."

"I know," replied Albert, putting his hand on the prince's shoulder to console him. "Let's go—best five arrows wins."

<hr />

Terryn knelt down and inspected Lynessa's body. "That's her," he confirmed.

Walking away from it, Terryn asked Roland, "What do we do now?"

Roland was a very experienced second in command to both the current and former Lord Rosser. He was not from a noble family, so he would never be a captain, though he was more than qualified. The best of soldiers, he always followed the rules without exception. These were the qualities any captain wanted in a lieutenant.

"The princess and the man she is with did not kill the servant," stated Roland. "I have seen these arrows before. They belong to the barbarians."

"The body was moved to this spot," added Terryn. "Why would they kill her and then bother to drag the body all the way over here?"

He pointed down the fifty-foot path made by the dragged body.

"I think they moved the body for us to see," speculated Roland. "It is a tactic designed to scare us with the hope that we will turn back."

"I think it was meant to scare, but not us," replied Terryn, looking at the old fire pit.

He picked a bone from the charred ashes. "These are fish bones," he said. "From what I remember my uncle telling me, barbarians would never leave this much evidence that they'd been here."

"You are absolutely right," replied Roland, impressed by his new commander. "They would have buried these ashes. Barbarians also would never take their catch inland from the riverbank. They would cook and eat right on the beach because it is much easier to hide the remains of a fire in the sand. This is most unusual behavior."

"The body doesn't show any signs of decay, which means this happened recently," said Terryn. "That also means we are not far behind them."

"Yes, but which direction did they go?" asked Roland.

Terryn called to the five soldiers who had accompanied them to the site of the dead body. The rest of the army had been held back a couple hundred yards.

When the scouts returned to the captain with news of a dead woman, Terryn didn't want to upset the crime scene with his whole host trampling the ground around the body and the fire pit.

"Look for evidence of which direction they went," commanded Roland.

Terryn was the first to spot the trail. It was not easily found because it started just over a dead log. "They probably jumped over the log as they fled the scene," he said to Roland.

The two leaders followed the trampled grass and bushes with the five soldiers close behind. They knew they were approaching the river when the sound of flowing water grew louder.

"This certainly complicates things," said Roland, as they reached the water's edge. "It will be impossible to track them if they entered the water."

A glimmer of hope filled Terryn when he noticed footprints in the wet sand of the riverbank. Their hope ended thirty feet down the beach as the trail made an abrupt turn into the water.

"It looks like a canoe was beached here," said Terryn.

"They could have gone in any direction once they were in the water," despaired Roland.

"Wait, what is that!" exclaimed Terryn, pointing at something like cloth dangling from an overhanging tree branch.

One of the soldiers rushed over and retrieved it. "Sir, it's some sort of small burlap bag," he answered.

"I know what that is," replied Roland, gravely. I have seen these covering the heads of dead soldiers. These are barbarians all right, and they have our fugitives. They are surely as dead as Lynessa."

Standing in silence for several minutes, Terryn pondered what to do next.

"We have to keep going," he said. "We cannot go back to the king empty handed. He would not forgive us. We will press on to the west," he commanded. "We will either find the princess and the man she is with or we will find the city he came from. Either way we will return to Westville with a prize for the king."

"An excellent plan, My Lord," replied Roland, slightly more optimistic.

After paddling the canoe for what seemed to Kelvin about twenty minutes, Borin guided it onto the beach. They were glad to get out of the cramped, narrow canoe, which was made for four. It had ridden low in the water, and the going had been slow with two additional passengers.

Four thin wooden planks spanning its width served as seats for their captors while Kelvin and Elizabeth were relegated to sitting on the floor. Elizabeth sat cross-legged between Borin and Algar, and Kelvin was sitting the same way between the other two men.

All senses were heightened due to the darkness they had been plunged into. Once they had taken their places in the canoe, canvas sacks were thrown over their heads. Borin had informed them that it was standard for any foreigner coming into their camp to be blindfolded so they would not know how to find it. The explanation was welcome, but it did nothing to offer them any comfort.

"We have a ten-minute walk from here," Borin said, hopping out of the boat onto the beach.

"Where are we going?" asked Kelvin.

"To our camp at Granite Lake."

Elizabeth and Kelvin turned toward each other, but neither could see the other's look of concern because of the sacks that covered their heads.

Borin reached for Elizabeth and helped her out of the boat while Algar grabbed Kelvin's arm with more force than necessary and led him onto the shore.

The mud of the beach quickly gave way to grass as they ventured away from the river. They clumsily followed their captors over the rough terrain, which gradually became steeper.

Kelvin took clues from what he heard around them to determine where they were headed. He figured this would be valuable information when the time came for them to leave. He wasn't quite sure if Borin and his companions were friends or foes, so he wanted to have a plan just in case things went bad.

Based on the force of the rowing and the slowing of the boat between pulls, he figured they had been moving upstream against the current. Even though they had left the beach and had been walking for a short while, they could still hear the flowing water. This told Kelvin that they continued traversing upriver.

The terrain was uneven with occasional stones and tree roots protruding from the ground, which made the going rough, especially because they were hooded.

"Ah!" screamed Elizabeth, grabbing her foot.

A rock with a pointy edge had caught her on the arch of her left foot. It didn't break through the leather sole of her shoe, but it did cause a significant amount of pain and discomfort.

"This would be a lot easier if we could see where we were walking!" she yelled.

"I am sorry, but that is not possible," replied Algar, unsympathetically. "In any case, we are close now."

As they hiked higher up the hill, the sound of the water grew louder and louder. To Kelvin's ears, it sounded like a waterfall.

After another twenty paces, they could feel the spray of water on their bodies, and Kelvin knew he was right.

It wasn't the water that caused them concern, but the sound of unfamiliar voices. As Kelvin listened to Algar explaining the reason for the hooded captives to the men at the gate, he deduced that the voices belonged to guards.

"These two are outsiders," said Algar. "I wish to take them to Meric."

Elizabeth was tense with nervous energy. *Who is Meric, and what does he want with us?*

She was startled when Borin once again grabbed her arm and pulled her forward.

The spray of water got heavier and then stopped completely. It sounded like they had entered a cave. The conversation and number of footsteps led her to believe that they were now following the guards. The echo of the voices only added to the tension in the captives' bodies.

The cool damp cave must not have been very big, because it wasn't long before they again felt the sun's rays on their skin. "It's a tunnel," she deduced.

Kelvin and Elizabeth were surprised when the canvas bags were ripped off their heads without warning. Appearing before them was a beautiful city of whitewashed stone buildings.

"Another city," marveled Kelvin. "How could all of these things exist in the world, and we didn't know a thing about them? I feel like a child first learning how to read."

Hearing this, Borin looked at them and smiled. "Welcome to Granite Lake," he said.

The town was built into the mountain with natural walls of black rock circling it. The mountain itself provided protection. The city was smaller than Triopolis or Westville, but it was every bit as modern.

"Why are you called barbarians?" asked Elizabeth, amazed at the sight.

"That is what you call us," spat Algar.

"Algar is right, we have never called ourselves barbarians," replied Borin, more diplomatically. Kelvin and Elizabeth were both reminded of their ignorance of the world.

"We must take them to Meric," said Algar.

"Who is Meric?" asked Kelvin.

"He is our leader," replied Borin. "He is wise and will decide your fate."

Borin then turned to give them a look of reassurance that everything would be all right. It was the best he could do without giving away to the other three that he knew Kelvin.

The captives were led to the center of town. Most of the buildings looked similar with the exception of only a few. These included the one they seemed to be headed toward. The difference was that it was much taller, having two floors, compared to most buildings, which were only one level.

The town center was graced with a beautifully manicured garden. Many different flowers, shrubs, and trees lined the walkways through and around it. A trickle of water could be heard coming from a gently flowing stream meandering around the many plants. The two-story house lay just beyond the green space.

Algar stepped up to the door and knocked. A servant answered and showed them to the receiving room. The interior of the building showed the importance of the occupant.

Not only was there a plethora of flowers and potted plants throughout the room, but the walls were filled with diagrams of plant life and their medicinal purposes. In the center of the room stood a pedestal with a single leafy branch enclosed in a glass dome.

Upon entering the room, Meric noticed Kelvin and Elizabeth looking at the solitary branch. "The foundation of all our knowledge," he said, approaching.

They looked at each other puzzled. "What?" asked Kelvin.

Meric was a small man with no hair left on his head. He looked as though his prime had passed him, but he still had some energy left.

"The leaf you look upon has restorative powers unseen anywhere else in nature," he explained. "Without it we could not have accomplished all that we have."

"Would you like a drink?" the host asked. Without waiting for a response, he motioned to his servant to bring them glasses. A cup of herbal tea was given to each guest.

"So, what can I do for you?" asked Meric. Algar moved Elizabeth and Kelvin in front of Meric so he could get a good look at them.

"We found these two in the forest," said Algar. "They are from Westville. There was a third, but we executed her because she was leaving a trail for the army to follow."

"We saw the army earlier this morning, and when we saw markers being left by the other woman, we followed them," clarified Borin. "That's when we came upon these two."

Meric looked at his two captives and asked, "Why is there an army coming here?"

"Sir," began Elizabeth, "we don't know why the army is marching this way."

Kelvin understood immediately that Borin and Algar didn't want to let on that the army was searching for him and Elizabeth. They didn't trust that Meric wouldn't use them in a trade.

"We have left Westville to find a city called Tripolis, which lies to the west," explained Elizabeth.

"Borin, you are familiar with Triopolis," said Meric.

"Yes sir," replied Borin. "I have been trading with them for years."

The leader pondered this information before making his decision. He looked at his guests as if there was more to them than it seemed. He sensed something strange about them. He had felt this before, but it had been many years.

"You will stay here as our guests for the time being," judged Meric.

He saw the look of disappointment on their faces.

"I can't let you go now because if the Westville army were to capture and question you, they might find our camp. We can't let that happen. Once the soldiers have passed and we are out of danger, we will let you leave.

"Borin, I would like you to bring our guests to dinner tonight. We can discuss what will be done about the army marching through our forest. Now show our guests to their rooms."

"Yes, sir," replied Borin, leading Kelvin and Elizabeth out of the leader's house.

Algar, content that he had satisfactorily completed his job, left the meeting and headed in the opposite direction of Borin.

"How long will we have to stay here?" asked Kelvin.

"I don't know," replied Borin. "I should be able to get more information tonight at dinner."

Kelvin put his arm around Elizabeth to comfort her. "It will be all right. We'll figure it out."

This gesture put a smile on her face. She felt safe with Kelvin even though she knew anything could still happen.

Walking into the small stone cottage, Elizabeth commented, "Well, it's better than sleeping in the forest!"

This received a smiling agreement from Kelvin.

The inside of the cottage was meager. There was a fireplace on one wall with a rack holding a large pot for cooking. The only furniture was a bed opposite the fireplace and a table large enough for two. The place was lit with candles placed throughout the room.

"I know it's not what you are accustomed to, but this is a standard guest cottage," said Borin. "Kelvin, I will have a pallet brought in for you to sleep on."

"Thanks, that will be fine," replied Kelvin.

Now that they were alone with Borin, Kelvin couldn't hold back any longer. "I thought you were dead!" he exclaimed. "Henry saw your body being dragged out of the pub."

"Oh," replied Borin, understanding what Henry had seen. "You saw my brother, Talan, who was in Triopolis with me. I was meeting him at the pub that night before we left town. He got there first, and when I entered, I saw two men forcing him into the kitchen. I listened from the kitchen door as they murdered him."

Borin had a mixture of sorrow and a thirst for revenge in his voice. "I watched through the door as the two men dragged his lifeless body out the back door."

"Henry was hiding around the corner, and that's when he saw the body he thought was yours," interjected Kelvin.

"I went back through the front door and came around the building to see the two men dragging him into the field behind the pub," Borin continued. "They were still a couple hundred feet away from their two partners who were digging the hole to bury him in.

"Here in Granite Lake, we believe that murder can only be punished by death! I had it all planned out. I could have killed all four of them I was so angry.

"The grass was high and gave me just enough cover to spring my trap. They were shielded from anyone walking past, but they were also hidden from me. I quietly moved through the tall grass toward the trailing man who was carrying Talan by his arms.

"He had no idea he was about to die until it was too late. I reached out for his arm and pulled him to the ground. He was so unaware that I easily knocked him off of his feet, and he fell into the high grass.

"The commotion was heard by the men digging the hole, and they rushed to their friend's aid. They were quicker than I expected, and I could not kill the other man holding my brother. The element of surprise was lost, and I had to get out of there."

Kelvin sensed that Borin was proud that he was able to avenge his brother by killing at least one of the murderers.

"It was the bishop," said Kelvin. "I overheard him talking about killing you because you had been seen by locals and they were starting to ask questions."

"I'm not surprised," replied Borin. "That man is evil."

Kelvin was disappointed in his father, but he couldn't bring himself to tell Borin he was also involved. His compassion, however, did not extend to the bishop.

"I have met the bishop," said Borin, with a grimace on his face. "He is a bad person. I sensed he was involved in things he could never hope to control."

Kelvin thought for a moment before answering. "Do you mean enlightenment?" Borin's head whipped around toward Kelvin.

"What do you know of enlightenment?" he asked.

"I have learned a few things since we last met," replied Kelvin.

"From who?" asked Borin. He was becoming concerned with this surprise turn of events.

"From the high priest in Westville," answered Elizabeth.

Before Borin had a chance to speak, Elizabeth told him some stories about the high priest. She spoke of the tales children used to repeat about the man, but as she told them, some of them seemed plausible now. *Maybe they were true*, she mused.

Her aim in telling these tales was to watch Borin's reaction. She had sensed that he was wise but not on the same level as Donovan. He seemed to have a lesser form of knowledge.

Ever since entering this town, her senses and intuition were overwhelmed. Her mind was overrun with thoughts and insights. She sensed that this was a place of great knowledge and great danger. It was only now that she was beginning to separate and make sense of this energy.

"He said his name is Donovan—one of the founders of Triopolis," added Kelvin.

Silence filled the room. Borin looked as if he had seen a ghost. The horrified look frightened his guests.

"He told you his secret?" he asked in a tone slightly above a whisper. It was as if he didn't want anyone to overhear them even though they were alone in the room.

"He helped you capture Luther," added Kelvin.

Again, Borin was surprised by the information these two possessed. "He told you that too?" Not waiting for a reply, he added, "He must have had his reasons to give you such secret information."

Looking suddenly distracted, Borin said, "Now I must go. I will return to escort you to dinner. Do not say anything about Donovan to anyone here," he warned.

"I can't tell if these people are our friends or not," said Elizabeth, after Borin left.

"I know what you mean," replied Kelvin. "I think Borin wants to help us, but I wouldn't want to cross Algar."

"He sure was scary!" replied Elizabeth, thinking about the very large brawny man that killed Lynessa.

"I still don't understand why she would betray us," said Elizabeth. "I wonder if she was ever my friend." Tears flowed as she considered the impact of such a betrayal.

Kelvin put his arms around her. "From now on, I think we can only trust each other."

Chapter 16

B orin was again at the house of Meric waiting for his leader to appear. He had no choice but to tell Meric all that he had learned. It was his duty as a citizen of Granite Lake. Questioning the leader was acceptable, even welcomed, but deceit was punished with banishment or worse.

He wondered how Meric would react to the news of Donovan hiding in plain sight in Westville.

"Borin, what troubles you?" asked Meric, entering the room. He knew something was on his subordinate's mind; otherwise, he would have waited until dinner to talk.

"I have unpleasant news, sir," said Borin, and he told his leader what he learned about Donovan.

"So, he broke his promise," answered Meric. "I had hoped this day would never come. Take Lucan and Owen to Westville, and bring Donovan to me."

Lucan, Owen, and Borin were the only three remaining hunters of the Enlightened called Chasers. A skill from a bygone age, Meric thought it important to keep a few men trained just in case the need ever arose.

"Many men in my council over the years have told me to let the trade die," preached Meric. "'We have no need of Chasers,' they would say. Well, they are proven wrong today!"

Borin knew Meric was not going to be happy with his news, but he was surprised that his leader immediately decided to send the Chasers after Donovan. It was almost as if he had been waiting for Donovan to make a mistake.

"Sir, maybe we should question him first before taking him into custody," offered Borin.

"No, remember the first lesson in your training, my friend," Meric instructed. "To be successful you must catch them off guard."

"I just don't understand, sir," said Borin. "After all these years, why would he tell his secret now, and why tell Kelvin and Elizabeth?"

"Because she has the ability to be enlightened," said Meric. "I sensed it the moment she arrived, and Donovan would certainly have known. The only question is has she been trained?"

"What will you do with them?" asked Borin.

"They will never leave Granite Lake," was Meric's definitive response.

What have I done? wondered Borin. He genuinely liked Kelvin, as much as he knew of him, and he counted Donovan as a friend. Taking this action would doom them both.

"Sir, can't we have her tested?" asked Borin. "If she has not been trained, can't they both be set free?"

"No, Borin. It's too dangerous to leave any loose ends. Even if she is not trained, if she has begun down the path, she will be able to learn more on her own. Now, gather the men and head out as soon as possible," commanded Meric. "This job needs to be done quickly and quietly. I will have Algar bring the captives to dinner tonight."

When Kelvin opened the door, he was startled to see Algar standing there and not Borin. "I am to take you to dinner," he said gruffly.

Kelvin turned back to Elizabeth with a look of concern, and they followed without a word.

Algar led them the short distance through the alley connecting their cottage to the main dining hall. They were happy the walk was short because rain had begun to fall. It wasn't a hard rain, but it was just enough to make the stones under their feet slippery.

The inside of the hall was not at all lavish. Bare wooden tables and chairs lined the hall, and several freestanding candles were placed throughout the room for light. On the walls hung modest tapestries, and the serving plates had no decoration.

"Sit here," directed Algar, pointing to two chairs just to the left of Meric.

As soon as they sat, the servers began their parade in front of the head table. Each server had a single item. The first carried a jug of red wine that he used to fill each glass.

Elizabeth couldn't tell if the food looked so delicious because it actually was or because it had been so long since she had eaten a good meal. They both took a little from each serving plate held out for them. Their plates overflowed with goat, venison, potatoes, and many different kinds of vegetables.

It was difficult for them to eat with dignity after the long journey. The pains in their stomachs were telling them to devour the entire plate, but they did their best to be polite and courteous.

Finally, Meric acknowledged them. Leaning over he asked, "How is the food?"

"Very good," they both replied, filling their mouths so quickly there wasn't room for more words.

Meric laughed, and then he described how the people of Granite Lake had taken certain things from each culture they had encountered.

"I thought this apple pastry looked familiar," commented Kelvin.

"That is correct," replied Meric. "Borin brought that back from Triopolis. The wine is from grapes grown on vines taken from the region just north of Westville, so this should taste familiar to you, Elizabeth," he added.

"Yes, it does taste similar to our wine," she answered.

"What is this black stuff on the meat?" asked Kelvin.

"Ah, that is called pepper," replied Meric. "It grows on a plant. We get it from some traders to the northwest of here."

"It gives the meat a whole different flavor," commented Elizabeth.

As Meric turned away to speak to the man on his other side, Kelvin whispered to Elizabeth, "Where is Borin?"

"It's strange that he brought us here and that he isn't coming to dinner," she replied. "He told us when he left that he would be taking us. What could have happened between then and now?"

"You are concerned about your friend," said Meric, startling them. He had overheard their conversation when they thought he was engaged in another.

"Yes," replied Kelvin. "He said he would be back to take us to dinner."

"I know that you are friendly with him," Meric said. "He told me about your meeting in Triopolis. Borin is fine. I had to send him on an errand that will take him away from Granite Lake for a short time."

Relieved, they finished eating their meal.

By this time, they were each on their fourth glass of wine. The music that filled the hall was intoxicating as well.

More and more people were filtering onto the dance floor that had been cleared in the center of the room. With the never-ending flow of wine making them more relaxed, people were drawn out of their chairs and onto the floor.

"Shall we?" suggested Elizabeth, offering her hand.

"What, you mean dance?" Kelvin asked, hesitantly.

"Yes, dance," she clarified. "Now come on!" Grabbing his hand, she pulled and he reluctantly agreed.

"But I can't dance," he argued.

"It's easy. I'll teach you," answered Elizabeth, not accepting his reluctance.

Elizabeth began by dancing in a circle around him. He watched as she circled, trying to remember every move she made. He focused on what her feet were doing, but then he couldn't remember what she did with her arms. Then, while he watched her arms, he forgot how she moved her feet.

As he was trying to figure it out, she swung around and grabbed his arm locking it in hers. He was so surprised that he almost fell as she dragged him into her circle.

With their arms locked, they were close but not quite touching anywhere else. Kelvin's clumsiness caused their bodies to occasionally rub together as they danced. Each brush against him made Elizabeth shudder in ecstasy.

She didn't want to let go of him as they danced around and around. So happy together, they didn't notice when the other people on the dance floor unlocked arms. Finally realizing this, Kelvin stopped and released her.

She continued dancing around Kelvin who stood in one position like the other men on the floor. They then switched and he danced around her. He no longer cared that he was a bad dancer. He just wanted to be near Elizabeth.

They were both excited when it was time to dance together again. This time Elizabeth did not lock her arm in his. She instead put her hand on his waist across his stomach. He did the same and it drew them even closer than before.

Their bodies were now continuously touching as they stared into each other's eyes. Everything they had been through disappeared from their minds as they were lost in each other. Side by side, they held each other dancing. Everything seemed to be moving in slow motion as the music played in the background.

Both had smiles on their faces, enjoying the moment. All Elizabeth wanted to do was stretch out her neck and touch his lips. Kelvin wanted the same, but he couldn't quite bring himself to make the move.

They continued to dance, holding each other close. Elizabeth's lips yearned for contact and her eyes begged, but Kelvin did not satisfy them.

The dance continued, and Kelvin was becoming upset with himself for not giving her what they both wanted. He acted the scene in his mind. *Why am I being so timid?*

Then his time had run out. The music stopped and was finished for the evening. Disappointment filled both of them, but neither showed signs of it. Kelvin was furious with himself for getting cold feet.

There wasn't much conversation on the way back to their cottage. Both wanted more, but it was too late.

The next morning they set out to find the library. At dinner the night before, they had overheard talk of the knowledge held in the library and thought it might hold answers to some of their questions.

The sun was shining today with only a few thin clouds in the sky. Without a map, they had no idea where they were going. They searched and searched as the sun slowly ascended higher in the sky.

Noticing that it was almost noon, they turned a corner and there it was.

"Of course it's in the last section we looked," said Kelvin, exasperated.

"Yeah, I thought it would have been a lot easier to find," replied Elizabeth.

Like most of the other buildings, the library was made of stone. There were no decorations or sculptures in front of it. The word *Library* was carved into the stone above the door. Like everything else in Granite Lake, the structure was simple and ordinary looking. They entered through the wooden door at the front.

"This isn't what I had imagined at all," Elizabeth said.

"It looks more like a museum than a library," replied Kelvin.

"You would be correct if you said that," said a quirky little man standing by the door. "Forgive me for being rude. I am Aaron, and I am the curator of the library."

They were overwhelmed with the energy and the speed with which the little old man spoke. He looked frail, but he was anything but.

Kelvin introduced them. "This is Elizabeth, and I am Kelvin."

"Welcome," replied Aaron. "Before we get started with the tour, I would like to tell you a little about myself. I have been a curator here for nearly forty years although not all forty as head curator."

Elizabeth and Kelvin glanced at each other as if to say, *We have to go on a tour of the library?* They had assumed they would merely enter the building and browse the stacks on their own.

"I became head curator after Bernie died when his house burned twenty years ago. Although, he probably would have died from that skin rash he picked up a year earlier!" Aaron laughed at his attempt at humor, but his guests didn't.

"He sure is odd," Elizabeth whispered to Kelvin, as they fell a little behind.

"I don't think he gets to talk to people very often," replied Kelvin, and they both giggled.

"Come on, come on," called Aaron. "We have a lot to see!"

"We begin in the Dark Days," he said. They were standing in front of a black wall. This time they understood his joke and laughed with him.

"Okay, so the Dark Days weren't that dark!" he exclaimed with a laugh.

To the right of the black wall there were many artifacts from that bleak period. Farming tools, weapons, machinery, and household items filled the exhibit. Not wanting to be rude, they followed Aaron as he spoke about each item.

Item after item, Aaron gave monologues that seemed to last forever. He droned on and on about a simple shovel or a cooking pot.

"This particular fork is fascinating," said Aaron, looking at a pronged utensil in a glass case. The fork occupied a case with a number of other types of kitchen utensils. "Notice the three prongs as opposed to the two prongs of the others," he pointed out, excitedly. "A brilliant creation, this one.

"It was discovered that a three-pronged fork was much better for stabbing meats or vegetables than a two-pronged one. Norbert the Bald, I believe, invented this little gem in the year three hundred thirty-two. It's also made of a thicker metal to better endure the force of the stab." He laughed again, but Kelvin and Elizabeth had long since lost interest in the fork.

Getting antsy and bored with the tour, Kelvin finally blurted out, "Who was Luther?"

Aaron stopped dead in his tracks and gave Kelvin a piercing look. The joking, high-strung little man vanished, and his face became grave and much more serious.

After a pause he said, "I guess you aren't here for the regular tour. Luther—that's a name I haven't heard spoken in many years. How do you know of him?"

"I am from Triopolis, and I recently came across his name in a text," replied Kelvin.

"Hmm," pondered Aaron. "I think we should go somewhere more private to discuss this matter. It would not be pleasant if the wrong person overheard our conversation."

He led them into a room at the back of the library. It looked like a scholar's workspace with clutter everywhere. Stacks of books, restored artifacts, items that needed restoration, and papers lined the floor and covered the desk and were even piled on the chairs. They had no choice but to stand.

"So you want to know about Luther?" he asked. "He is one of the worst men this world has ever known. He was manipulative and cruel, and had an unquenchable thirst for power. I have not heard his name spoken in quite a long time. Most shameful for our people is that he was one of us. That is why we must talk in private. If the wrong person were to hear us speaking of Luther, it would be very unpleasant for me.

"His life began as an alchemist, but not like any other. He studied medicine along with alchemy to devastating effect. His powers of foresight were strong, and he could control an adult with a whisper when he was just a boy.

"Our elders argued over whether or not the boy's abilities should be cultivated. Some said his personality was not the right fit to become one of the Enlightened. He had a concerning trait that exposed itself when working with other students. He always wanted to control the other kids.

"Others thought that with the right guidance and teaching, he would learn how to harness his demons. These leaders of ours were not aware that Luther was already beginning to control them. He had entered their minds and convinced them that he must be trained.

"It was almost as if he was being influenced by a much more negative force. His words, his mannerisms and some of his abilities almost reminded me of the most evil enlightened the world has ever known, Arnaud the Black.

"Is Arnaud the Black still alive?" asked a worried Elizabeth.

"No, no, he died many years ago," replied Aaron. "Long before Luther's time, so it would have been impossible for Arnaud the Black to train him. It just felt similar."

"You speak as if you experienced it yourself," said Elizabeth.

Aaron looked her in the eye and said, "I did experience the horror he brought to the world."

"How?" asked Kelvin. "That had to have been hundreds of years ago."

"Seven hundred fifty-nine to be exact," he replied. "I have the gift of long life."

"So, you are enlightened then?" asked Kelvin.

"Me? No, I am not enlightened."

Seeing the confused look on their faces, he explained. "I have the ability to be enlightened, but was never taught."

"Why aren't people taken down the path of enlightenment anymore?" asked Elizabeth.

"It is illegal," he answered. "It has been a law for more than five hundred years. After Luther, Meric's father, Jorin, decided it was best to no longer teach enlightenment as a precaution against anyone who might go down the same path."

"It almost seems like he wanted to stop intellectual growth," Kelvin commented.

"In a way he did," responded Aaron. "Many people, including myself, didn't agree with this approach, but as our leader, we eventually yielded to his judgment.

"He ordered that there was no way to prevent another from going down the path that Luther had taken, so the Enlightened had to be eliminated. A few of us realized that paranoia had overtaken him, and we questioned his sanity.

"Meric was one of us who tried and failed to convince his father to see reason. In the end, he was not saddened when Luther took his father's life."

"Wait a minute!" interrupted Kelvin. "You are Aaron!"

"Yes," he replied, a little confused.

"What is it?" asked Elizabeth, not following Kelvin's line of reasoning.

"Donovan told us to seek out Aaron," he explained.

"Donovan!" replied Aaron, surprised. "You know Donovan? He is a good friend of mine. How do you know him?"

"I know him from Westville," Elizabeth responded.

"Yes, I have heard where you are from," said Aaron impatiently. "And I know you are from Triopolis, Kelvin."

"Yes . . ." Kelvin said, not sure where Aaron was headed with this.

"If this is true, Meric no doubt sensed it," said Aaron.

What he didn't tell them was that if Meric *did* know that Elizabeth had begun her training, not only were they both in danger, but Donovan was as well.

"What happened with Luther?" asked Kelvin. How did he end up in Triopolis?"

"So many questions, my young friend," said Aaron, stalling to collect his thoughts. "The path to enlightenment includes learning in many different areas. They were taught how the human body worked and how to use nature to cure disease and mend wounds. Alchemy, along with the study of how various elements and forces interact with each other and can be harnessed, was also an integral part of the learning.

"The children were thoroughly screened before their instruction began to verify that they would use these powers for good. The purpose of this knowledge was to help people live better and longer lives, but Luther fooled everyone. He wasn't interested in helping people. He only wanted to control them.

"The story goes that one day during instruction, he used his mind to overpower his tutor, causing the man to collapse unconscious to the floor, where he lay for nearly an hour. Well, when the elders heard of this, they began to worry.

"Numerous incidents like this over the next few months increased their concern. He not only manipulated his educators, but he also began to control a large group of students. He was taking over the school.

"Never before had an apprentice been unable to be directed and taught. The elders were unanimous. Luther had to leave never to return."

"How could they expel a man so powerful?" asked Kelvin.

"There were many powerful Enlightened here," answered Aaron. "He knew he couldn't fight them all. His only choice was to leave. Luckily for us, we were able to expel him from our land before he became too powerful."

"Where did he go after he was expelled?" asked Kelvin.

"He found his way to Triopolis," replied Aaron, looking into Kelvin's eyes. "But I think you already knew that."

Kelvin remained quiet, thinking it best to let Aaron keep talking.

"Luther was one of your founders, although his motives were somewhat different from the others. Nelson, Donovan, and Rowen didn't have anyone experienced in medicine. That was the one thing they needed to hold their people together. He used a network of spies to learn this information, and then he used it to his advantage."

"He had spies?" asked Elizabeth.

"Birds, no doubt," answered Aaron. "They are the most effective at gathering information. People don't pay any attention to a bird perched nearby."

"Luther can talk to birds?" Kelvin asked skeptically.

"The Enlightened can speak to any animal they choose, if they only learn the language," he answered.

Looking at Elizabeth, he could see that she too questioned Aaron's sanity.

"One day the four were walking on the beach where your docks are today. They heard the screams of a boy in the forest. Reaching him, it looked like he had been attacked by some sort of large animal. His arm and leg on the right side of his body were badly maimed.

"Luther immediately knelt down and administered medicines he mysteriously had in his pocket. Nelson, Donovan, and Rowen were so impressed with Luther's compassion and ability to ensure the boy would survive that they immediately invited him to be an equal.

"What the other three men didn't know was that Luther had taken control of a giant wolf and commanded it to attack the boy just before they met on the beach. He set it up perfectly so they wouldn't hear the boy scream until they walked down the beach."

"That's horrible!" exclaimed Elizabeth in disgust.

"I could tell you many more loathsome stories about Luther," replied Aaron. "He is an evil person."

In the silence that followed, they heard a knock on the door.

"I thought I might find you two here," said Borin. "Thank you for speaking to my friends, Aaron."

"It's been a pleasure," he replied, noticing more guests in the library. "Oh dear, more inquiring minds I must attend to."

"Borin, what happened to you at dinner last night?" asked Kelvin, as the three of them left the library.

"My leader gave me a task," he answered, solemnly. "A task I am not sure is the right thing to do. Come, I will have dinner with you tonight."

"This is the hall I eat in most nights," Borin pointed out as they entered the cafeteria-style food line.

"I am not sure I can eat yet after the banquet last night," exclaimed Elizabeth.

"Oh, I think I can find room," replied Kelvin. "One thing I have learned since leaving Westville is you never know when the next meal will be, so eat while there's food!"

"Try the pork," yelled a woman familiar to Borin, who worked behind the buffet. "It was just brought in this morning."

"Oh, what a treat!" he replied excitedly.

Kelvin and Elizabeth followed and each took a healthy portion of the fresh meat. Wild rice and steamed corn completed the meal on their plates.

"I don't know why, but I always sit at the same table," commented Borin as they took their seats.

"I do the same thing at the ale house back home," said Kelvin, with a laugh.

"So, what did Aaron show you at the library?" asked Borin.

"That guy sure knows his history," said Kelvin.

"Well, he is our leading scholar on the topic," answered Borin. "In fact, Meric even goes to him when he suspects someone is practicing the art."

"So it really is illegal . . ." said Elizabeth.

"Oh, yes," replied Borin sternly. "If found guilty, you will be locked up for life, and if you have learned too much, you can be executed."

"That seems rather harsh," commented Kelvin.

"It really isn't," Borin replied, "when you think of the havoc a person so powerful can bring upon a people. Luther's foul deeds forced our elders to reconsider the training that occurred here. Their conclusion was that they could not take the chance of another pupil going astray.

"Not only did the training end, but people called Chasers were sent to hunt down all the Enlightened that roamed the world at the time. Aaron was one of these Chasers."

"That explains his vast knowledge," said Kelvin.

"The oldest living of the Chasers, he may not look it, but he is tough as iron," added Borin.

Changing the subject, Elizabeth asked, "What is the connection your town has with waterfalls? I saw them referenced many times in the library."

Borin looked surprised. "Very impressive, Elizabeth. Most people don't recognize the connection, but that knowledge makes you even more dangerous." Noticing her fearful expression, he lowered his voice and said, "Don't worry, I want to help you. Let me answer your question. The entrance to Granite Lake is hidden behind a waterfall. Your secret is safe with me, but do not speak of this to anyone else. It would not be good if the wrong person knew you had this information."

"Thank you for the warning," replied Elizabeth, wishing she hadn't said anything.

As Borin went to get another plate of food, Kelvin pulled out the map that he and Henry found in the maze under the schoolhouse in Triopolis. Elizabeth knew of the map, but this was the first time she had actually seen it.

"Do you know where it leads?" she asked.

"The inscription just said it leads to the truth," replied Kelvin. I am hoping it will be what I need to bring down the bishop. I will do whatever it takes to destroy that man."

"Look," said Kelvin, pointing to a picture of a waterfall on his map, and he leaned closer to Elizabeth.

"This map begins near a waterfall. Since this is where Luther is from, I bet this waterfall and the one Borin spoke of are the same!" The excitement built in both of them. This was their first glimmer of hope in days.

Borin returned with another full plate of food. "I have to fill up because I am being sent back out tomorrow morning," he justified.

"Where are you going?" asked Kelvin.

"I have been sent to arrest Donovan," he replied. "This is the task I do not agree with. I will not arrest him. I only want to talk to him."

"What will happen to us?" asked Kelvin frantically.

Before Borin could answer, Elizabeth said, "Meric will not let us leave. That is what Borin has not yet told us."

"So, it is true then," replied Borin. "You do have the Blood of Alemon in you."

"The Blood of Alemon?" she asked.

"Yes, only people who have the Blood of Alemon in their veins have the ability to be enlightened. You knew what I was thinking before I said a word. You read my mind, didn't you?"

"Things just appear in my mind," answered Elizabeth. "I don't know how it happens, and I can't control when it happens."

"It is the gift," said Borin. "Alemon lived more than a thousand years ago, and he was the first to understand the power of the mind. Every one of his descendants has had his ability, and when taught to harness their power, they have become the Enlightened."

"So, Aaron has the Blood of Alemon and will not die of old age, but he was not taught to be enlightened," she deduced.

"Yes," confirmed Borin. "Your ability comes from your mother."

"How could you know that?" she asked, shocked.

"You forget that I was the one who saved you in the Midalo Forest," he answered. "I know who your mother was. At Meric's request, I was following her so I could bring her back here. Unfortunately, the wild men found you first.

"I did all I could to save her, but I was too late. You were the only one still alive when we arrived. We were able to overpower them and save you.

"I made sure you ended up in Westville, and Donovan did the rest," he continued. "We didn't think you would be safe back here without your mother, so Donovan made sure you ended up in a good home."

"I am grateful for everything you have done," she replied. With all the new information she had learned about herself, and all the changes in her life, she was almost becoming numb to shock. The more she heard the more she expected the puzzle of her life to unfold.

"It's sad, then," she continued. "All the work you and Donovan did to keep me out of here and this is where I ended up anyway."

"Elizabeth is correct," replied Borin. "Meric intends to keep you imprisoned here, but I will not let that happen. Go back to the cottage and gather your things. I will come get you after the sun has set. This endeavor would be impossible in the daylight, but it might be successful in the darkness of the night."

Chapter 17

The door flew open and Borin entered hastily. "This bag is full of dried meat," he announced, setting it on the table. "Fill your pockets with as much as they will hold. This will be enough protein to sustain you for a while."

Complying, they stuffed their pockets. They each attached a water skin to their belt. Kelvin made sure he had the flint and steel he had taken from the mantel in the Great Hall in Westville.

"My dagger was taken when we were captured," said Kelvin.

"Here take mine," replied Borin, handing it to Kelvin. "Let's go, we haven't much time."

Walking through the streets, heading in the opposite direction of the front gate, Borin said, "We can't go through the gate. There are too many guards."

"What other way is there?" asked Kelvin. "The camp seems to be encircled by these cliffs."

"We will climb out," answered Borin. "This place was chosen for our home because of the cliffs. The only way in or out is through the waterfall, which is heavily guarded. The cliffs and the waterfall are the reason no one has ever found us. That was the lesson learned from the Battle of Loran."

Kelvin looked at Elizabeth nervously. He reached out and held her hand to reassure her that everything would be all right. This little bit of comfort was just as much for his sake as it was for hers.

They made a quick turn to the left and headed for the sheer, black wall. Reaching it, Borin said, "This is the most eroded section of the cliff, so it shouldn't be as difficult to climb."

Kelvin's eyes followed the strange black granite higher and higher until he finally saw the top. "What have I gotten myself into?" he asked himself.

"Before we start, I want you to know that there is much danger in what we are about to do," warned Borin. "Not only is there a risk in falling to your death, there is also a risk we will be caught. If that happens, we will all be executed."

Elizabeth looked at Kelvin. "This may be our only chance of getting out of here. I am worried about what would happen to us if Borin were no longer here to protect us."

"I am worried about that too," replied Kelvin. "As much as I don't want to climb this wall, I don't think we have any choice."

"How are you going to get back into the camp without being noticed?" Kelvin asked Borin.

"I will just say I was out hunting. I chose this time of day not only for the cover of darkness it provides, but because I often hunt during the afternoon and return after dark. The guards won't question me."

"That's brilliant," replied Kelvin.

Borin heaved a long, thick, coiled rope onto his shoulder. "There is no time to waste." He put his right foot on a small ledge about two feet above the ground and began his ascent.

The rock face was sheer, but it did have many cracks, crevices, and small ledges from the weathering it had endured over time. This made it possible to climb, though it was no easy task. Borin looked like an experienced climber as he moved up the rock face with relative ease. The two first-timers labored with every step.

Kelvin and Elizabeth followed as Borin moved higher up the cliff. Their muscles ached with every movement. Many times their full weight was supported only by their toes or a small portion of the foot, based on how large the crack or ledge was.

They had to pull their body up using only the strength in their fingers, and all this while battling the fear of falling. One misstep or loss of concentration and death would follow.

Kelvin trailed with Elizabeth just above him. He wanted her to feel as comfortable as possible with him below to protect her. In reality, he knew that if she fell, he would not be able to catch her, and they would both plummet to the ground.

"We are about halfway," Borin said in a quiet voice. He stayed close in case either of them had a problem.

Kelvin turned and looked down. "Oh, I shouldn't have done that," he said feeling nauseated.

"I need to rest," said Elizabeth, her legs feeling like jelly.

"We can rest on that ledge," Borin said, pointing to their left.

"This looks like a cave," Elizabeth commented, pulling herself up onto the ledge.

The hole was only large enough for the three of them to stand at the entrance, but it opened wider as it snaked deeper into the side of the mountain.

The ledge was just wide enough for the three climbers to rest their weary muscles. They each took a long drink of water to quench their thirst.

"Every muscle in my body aches," complained Kelvin.

"Mine too, but we can't stop now," replied Elizabeth, trying to motivate them both.

"Trust me, we don't want to stop now," commented Borin. "I have seen what lives deep in this cave, and she will not like us being here."

Kelvin and Elizabeth exchanged looks of dread.

"That's enough rest, let's go," said Borin, noticeably worried. They knew they had overstayed their welcome when the high-pitched screech of the creature that called this place home echoed through the walls of the cave. "We have to go," yelled Borin.

Within seconds, he was off the ledge and back on the sheer rock face. "Quickly!" he yelled. Elizabeth was next and Kelvin about to follow.

Kelvin felt a rush of air hit him, nearly knocking him off the mountain. He caught himself just in time as he swayed on the edge of the cliff.

Elizabeth and Borin turned back to see an absolute monster of a bird exiting the cave. It must have had a fifteen-foot wingspan and looked like it could easily eat one of them for a midnight snack. In awe, they watched the magnificent yet terrifying bird fly out over the camp.

"I have never seen a bird that big," exclaimed Kelvin.

"Haast has lived in that hole for many years," explained Borin. "She is usually out hunting by now; otherwise, I never would have taken us there."

Haast was an eagle but much larger than the eagles they were used to. She had all brown feathers, a beak that looked like a meat hook, and large sharp talons for gripping her prey.

"She is what mothers in Granite Lake use to scare their children into getting home before dark," he continued. "If you aren't home before the darkness comes, Haast will snatch you up and eat you, they say."

With this image occupying their minds, they forgot about their aching bodies and scurried up the rock wall faster than they thought possible. It was another hundred feet before they reached the top.

"We are almost there," said Kelvin, relieved.

Their legs were on fire, their muscles felt as if they were engulfed in flames, and they could no longer feel their fingers and toes.

"Ah!" screamed Kelvin, as an arrow narrowly missed his hand and crashed into the rock.

"He is shooting at us," yelled Elizabeth, looking at a man with a bow and arrow on the ground.

Borin watched the man fire another arrow into the sky, but this time it broke apart when it hit the rock face a long way from where they were.

"No, look," said Borin, pointing at the bird still flying overhead. "He is shooting at Haast. I don't think he can see us in the dark. I am going to climb down and make sure of it."

"Are you going to kill him?" asked Elizabeth.

"Not if I don't have to," replied Borin. "You don't have time to wait. You must go on without me."

As he was explaining this to them, he tied the rope he was carrying over his shoulder to a pointy piece of rock jutting out from the wall. "When you reach the top, listen for the sound of rushing water, and stay away from the waterfall. There will be many guards around the gate."

As they watched Borin rappel down the rock, Elizabeth said, "I am scared."

"I would be lying if I didn't agree with you," replied Kelvin. "We will be okay. I have spent enough time in the forest to be comfortable navigating it."

Feeling resolved to conquer this challenge, Elizabeth suggested, "Let's get to the top before we are seen."

Kelvin snuck a glance down to see if Borin had made it to the bottom yet. He had, but the man with the bow was already walking away, or stumbling rather. He looked as though he was drunk as he labored downhill.

Elizabeth pulled herself up and over the last ledge, making it to the top of the mountain, where she rolled onto her back and let out a huge sigh of relief. Not more than a minute later, Kelvin joined her. "Whew, I don't think I have done anything that difficult in my life!" she exclaimed.

Lying on their backs, they both stared at the stars above. Neither said a word for the next few minutes until Elizabeth's hand caught Kelvin's and held it firmly. They enjoyed this moment together allowing their thoughts to remain on each other instead of the perils that lay ahead.

Sitting up and with a full view, they saw the impregnable nature of the town. It lay at the bottom of a gorge that looked like it was carved out of the mountain just for the purpose of hiding the town. It was circular and had black sheer rock walls all the way around.

"It looks like a prison," observed Elizabeth.

"I can see why no one has ever found it," he replied. "It's a fortress!"

One could walk continuously around the camp on top of the rock walls. They were on a large plateau. On the other side of the gorge, the mountains continued to rise into the sky. The river that ran over the falls could be heard in the distance.

"That must be where the guards are stationed," observed Kelvin, pointing to the opposite end.

"We have to get out of here before the sun comes up," said Elizabeth.

"Let's go this way," suggested Kelvin, and they got to their feet.

There was enough light from the camp below and the stars above to allow them to see well enough to navigate the foreign terrain. The rock they were walking on soon turned to dirt and grass as they walked away from the camp. They could hear the soothing sound of the river getting louder as they approached it.

"Let's fill our skins while we can," recommended Kelvin. "You never know when we will have another chance."

Reaching the river, they could see a dense forest on the other side. Beyond the trees, the mountain rose again. The plateau they were on was in the valley between two mountain peaks.

It would be expected of them to take the easier route down the mountain, which was exactly why they intended to climb higher.

"We need to cross," said Kelvin, as they crouched over the river taking in large gulps of water from their cupped hands

"The current seems too strong to cross here," Elizabeth noticed. "I would hate to get pulled over the waterfall!" They both cringed at the thought.

"What's that?" whispered Kelvin, turning toward voices he heard upriver but staying in a crouched position.

"Guards," she replied. "They're walking this way. Run!"

They both shot to their feet running as fast as their tired legs would take them. "You there, stop!" shouted the guards as they gave chase.

"How many are there?" asked Elizabeth, panting for breath.

"I see four," yelled Kelvin.

"That's too many to try and overpower!" she yelled.

The guards had the advantage and they knew it. They were herding them toward the lights and two of their fellow wardens like cattle.

"We're going the wrong way!" yelled Elizabeth.

"We're trapped!" realized Kelvin.

The waterfall was coming into view with more guards converging in front of them from the left. They were blocking the small sliver of rock between the cliff and the waterfall at this end of the gorge.

"There is nowhere to go!" yelled Kelvin. "The guards will kill us if they catch us, and if we jump into the river, it will take us over the falls!"

Needing to make a decision, and without warning, Elizabeth yelled, "Jump!" Leaving no time for Kelvin to argue, she reached out with both hands and pushed him with all her might.

The force of the impact propelled both of them into the river just out of the reach of the pursuing guards. With adrenaline filling their bodies, they didn't even notice the ice-cold water as they plunged in. It all happened so fast. They didn't have time to think about their fate before slipping over the edge of the waterfall.

Screaming, with arms and legs flailing about trying to find something to grab hold of, they fell. With all the noise around them from the water, the wind from their fall, and the screams coming from their mouths, inside their heads was surprisingly silent. It was as if they were somehow separated from themselves as a deep sense of calm came over their bodies.

The crash brought them back to reality as their feet plunged into the frothy water at the base of the waterfall. Luckily, they landed in a small area free of rocks and debris, and the falling water broke the surface, padding their fall.

The guards at the top watched them plummet, but it was too dark to see the bottom. They yelled down to their comrades who had now appeared from behind the waterfall. Shining their torches over the water, they searched for the fugitives.

They saw nothing but dark frothing water.

The momentum of the fall drove the divers to the riverbed. It was only when their feet touched the bottom that they realized they were still alive. Landing not far from each other allowed Kelvin to reach out and grab his partner's hand before she surfaced.

He motioned for her to swim underwater toward the rocks ahead. With lungs burning due to a lack of oxygen, they slowly swam the ten feet to the nearest collection of stones.

Thoughts of his brother ran through Kelvin's mind. Holding Elizabeth's hand tight so he wouldn't lose his grip, they moved onward together. He was determined not to lose her.

Funny, Elizabeth mused. *I feel strangely safe even though we are so close to death.* The feeling grew as Kelvin looked back to check on her repeatedly.

"I don't see them," screamed a guard.

They were holding their torches and frantically changing positions to see from every angle. Guards were on both sides of the waterfall now trying to locate any sign of them.

"They couldn't have survived that fall," said a guard. "If they weren't killed by the rocks, they surely would have drowned. I will tell the captain they are dead, and we can look for their bodies in the morning."

Reaching the boulders, Kelvin saw the flashes of light from the guards' torches. He immediately noticed a stretch about a foot wide in the middle of the river where the glow of the torches from either side did not reach. Pointing to a collection of large rocks within that area, he led Elizabeth underwater.

Elizabeth surfaced first, gasping for air. "Are you okay?" asked Kelvin, when his head appeared above the water.

"Yes," she replied between breaths.

"I can't believe we survived that," he said in amazement, while looking back at the waterfall.

"Sorry for pushing you over," she said with a smile. "It was the only option we had."

"I am glad you did," he replied. "If we had stopped, they would have caught us for sure."

Kelvin slowly surveyed the situation planning their escape.

"The guards seem to be giving up," he noticed. "To be safe, I think we should swim a little farther downriver underwater."

Elizabeth wasn't too keen on submerging herself in the water again, but she knew he was right.

As they moved down the river, they didn't see any more beams of light dancing on top of the water. Feeling confident that their pursuers had given up, they swam toward the shore.

When the cool night air hit their wet clothes, it felt like an arctic blast. The pain of the cold wet clothes against their skin made them completely forget about the fall they had just survived.

"We have to keep moving," said Kelvin, finally able to get a few words out through chattering teeth. "If we keep moving, our bodies will produce heat. And if we stay here, they will catch us." He was trying to motivate himself as well as Elizabeth.

"The men won't go any farther, My Lord," said Roland to Terryn. The two commanders were looking out over the Valley of Death as the morning sun had just risen above the eastern peaks in the distance.

"They are afraid of what happens to people who enter the valley, at least according to the legend they have all heard," added Roland.

"Oh, yes, the legend of Damien Fisher," remembered Terryn. "A useful story when you want to keep people in Westville, but it seems to have the opposite effect today."

The story of Damien Fisher was one every child heard growing up. It was used to keep people from wandering too far outside the city walls. The kings of Westville had always thought it in their subjects' best interest to stay within the city. They knew that if they controlled the information, they controlled the people.

Adventurous young men were always recruited into the army so they didn't try to explore the surrounding area on their own. Damien Fisher was a soldier in the army about a hundred years ago. He was sentenced to death for being a coward by deserting the army during a battle the previous day. Death was the only option for desertion, but Damien was very popular with his fellow soldiers and had shown great courage in many other battles.

It was a mystery as to why a soldier of his quality ran away from the fight on that day. Maybe it was simple battle fatigue. His mates begged the commander for mercy, and eventually they won him over. The commander's compromise was to send Damien into the valley where he was left to his own devices.

The whole army was lined up on top of the mountain, watching as he walked down into the valley. Grasses and trees grew a few hundred feet from the top with the exception of the areas where lava had flowed recently.

As soon as Damien disappeared behind the first trees, the soldiers heard loud, blood-curdling screams. It was almost as if the creature that mauled him was watching and waiting for its prey.

Although nothing was seen by the soldiers, many stories and legends had developed from this incident. Some soldiers claimed they saw a large, ten-foot-tall, manlike creature covered in hair and grunting like an ape. Others claimed to have seen an ogre with horns coming out of its head and large fangs protruding from its mouth. Some even claimed to have seen a large bird swoop down and land on Damien with its sharp talons extended.

"Those stories were encouraged by our leaders to stop people from doing exactly what we are trying to get them to do now," said Terryn. "We could force them."

"We could, My Lord, but that would create discontent within our ranks," replied Roland. "We need our soldiers to be completely engaged in order to fulfill our mission."

Terryn's second in command was trying to coach the young captain into making the right decision. Even though he was the leader of the army, he still had to sell the soldiers on their mission and convince them it was for the greater good to prevent desertion or mutiny. This was something the battle-tested lieutenant knew all too well and wanted to impress upon the green captain.

Terryn called for his soldiers to move into formation at the top of the mountain. With the volcanoes falling silent nearly fifty years ago, grass and trees were beginning to completely cover the mountaintop.

The mountains were rounded at the top by the constant volcanic activity over the years. This allowed for plenty of space for the army to form.

Terryn mounted his black battle horse and trotted slowly to the front of the formation. The soldiers watched their commander with awe. He was truly a symbol of what a knight of Westville should be, with his silver armor shining in the sunlight and his marvelously decorated sword and sheath at his side. Reaching the front, he slowly turned his horse and looked upon his army, preparing to address them.

"I know what you have heard of this place. The mere mention of the Valley of Death brings fear to every man, woman, and child in Westville. This is what we have grown up believing.

"Knights of Westville, it is our duty to put ourselves in harm's way for the good of the realm and for the honor of our families. I am not here to tell you it won't be dangerous. You can be certain it will be. What I will tell you is that we are the Army of Westville. We may fear, but we back down from nothing!"

Every man listening to the captain raised his weapon and cheered with inspiration. Motivated by their leader's words and actions, they prepared to depart. Terryn called to his lieutenant to follow him as he turned and started down the mountain.

It looks like our captain is a fast learner, thought Roland.

216 | GREG JOHNSON

The men were so motivated by this action that they cheered again. Terryn had appealed to their courage and honor. No man was going to stay on top of the mountain while the leaders moved into the valley.

Chapter 18

Kelvin and Elizabeth walked slowly away from the camp that was their prison. They both worried about what lay ahead of them on their journey. Elizabeth's fear came from not having spent a lot of time in the forest, while Kelvin's came from his vast knowledge of the dangers the woods presented.

The leaves, grass, and twigs on the forest floor crunched under each step. A light breeze rustled the leaves in the trees as the moon and stars lit their path. The unnerving sound of an owl hooting high up in a nearby tree kept their tension high. Concern for man-eating wild animals kept them from feeling their cold and still wet clothes clinging to their skin.

As they made their way west of the river, they noticed that the ground sloped upward toward the summit. The thick forest was not so dense that it was difficult to navigate, but it provided good cover from their pursuers, who undoubtedly would be looking for them.

"I have to rest," said Elizabeth, after they had been walking up the mountainside for nearly two hours.

"I could eat too," Kelvin replied.

Flopping down on a nearby fallen tree, Elizabeth took off her shoe and rubbed her foot. "My feet are killing me!"

"Yeah, but the good news is our clothes are finally dry," answered Kelvin, with optimism. "What would you like for breakfast?" he asked, jokingly. Elizabeth laughed out loud in response.

"That was just what I needed after the stress of last night," she said. "We haven't had much to laugh about lately."

The conversation remained light as they finished their meal of jerky and water while resting on the log.

By the time they were up and moving again, the sun had completely risen giving them a full view of their surroundings.

"So, this is what it was like for my mother when she was stranded in the forest," wondered Elizabeth.

"It must have been even more frightening trying to protect a baby," replied Kelvin.

Elizabeth nodded in agreement.

"Growing up in Triopolis, we knew nothing about what lies beyond the Red Mountains," said Kelvin, pondering the ramifications of what he had learned. "Our teachers and parents told us about horrible creatures in the forest. Some could swallow us whole, and others would tear us apart just for fun."

Noticing that Elizabeth was looking around with concern, he softened the story. "I am sure they were just trying to keep us from venturing too far from home."

"It wasn't much different in Westville," explained Elizabeth. "Of course, we knew other people existed, but we were also told of the monsters that inhabited the forest. Only barbarians could survive because of their brutality, and armed soldiers because of their training and weaponry. So anyone who was adventurous joined the army."

Changing the subject, she said, "Tell me more about Triopolis."

"It's a beautiful place on a charming bay with white, sandy beaches," began Kelvin. "Acres of fertile farmland provide plenty of food for everyone. The people are very nice, and I am sure once they know who you are, they will welcome you with open arms."

"It sounds wonderful," she replied with a smile. Hearing Kelvin talk about their destination helped her cope with the journey, and being able to visualize her new home made her more optimistic.

"The only negative thing I would say about my home is what the bishop has done to it," he said with disappointment.

"Maybe you can talk to your father about him," she responded. "I sure would like to tell him what that man did to my mother and me."

"Wait a minute!" he exclaimed. "Putting together everything that we have learned, I think there might be something else going on there."

"What do you mean?" asked Elizabeth, confused.

"The Enlightened," he said. "The bishop found Luther's laboratory in the archives. He used what he found to guide himself down the path of enlightenment. I saw books with spells and recipes for potions on his table."

"So, are you suggesting that he is controlling your father's mind and actions?" she asked.

"It all fits," he said. "When I think back to what Henry said about some of the decisions my father made in the Assembly, the bishop was always the one who benefitted the most."

"I hope there is something left in Luther's cave that will help us rid Triopolis of that man," said Elizabeth, climbing the last few feet of the slope.

"We made it!" exclaimed Kelvin when they reached the top of the mountain.

Grass had grown almost to the top on the side they had just traversed, but the terrain on the other side was much different. No vegetation grew for the first few hundred feet down the slope into the valley.

"This must have been a more recent lava flow," said Kelvin. "I remember when I was very young we would occasionally have an eruption in the Red Mountains. The liquid fire would flow like water down the mountainside, destroying everything in its path."

"I have never seen such a thing," said Elizabeth. "In Westville these things did not happen."

The ground was devoid of color. Gray rock with a thin layer of loose shards covered this side of the mountain. They could see a clear line ahead where the vegetation started to grow again.

"Wow!" exclaimed Kelvin. The view of the valley was spectacular as they looked out over the treetops.

He turned toward Elizabeth. Her face looked as if she had seen a ghost. "What is it?" he asked.

"The story we were told as children about monsters in the forest," she recalled. "In the story the monsters originate in a valley beyond the mountains. This is the Valley of Death!"

Suddenly, it didn't seem so spectacular to Kelvin. They both stared into the valley wondering what lay ahead.

After having a lunch of the usual jerky and water, they were ready to enter the valley. The midday sun felt warm on their skin as they took their first steps down the mountain. The loose gravel made it difficult to get a firm footing on the old lava flow. Many times they had to help each other regain their balance.

"I think it would be easier if we got off the rocks," said Elizabeth, after another near fall.

"I agree," replied Kelvin. "Let's go this way."

He led her toward the nearest edge and onto the firm dirt floor of the forest. "Much better," she said.

<hr />

"She trusted you!" screamed Richard at the high priest. "How could you betray Elizabeth? And now because of you Lynessa is dead!"

Richard continued his tirade, and the high priest listened expressionless and silent. *It doesn't come out nearly as often, but he definitely has his father's temper*, he observed with wry amusement.

"You both should have come to me first," said Richard. "I could have helped cover up Henry's involvement and identity. Now she will surely hang when they catch her."

The high priest was surprised by the news of Lynessa and thought it was time to calm the young prince and take control of the conversation. "How did she die?" he asked.

"She was shot with an arrow," replied Richard.

"Shot by the army?" asked the high priest.

"No. It is thought that a barbarian shot her. Terryn's message says that she was leaving a trail of torn bits of cloth for the army to follow," continued Richard.

I was wrong about Lynessa, thought the high priest. *I didn't think she would have had any important friends. Apparently her ties go much higher than I realized.*

Doing nothing to betray his thoughts, he merely said, "Hers was the only body found?"

"No other bodies or signs of others being injured were reported," answered Richard.

He continued to give the high priest the rest of the information contained in the report. The only other piece of information that got Donovan's attention was the location. They had been on the upper part of the Misty River.

The Misty River was named for the unusual amount of fog that seemingly came out of nowhere to engulf travelers. It ran from the mountains all the way down to the ruins of Midalo.

That's near Granite Lake, the high priest mused as Richard prattled on about some unimportant bits of information. *They could have shot Lynessa if they thought she was leading an army too close to Granite Lake, and they would never allow barbarians that close.*

The high priest was now confident that Kelvin and Elizabeth had made their way to Granite Lake. This filled him with a great deal of relief knowing they would be safe there.

"Sometimes I feel like I got Henry killed," bemoaned Richard. "Lord Rosser had been following me and Albert, and he must have seen us with Henry earlier that day. After that, he must have followed him."

"These events are not your fault," replied the high priest. "You must remain strong in these difficult times. Remember our lessons from your younger days—the ones you thought were pointless. I was preparing you for kingship in a time that would be very different from your father's."

Richard reminisced. "Yes, I do remember. We used to discuss the potential for life outside our borders, the ability to sail across the ocean, and the type of knowledge a foreigner might possess."

Thinking about the memories gave him a moment of revelation. "You were right!" he exclaimed. "They were all true."

"Richard, you will be king soon, much sooner than you think, in fact. You must be prepared to rule in this new world we have entered."

Feeling that they were safely far enough away from Granite Lake and their captors, Kelvin thought it was time to refer to the map. It was mid-afternoon, and a little, grassy clearing provided the perfect spot to sit and rest their exhausted legs.

Kelvin immediately unfolded the piece of paper containing the rubbing he made of the map in the House of the Founders. Elizabeth scooted closer to him so she could see.

Studying the markings on the map, Kelvin tried to remember if any of the land features looked familiar. The chart was of a geographic area with landmarks determining whether you were on the right path or not. It did not contain a marked trail.

"I think you were right about the waterfall at Granite Lake being the first marker," Elizabeth said, pointing at a formation near the bottom corner. "These black lines look like the walls of Granite Lake, and that looks like a waterfall. It has to be Granite Lake."

"That means if we continue to walk southwest, we should find the next marker, which is the Giant's Legs," replied Kelvin, drawing a line on the map with his finger.

"The Giant's Legs, that's funny," said Elizabeth. "I wonder what happened to the rest of him!"

Laughing, they jumped to their feet, energized from their discovery.

Walking through the forest always gave Elizabeth a certain amount of calm. Being surrounded by the abundant life and the wonderful fragrance of the various trees, bushes, and flowering plants invigorated her. It was easy to have pleasant thoughts with the sun shining down through the canopy of trees.

"I wonder when our next full meal will be?" said Kelvin. "I am dreaming of the wonderful feasts we have during our Founders' Day celebrations. Ms. Parkinson always serves roast chicken, fresh green beans, carrots, and diced potatoes cooked in butter. For dessert she serves the best apple cake I have ever eaten."

"Mmm, that sounds good," replied Elizabeth, her mouth watering at the thought of so much good food. "Is Founders' Day coming up soon?"

"No, unfortunately. It is still a few months away. Maybe we can get Ms. Parkinson to make us a feast anyway."

The terrain was becoming rocky, but vegetation still grew everywhere as they made their way around a large outcrop. The forest was still dense, but the ground looked like it had experienced a vast amount of upheaval.

All around them large slabs of rock jutted out of the ground. This chaos had happened many centuries ago because grass, bushes, and trees grew all around and on top of the massive rocks. Layers could be seen higher on the cliff face.

Their path took them between two high cliffs towering hundreds of feet above them on both sides. The path was only three feet wide.

Coming to the end of the roofless tunnel, the sun became brighter as the trees overhead backed off to allow the rays to reach the forest floor. Passing the threshold of the two large cliffs, they entered a small plateau.

Kelvin and Elizabeth looked out over the edge of the plateau down to the forest below. They were twenty feet higher than the tallest trees.

"There is so much land," he commented, unable to comprehend the enormity of the world until this moment.

He now knew that their journey was going to be much longer than he'd originally thought. As he looked west and pondered the size of the world, he hadn't noticed Elizabeth.

"I have seen this before," she said, remembering. Kelvin turned to his left to see what it was. Elizabeth was motionless, gazing at an oddly shaped stone arch.

The arch looked like a man cut off at the waist. It was natural, but the legs looked almost perfectly carved. You could see what looked like knees and feet at the bottom.

"This must be the Giant's Legs," said Kelvin, consulting the map.

"It almost looks as if it was created by man," she replied, and then she gasped. "I have seen this exact formation in a dream!" she exclaimed. "It would be impossible for another arch like this to exist anywhere else." She stared at it trying to understand.

"Could it have been a memory from when you were a baby?" asked Kelvin. "Maybe your mother passed through here with you."

"It's possible, but I didn't sense my mother in the dream."

Thinking about this, she suddenly became panicked. "The dream was terrifying, but I don't know why. I had a feeling of complete dread. I felt like I was being watched by a beast waiting to attack."

Hesitating for a moment, they looked in all directions to verify that the dream was not a premonition.

"We should turn right," he said, feeling comfortable that they were safe. "The map says we should go through the Giant's Legs, but that would only be if we were coming from the other direction."

She followed him as they turned right.

The line of soldiers marching through the forest had lengthened and thinned due to the thick vegetation. Because it was nearly impossible to ride through, the men dismounted and walked their horses. This slowed their progress, but it was much easier on the horses.

"How is the morale of the men?" Terryn asked Roland.

"Morale is increasing, sir. The farther we move into the valley without incident the more comfortable they become."

"They must not have seen the size of that weasel back there," commented Terryn.

"No sir, I believe we're the only ones who saw it," replied Roland.

"Good, I would like to keep that secret as long as possible," answered the captain.

"Sir, sir!" yelled a soldier, running up to his leaders.

"What is it, soldier?" asked Roland in a commanding voice.

"A man has been attacked!" he said, pointing toward the front of the line.

All three men ran to the crowd that had gathered around the injured man, who was lying on the ground. Seeing the captain arrive on the scene, the crowd backed away and allowed him to approach.

"What happened, Doctor?" he asked the man attending the mutilated soldier.

"The men who witnessed the attack say it came from a large wolf," replied the doctor.

"This is what we feared," Terryn whispered to Roland. "The valley is coming alive."

"Can you save him?" asked Roland.

"He will live," answered the doctor. "No major organs were damaged. The only question is whether these wounds will heal without becoming infected."

"I know you will do your best, Doctor," replied Terryn. He nodded to Roland, and the two walked away from the injured man to discuss the wolf attack, specifically, how it could have been avoided.

Moments later, the soldiers began to yell hysterically. Turning to look, Terryn and Roland saw what was causing the excitement.

The wolf attack was not a lone incident but a reconnaissance mission. That wolf was only one member of a much larger pack, and that pack now stood on a small hill overlooking the army.

Every member of the pack looked down upon the men, snarling and showing their teeth ferociously. The average height of the wolves was four feet, and they had broad muscular shoulders. The men could see their black eyes staring down upon them with blood lust.

Then, with one voice, the wolves emitted the most dreadful howl.

"Arm yourselves!" yelled Roland.

"Prepare to fight!" yelled Terryn.

The men fell into unit formation with weapons ready as they awaited the attack. Then it happened.

Charging down the hill, the wolves leapt toward the soldiers. Some men were prepared for the speed of the animals and some weren't. The prepared soldiers were able to get their swords up in time to repel the attack, while the unprepared men were overtaken by the powerful animals.

The battle was short but very bloody. Of the thirty wolves that attacked, ten were killed and another five were seriously injured. Seven men perished at the hands of the beasts. Even with the casualties, the men rejoiced in their victory. Elation spread through their ranks as the animals retreated up the hill.

"Our first encounter with the beasts of the Valley of Death, and we are victorious!" yelled Terryn, waving his bloody sword in the air.

The men replied by throwing their hands in the air and cheering wildly. "That should help morale," he said to Roland.

Chapter 19

Looking up at the sun, Kelvin noticed it had begun its downward journey in the west. "I have been thinking about your dream with the Giant's Legs in it," he said.

Satisfaction filled Elizabeth, knowing that he didn't think she was crazy for what she had said. It also reassured her that she wasn't crazy. Despite what Donovan and Aaron told them about being enlightened, she was still a little unsure of how people would react to her visions.

"I have been thinking about what Donovan told us about the abilities some people are born with," Kelvin said, breaking their silence after a difficult stretch of terrain. "Maybe it's not so far-fetched. After all, we have heard some pretty crazy things about our world lately."

"I stopped telling people about them when I was twelve," she explained. "When I was young, people just passed it off as a child's active imagination, but it became less acceptable as I got older.

"Just past my twelfth birthday, I told my tutor, Louise, about a dream. She slapped my hands and told me that a lady did not speak of such things. It truly frightened her, and I think she thought I might be crazy."

Kelvin listened intently as she shared an obviously very emotional memory from her past.

"I too thought I might be mad, so I did everything possible to block these thoughts from my mind," she continued. "For years I struggled to force them out of my head, but it was useless. Eventually, I just learned to ignore them and not let them affect my life."

"Well, we know the truth now," replied Kelvin. "You aren't mad at all. I want you to tell me when you have a vision. It could help us make it out of this forest alive."

The sun was now only slightly above the horizon. "We should find a place to camp for the night," suggested Kelvin.

"Yeah, I don't want to be walking through this place at night," Elizabeth replied. Suddenly, she stood perfectly still.

"What is it?" asked Kelvin.

"I don't know," she answered apprehensively. "I heard something over there."

They were both silent as they watched in the direction of the noise. Leaves rustled just before they heard the most grotesque mixture of a grunt and a screech. There wasn't time to react between the frightening wail of the beasts and the sounds of them charging closer.

A pack of wild boar came crashing through the bushes intent on impaling the two intruders with their tusks. The massive beasts trampled everything in their path, their great heads slashing side to side.

"Run faster!" screamed Kelvin, as they ran for their lives. "They're catching us!"

"I am running as fast as I can" she screamed with labored breath.

They could feel the pounding hooves on the ground and smell the animals' foul odor as the predators narrowed the gap. "We can't outrun them!" yelled Kelvin. "Do you see the tree ahead? Jump up and grab that low-hanging branch!"

Kelvin wasn't sure if they would beat the animals to the tree, let alone reach the branch. With each step they took, it seemed the boar took two. They were quickly gaining ground. The animals plowed through small bushes and tree branches that their prey had to go around.

"Jump!" screamed Kelvin, reaching the targeted tree limb.

His hands firmly landed on the branch. The momentum of his body kept his legs swinging forward allowing him to pull his whole body up into the tree.

Remembering his tree climbing days in his youth he spun his hips and landed in a sitting position on the branch.

"Help!" screamed Elizabeth.

Kelvin looked down to see Elizabeth hanging from the branch by one arm.

"Give me your other hand!" he yelled. Reaching up, she gave him her hand and he pulled. Her feet just cleared the top of the lead beast's large tusks as they charged past. A loud screech could be heard from the disappointed boar as the herd ran off in anger.

"What is this place?" asked Kelvin. "I have never seen wild pigs that big. They're twice as big as any I have seen!"

"We should stay up here for the night," said Elizabeth, concerned about what else might be out there. They slept leaning on each other, shoulder to shoulder, with two arms locked and their legs straddling a branch. This would force them awake if either of them leaned too far on either side.

The next morning, Kelvin was startled awake by Elizabeth pulling on his arm. "Good morning," she said sleepily. "Are you as hungry as I am?"

"I could sure go for some eggs and bacon," said Kelvin, as he dug into his pack and produced a dried-out piece of meat for each of them.

"Yeah, I am sick of jerky," she replied. "Maybe we can at least find some fruit today."

"Anything different would be fine by me," replied Kelvin. "Hey, did you hear those strange noises last night?"

"I don't know what I was more afraid of, the noises or falling out of the tree," she said.

"I think all of the rumors about this valley are true," he said. "With the boar yesterday and the noises last night, we better not lose focus today."

The morning proved to be uneventful. A light drizzle accompanied their walk. The usual crunch of leaves and dead tree branches beneath their feet was muted from the rain. This didn't make them feel any more comfortable though. The silence due to the lack of wind was unnerving. In the quiet, they felt as if their voices and footsteps carried for miles. In a forest full of predators, this was a distinct disadvantage.

By midday, the sky had completely cleared, and the ground was dry again. It was much more pleasant walking on dry ground.

"Ah, the sun has returned!" said Elizabeth. "It will be nice to have dry clothes again. Hey Kelvin, what is the next landmark we are looking for?"

Opening the map, Kelvin studied it and replied, "The river."

"Great, another river," Elizabeth muttered.

"The map says we should cross it," Kelvin said. "It looks like there is a clearing ahead."

When they got to the river, they both slid up to a tree so they could determine if it was safe to cross without being seen. "Wow!" was their reaction to what they saw in the small field.

A herd of the most massive animals they had ever seen was roaming the small meadow. "They look like buffalo only bigger," marveled Kelvin.

They were mostly covered in brown hair and had very strong shoulders and a thick growth of hair protecting their neck. As two younger members of the herd chased each other playfully, they could see that the beasts were gathered around a small pond.

"They are so big," commented Elizabeth. "They must be ten feet tall!" They admired the impressive animals, but they did not want to startle them. Kelvin wondered if even these trees would protect them from a stampede.

They snapped to attention when they heard the crack of a dead tree branch behind them. Spinning around, their lives flashed before their eyes.

The first thing they noticed were enormous teeth protruding from the cat's upper jaw. A low growl from the feral feline's throat sent shivers up their spines. Its shoulder muscles rippled as it inched toward them.

Kelvin put his hand behind his back and gripped his dagger, certain that it would be the only chance he had against the large cat. *Built more like a bear than a cat*, he thought, as he sized up his opponent.

Saliva dripped from the cat's mouth as if it could already taste their flesh. Focused on the beast, they didn't notice the man crouched alongside it.

"You don't look like barbarians," said the man.

"We're not," replied Kelvin, still watching the large fangs in front of him.

"We are from Triopolis," Elizabeth announced.

"I have never heard of Triopolis," replied the old man.

"It's over the western mountains," explained Kelvin.

"Over the western mountains, eh?"

"Come, Brutus," the old man commanded the large feline. It immediately backed off and retreated behind its master.

Kelvin and Elizabeth let out a sigh of relief, making the old man laugh. "You should have been scared," he warned. "Large-toothed cats are the most evolved killers in the valley."

Unsure of their current standing with the old man, his comment didn't make them feel comfortable.

Even though the cat backed off, it kept its unflinching gaze on Kelvin. The spooky yellow eyes continued to evaluate him. Brutus would occasionally lick his lips causing a horrified pulse to shoot through their bodies.

"If you aren't wild men, then why are you walking in this forest alone?" asked the man.

He seemed to miss the irony of his question, considering that he looked like a wild man. He was covered in the skins of animals he had probably killed and eaten. He retained the muscle mass of a younger man, but the thinning gray hair on his head gave away his true age.

The man's piercing gaze and the hungry glare from the oversized cat made it nearly impossible for Kelvin and Elizabeth to develop a fake story as a ruse. Fear controlled them, and any attempt to cover up the truth would have been feeble.

"We escaped from Westville," answered Kelvin, finally.

"Well, then, I guess that makes us friends," replied the old man with a smile. "My name is Forwin." Kelvin and Elizabeth returned the introduction.

The look of these two did not concern Forwin. He was not being overly trusting; they just didn't give his keen intuition a feeling of danger. They simply looked like lost travelers.

"You must have been walking for days," concluded Forwin. "Westville is a long way from here."

"We crossed the mountain two days ago," replied Elizabeth.

"You must be hungry then," said Forwin. "My home is not far. I will take you there."

He led Kelvin and Elizabeth around the edge of the small field so they wouldn't disturb the buffalo. This was unsuccessful because their heads were raised as they followed the three odd-looking creatures with their eyes. Kelvin thought they probably smelled the old man's oversized pet padding alongside his master.

The old man was right; his house wasn't far. If you didn't know it was there, you would walk right past it. The shelter was built into a hill with trees and thick bushes grown in around the opening. It looked like a dense patch of bushes to a stranger, which is exactly what Forwin wanted.

The door was around the side, right next to the hill, with tree branches fastened to it so it didn't look out of place. Forwin led them into the perfectly camouflaged cabin while Brutus lay down just outside the door to protect the inhabitants of his home.

"So how did you escape Westville?" asked Forwin.

"We had the help of a friend," replied Kelvin.

"I have never met a man from there I could trust," answered Forwin, skeptically. He was in the process of lighting a fire as they spoke.

"They aren't all bad," explained Elizabeth. "I don't think we would have been able to escape without his help."

"You sound as if you have been there," Kelvin ventured.

"Not in a long time," he replied. "It has been many years since I last crossed the mountains."

"Why don't you cross them?" asked Elizabeth. "It seems this is the more dangerous side."

"You are mistaken," answered Forwin. "It's not what lies on the other side that scares me. I do not cross them for the same reason none of the creatures in the valley have crossed them—you never know when the mountain itself will come to life spitting fire into the air. I have seen thousands of trees and animals burn in the liquid fire that spews from its angry mouth."

"We saw the rockslides that resulted from the cooling liquid fire," replied Kelvin.

"Do you have family here?" asked Elizabeth, looking around the hut.

Their host put three large pieces of meat on the spit and hung it over the fire. "My wife and child were killed by a bear some years ago," he answered, staring into the fire as if he would see them there.

She gave the old man a moment to remember his family before asking another question.

"Brutus is my only family now," he stated.

"I can't imagine better protection than that!" exclaimed Kelvin, to lighten the mood.

"Brutus is a good and loyal companion," Forwin said proudly.

"How do animals get so big here?" asked Kelvin.

"This is normal," replied Forwin. "They are this big everywhere. I guess the only reason they haven't grown this large on the other side of the mountains is because they are contained in a small area between the mountains and the sea. Your people have been hunting them for hundreds of years, so they aren't alive long enough to grow this large."

"How did you train Brutus?" asked Elizabeth.

"Oh, I wouldn't say he's trained," answered Forwin, with a chuckle. "We have more of an understanding than a master-servant relationship. Just a baby when I found him. He couldn't have been more than a couple of months old.

"His mother had been killed, and I found him sitting by her side. I didn't want him to get eaten by the scavengers that would soon arrive, so I took him home with me. We have been together ever since."

Turning the meat one more time, he announced excitedly, "Looks like supper's ready!"

The smell of the cooked meat permeated the room, causing their stomachs to growl and mouths to water. He brought three plates to the table, setting one in front of each of them. The meal consisted of a large piece of meat, which looked like pork, and a mixture of vegetables and potatoes that he had steamed over the fire.

They savored their first bite for an extended period as they had done with every hot meal since leaving Westville.

There were no more questions as they devoured the food on their plates. The pork was so tender that its juices dripped onto the plate after each bite. The juices saturated the potatoes giving them a heavenly flavor.

"You must have liked it," said Forwin, with a smile, looking at their clean plates.

Having been a man of the woods for so long, he understood what it was like to go days without a hot meal. He gave them each another serving of vegetables and potatoes.

"How did you come to live in the valley?" asked Elizabeth.

He carefully studied Elizabeth before answering. She didn't seem to have the arrogance of most people from Westville. *Those wretched people*, he mused with grim disdain. He wondered if she was different from most, or if they were becoming more tolerant of other people. It had been twenty years since he had encountered anyone from that city.

"I was run out of my home by an invading army," he stated, showing no emotion.

Elizabeth gasped. "That's terrible!"

"A small group of us made it out alive," he continued. "My dear wife had prepared our son and packed a survival kit just in case the battle didn't go our way.

"The fighting was brutal that day. As soon as the bombardment from their catapults ended, the enemy was over the wall. We couldn't stop them. They were too many. With twice our numbers, they hacked and slashed their way through our columns with ease.

"I fought as long as I could until it became pointless. If I had stayed, it would have been only to sacrifice myself. I couldn't do that with my wife and son waiting for me.

"My indecision soon dissipated as I watched the brutality of the invading army. A man ten feet from my side was injured and kneeling on the ground when a large man covered in silver armor approached. 'Please don't,' he yelled, holding his bleeding arm. The knight didn't care. With one swipe of his sword, the lame man was gone.

"Women were cut down as they fled. Babies and young children were ripped from their mothers' arms. The elderly didn't stand a chance either. The soldiers were ruthless with cruel efficiency. When they were done with us, the trailing soldiers set fire to our homes. Soon the flames reached the clouds, and the smell of burning wood reached my nose. It was time to leave.

"Finishing off the man attacking me, I quickly turned and fled to find my wife and son. As I ran, I knew that I would never return. This was an army of annihilation. They were sent here for one purpose, and that was to destroy every one of us."

Elizabeth gasped with a look of horror on her face. "You are Midaloan, aren't you?"

She looked upon him with sad eyes as if to say, *I am so sorry we did this to you.* She felt guilty for having grown up in Westville even though she had never set foot on the battlefield. What made her feel worse was that she knew how the people of Westville celebrated the victory that was really just a massacre.

"I am the last of my people," he said, proudly. "Over the years the forest has taken each of the three families that escaped our homeland that day."

Forwin sat in silence for a moment as he recalled his former friends. His two guests sat in the uncomfortable silence, listening to nothing but the crackling fire.

"The wilds are very dangerous for two people such as you," he said. "At any moment the most ferocious of beasts may attack, the ground can open up and consume you, or you could be plucked from the sky by a great winged beast. So again I ask, why are you out here all alone?"

Elizabeth looked at Kelvin before answering. With their eyes, they communicated agreement that Forwin could be trusted. Being from Midalo, he had no interest in meeting anyone from Westville.

Elizabeth repeated the story of who she was and her upbringing as a future princess of Westville. She noticed Forwin's eyes narrow as anger filled him, knowing he had a member of Westville's royal family sitting in his kitchen. She understood that even though it had been twenty years, Forwin still held much contempt for the people who destroyed his life and banished him to this place. Elizabeth quickly got to the part where she discovered that she was not from Westville at all.

"I have never heard of Triopolis," he replied, unconvinced.

"Most people haven't," replied Kelvin. "We think it lies to the west over the mountains. That is where we are headed."

"Very dangerous to the west," replied Forwin. "Even the barbarians don't dare venture too far west. Strange beasts and odd sounds come from over the river. But that is a tale for another day. I will show you to your beds."

Kelvin's wish came true the next morning as Forwin had prepared eggs and bacon for his guests. All three were seated at the table scarfing down their breakfast when they heard a scratching at the door. The scratching was so forceful that it sounded as if the door would come crashing down. Kelvin and Elizabeth both looked up in surprise.

"It's just Brutus," said Forwin. "Hold on, you mangy cat!"

He grabbed a large slab of uncooked bacon and tossed it out the door to his companion.

"Cat loves his bacon!" he said with a chuckle.

"So, you want to cross the river?" asked Forwin, as he sat back down.

"Yes sir," replied Kelvin.

"Well, that's easier said than done, but I can help you."

"Why is it so difficult?" asked Elizabeth.

Forwin went over to a shelf and retrieved a well-worn notebook. Returning to the table and opening the notebook to the third page, he showed them a picture of what was in the river. It was a drawing of a fish with an extra-large mouth wide open and a man standing inside.

"Of course, man-eating fish," Kelvin said in a deadpan tone.

"They're so big that they don't have any natural predators," said Forwin. "They aren't afraid of anything, and they investigate everything that enters the water. I once saw one ram a boat, dumping the two barbarians into the water, where they were easily gobbled up."

"This place is a nightmare!" exclaimed Kelvin.

Elizabeth's face was ashen. She just sat there silent, contemplating the horror of being eaten alive.

"There are many creatures in the rivers of the forest," continued Forwin. "Some are known, but more are unknown. It is the unknown creatures that I fear."

They sat in nervous silence at the thought. Finishing breakfast, they walked outside to plan their crossing. Brutus was there to greet them, and he followed them down to the water's edge. Kelvin and Elizabeth stared into the dark blue water, wondering what lurked beneath its smooth surface.

"This is a very deep river," Forwin said. "That's why so many large creatures can survive in it. We will not cross here."

Kelvin and Elizabeth turned in surprise. "It looks so calm here," said Kelvin, doubting Forwin's suggestion.

"Calm!" Forwin exclaimed. He ran up to his house.

"He's crazy," Kelvin joked.

Forwin soon returned with a piece of uncooked bacon left over from breakfast. Brutus, thinking it was for him, followed closely.

"Oh, you darn animal," Forwin cursed his cat jokingly and tore off a piece of meat for him.

"You think this river is safe?" he asked. "Watch this."

He tossed the raw meat into the river. Before the meat hit the water, a fish with very large prehistoric-looking teeth leaped from the water and snatched it out of the air.

Before that fish landed back in the river, a much larger fish jumped clamping its jaws around the smaller fish's body. It all happened in a split second, but what a sight it was. Forwin stood back with a smirk on his face, waiting for a reaction from his guests.

"That was unbelievable!" exclaimed Kelvin.

"This is no place for humans," said Elizabeth, stunned.

Forwin laughed and said, "There is a better place to cross."

After what they had just witnessed, there was no argument. Following Forwin, they marched up the riverbank to a section of the river where the water was shallower but faster moving.

"Are we going to walk across the river?" asked Kelvin, looking at the water rushing over and around a line of large rocks protruding from the water.

"Yes," replied Forwin. "This is the safest place to cross because the large fish cannot navigate the rapids."

The large stones stretched the entire width of the river, slicing it in half. The rapids, however, were no wider than the width of a man's arms stretched out from either side of his body.

Kelvin was the first to test the rocky bridge. "Walk slowly and mind your footing," directed Forwin. "The rocks are very slippery, and you saw why you don't want to end up in the river!"

"Did we ever!" replied Elizabeth. She stepped onto the rocks, testing how well her shoes would grip them before proceeding.

Slowly, they traversed the wet rocks. Every step was cautious, and they remained silent to stay focused. Forwin watched as they inched their way across. By the time they reached the halfway point, it seemed like they had been walking for hours. Already starting to feel the effects of mental fatigue, they stopped to take a break.

The water was loud as it crashed into the rocks, making conversation difficult. Yelling was the only way they could hear each other.

"Just focus on the other side and don't look into the water," yelled Kelvin, trying to keep the thoughts of the large-toothed fish out of their minds.

Again moving toward their destination, they watched the rocks in front of them. What they didn't see were the hungry reptilian eyes just above the surface of the water, fixated on every move the humans made, waiting for a misstep. As they slowly continued forward, the eyes followed.

The reptile could wait no longer. Like a rocket, it shot out of the water. The enormous water snake hovered five feet above their heads.

Panicked, they ran. The snake attacked with its mouth slamming down on the rocks just missing them. Again and again, it lunged.

Brutus and Forwin ran toward the fight hoping they would make it in time. Kelvin and Elizabeth were screaming as they tried to outrun their attacker. They couldn't think about the wet rocks; they just had to move quickly, jumping from one to the next to make it to the other side.

Brutus was the first to arrive, showing his teeth and growling. He swiped at the snake with his razor-sharp claws making contact. His claws dug into the serpent's thick skin, drawing blood. The beast let out a horrific shriek as the pain set in.

By this time, Forwin had arrived. "Keep going!" he yelled to Kelvin and Elizabeth. "We will hold him off while you finish crossing."

The snake, recovering from the shock of being wounded, lunged forward again, but this time its head landed between the cat and its master.

Brutus swiped at the snake's head for the brief second it was on the rocks, but he wasn't quick enough. Forwin had his sword out and was ready for battle. He jabbed it into the snake's lower body drawing more blood. The snake backed away until it was just out of reach of Forwin's blade.

Kelvin and Elizabeth stepped onto the shore and turned to watch the fight. The snake lunged toward Forwin again. He thrust his sword at the snake's belly, making contact and letting the force of the snake's lunge do the rest. Impaled on Forwin's sword, the snake's momentum continued. Forwin dove to one side, but he wasn't fast enough.

The snake's fangs caught Forwin's right leg causing a significant gash and weakening its opponent. The force of the impact knocked Forwin over the rocks and into the river. Kelvin and Elizabeth gasped at the sight.

The snake kept lunging but was getting weaker and slower from its wounds. Again, the serpent's head slammed down on the rocks, missing its target, but this time Brutus timed it perfectly. Catching the snake in his jaws his long sharp fangs sank into its body, severing its head.

For several minutes, the large cat stared into the water looking for his friend, but Forwin did not appear. Elizabeth could sense the sadness in the animal and wished there was something she could do, but they were powerless to help.

Walking to the west, away from the water, a splashing disturbance in the river made them look back. "He's alive!" shrieked Elizabeth.

Ten feet downriver on the other side, Forwin was pulling himself out of the water. Brutus took off in a full sprint over the slippery rocks. They watched as the cat leapt excitedly on top of Forwin.

When Forwin looked up and spotted them on the other side, Kelvin waved as if to say, *Are you okay?* Forwin waved back, and they knew he was. Relieved and happy for both Brutus and Forwin, and thankful that those two brave souls had saved their lives, they continued their journey home.

Chapter 20

It had been two days since they left the river. Kelvin and Elizabeth had trekked through forest and field covering much ground. The weather had not cooperated on the first day, and a steady rain had beat down on them the entire day. Clearing up overnight, the second day was much more comfortable.

The sun had begun its descent, and dusk was upon them. They had reached the edge of a bluff that overlooked a large meadow. The bluff was not high or steep, but it did give them a good vantage point to survey the green grass below.

"Look!" yelled Kelvin, pointing. "That has to be the Lone Soldier!" He took the map out of his pocket, opened it, and verified his theory.

"It's labeled the Lone Soldier and has a small drawing of a tree next to it," said Kelvin. "I guess that means the soldier is a tree."

A sense of accomplishment overcame them as they looked upon the final marker on the map. Even though they were a long way from their destination, they needed the satisfaction of this small victory.

"I wonder why no other trees grow around it," said Elizabeth. "It's just a single tree in the middle of an open field." They both stared out over the cliff as they pondered the question.

"I don't like this place," she commented. "I can't put my finger on the reason, but it just doesn't feel right."

"I think we should rest here before entering the plain," said Kelvin, realizing how dark it was getting. "Once we get out there we will be exposed, and I would rather do that during the daylight and with fresh legs."

"You're right," she agreed. "Let's find a good tree for the night."

Once again, sitting up against each other in the crook of a tree roughly ten feet above the ground, the two weary travelers were ready to sleep.

There wasn't a whisper of wind on this night. The dead silence was enough to strike fear into even the most hardened woodsman. Elizabeth began fidgeting as the nervous energy built inside her.

A thousand stars were visible in the night sky with the occasional flash of light streaking between them. *It's so beautiful here*, she thought, trying to put her mind at ease.

Back in Westville, she would sometimes go out onto her balcony and stare up at the stars wondering how they got there. To coax herself to sleep, she tried to take herself back to those safe nights in the castle.

She was almost asleep when the sound of a twig cracking echoed through the night. Her eyes flew open in fright. She tried to twist and turn her body to see what it was, but she couldn't turn far enough because she didn't want to disturb Kelvin.

The unknown animal below entered her mind, bringing her into a state of paranoia. All of the large terrifying beasts of the forest that they had heard about over the past several days came rushing into her mind.

Frightening images passed through her mind—the snake from the river with fangs the length of her arm, the fish that looked like it could bite a person in two, the charging wild boar. Then, the frightening beast from childhood stories stood out among the rest.

Was it a bear that could stand on two feet and pluck her out of the tree?

A picture of the fearsome head of a mammoth bear filled her mind. The large claws were reaching out ready to pull her into its open mouth. Its teeth were dripping with saliva in anticipation. She fought to hold back a scream.

Her head was pounding and her hands sweating as she imagined the worst. Then the sound of an owl drew her attention to her left. Suddenly the bear was gone, and the horrifying bird from Granite Lake filled her head.

Haast was coming straight toward her, the eagle's long sharp claws outstretched and ready to clamp down and carry her away to its nest.

The owl hooted again bringing her fear to a frenzy. Back and forth her head went, waiting for the clawed creature to appear from the darkness. When it landed in the tree above, a loud shriek escaped her lips startling Kelvin and waking him from his slumber.

"What is it?" he asked, opening his eyes.

The owl flew away no doubt because of the noise disturbing his hunt. "Elizabeth, are you okay?" he asked. "You're shaking."

"I am sorry," she said. "I couldn't sleep. I was hearing noises and thinking of the horrible beasts we have encountered. My mind is driving me crazy!"

"Don't worry," he said, putting his arm around her. "The darkness can play cruel tricks on anyone. I will keep watch for a while so you can sleep."

"Thank you," she said, closing her eyes, now feeling safe.

The rest of the night was filled with dark dreams, but none were bad enough to wake her again.

The morning sunlight woke Kelvin first. The slight twisting of his cramped body opened Elizabeth's eyes.

"Sorry for waking you up," he said.

"It's okay," she replied. "After all, anytime you move I am supposed to wake up so we don't fall out of the tree."

The morning was a little slow after the disturbing night they'd had. This made for a quiet breakfast, as neither was interested in much conversation. It wasn't long before they were on their way down the small slope and into the grassland below.

"This place doesn't feel right," said Elizabeth, taking her first step onto the plain. "I haven't felt right ever since we reached the cliff last night. My head immediately began pounding, my thoughts darkened, and my dreams last night were unbearable."

"We could go around," offered Kelvin. "It would take a little longer, but it would be worth it if your headache went away."

"That's just it," she answered. "All these things are telling me we should stay away, but for some reason, I feel that we must reach the tree in the middle. I have an overwhelming feeling that tree can tell us something."

Kelvin knew the power of her insight and believed immediately that they should follow that intuition. If something was telling her they should go to the tree, then that's exactly what they would do.

The grass was waist high and thick as they started across the plain. A slight breeze blew the blades from side to side, and a partly cloudy sky allowed occasional rays of sunshine to reach the ground.

Kelvin tried to stomp down some of the grass to make it easier for Elizabeth to follow. Frustrated, his attempt was in vain because the grass was simply too dense.

Keeping an eye on the Lone Soldier, they plodded through the heavy turf. By the time the sun was directly above, they were each on their second piece of jerky.

"I can't believe we've been walking all morning and we aren't there yet," complained Kelvin.

Taking a bite of jerky, Elizabeth answered, "The grass didn't look this thick from the clifftop."

Each step was becoming more and more difficult. It was as though the grass itself was reaching out and pulling on their feet as they lifted them for the next step. When their shoes hit the ground, the thick turf swallowed them whole, making it a fight to save each foot from the voracious grass.

"Does it seem like this is getting more difficult as we get closer?" asked Elizabeth.

"It does," answered Kelvin, watching his feet sinking to the ground and being covered by vegetation. He could swear the weeds were moving, but he thought it was only his imagination until a tall length of grass formed a vine that rubbed against the back of his ankle and curled itself around his leg.

"Ah!" he yelled. "It's alive! Run!"

It was too late. The vine quickly wrapped itself around his leg holding him in place. He pulled and pulled but could not break free. The vine was too strong.

Tearing at it with his hands, Kelvin watched as more were coming. Fear gripped him as Elizabeth came to his aid. Just as she was reaching out to help, he broke free from the assaulting weed and broke into a sprint. They were headed for the Lone Soldier.

As soon as Elizabeth began to run, the vines reached out to entangle her. The faster she and Kelvin ran, the faster the vines followed, with more of them joining the hunt. It wasn't long before a tangled web of greenery was on their heels.

The ground encircling the Lone Soldier was strangely bare and free of grass. No time to think about why, Kelvin hoped their attackers could not reach them there.

The abrupt border of the grassland was within reach, and they ran as quickly as their legs would take them.

"Jump!" yelled Kelvin, and they flew over the edge of the vegetation. The rough landing on the hard dirt didn't bother them because of the elation they felt watching the attacking vines slither back into their hovel.

Relieved he was still alive, Kelvin lay face down on the ground to catch his breath. Elizabeth had rolled onto her back to break the fall from her dive, and she was staring up into the sky regaining her strength.

His breath returning to normal, Kelvin finally opened his eyes. The ground was hard as rock but covered in a layer of fine sand. The force of his heavy breathing had disturbed some of the sand, and he thought he saw a finger protruding from it.

He wiped the spot with his hand and screamed, mortified at what he uncovered. First he saw a finger, then a hand, then an arm and a face. After several minutes of desperate digging, a dead man lay face–to-face with him. He jumped to his feet in alarm. Without thinking, he took off in the direction they came.

"Kelvin, the vines!" yelled Elizabeth, not sure what was wrong.

Coming to his senses just in time, he stopped. Staring into the grass, he saw the ravenous plants moving into position ready to pounce again if he entered their lair.

"What is it?" asked Elizabeth.

He turned and pointed to the spot where the sand was cleared. Walking up to it, she realized why he was so freaked out.

"My god!" she exclaimed. "It's a dead man!"

"Dead?" said a deep voice. "No, he is not dead. He's sleeping."

Slowly, they both turned toward the voice with a look of dread on their faces. The tree had eyes, a nose, and a mouth, and was looking right at them.

"Is this real?" asked Kelvin out loud, when he really meant to keep the question to himself.

Laughing, the tree answered, "Oh, yes, I am quite real."

"But . . . how?" stammered Elizabeth, unsure of what she wanted to ask.

"I was a man once, before I was deceived by an evil sorcerer of the dark arts who confined me to this tree and my brothers to the dirt."

"Your brothers?" asked Kelvin, looking pointedly at the man in the ground.

The ground seemed to be covered in glass. The body could be seen clearly, but it could not be touched.

"Yes, my brothers in arms," the tree replied. "My name is Vannes, and these men are my army."

"The Lone Soldier," commented Kelvin, now understanding the title.

"That is correct," replied Vannes. "I was left here to watch over my men who lie in eternal sleep."

"Why would someone do that to you?" asked Elizabeth.

"Many years ago when the sky was still dark, we were marching across this land when we happened upon an old man traveling alone. We were riding to the aid of Hugh of Loran who had moved to Granite Lake."

"That must be Meric's grandfather," Elizabeth whispered to Kelvin. "I saw the family tree when we were in the museum with Aaron."

"War waged between Granite Lake and an Enlightened named Arnaud the Black," continued Vannes. "My men were regarded as the greatest fighting force in these lands, and he knew he could not let us reach the fight."

They could see the memories tearing at Vannes from the inside. Every word he spoke was like a dagger piercing his skin. Hundreds of years had passed, but he had nothing else to think about, and he spoke as if it happened yesterday.

"The old man convinced me he was a warrior from the past. I foolishly believed him and took his counsel. He said he knew of a shorter path to the besieged Granite Lake. His path led us here.

"The soft sands that used to cover this land devoured my men. While we were all sinking in the fine sand, the old man transformed himself into the conjuror we knew as Arnaud the Black.

"Laughing as we sank, he did not lift a finger until we were completely submerged. Then he raised his hand and cast three spells. The first raised me up and placed me here, stuck in this form forever. The second cast my army into eternal sleep. With the third spell, he summoned lightning from the clouds.

"The bolt flashed down with such force and heat that it melted the sand above their heads. It created this glassy substance you see today."

"That's horrible!" exclaimed Elizabeth. "Is there anything we can do to help?"

"I am afraid not," replied Vannes. "This is how we will end our days in this world. We have had very few visitors except these blasted birds," said Vannes, shaking off a bluebird trying to build a nest high up in his branches.

"How did you pass through the vines so easily?" he asked. "They have taken many men over the years, but why not you?" Vannes was puzzled by this.

"It was not easy," answered Kelvin. "They chased us, but we were able to outrun them."

"The only people who have ever visited us are enlightened," he pondered. "Yes, the vines will not attack them. It must be part of the spell."

"One almost wrapped itself around my leg," said Kelvin. "I thought I was caught, but I managed to break free."

"The vines do not let go and are much stronger than a man," said Vannes. "It was something else."

"What do you mean?" asked Kelvin.

"Did any of the branches touch you?" Vannes asked Elizabeth.

"No, they didn't."

"Was it because you got closer to Kelvin that the vines released him?"

"Maybe," she answered, knowing where he was going with his questions.

"You have the Blood of Alemon in you," he declared definitively.

"I have been told that, yes."

"It must be true," he said. "Otherwise the vines would have tied you up and dragged you underground to a slow, suffocating death."

Kelvin and Elizabeth shuddered at the thought. Neither had thought about what would have happened if they'd been caught. They hadn't had time to do anything but run.

Changing the subject, Kelvin asked, "Why was Granite Lake at war with Arnaud the Black?"

"The story of Arnaud the Black is a tragic one," said Vannes. "Once someone I called friend, he was no longer the same man."

"Your friend did this to you?" asked Kelvin.

"His anger and thirst for revenge changed him," said Vannes. "It made him the vengeful and distrusting man who did this to me."

The wind blew through his branches, and it almost sounded like a heavy sigh. "The story really begins with Hugh of Loran. Being the leader of that city, he was in charge of the mentors who brought the apprentices down the path of enlightenment.

"Occasionally, a student would veer from the path, but there was no common man who could stop the Enlightened. They were too powerful, even early in their training, so it was necessary to bring in a Chaser to help rein in the wayward apprentice."

"Chasers have the Blood of Alemon but are not enlightened," remembered Elizabeth.

"The leaders were not enlightened, and that made Hugh bitter. He did not like that he could not control some of his own people."

"How could the leaders be weaker than their subjects?" asked Elizabeth.

"Exactly what Hugh wondered," answered Vannes. "The relationship between the leaders and the Enlightened goes all the way back to Alemon, the first known of the Enlightened. He and Galahad, the first leader of Loran, made a pact. Alemon was looking for a place to train people of his blood, and Galahad wanted Loran to grow strong enough to protect itself.

"The perfect match lasted for many years before Hugh's jealousy consumed him. He set out on a mission to find a way to fight the Enlightened. It was when he found the White Light of Florin that he began his war."

"The White Light of Florin?" asked Kelvin.

"Yes, it is the only substance known to man that can contain the Enlightened," answered Vannes.

"How did Hugh find it?" asked Elizabeth, interested because of the blood that ran through her veins.

"That task fell to me," he replied. "I was only a common soldier then, but he bribed me by telling me that I would be lord of my own land. Of course, I took him at his word and set about my mission.

"I read through as many of the old books as I could find. Scouring the vaults below Loran, I kept seeing a reference to the White. At first, I didn't even notice, but then I saw that it was always used in the context of scaring the Enlightened.

"I soon learned that the White was a bright light that emanated from a crystalline stone that could only be found near the town of Florin. So I made the trek to the northwest.

"Florin is covered in ice and inhabited by the people who work in the mines. The only way they survive in the extreme conditions is by working so far beneath the surface. The farther you go down into the dirt, the warmer it gets."

"I have never seen enough snow and ice to cover a town," commented Kelvin. "We get some during the winter, but it's never much and it never stays long."

Elizabeth nodded in agreement, remembering the winters in Westville.

"Underneath the ice and earth of the Northwestern Mountains lie great riches," continued Vannes. "Some have been discovered, and many have not been. The White Light of Florin comes from a rare form of quartz. The miners of Florin found it near the center of the earth. At that depth, it is in a liquid state. When it is brought to the surface, it cools and emits a constant and very bright, white light."

Kelvin and Elizabeth stood amazed at what they were hearing. Killer vines, talking trees, and now magic rocks; it was almost overwhelming for two who had lived such sheltered lives.

"Now that Hugh of Loran had a way to control the Enlightened, he set out to enforce his will," said Vannes. "Like a schoolyard bully, he waved his sword made of the white light at any Enlightened who crossed his path. It didn't matter if they were approaching him or just minding their own business. One flick of his blade in their direction would send them running."

"Why was he so cruel?" asked Elizabeth. "Did he have a reason to hate the Enlightened?"

"His mind wasn't right," answered Vannes. "He was constantly developing conspiracies about people trying to kill him. It wasn't long after he acquired the White Light that he completely snapped. Paranoia drove him to cast the enlightened out into the wilderness. Instead of sticking together, they scattered. This included Arnaud and the family he started in Loran."

Vannes paused then continued. "Arnaud was Alemon's ambassador to Loran ever since the initial pact with Hugh's ancestor, Galahad. He had done many things to help Hugh and the people of Loran, but Hugh was driven mad by power and forgot those things. They were given nothing but the clothes on their backs, which wasn't enough to brave the elements. That night was one of the coldest ever seen, and his son, who was just shy of his first birthday, died of exposure. When he returned from gathering food for his wife and daughter, they were gone too. Taken by wild animals.

"Arnaud blamed Hugh for his loss, and that is when the war began. Arnaud the Black's transformation into the evil man who did this to me was quick and complete. For the next year, he brooded in his homeland in the west. He plotted, planned, and gathered his army of disgruntled enlightened.

"His war began with small skirmishes that moved closer and closer to Loran. Hugh soon figured out that he was coming for revenge, so he readied his men, but they were no match.

"Arnaud's retribution was ruthless and efficient leaving the city destroyed and its citizens fleeing. That is when I arrived with these brave men. We were too late to save the city, but we fought off his army. For miles, we chased them. We were not going to let them kill any more of Loran's citizens.

"Hugh's people made their way to Granite Lake, but Arnaud never forgave me. He thought I betrayed him, but I just couldn't bear to see any more innocent people die. I didn't agree with Hugh, but I also didn't think the people of Loran should suffer for his mistakes."

"Why couldn't Hugh have used the White Light on Arnaud?" asked Kelvin.

"Hugh only had one sword made of the White Light," answered Vannes. "It was enough to fight one Enlightened but not a whole army. Knowing the weapon Hugh had acquired, Arnaud never presented himself to him.

"Legend says they did finally meet on the plains below Granite Lake. There, Hugh used his sword to bring the great Arnaud the Black to his knees. Arnaud was never seen again after that encounter. Hugh of Loran ended the black sorcerer's life and saved his people.

"Hugh succumbed to his own wounds from the battle and died shortly after. His son, Jorin, made peace with the enlightened and apologized for all of his father's wrongs. They were welcomed into Granite Lake where their teaching continued."

"Well, until Jorin fell victim to the same disease as his father and decided to eliminate the enlightened too," commented Elizabeth.

Kelvin noticed a small bird fly past Vannes just above his top branches. It glided by ever so peacefully, not seeming to notice its surroundings.

"What a pretty bird," commented Elizabeth.

"What was that!" exclaimed Vannes, overly suspicious. "Was it a black bird with a red chest?"

"Yes," replied Kelvin, looking at Elizabeth.

"Spies!" yelled the paranoid tree. "That is how he keeps an eye on me. Those red-bellied birds are the only ones to never land on me. The only explanation is that they are spies."

"Maybe they just aren't tired," offered Kelvin.

"No," he answered. "Those flying vermin are watching me. You should go before he gets a good look at you."

Elizabeth looked at Kelvin, her eyes conveying what he was thinking. How could a man so intelligent and with such a good memory be so paranoid? Maybe it was because he had come up against a force so strong that it had forever rooted him to the ground as a tree.

Not wanting to appear disrespectful, Kelvin nodded his understanding, and they proceeded into the thick grass on the opposite side they had come from, hand in hand so she could protect him from the vines.

Chapter 21

Borin, Lucan, and Owen marched onward through the overgrowth of the forest headed toward Westville. This was no leisurely stroll. They were fixated on the task given to them by Meric: to bring Donovan in for questioning.

Borin struggled with his leader's decision to detain his old friend. *What have I done to him? What will Meric do if we bring him back? Does he mean to destroy Donovan? Will we even be able to contain him? He is so powerful.*

Pondering these questions, Borin made up his mind. He could not betray his friend for a decision he did not believe in. Never before had he questioned his leader in this way, but this did not sit well with him. He did not understand or agree with Meric's motivation to be so quick to arrest Donovan.

He had to figure out a way to warn the high priest before they arrived. Interrupting Borin's thoughts, Lucan asked, "Will Donovan fight?"

"If we surprise him, yes, he will fight," answered Borin.

Lucan and Owen were both much younger than he was. Having finished their training only five years ago, they were just becoming used to the lifestyle of a Chaser. Not only were Chasers called upon to detain the Enlightened, but they were also charged with seeking out any signs of the craft being practiced in the world.

The younger men looked up to Borin. He was the only one of the three who had actual experience fighting the Enlightened. He had helped Aaron and Meric train them, and as a result, they came to him whenever they needed help.

The life of a Chaser was a solitary one. The land was divided among the three, and they crisscrossed it searching every corner, crevice, and alcove for the slightest hint of a greater knowledge. Any suspicious activity was immediately brought back to Meric at Granite Lake. He alone decided on a course of action.

Chasers were not enlightened, but they did have the Blood of Alemon in them. These three plus Meric and Aaron were the only Chasers left in Granite Lake.

"I have known Donovan a long time," said Borin. "He is very powerful and dangerous when crossed. He will be the most formidable opponent I have ever faced."

This statement sent shivers down the spines of the two younger men. They wondered if they were prepared for what they were about to encounter.

Borin was happy that his answer scared them into silence. This gave him time to develop his plan.

An hour went by without a word. Lucan and Owen dwelled on the powerful man they were going to try to detain, and the fear was evident on their faces. It only dissipated when they broke through the last bit of foliage and emerged onto a beach staring at nothing but blue water as far as they could see.

"Did we miss the city?" asked Owen, surprised.

"No," replied Borin with a chuckle. "The best way to enter the city unnoticed is from the east. The trail leading into town lies just down the beach." He said this as he pointed toward it.

"I want you two to stay hidden in the forest while I go speak to Donovan," Borin said. "As I said earlier, surprising him would be a mistake. I want to try and convince him to come and speak with Meric."

Completely trusting their mentor, Lucan and Owen didn't question him. They agreed and went back into the forest to wait. In fact, they were relieved that there might be an easier way to bring their powerful enemy to Meric.

Setting out on his own, Borin walked down the same path Henry and Kelvin had taken into Westville. He was not as cautious, however, as he knew exactly where he was headed.

Opening the large oak door, Borin entered the Temple of Apollo. Donovan froze, surprised to see his old friend. He had been milling about the worship chamber doing nothing in particular.

"Borin, my old friend!"

Smiling, he replied, "It's good to see you, Donovan."

"So, what brings you here?"

"I am afraid I do not bring happy tidings," answered Borin. "Is there somewhere private we can talk?"

Donovan led his guest past the statue of Apollo, down the hallway, and into his study. He took a seat next to his friend in the chairs in front of his desk.

Without wasting any time, Borin explained the situation to Donovan. He took him through everything that had happened since Kelvin and Elizabeth had been found in the forest.

"Thank you for helping them escape Granite Lake," said Donovan, after hearing the story. "They both have special qualities, and I believe they will play a part in what is about to befall our world."

Shifting in his chair to better face Borin, Donovan said, "So, it seems Meric has finally found a reason to have me eliminated. He has wanted to do that for many years. It was the other elders, most notably Aaron, who spared my life. Because of their support, Meric was powerless against me."

"You should not have begun training the girl," said Borin. "Now he has his reason, and it is valid according to our laws."

"My life is not my concern," answered Donovan. "I have envisioned dark times ahead, and she will play an important role in the outcome."

"I'm here to help you, old friend," replied Borin. "The other two Chasers are hiding in the forest near the beach. I will tell them you were already gone when I arrived."

Donovan looked at his friend as if to say thank you. He had always known Borin to be a good and loyal friend, and now he was again proving it.

"If Meric finds out about you helping me, he will execute you," warned Donovan.

"Like you, I have to do what I think is right," he answered.

Donovan put his hand on Borin's shoulder and nodded his thanks. Leaving, Borin felt good about his talk with Donovan. He knew he had made the right decision, and he wasn't worried about his two companions. They looked up to him and would never second-guess his decision.

Terryn looked out into the valley below at the city of Triopolis. The setting sun glistened off the deep-blue water of the bay to his left. He now understood why no one had ever conquered these people. Mountains completely encircled the city. He guessed that because of this protective barrier, the beasts from the Valley of Death did not disturb them either.

Roland joined his commander at the top of the mountain. "Naturally fortified," he commented. "This is where I would build a city."

"It's perfect," replied Terryn, savoring the view for a minute before asking his next question. "Have our scouts been sent out?"

"Yes, sir," answered Roland. "We had to send them through that sliver of forest between the fields and the beach on the southern edge." He pointed to the area to give Terryn a visual of the route.

The army would camp on the backside of the mountain just below the summit so their fires would not be seen from Triopolis. The element of surprise was crucial, and that was why Roland directed the scouts to go around the crop fields. He didn't want to alert the farmers of their presence.

As darkness fell, Terryn and Roland continued to develop their strategy over dinner in the commander's tent.

"I think we should attack through the forest on the north side of the city," suggested Roland. "A river runs through it from the mountains to the sea. It must be their main water supply, so I think it is imperative that we control it."

"I agree," replied Terryn. "We could also launch a silent attack from the river using boats. We would be in the heart of the city before they had time to react."

"A brilliant plan, My Lord," replied Roland, playing to his commander's pride. "The difficulty in that would be building the boats. It would take weeks to build enough boats to hold the army."

"This is true," agreed Terryn. "It would take too long. These men are best when riding into battle atop their warhorses anyway. Putting them in boats would only lessen their effectiveness."

Roland was impressed with his master's grasp of military strategy. This was a most unusual trait in a commander so young. It was true that Terryn was prone to overreaction and over zealousness, but when he was calm, he was very adept at developing strategy.

"In any case, a decision can only be made once our scouts return," stated Terryn. "The information they bring back will decide whether we attack from land or water."

"I agree, My Lord," Roland replied, taking a large bite of bread.

There was a moment of silence as the two men scarfed down the food in front of them. A deer had been taken earlier in the day, bringing a welcome treat of venison stew with brown bread to soak up the remaining sauce, all of it washed down with the last of the ale.

"I have heard that you began your military career as a scout," ventured Terryn.

"That is true," replied Roland. "I was a scout for four years during the Midaloan wars. For my success during the final battle, the king gave me a promotion to Knight, and I was able to work my way to my current position."

Terryn looked at Roland in disbelief. "You are the one who found the weakness in the walls of Midalo."

"Yes, sir, it was me," replied the humble soldier.

"Well, I didn't know I was in the presence of a hero of Westville!"

"I don't know about a hero, but thank you, My Lord," replied Roland.

Roland was a person who didn't like to be in the spotlight. Perhaps this was a trait learned during his time as a scout. He always felt a little embarrassed when being showered with praise, and he prided himself on his ability to stay out of the politics of his position.

"So tell me, based on your experience, how will our scouts enter the city?" Terryn bit into a tender piece of venison and chewed with vigor while he listened.

"It will not be difficult for them to move through the forest unseen," answered Roland. "They have had extensive training and practice in this art over the years. As they approach the city, they will find a place to hide and watch. They will be looking for the way people dress, act, and speak so they can mimic those traits to blend in. Clothes will be the first priority. They will acquire them by any means necessary. The easiest and quickest way to do this usually is to take them from someone."

Terryn understood what he was saying. The clothes would be taken from the unfortunate souls who crossed paths with the scouts.

"Once they look like the people they are spying on, they can enter the city. They will be looking for information on the enemy army, the availability of food and water, and how the people will react to an attack—whether they will fight or not."

"Sounds good," said Terryn. "What else?"

"We know food is prevalent with the many fields we have seen, so they will focus on the size and strength of the army and the general feeling among the populace."

"I hope all the people don't have the grit of the man who killed my uncle," responded Terryn.

"That is my concern as well, sir."

"Well, we won't be able to complete our plan until the scouts return," said Terryn. "So, let's continue in the morning." Agreeing, Roland left his commander for the night.

The night was uneventful as the army slept. Wolves howled in the distance alerting the guards, but they never came close enough to cause concern.

After having an early breakfast the next morning, the two leaders were once again standing on the rounded top of the mountain overlooking their target. The sun was just rising over the western peaks shining a spotlight on Triopolis.

"I have been informed that our scouts returned in the night," stated Terryn. "What have they discovered?"

"Yes, sir, they did return, and the information they brought back is most promising," answered Roland. "They don't seem to have an army at all, sir. Our scouts saw a few guards, but they seem to be more like local constables rather than soldiers, and only a few of them were seen patrolling the streets. Food seems to be plentiful, as we suspected, so it would be very difficult to starve them out if we were to be stuck in a long siege.

"The river does seem to be the main water supply, so we could use that to our advantage. We could cut it off or poison it in a siege, or we could attack from it with boats."

As always, Roland was a very thorough battle strategist and had looked at this siege from every angle. This was the main reason he'd had such a long and successful career in the army. He was viewed by the king as an indispensable asset to the security and stability of Westville.

"Since they have no army, we could walk in and take the city whenever we wanted," gloated Terryn.

"Possibly, but I think we should use caution," replied Roland.

"Roland, you are always so cautious," said Terryn. He was exuberant upon hearing that there didn't appear to be an army in this beautiful city they were about to invade. He had already decided what they would do.

"The king wants this city, and I will bring it to him!" he exclaimed. "We will move into position and attack today. Get the men ready and leave the provisions behind. We will ride at first light and take the city by nightfall!"

"Yes, sir," replied Roland, knowing he would not win this argument.

He had been with young, exuberant commanders before, and he knew that when they got excited about battle, nothing would change their mind. Some of them had been successful, and some had made fools of themselves. Roland wondered which one Terryn would be as he left the tent to prepare.

The sounds of armor being strapped on and blades being sharpened filled the camp. None of the men would admit it, but everyone was nervous for the coming battle. The morning dew covered the grass as soldiers scurried about in preparation. The hot breath of men and horses turned to a white mist as it breached the morning chill.

With the camp having been completely disassembled and packed into carts that would follow in the rear of the attack, Terryn prepared to address his troops.

"Men of Westville, you have braved the Valley of Death. You have beaten back the beasts that dared attack us. You have come so far and endured such hardships. I tell you now it will be worth it by the end of the day. I am so proud of every one of you for what you have achieved. Now it is time to reap the rewards of your struggle. The city below will be overwhelmed by our surprise, and we will plunder it. Now you shall have your reward!"

Excited and motivated by their commander's words, the army set off toward the forest at the base of the mountain to the north of the city. Terryn deferred to Roland on where the point of attack should come from. There was much less open space to cover by going through the woods, which would make the element of surprise more effective.

By early afternoon, they had reached the edge of the forest that lay at the northern doorstep of Triopolis. The only thing that lay between them and their prize were open fields, which their horses would cross with ease.

Each soldier dismounted and allowed his horse to eat, drink, and rest in preparation for the coming battle. Roland was giving instructions to each unit as the soldiers gnawed on lumps of bread they had brought with them.

Standing alone, Terryn looked out at the city in the distance, pondering his first big moment leading an army into battle. What would be his fate? Victory would mean returning as a hero of Westville, but if he suffered defeat, the people's judgment would be cruel.

"Sir, the men are mounted and ready," Roland announced, interrupting his thoughts.

"The calm before the storm can be so lonely," commented Terryn.

Turning around, he was surprised to see his army so quickly ready for battle. The awe-inspiring sight broke Terryn from his questioning thoughts. His confidence was returning as he jumped on the back of his Destrier.

Riding between the columns of his army in silence, he inspected his men nodding at some while patting others on the shoulder. Reaching the middle, he stopped and addressed the army.

"Soldiers of Westville, today you are not men. As the symbol on your chest represents, today you are bears! Fight like it and the day will be ours. To the prize!"

With that, his army stirred into action. Forty horses burst from the forest thundering toward the tranquil city of Triopolis. It wasn't long before they were at a full gallop tearing through a wheat field.

Farmers watched out of their windows as the magnificent-looking soldiers in silver armor rumbled past astride their battle horses. The sight was stunning and the sound was deafening. The people of Triopolis had never witnessed the sights and sounds of war, and they were terrified.

The soldiers were ordered by Roland not to kill the farmers and to destroy as little of the crops as possible. He understood the need for food once the city was taken. Without a good supply of food and water, the army would not be able to remain and would have to retreat.

By now, the people in the city heard the noise and felt the tremors as the horses rumbled closer. Roland was surprised that there was still no opposition. He couldn't believe no one was trying to stop them from taking the city. In the middle of this thought, he got his answer.

From around a row of buildings, he saw the soldiers of Triopolis coming to meet them. "I knew it was too good to be true," he murmured.

As they got closer, he saw only twenty poorly armed men. He wondered if this was a trick.

William Ward was at the head of his makeshift army as they rode out to meet Terryn. He was dressed in the blue uniform of the Guard of Triopolis. Their leather protection on the chest, forearms, and thighs was nothing compared to the steel-plated armor that the Army of Westville wore. Nonetheless, William marched his men with pride.

Terryn and Roland both rode to meet William with two soldiers for protection. Seeing this, William took his two most experienced men and rode out to parlay.

William was nervous and scared, but he would not show it to his men. He was in awe of the strength of the enemy army. Knowing he could never defeat them, he was trying to envision how he would win the discussion.

"My name is Terryn Rosser," the attacking commander announced as William approached the center of the field.

"What are your intentions here?" asked William.

"Are you the leader of these people?" asked Terryn.

"No, I am not," responded William.

"Are you able to speak on the leader's behalf?" asked Terryn, slightly irritated.

"Yes, my name is William Ward, and I command the City Guard."

"With this army?" replied Terryn, sarcastically.

William was smart enough to know he didn't want to get into an argument with the man leading this war machine. That would only lead to a battle he couldn't win.

"What is it you seek in Triopolis?" he asked.

"Our princess, Elizabeth, has taken up with a man from here named Kelvin," said Terryn. "He and his companion Henry murdered my uncle, and I seek revenge."

William's eyes grew wide at the mention of his friend Henry. *What has Henry gotten himself into now?*

Movement in the enemy lines caused Roland to look at his men to make sure they were ready. Tensions rode high wondering what the other side would do. The defenders parted down the middle and a man appeared from behind them. Carl Drake slowly rode toward the commanders.

When he joined them, William announced him as their leader. Terryn gave a slight bow in greeting. William quickly updated Carl on the information about Henry and Kelvin.

"The three of them are together on the loose?" asked Carl.

"Henry's body was discovered with my uncle's," responded Terryn. "We believe it is just Kelvin and Elizabeth in the wild. We were hoping they would have come here by now."

"They have not," replied Carl.

Terryn looked into Carl's eyes skeptically, trying to determine the truth. "My intention is to remain here until the murderers arrive," he stated.

"What makes you think they will come here?" asked Carl. "They are probably dead somewhere in the forest. Kelvin wouldn't know how to survive out there."

"Nevertheless, we will stay," replied Terryn. "My army will remain camped outside the city, but I would like accommodations provided for my lieutenant and myself," commanded Terryn.

Carl had no choice. He had to give the captain whatever he wanted because they had no force to oppose them. His twenty-man guard were little more than merchants with clubs, and everyone present knew that.

Following William and Carl, Terryn entered Triopolis accompanied by Roland and ten soldiers for their protection. The first thing Roland noticed was that the city had no wall. The land transitioned from field to city. *One will have to be constructed,* he mused. *Otherwise, it will be difficult to defend the city.*

Carl led them to a house owned by Eric Feldstein, which was situated many blocks from the city center and hadn't been used in over a month since the Feldsteins had moved into a new larger home near Town Hall.

Later that evening, Terryn and Roland were having dinner. Their guards were stationed outside. "I am surprised they were completely unprepared and gave in just like you thought they would," Roland praised his captain.

"I remembered my uncle's teachings," he replied. "He taught me about the Battle of Winslow."

"I have never heard of it," said Roland, surprised.

"That's because it wasn't a battle at all," replied Terryn. "Your studies focused on the major battles our ancestors fought. Winslow was a place taken by Apollo during the early years. Similar to our current situation, the town of Winslow had no army and never suspected a conquering force would approach them. The key was getting a small group into the city. These people don't realize it yet, but their city is already lost.

"Just like Winslow, Triopolis has been so isolated from the rest of the world that they have no idea armies like ours exist. Because of this, they have only needed a small number of guards to keep the peace and fend off the occasional wild animal."

"A great intelligence victory, My Lord," responded Roland. His respect for his new captain was growing significantly.

"Tomorrow our men will enter the city," commanded Terryn. "They have let us in, and now we will make them submit to our will. They will recognize King William as their sovereign and me as their new leader."

"I will prepare the men, sir," replied Roland.

"Where is the bishop?" yelled Carl Drake, as he paced in his office at Town Hall.

"My men have not been able to find him," replied William.

"How could he abandon us in this time of need?" lamented Carl.

William was secretly happy that the bishop wasn't there. The power he had over Carl maddened him, and he hoped that the assembly chief would now see the bishop for who he truly was.

"How did my son end up in their city?" asked Carl.

"They were last seen on the morning of that big storm," recounted William. "They must have survived the storm, and it carried them to wherever this army is from."

"It had to be Henry," said Carl, not really listening to what William was saying. "My son couldn't kill anyone. Henry dragged him into this mess." Carl was very angry at being stuck in this impossible situation.

The day when Kelvin and Henry went missing, Carl did not mourn. Even with the thought of his only surviving son dead, he could not bring himself to tears. The man had hardened himself toward his son, and not even death could change that.

The death of his wife, when his two boys were very young, had taken a toll on Carl. He mourned for months, battling depression with bouts of rage. The loss was difficult, but it was only after the death of his younger son that he vowed to never let himself get that close to anyone again. Unfortunately, Kelvin bore the brunt of this decision being the only family member still alive.

William was pained to know that Henry really was dead. The confirmation given by the enemy commander started the mourning process all over for him. Henry was and always would be his friend.

"What do we do now?" Carl asked William. "We don't have the means to fight them."

"Maybe we can help them find their princess," suggested William. "We know the forest around here very well, and if she and Kelvin are hiding in the hills, we can find them. At the very least, it will buy us time to figure something else out."

"I suppose you're right," answered Carl. "They must be somewhere around Triopolis if the army is here. They were tracking them after all."

The wooden door suddenly flew open slamming loudly against the wall. Six large, armed soldiers entered the room.

"You are to be detained at the pleasure of Terryn, commander of the Army of Westville," said the leader of the group.

Their panic-stricken faces were obvious. Trying to speak, no words came out as two soldiers apprehended each detainee. With hands tied behind their backs, they were escorted out of Town Hall.

The bishop fled the city with five of his most loyal men when he saw the army approaching. Like everyone else in Triopolis, he had never seen such a spectacle. Knowing it wouldn't turn out well for them, he headed to his retreat in the mountains to the west. This was the lab where his real experiments took place.

It was ten years ago when the bishop discovered the room beneath Town Hall. It all started with a dream. He was lying in bed one night tossing and turning, unable to sleep. The window was open, but the summer air outside was completely still. He stared at the ceiling begging for sleep when all of a sudden a single gust of wind entered the room, circled his bed, and left through the same window.

When he woke the next morning, he remembered a very vivid dream. He was in the dream, but it was as if he was watching himself from a distance. He was walking through a dark room filled with clutter. Even though he didn't recognize the room, he felt that it was the basement of Town Hall.

Walking directly toward the north wall, he entered a most amazing room. He didn't stop until he was directly in front of the large painting of Luther. At the time, he didn't know who Luther was, but he would soon learn.

That day he went into the basement archives of Town Hall and began his search. Knowing which wall the room was behind, he went straight to it. A large bookshelf was covering the place he entered in the dream. Each item had to be taken off the heavy shelf before he could move it. After sliding one side away from the wall, he had room to work.

He used a large hammer to search for the entrance to the room. Swinging with all his might, he tore into the wall. It didn't take long to puncture it, revealing the narrow corridor.

Entering the room, he knew that if he walked forward, he would come upon a circle of torches, and that was exactly what happened. He lit the torches surrounding the basin, and the room came alive.

The bishop was amazed at the various instruments and symbols written on the walls. Making it to the desk at the back of the room, he looked up at the painting he remembered from his dream.

He wondered who this man was. He instantly felt the same strange breeze he'd felt the night before, but this time it blew past him toward the painting. As he watched, the word *LUTHER* was slowly etched into the bottom center of the canvas in a chilling red color.

By the time the *R* was written, the breeze was gone. *What kind of sorcery is this?* he wondered, remembering the strange breeze the night before.

The bishop recalled these things as he headed to his mountain retreat, which was located to the west of Triopolis inside a cave cut into the mountain. The natural feature had a number of tunnels that he had converted into rooms. Much of his experimental work took place here, far away from anyone who might question it.

The bishop's man, Baldwin, entered the room. "What have you learned about the army?" asked the bishop.

"They have moved into the city," Baldwin replied. "They marched straight to Town Hall this morning. In front of the statue of the gods, their commander claimed the city for his king. He met with Assembly Chief Drake, but when they adjourned, Drake came back to the statue and swore allegiance to King William of Westville!"

"He was no doubt forced to do so," responded the bishop. "We could never fight against an army of that size."

"Have you ever seen such an army?" asked Baldwin.

"No," replied the bishop, pondering his next move.

Chapter 22

The two weary travelers gazed up the steep cliff, both grumbling silently. "I don't know if I can do this again," commented Kelvin.

"It looks like the right spot," Elizabeth replied, looking at the cave about halfway up the cliff. "The picture looks identical to this rock. We haven't seen anything even close to that description until now," she added.

Knowing she was right, he stopped his complaining and planned the best way to tackle the climb.

Kelvin looked at the map and again at the cliff. He sighed knowing that this was the correct cave.

"At least it doesn't look like a difficult climb," he grumbled.

They stood before what looked like a single large rock structure jutting up from the ground. About fifty feet up from where they stood, a cave was carved into the rock.

The rock face was jagged and uneven leaving many places to grab onto and many crevices perfect for footholds.

"This actually looks like an easier climb than the black wall at Granite Lake," said Elizabeth, optimistically.

She was the first to grab onto the mountain and take a step while Kelvin followed closely behind. They easily scaled the rock wall because the cracks were positioned to almost perfectly resemble a ladder.

Reaching the top, they sat on the ledge that led into the cave to catch their breath and have a drink of water. "So, this is where that madman Luther was imprisoned," commented Elizabeth.

"I guess so," replied Kelvin, feeling a little nervous.

"Do you think his body is still in here?" she asked.

"I never thought about that," he replied, thinking about the unpleasant sight of Luther's bones. "I am just hoping to find something that can help in my fight against the bishop."

The outside of the cave looked unspectacular. There really weren't any features to speak of. It simply looked like a hole in a mountain. They took their first step in and jumped backward as a group of startled bats flew out.

They both laughed nervously to relieve the tension. "Let's try that again," said Kelvin.

The inside of the cave was dark and cool. The bright sunlight did not penetrate more than a few feet in, but Kelvin was prepared with his flint and steel. Wrapping what was left of his char cloth around the end of a stick he found outside the cave, he lit it.

"Much better," Elizabeth responded when the cave was suffused with light.

They breathed in the stagnant air that smelled like dry rock dust. This cave had not seen water in many years. The watermarks on the walls proved that water had once flowed here, but it had been hundreds of years since it dried up. Kelvin hoped this meant there were no current residents.

Walking cautiously as if something was going to jump out at them, they moved deeper into the cave. The excitement of finding it was quickly wearing off as they trudged onward, finding nothing.

"I expected more," said Kelvin, disappointed.

"Me too," she replied. "I guess it is fitting since we are entering a tomb."

"I never thought of it that way," he said.

Coming upon a fork in the path, they didn't know which way to go. Kelvin looked at the map, but it said nothing about the inside of the cave.

"We could always go one way and turn around if it isn't right," Elizabeth suggested.

"In the maze below the school, every wrong turn led to a trap," Kelvin replied, nervously. "The Enlightened don't allow for mistakes."

They scanned the walls looking for a clue as to which direction to go, but there was no indication. The only thing they discovered were thick cobwebs that covered them like wallpaper.

"I hope we don't come across the creature that spun all these webs," said Elizabeth.

Kelvin didn't respond but shuddered at the thought.

"I feel a sense of foreboding, like we are in danger, but I can't tell which direction it's coming from," she alerted him.

Elizabeth's inability to control her insight sometimes frustrated her. Knowing she could see into the future was one thing, but controlling it was quite another. Now that she was comfortable with her abilities, it was discouraging when they could not be used at her command.

"I think it might be the cave," he said. "It's a little spooky in here."

"Yeah, you're probably right," she replied. "Let's try this way."

Walking into the right tunnel, they took an immediate left turn and then a sharp right that left them staring at a small vertical crevice.

"Is this the end?" asked Elizabeth.

"I think the cave just narrows," he answered, holding the torch in the gap. "It looks like it opens up again."

Elizabeth, taking the lead, turned her body and side-stepped into the tight space.

"You have no fear, do you?" Kelvin asked.

She laughed. "It's from growing up with all boys. Most of the noble kids my age were boys. I would have been teased if I was afraid to keep up with them."

"Well, I'm glad you're so brave," Kelvin said with a laugh.

The space was slightly bigger than the width of their bodies, so it was a little claustrophobic, but they didn't have to squeeze. They only had to go about fifteen feet before it opened into a larger area.

"You were right," said Elizabeth. "There is another room. Hand me the torch."

Carrying the light, she looked around the chamber. The first thing she noticed was a large pile of old dead wood, branches, and leaves. It was on their left against the wall and almost reached the ceiling.

"I wonder how all that got here," said Elizabeth. "Nothing is growing in here, so someone had to have brought it in."

"Is that water?" asked Kelvin, as they made their way to the back of the room.

A small trickle of water ran down the wall into a pool on the floor. Based on the stains on the wall, it looked like this stream had been flowing for quite a long time. The flowing water had also worn away the floor where it landed, creating a small basin.

"It's strange that there would be water here when the other part of the cave was so dry," commented Kelvin.

He was answered by the loudest scream he had ever heard. The ear-piercing wail echoed throughout the chamber. "Scorpion!" she yelled.

As Kelvin turned to see the beast, it matched Elizabeth's scream with another horrific screech. He was surprised to see the terrifying arachnid's head scrape against the ceiling. It was standing on the back four of its eight legs towering over them.

"It must have come from behind that pile of wood," yelled Kelvin.

The solid black scorpion struck a menacing pose with its outstretched claws opening and closing in anticipation. With it slowly moving closer, they could see the massive size of its clamp-like claws. The terrifying creature approached with the confidence of knowing there was nothing in the cave to match it.

It was now close enough for Kelvin and Elizabeth to see the beak-like mouth of the beast. Standing on all eight legs the scorpion was the same height as a fully-grown adult, and it stared into Kelvin's eyes.

Then, in a show of force, it raised its two tails scraping them against the roof of the cave and showering its victims with dust and debris.

"It has two stingers!" yelled Kelvin, reaching for his dagger ready to do battle.

Each tail was tipped with a large barb used to inject a poison that would kill within seconds.

"Stay away from its tails!" shouted Elizabeth.

She was proud of Kelvin as he strode into battle without hesitation. For the first time since she had met him, he didn't concern himself with the danger of the situation. He just jumped in knowing what had to be done.

The scorpion made the first move thrusting one of its large claws at Kelvin. Missing him it struck the rocky floor of the cave causing shavings of rock to fly up. Kelvin evaded the attack by stepping to the right, but the other claw was bearing down on him. Moving to the left, he avoided contact, and more rock shards flew up into the air.

Elizabeth didn't know what to do. With no weapon to help fight, she watched as Kelvin tangled with the beast.

In between thrusts, the scorpion bellowed that piercing shriek, which echoed throughout the cave, making it sound even more terrifying.

It proved to be intelligent, learning from its unsuccessful attempts to thrust at its prey. Kelvin stood waiting with dagger in hand for the creature's next move. This time the scorpion used its claw in a swiping motion, knocking Kelvin off his feet.

"Ah!" he screamed, as his back hit the ground.

In a continuous motion, while its right claw was knocking Kelvin off his feet, the left claw was wide open and bearing down on him. Before he could react, the left vise of the beast gripped his body. Lifting him off the ground, the scorpion let out another terrifying, victorious scream.

In over confidence from besting Kelvin, the scorpion had forgotten about Elizabeth. She had not been noticed as she quietly moved around the side of the beast. Wedging the torch between two stones and picking up a large stick that was lying at the base of the wall, she swung it with all her might.

The stick connected with the leg holding Kelvin. The force of the blow caused the claw to release, and Kelvin fell to the ground. Anger was in the creature's voice as it bellowed loudly. It turned toward Elizabeth, and she could see a thirst for revenge in its eyes.

Before it could strike at her, Kelvin jumped on one of its tails. He latched on just below the fearsome barb. The scorpion thrashed about trying to free itself from Kelvin's grasp. Out of the corner of his eye he saw the other tail coming toward him.

He used one hand to hold on and the other to attack the second tail. The strength of the beast was overwhelming, causing the dagger to turn in his hand. It was now parallel to his arm with the handle still in his palm and the point further down his arm.

Kelvin's hand slowed the tail's descent, but it wasn't enough. The scorpion was too strong. With the barb approaching his head, Kelvin had to act quickly. He pulled his hand off the tail, spun the dagger around, and in one smooth motion, sliced off the spike.

The beast lifted its head and shrieked in pain and anger, but the attack did not abate. It swung its barbless tail at Kelvin, knocking him to the ground.

Elizabeth saw her opportunity and charged toward the creature's head. She thrust upward with the stick as its head came falling back down, a blood-curdling scream emitting from its throat.

The stick penetrated the hard exoskeleton and into the creature's soft tissue leaving its head impaled. The scorpion was dead.

Elizabeth ran around the carcass of the beast, reaching for Kelvin as he sat on the ground dazed. "Are you okay?" she asked, her eyes filled with concern. Falling to her knees next to him, she embraced him, pulling his head close to her chest.

"I am much better now," he said, enjoying the loving embrace. "And I'm impressed that you got in the kill shot."

Elizabeth shrugged off his compliment and held him tight, so proud of his daring and fearlessness in fighting the beast. A light kiss on his head brought frenzied emotions. He could feel the love in her embrace.

No longer wanting to control himself, he reached his lips to hers and gazed at her longingly. Seeing the lust in her eyes, he fulfilled their mutual desire. The passionate kiss only intensified as he put his arms around her. His fingers ran through her hair, pulling her head close.

Elizabeth felt things she had never felt before. The once strong woman now felt helpless in his arms. The feeling was exhilarating as they conveyed their passion through their lips. Words were not necessary as feelings and emotions were shown through their tender embrace.

When the kiss ended, they remained on the floor leaning against the wall, not noticing the chill from the cold stone. It couldn't penetrate their bodies, still overwhelmed from the heat of passion.

Basking in the glow of each other, Kelvin held her tight. Elizabeth nestled her head in the crook of his neck, and they enjoyed the moment together.

As the heat of their passion slowly subsided, they felt the cold from the floor seeping into their bones. Kelvin was still in pain from his battle with the massive scorpion. He inspected his body for damage. Looking at a colorful bruise on his arm, Elizabeth asked, "Is it bad?"

"No, it's just a bruise."

With that, they stood and only glanced at the scorpion as they left this part of the cave. Neither said a word as both were secretly worried that the terrifying beast would come back to life.

Backtracking, they found themselves at the fork in the cave, and this time they headed to the left. Kelvin was in the lead and carrying the torch.

Elizabeth was proud and excited at the prospect of Kelvin becoming more confident in his abilities. She wondered if he had finally broken from his past and moved on from the guilt of his brother's death.

They were again forced to make two quick turns, the first to the right and then to the left. Upon turning left, they entered another large chamber with a green glow emanating from the walls.

"This is what the walls of the maze below the school looked like," said Kelvin. "Do you sense anything in here?"

"No, I have no insight at all," she responded. "It's almost as if I have completely lost my gift. I don't feel fear or danger either. I feel nothing at all."

Perplexed, they walked into the room looking in all directions for any clue of Luther's presence. They saw nothing. The walls and floors were clear.

"At least there's nowhere for a giant scorpion to hide," commented Kelvin with a laugh.

"That's a very good point," she replied, returning the laugh.

Circling the room a couple more times, they did not find another doorway. "Where do we look now?" asked Elizabeth. "There has to be a doorway somewhere."

"If Luther really is here . . ." Kelvin said.

They continued to search every crack and crevice for a clue that would answer that question. Hours went by and their frustration grew.

Finally, Kelvin flopped onto the floor and sighed. "This is hopeless," he said. "I don't know where else to go."

Elizabeth walked over and sat on the floor next to him. "Let's take a break," she suggested.

They both wondered if the map was wrong.

"How will we ever stop the bishop if we can't find Luther?" Kelvin said. "What if the bishop found him first?"

He was consumed with dread until Elizabeth asked, "Is there anything you remember from the maze that might help us here?"

"Not that I can think of. Everything in the maze referred to finding the map."

Kelvin took a long refreshing drink of water from his water skin. It felt good flowing down his parched throat. They had been so focused on finding the passageway that they hadn't realized they were becoming dehydrated.

Rest and water had a rejuvenating effect on the explorers. They jumped to their feet and began the search anew. They each took a side and began looking at every square inch of wall for any sign. It wasn't long before Elizabeth yelled, "Look, it's the sign of the Enlightened—the same one we saw in the temple!"

Kelvin ran over to her, and they stared at the eye encircled by two golden rings. It was near the left corner at about eye level on the wall. The feelings of doubt that had crept into their minds instantly vanished.

They inspected the wall around the symbol more closely without success. No other writings or drawings were there to give them guidance. The wall gave them no clues other than the symbol of the Enlightened.

Again becoming discouraged, Kelvin leaned his back against the wall, only to discover that this part of the wall was not solid at all. A quick scream escaped his lips as the wall seemed to suck him in, and then he was gone.

Elizabeth tried to grab his leg as he fell backward into the wall, but she was too late. Touching the exact spot on the wall, she realized what happened. The wall was not solid here. It was some sort of doorway.

It felt like water, but when she pulled her hand back, it wasn't wet. Without any hesitation, she went head first into the wall.

It felt as if she was swimming underwater with her eyes open. There was Kelvin lying on his back on the floor looking up at her. Coughing, she came through on the other side.

"I didn't think to hold my breath, but it is liquid," she said, feeling foolish.

"I did the same thing," replied Kelvin, trying to make her feel better.

Because of their excitement from walking through a wall, they didn't realize they were being watched. Elizabeth offered her hand to help him to his feet all the while not noticing the old man staring at them.

They both looked at the room in front of them. They met the eyes of the old man.

Kelvin immediately recognized Luther's facial features from the painting underneath Town Hall, but he looked much older.

The once great sorcerer looked like a shell of his former self. Gray hair had overtaken him, and he was hunched over like the toll of hundreds of years were finally defeating him. Wrapped in a tattered brown robe, he stared in shocked surprise at his guests.

"Is he a ghost?" whispered Elizabeth.

"Ghost, ha!" exclaimed the old man. "Although I admit some days I do feel like a ghost."

They stood watching the old man mill about, seemingly doing nothing at all. He wandered aimlessly from his bed to his makeshift kitchen to his table all the while talking to himself. At times, he acted like they weren't even there.

What a lovable old man, thought Elizabeth.

They were standing in an area about ten feet wide with the wall they came through behind them and a wall of bright white light separating them from the old man.

The wall of light spanned the distance between the two sides of the cave. The light emanated from three small stones on the floor at evenly spaced intervals.

Stepping closer to the white light, Kelvin held out his hand. He didn't feel anything as his fingers pushed through the rays. Multiple times he put his hand into the light and quickly pulled it out, inspecting it to see if it was burned or otherwise affected by the light. Each time he found nothing wrong with his hand.

Looking over at Elizabeth, he noticed it clearly affecting her differently. She was writhing in pain holding her head in her hands. Kelvin quickly jumped between her and the light. Putting his arms around her, he guided her away from the dangerous rays.

Neither had seen that the old man had taken notice of Elizabeth's reaction to the light. A slight smirk crossed his lips as he pondered the implications of her body's response to the radiant stones.

Kelvin could feel her strength coming back as he held her upright. "What happened?" she stammered, now able to open her eyes.

"The White Light of Florin," answered Kelvin, pointing at the stones producing the wall of light. "Vannes told us about this powerful weapon against the Enlightened. I remembered his story as soon as I saw the clear stones."

Looking back at the light, they saw the old man still about his business. Noticing a pot of water over the fire, it looked like he was making tea.

Seeing a stick in the corner, Kelvin retrieved it and walked up to the light. Reaching the old tree branch into the light, he moved it down toward one of the clear stones. The stones were easily accessible from this side because there was no protective barrier.

The old man, however, could not see the stones from where he stood. His captor had sunken them into the floor and secured a larger stone to the floor directly in front of them.

For someone who didn't have the Blood of Alemon, there was no harm in touching the stones, but Kelvin was a little unsure if there was any danger in moving them. Using the stick, he pried it out of the small recess and slid it far enough to allow Elizabeth to enter the cell.

He quickly followed not wanting to give Luther any chances to escape. Now knowing the stones were safe to touch and move, he easily slid the stone back into its position with his hand.

The old man was the first to speak. "I haven't seen another human being in five hundred and twenty-one years. Who are you?"

Elizabeth introduced herself and Kelvin before asking him the same question. "This is Luther," answered Kelvin before the old man could reply.

"Ah, so Donovan didn't succeed in wiping my name from existence," replied Luther. "You know who I am." He showed obvious pleasure in that fact.

"Young man, I am the Luther of whom you speak," he confirmed, looking directly into Kelvin's eyes. "Although, I am much older and weaker now, I'm afraid. I don't have much strength left in me."

Elizabeth noticed Kelvin rubbing his forehead as if he was in pain. "What is it?" she asked.

"Nothing, I just have a bit of a headache."

Breaking his gaze, Luther groaned as if the pains of growing old were overtaking him, and he hobbled over to the pot of water hanging over the fire. "Would you like some tea?" They both accepted their host's hospitality.

"How is it that you have tea after having been imprisoned here for so long?" asked Elizabeth.

"Oh, I have friends who bring me gifts from time to time," he answered, walking toward a grouping of three chairs.

Kelvin and Elizabeth looked at each other. Both were thinking the same thing. *He said he hadn't seen anyone in over five hundred years. Who are his friends?*

Feebly shuffling his feet, Luther finally made it to a chair and flopped into it. He motioned with his shaky hand for them to join him in the other two chairs by the fire.

How could this weak old man have been the most powerful Enlightened in the world? Kelvin asked himself. *He seems so kind and gentle. Could he really be a threat anymore?*

It was almost sad watching the old man as he tried to spread a blanket over his legs. His hands were not as dexterous as they once were, causing him to fumble with the torn and shabby old thing.

It must be difficult for a man who was once so powerful to have succumbed to the effects of time while being imprisoned here, empathized Kelvin. They watched and waited as he stared at the ceiling mumbling incoherently.

"And where are you from?" asked Luther, finally getting settled with his blanket.

They looked at each other briefly not knowing how to answer then Elizabeth took the lead. "We are from Westville," she said, not wanting him to know their destination.

"Westville . . . I have only been there once many, many years ago," he replied, catching her gaze and holding it for a moment. "Tell me about your homeland."

"It is a rocky place east of the mountains right on the Great Sea," replied Elizabeth. "Most days are gray, but when the sun does shine, we have a wonderful beach to enjoy."

Kelvin was looking around the room for clues that could help in his fight against the bishop. He was certain that in finding Luther, he would find a way to defeat the man in control of Triopolis.

Elizabeth was also searching the room with her eyes. The walls were mostly empty except for a small cloth hanging in the center of the opposite wall. She stared at it trying to make out the faded design when she saw it rustle slightly.

The first thing she saw was its small black beak, then its eyes, and finally the bird's head. A small black bird was peeking around the cloth, and as it did so, she saw sunlight.

The birds are his friends!

Remembering the paranoia of Vannes and his story about Arnaud the Black's spying birds, she put it together. Looking at Kelvin and Luther, she realized that they did not see it. Locking eyes with her, the bird quickly pulled its head back behind the cloth without a sound.

"It sounds like a wonderful place," said the old man, sipping his tea. "And how did you find me?"

"We just happened upon this cave and decided to explore it," Kelvin said in a casual tone. He knew that mentioning the map would give away the fact that he was from Triopolis.

"Hmm," muttered Luther, knowing this wasn't the truth. "How did you know how to get through the wall?"

Looking at Elizabeth, Luther said, "Because of the Viridian Powder, you would not have been able to see behind the wall."

Panic showed on her face. "How did you know about my abilities?" she asked.

"We always know one of our own kind."

"He saw your reaction to the stones," said Kelvin, confidently.

"What is Viridian Powder?" she asked.

"It's what causes the green glow in the outer chamber," answered Luther. "I am sure you noticed that the walls were lined with brick. These bricks are made with the green powder that causes them to glow.

"When an Enlightened is surrounded by the green glow, they lose their abilities of foresight. It's why you could not see this room behind the wall."

Realizing he was going too far, Luther sat back in his chair. He didn't want to alarm them and ruin the only chance he might ever have of escaping this place. Falling back into his murmuring, he fumbled with his teacup to prove his feeble state.

"Who imprisoned you here?" asked Kelvin.

"A man I once called friend," he answered. "I was a fool. I was over confident, and he tricked me."

"Who tricked you?" asked Elizabeth.

"My mortal enemy, Donovan." Luther stared at the floor as the anger and pain of betrayal swelled inside him.

"One day, the two of us were walking along a path in the forest when a group of bandits attacked us," he began. "I felt confident that these raiders would be no match for two powerful Enlightened.

"A struggle ensued, and we fought side by side. Each man that attacked was quickly repelled. It was only when three of the men simultaneously attacked me from the front that the deception was complete.

"I felt a stinging sensation in my back from the spell hurled at me from behind. The traitor Donovan had caused every muscle in my body below my head to go numb. I was frozen. I could do nothing but blink. It is a frightful feeling to see your enemies coming and be unable to protect yourself.

"Unable to move, I watched as the three men approached me. This time they did not carry their usual weapons. In their hands were the round white stones you see here on the floor. I pushed and pulled, trying to break free from the unseen force, but it was useless. My body did not move.

"Fear gripped me as my captors moved in with their glowing white trap. I tried to fight to no avail. My fear turned to anger as I looked upon Donovan with his smirk of success. Then the walls of my prison connected while the three men encircled me."

"We know the feeling of betrayal," sympathized Elizabeth. "We almost fell victim to the third member of our party's deceit."

Kelvin nodded in agreement as he considered what Lynessa's actions could have brought upon them.

"I was then put in a cage and brought here," continued Luther. "You have felt the pain of the light, Elizabeth. You know what brutal misery I endured on my journey here. I was almost happy to be thrown into this cell just so the suffering would stop."

He slowly got up from his chair and headed over to the pot of hot water to refresh his tea.

While Luther worked near the fire, Kelvin and Elizabeth felt much sadness for the lonely old man. "Should we help him leave this cave so he can spend what time he has left in freedom?" asked Elizabeth.

Luther's ears perked up when he heard her question. He wondered if his ruse had been successful.

"I feel bad for him," she said. "He doesn't look like he could still be capable of the horrible things he did hundreds of years ago. It seems as though the stones have taken their toll on him."

"Oh, the years have not been kind," said the old man, as he came back to his chair and sat down with the occasional sound of creaking joints. They watched as Luther's shaking hand lifted the teacup to his mouth.

Elizabeth looked at Kelvin to see if he was in agreement that they should free the old man. He nodded his agreement.

"Well, we should be going," said Elizabeth, getting up from her chair.

"Yes, we have put you out long enough," replied Kelvin, grimacing in pain from his now throbbing head.

"No trouble at all," said Luther, remaining in his chair. "I would give you a proper send-off if I could, but I just don't think my old bones can get back up."

They both looked on with pity, and Kelvin offered, "We think you have served your time for your past crimes. We think that you should spend your remaining days in freedom."

His eyes lit up at the prospect of being free. "Oh, you are too kind. I would very much like to see the sun again, as I do not have much time left in this world."

Knowing it was safe, Kelvin walked over to the middle white stone and picked it up. He moved it next to the stone on the left creating a clear space for Elizabeth and Luther to exit unharmed.

As the gap in the wall of light grew, Luther prepared himself by standing and slowly walking toward the exit. Wanting to run, he managed to remain calm. The moment Kelvin dropped the stone and made an opening wide enough, Luther was gone.

"He tricked us!" yelled Elizabeth, embarrassed.

The minute the old man was out of sight, the pain in their heads diminished. They both stood in anticipation of something else happening, but nothing did. Disappointment soon overtook them when they realized he was not coming back. They hung their heads low in dismay, walking back through the wall and into the cave.

"I can't believe we fell for that," groaned Kelvin, upset with himself.

The climb down the cliff was silent as they both mentally replayed the event. Each was pondering the ramifications of what had just happened and how disappointed Donovan would be.

When Elizabeth reached solid ground, they turned to see Luther appear from behind a nearby tree. He looked much younger. The gray hair had turned black, the wrinkles on his face had gone, and he was no longer slouched over.

"You tricked us!" yelled Kelvin, angrily.

"Yes, I did," he admitted. "I am sorry, but I had to get out of that place." His red robe rustled in the light breeze as he stood before them.

A black bird swooped down from the cliff and landed on Luther's shoulder. Elizabeth recognized it as the same bird that she had seen in his cell.

It looked as though the bird whispered something in Luther's ear before flying away. That's when they heard the sound of approaching hoofs. From around the side of the rocky cliff trotted a solid black stallion. Knowing who its master was, it walked directly to Luther.

"Because of your generosity, I will grant you one favor," he offered, mounting the powerful animal.

Looking at each other, they tried to think of something they might want. Not letting them answer, Luther said, "At a time when all hope is lost, seek me out and my help shall he yours."

Chapter 23

Carl felt a strange sense of relief as he looked out the window of his office from Town Hall. He couldn't explain it, but it was as if his mind was becoming clearer. The constant headache he had endured for over a year was finally beginning to diminish. He assumed it was because of the stress of his job, but there had been no time more stressful than now, and it was finally going away.

Upon mentioning this to William, who was with him in the office, his reply was "I have noticed that your eyes have recently turned blue."

"Really?" he exclaimed, running to the mirror he kept on a shelf to his left. "It is true, they have changed back!"

"It was about a year ago they curiously turned to this cloudy brown color," continued Carl. "I just assumed it was from the stress too."

"Strange that they both happened at the same time," replied William.

They both pondered the physical change in Carl, but neither had any ideas as to why it happened. Carl was just happy he was beginning to feel normal again.

"Funny that the sun is out but the feeling is so gloomy," commented Carl, staring out the window. "People move about their normal business, but there is no cheer. You can see the despair in their faces."

Carl watched as a husband and wife walked down the street with their two children. They didn't even look at Town Hall or the statue of the founders out front. This was the way of things now, being occupied by the foreign army.

After being arrested by soldiers the day before, they were taken to the house commandeered by Roland. There the two captives were interrogated as to the nature and personality of the high-ranking officials of Triopolis. It was Roland himself doing the interrogating while Terryn watched.

Roland wanted to know who would submit to their will and who would fight. He knew all too well the importance of taking out rebels as quickly as possible. Otherwise, they would fester and grow, bringing more and more rebels to their cause.

They could hear the busy soldiers on the other side of the door of the room they sat in. Orders were being shouted down the hall and into the other rooms on the ground floor of the house. It had been transformed from a quiet living space into a bustling office building.

William thought he recognized this as the sitting room of the Reynolds' house. He had only been to the house of Gerald Reynolds a couple of times, and this looked like a room in which he had once shared a drink and cigar with him.

Now an elderly man, Gerald had specialized in the farming tools trade and made a nice living for his family, as evidenced by the large house he had built.

He wondered what had happened to the poor man and his family.

Their interrogation was not too unpleasant. In fact, they were treated fairly well, having been given bread and wine. There was no physical element to this questioning. It was quite civil.

After William and Carl gave the names of the other members of the Assembly, Roland addressed each of them individually. They were both surprised at how easily the information flowed from their mouths. Neither of them sensed much danger in the questions being asked. They were only concerned with the safety of the people, and Terryn assured them that, unless provoked, the army would harm no one.

After a short period of questions, Roland finally came to the purpose of the meeting. "My captain would like to address your assembly," he said.

William looked at Carl and nodded his counsel. In reality, approval was not needed. This was more of a command than a question.

"That can be arranged," answered Carl.

Watching a family walk past Town hall, Carl wondered what the common folk thought of this occupying army. He was certain they were frightened. They had probably never seen soldiers such as this, and like their leaders, they had no idea what the future held.

Do they even trust their leaders anymore? He was horrified at the answer most would give to that question.

William returned to the room, startling Carl. "Sir, they are ready," he announced.

The Assembly had been gathered in their chambers below on the first floor of the building. Not knowing why they were there as the conquering captain had requested.

"Very well," replied Carl. "Let us join them and see what Terryn has in store for us."

The dejected assembly chief left his office and headed down the hallway toward the stairs leading to the first floor. Today, Carl felt like this walk was happening in slow motion, as if he were a condemned man heading to the gallows.

Entering the meeting room, the chief looked around, making a mental note of each member present. "Walter, Kevin, and William are here," he mumbled to himself.

One by one, he checked them off the list as he circled the table. The obvious empty chair of Henry's and a second empty chair caught his eye.

Henry's seat on the Assembly had not been filled in the hopes of some that he would return. Much debate took place over the time that he had been missing about how long they should wait and who should replace him. Of course, the bishop had a preferred candidate, but the members loyal to Henry were able to hold out. All talk had ended recently with the arrival of Terryn and his army.

The other empty seat was causing Carl much concern. Where was the bishop? He had not been seen since the army was first spotted approaching over the fertile plain. Had he deserted the city he claimed to love?

Despite these ruminations, Carl's head was becoming much clearer, and the pain that had plagued him had now completely subsided. This clarity had brought with it anger against the bishop.

Why is this anger overtaking me? Where did it come from?

Carl finally circled the table and stood next to his chair. He did not sit because this would not be his assembly to lead anymore.

"We are here at a grave time for our people," he addressed the members. "Our very existence hangs in the balance."

This was not news to anyone seated at the table. They all had their own terrible experiences during the invasion and knew exactly what was at stake.

Before Carl could say another word, Roland burst through the door with Terryn close behind. He introduced Terryn as Captain of the Army of Westville and protector of Triopolis. Walter turned toward William with a sad look of defeat.

"Leaders of Triopolis," began Terryn, "I have summoned you here to come to an agreement on our new arrangement."

Arrangement? questioned Carl to himself. *There will only be one way—his way.*

With the room remaining silent, Terryn explained the terms of the arrangement. "I wish to have a peaceful transition of power. I do not want to unleash my army on your people. These men are highly skilled warriors, and I fear they would completely destroy Triopolis with ease. You have not the means to compete with such a force. I ask you to agree with me, and we shall have peace."

Each member of the Assembly was having the same thought. *We have only one choice, and that is to agree with this man. He is right; we cannot fight. William and his small force of guards are no match for the knights in their shiny armor.*

Terryn laid out his terms. "You will continue to govern as you always have. I do not wish to change the process. I wish the people to see their leaders as they always have. I will attend the assembly meetings to offer my counsel, and my army will stay for the protection of the city."

Having no choice, all members of the Assembly announced their agreement to the deal. The somber mood at the outset of the meeting was now showing some signs of optimism, but it wouldn't last. Terryn did indeed want to leave the Assembly intact, but he would have absolute control over it. The Assembly would become his face and voice to the people.

Each topic of discussion ended with Terryn dictating what his wishes were. After a somewhat lengthy debate about how citizens displaced from their homes by the invading soldiers would be cared for, the answer was given by their new master.

"My soldiers will be given lodgings appropriate to their rank," he dictated. "Furthermore, a levy of one-fifth of the output from the harvest and hunt shall be forfeit in order to feed the army."

The assembly members were astonished, but no one dared to contradict him. He watched their faces as he issued his command and was pleased with the unanimous acceptance of the inevitable.

Anger burned inside Carl. As the former leader, he felt an obligation to do something, but what could he do against such a powerful force?

Terryn and Roland left as swiftly as they entered. Each member rose and stood in complete silence except for a collective sigh of relief when the door shut behind them.

"What do we do now?" asked Walter, looking to Carl for leadership.

"Let's meet at my house in thirty minutes," suggested Carl. "It might be safer there." With that, the room emptied.

William and Carl made the ten-minute walk to Carl's house together. "Where do you suppose the bishop went?" asked Carl.

"Baldwin is missing as well," added William. "They must be hatching a plan somewhere. He always has a plan."

Kevin was the last to arrive at Carl's home. The four men stood around the large antique desk that was the focal point of the room. The office was dark even though the sun was high in the midday sky.

Carl had drawn the curtains shut to keep their meeting secret. The wrong eyes seeing or ears hearing what they were about to discuss would mean death to them all.

"I think we have to find their missing princess," said Carl. "If we find her, she will be the bargaining chip we need. We can trade her for our freedom."

"How would we know where to look for her?" asked Kevin.

"We know she's with Kelvin," answered Carl. "Terryn said that she helped Kelvin escape after Henry was killed. I can only guess that he would lead her here. This is all he knows, so I can't think of any other place he would go."

Surprisingly, the disappointment in his son was no longer present. *Is there a correlation with my headaches going away?* he wondered to himself. *Or is it that he finally did something to prove himself as a man?*

"I know the forests around Triopolis better than anyone, so I will lead the search," offered Walter.

"An excellent idea," replied Carl.

"I know of a few hiding places in the fields that I will search," added Kevin.

A smile came to Carl's face as each man committed to his plan.

"I think we should fight," said William, who had been quiet to this point.

Surprised looks came from the other three. Before they could respond, William explained his reasoning.

"I don't mean fight in a head–to–head battle," he continued. "We could never compete with them on a field, but we could surprise and ambush them. Remember the founders and the Battle of Loria Forest."

"What was the Battle of Loria Forest?" asked Kevin.

"Yes, please explain," replied Carl, knowingly, but he wanted William to explain for the benefit of the others.

He knew of the battle from one of the many late-night discussions he'd had with William. The two men had both served on the Assembly for many years and had become good friends.

In years past, before the bishop took control, it was common for the two to burn the midnight oil with an ale or two, discussing many topics that interested them, including history. The Battle of Loria Forest came up many times, as it was the only true battle fought during the founding of Triopolis.

"It wouldn't take much for fear to grow and fester within the ranks of their army," said William. "We will need to arm as many men as possible. Bows would be best. That way we can take them out from a distance. It's clean and stealthy."

Kevin was unsure of the probability of success. "Their retribution would be terrible," he commented.

"They wouldn't be able to retaliate," replied William. "Who would they retaliate against? They couldn't kill everyone or even pick people at random. The last thing they want is a full-scale revolt.

"Kevin, do you remember the panic that spread through the city last year when the wolf killed that boy in his sleep? No one saw the wolf sneak through the old city wall and into the family's house. The boy was viciously attacked in his sleep by the hungry beast.

"People all over the city panicked and overreacted thinking the wolves would take over and there was nothing we could do. We didn't round up all the wolves and kill them."

"Yes I remember," Kevin replied, now understanding what William planned.

"We should do both I think," announced Carl, after all debate was over. "We could use the ambush attacks on the soldiers as insurance for our negotiations when handing over the princess."

Gaining agreement from everyone present was a good start. Carl was happy that they could all agree in this critical moment. It gave him the slightest amount of hope.

"Walter, your men would be best for this job," said William. "They are accomplished marksmen already. We just need to teach them how to kill enemy soldiers instead of animals."

"I agree," said Walter. "For some it will be a difficult change, but I can think of a few savage hunters who will find it frighteningly easy to launch their arrows at human prey. I have twenty extra bows and many thousands of arrows."

"My farmers also have bows, and I know they will be eager to help," added Kevin. "Though they are not as accurate as the hunters, they have been protecting their crops from wild animals for a long time."

"Excellent," said Carl, happy that for the first time since he could remember, the Assembly was coming together in full agreement. "Walter, send your best trackers out to find the princess and Kelvin. William, you will train the other hunters and farmers that are willing to participate and plan the attacks. Let us continue to meet here until our mission is accomplished. Town Hall is no longer safe for us."

<hr>

Richard shifted his weight and pulled on the reins, and his horse came to a stop just under a tall birch tree.

"This should be far enough," he said to Albert, who wasn't far behind.

"I didn't see anyone following us," replied Albert, who had been turning around every few minutes to see if anyone was in pursuit.

"It's not safe for us to speak freely in the castle anymore," said Richard. "My father has his spies everywhere."

"That's true. Now that Lord Rosser is dead and Terryn is leading the army, he could have assigned anyone to follow us," replied Albert. "But why have we come all the way out here?"

"Terryn has taken the city of Triopolis," answered Richard.

Albert let out a gasp. "What about Elizabeth and Kelvin?"

"I don't know. I haven't heard anything about them yet."

"Bringing your wife back would be the king's first priority," said Albert. "I think everyone would know if Terryn had captured her."

"If he does capture her, I don't know how I could save her from the noose," lamented the prince.

The two friends dismounted their horses to give the animals a chance to graze on a small patch of grass.

"I wish my father would just die," complained Richard. "I am his only son and heir, yet he treats me as though I am a peasant."

"He will die soon enough," replied Albert, trying to comfort his prince.

"Who goes there?" yelled Richard, unsheathing his sword.

"I heard it too," said Albert, also pulling out his sword.

Twigs cracked underfoot, and a branch snapped back into its original position as a cloaked man ran behind a lush pine tree and remained hidden.

Richard and Albert approached the tree with swords held out ready to strike.

"Show yourself!" yelled Richard. "I am Richard Westville, prince of these lands, and I command you to present yourself to me."

Out came an old man wrapped in a tattered gray cloak with the hood pulled over his head. He slowly moved into view with a slight limp probably caused by his old age more than anything else.

"Please don't hurt me, sirs," he stammered. "I mean you no harm."

"Why are you sneaking around?" asked Albert, as he and Richard returned their swords to their sheaths sensing no danger.

"I was here when you arrived," answered the old man. "I saw your big horses and your swords, and they frightened me."

"Well, sneaking behind the tree instead of staying where we could see you was a dangerous move," said Richard.

"Yes, sir," said the old man, bowing.

"Now move along," commanded Richard.

"May I ask a question, sir?" inquired the old man.

"As you wish," allowed Richard.

"What city is this?" he asked.

"Where are you from, old man?" asked Richard, curious as to the nature of the question. "How could you not know our city?"

"I am from somewhere and yet nowhere," he replied, cryptically.

"Don't toy with me, old man," exclaimed Richard, irritated by his answer.

"I meant no disrespect, sir," he answered. "I just mean that I live in the forest."

"You are a barbarian then?"

"Barbarian?" asked the old man. "No, no, I am no barbarian. Many people other than barbarians call the forest home, you know."

Richard, getting angry, stepped toward the old man, and Albert followed. Albert, knowing what his master wanted, hovered over the old man saying, "When Prince Richard asks a question, you will answer him honestly, or I will cut off your head. Do I make myself clear?"

They had fallen right into the old man's trap. From his cowering position, he sprang up and in the same motion reached for Albert's head. His hand landed precisely where he wanted it to, ripping a chunk of hair as it recoiled.

"Ah!" screamed Albert, as the hair was wrenched from his head.

He pulled back and away from the attack. Richard lunged for the man. He could almost feel the man's cloak in his hand, but a quick jump backward by the old man left him with a handful of air.

"You are not what you seem, old man," said Richard. "That was the quickness of a much younger man."

"Right you are," replied the stranger, lifting his hand up to a giant oak tree as if to command it.

In horror, Richard and Albert watched the lowest branch of the tree come alive. Like a snake, the wooden leafy branch rapidly slithered its way closer to the two young men. Before they could react, the extended arm of the tree split in two each wrapping itself around one of its adversaries' ankles. With a powerful jolt, the branch recoiled with the two men hanging upside down from their ankles.

Richard and Albert looked at the old man in disbelief. "Who are you?" asked Albert.

The old man gave them a quick smirk and quickly disappeared from sight. Richard, surprisingly calm, observed, "Strange things have been happening of late in the world. I must speak to the high priest about this."

After a couple of minutes of the men being suspended in the air, the tree let go. Not expecting it, they landed with a thud.

"A little warning would have been nice!" exclaimed Albert, rubbing the back of his neck.

Jumping on his horse, Richard yelled, "Come, Albert, we must go to the temple."

Luckily, their horses had plenty of rest and were ready for a full gallop. They needed every bit of energy for this trip because their riders pushed them hard. A pure sprint all the way back to the city got them there in half the time it took on the way out.

Quickly dismounting and loosely tying their horses to a post, they ran up to the front door of the Temple of Apollo. Pulling it open, Richard entered the hallowed building with Albert close behind. Without hesitation, they headed directly to the high priest's study.

Hesitating at the door, Albert said in a low voice, "I don't understand why there is a need to speak to the high priest."

"He has knowledge and wisdom," replied Richard. "I think he can help us explain what happened by the lake."

Albert looked at Richard, wanting to ask another question, but he didn't. When the prince was this determined, it was best to let him finish before bothering him with more questions. It was another trait picked up from his father.

The door to the study was slightly cracked open, so they entered. The high priest was pacing back and forth as if in a trance, not even noticing his two visitors. From one side of the room to the other he stalked, lost in his thoughts.

"Sir," said Richard, but there was no response. "Sir," he said louder. Finally, on the third "Sir," which was even louder, the bonds of Donovan's trance were broken.

As if waking from a nap, he said, "Richard, I didn't hear you come in."

"Sorry to bother you, sir, but we had a disturbing discovery today," began the prince. "We were out by the lake and stumbled upon a most curious old man. He seemed like a frail old thing, but it was only a ruse."

Fear spread over the high priest's face, for he already knew what Richard was about to say.

"He was quick when he wanted to be, and very cunning, but the most amazing thing was he seemed to have control over the trees. He seemed to be able to command the tree to do his bidding."

"It is as I feared then," declared the high priest. "He has escaped."

The high priest turned and walked away from his guests toward the back of the room. Taking a book from a small table, he opened it, returning to Richard and Albert as he leafed through the pages.

"Is this the man you saw?" he asked, showing them a hand-drawn picture in the book.

"Yes, that's him," confirmed Richard.

"I have foreseen his escape," stated the high priest.

"Whose escape?" asked the prince, confused.

"Luther," answered the high priest. After his response, there was a moment of silence as he pondered the implications.

"Who is Luther?" Richard asked.

"He is an ancient, sinister man with great power," answered the high priest. "He is someone we would rather have imprisoned than running loose in the forest."

"Can we send the army to kill him?" asked Richard.

"No, that will not work. They would all perish by his hand."

"Impossible!" exclaimed Albert. "One man would defeat a whole army?"

"You saw the way he commanded the tree," replied Richard. "What if he could do that with all the trees in the forest? Swords won't help against an army of oak trees."

The high priest was so proud of Richard at this moment. He was able to look past the unbelievable nature of the things he'd just heard and make good decisions. Donovan was proud that the prince did indeed possess the leadership skills that would be needed to advance the kingdom toward a better future than their past had been.

"You haven't known it, but I have prepared you for this day," said the high priest to Richard. "I have always taught you to allow yourself to see past what is on the surface to find the real truth hidden beneath."

Richard thought back to his youth when he would come to the temple for his lessons. They were not lessons sanctioned by his tutors or even his father. No one else even knew they were taking place.

He remembered every Saturday morning he would rush out of bed and come here. It was so exciting to anticipate what new thing he would learn from the high priest that day. His instruction in the temple was always so interesting and different. It went far beyond the math and language he learned from his tutors. It was even more exciting than practicing with his sword.

His teachings centered on the different elements that existed in the world and how to use them. He mixed minerals together that when sprinkled over a horse's head would immediately calm him. One concoction turned water red, and another increased the height of the flowers in the garden.

"I was teaching you the knowledge of the Enlightened," said the high priest.

"Who are the Enlightened?" asked the prince.

"We are the keepers of wisdom, such as the ability to command a tree like you witnessed today. Although, commanding multiple trees or a grove, as you suggested, is not possible."

"So, you were teaching me to be an Enlightened?" asked Richard.

"No, unfortunately, only a very rare few with the proper blood may be enlightened," answered the high priest. "Knowing you would be king, I thought it was important for you to be aware of certain things in this world.

"When I first laid eyes on you after your birth, I had a vision of Luther roaming the world a free man again. Unfortunately, you have just confirmed that my vision was correct.

"This is why I tutored you in the knowledge of a more powerful wisdom than any known to man. I wanted to make sure you were aware that the possibility existed so you would be able to act when the time came."

"Thank you for preparing me," Richard said, still taking it all in. He didn't know what else to say. He felt humbled and amazed that all this had transpired without him knowing it.

"Did Luther tell you what he was looking for?" asked the high priest, getting back to the matter at hand.

"No, he didn't ask us any questions at all. It looked like we startled him, and he was only interested in getting away from us."

"Did he touch you or throw any dust on you?" he asked.

"No, not that," began Richard, when he was interrupted by Albert.

"He grabbed my hair," he blurted.

Panic overtook the high priest. He rapidly approached Albert, put both hands on his shoulders, and looked him straight in the eye. Albert was scared. He had never seen the high priest act this way.

"Was it a pat, or did he intentionally rip the hair out of your head?"

"Umm . . ." was all he managed to say.

"Quickly, answer the question!" commanded the high priest.

Replaying the scene in his head, he answered, "He most definitely was ripping hair out of my head."

Upon hearing what he didn't want to hear but suspected, the high priest's hope deflated as he released the young man and returned to the back of the room. He summoned them to join him around a medium-sized bowl sitting on a small table.

"Luther wanted your hair so he could watch your movements," he explained.

"Watch his movements?" questioned Richard.

"Yes, I fear we are all in great danger," answered the high priest.

Reaching the bowl, they looked in and saw a thick clear liquid. It looked like water, but it wasn't. It had the feel of lamp oil but was perfectly clear.

"Luther is looking for me," explained the high priest. "Since I am the one who caused his imprisonment, he will want revenge. He must know I am here, and that is why he approached you in the forest."

"I don't think he meant it to happen," replied Albert. "We startled him."

"The Enlightened are never startled," he answered, sternly. "If you encountered him by the lake, then he meant that to happen. He planned it."

Taking a vial from a nearby shelf, he plucked a single hair from it and dropped it into the liquid, which immediately turned cloudy. Seconds later, a picture emerged as the water cleared.

A man dressed in red with black hair appeared before them.

"I have never seen this man, but his face looks familiar," said Richard.

"But you have seen him," replied the high priest. "That is the true look of the man you saw in the forest."

"This is Benzatine liquid," explained the high priest. "Very little of it exists in the world. When a piece of hair is put into it, the person whose head it was plucked from can be seen. This is what Luther is seeing right now."

"That's incredible," exclaimed Albert.

"That means Luther would be able to see us right now if he had some of this liquid," said Richard, gravely.

"That is correct," confirmed the high priest.

The three of them watched as Luther moved about. "That is not the room I left him in," said the high priest. "What is that in the middle of the room on the table?"

Luther was walking toward a table. As he got closer, the high priest became more anxious. "I think our luck just ran out," he said.

It was a bowl of similar size to the high priest's, but it was much more elaborately decorated. It was encrusted with sparkling jewels, whereas the one in front of them was very plain with a dull finish.

They watched a hair that looked about the same color as Albert's float ever so lightly into the gelatinous substance. It didn't sink. Instead, it lay suspended on top of the liquid.

As soon as the hair hit the liquid, fire encircled the rim of the bowl, and they could see each other! Luther was looking directly at them through their bowl, and they were looking at him.

All four men watched, mesmerized by the confrontation. In a deep raspy voice, Luther uttered, "I see you!" in comical derision.

Richard and Albert jumped back while the high priest plunged his hand into the liquid retrieving the hair. Quickly placing it back into the vial, he flung a cloth over the bowl.

"We are all in danger," he exclaimed. "I must leave Westville!"

"Where will you go?" asked Richard.

"I have to find Luther before he finds me," answered the high priest. He frantically ran around the room gathering the things he would need for his journey. Richard and Albert looked on concerned for their friend.

As he finished gathering his things, he stopped in front of Richard and said, "This is the moment I have prepared you for. You will be king soon. Remember what I taught you."

"Will you come back?"

"This will be the greatest challenge of my many years," said the high priest. "I don't know if I will survive, but I promise you I will do my best to keep Westville safe. Use the knowledge I have given you. You have it in you to be a great king. Realize your potential!"

With that the high priest was out the door and gone.

Chapter 24

Around the bishop sat twenty men, rounded up by his henchman, Baldwin. They were a ragged-looking bunch, most of them criminals, according to the occupying army. These were the exact type of men the bishop wanted. They were loyal to Triopolis, and were not afraid to take matters into their own hands.

The occupying army had only been in control for a short time, but they had already made their presence known to all. Not only was Terryn making all political decisions, but he had imposed taxes on food, wine, ale, and even fresh water. All taxes were paid directly to the army.

Houses were confiscated at will from the people who owned them. Some had been in their families for generations, but they were evicted merely because the soldiers needed roofs over their heads. If a house so much as caught a soldier's eye, it would immediately be taken and the inhabitants kicked out into the street.

The usual happy gathering places such as pubs and parks were vacant now, as all fun and laughter seemed to have disappeared from the once vibrant city. Small groups of soldiers, usually two or three, continuously walked the streets reminding the people who was in charge.

The men enlisted by the bishop were already taking matters into their own hands. Isolated, random attacks on drunken soldiers or soldiers walking alone at night were occurring in the dark alleys of Triopolis.

The renegades were doing their part to fight back, but only when they had the physical advantage and the ability to remain unseen. If a soldier stepped out alone or too arrogantly walked in dark places without his weapon, the citizen militia would pounce. The attacks were few but beginning to get the attention of Roland and Terryn.

The morning sun was just beginning to show itself over the mountains to the east. A small fire was crackling as the men filled themselves with salt pork and bread.

The bishop provided the food and ale to wash it down. Since his men were not trained soldiers, he thought a little ale to take the edge off would be just what was needed to accomplish the task ahead.

As the men ate, they were given their orders. They would cause diversions throughout the city while the bishop and Baldwin sought out the leaders. Guerilla tactics combined with surprise were the only way they would successfully overtake the army. They would hide in the shadows and only appear long enough to ignite the bishop's explosive black powder, and then they would vanish again.

The previous night, the bishop brought his group of men the short distance to the top of the mountain and over to the other side. Gathering just over the peak so they would not be seen from the town below, the bishop unveiled his secret weapon.

He set a small clay jar against the trunk of an adolescent tree. A white wick bent from the top of the jar down to the ground. His men watched as he poured a line of mysterious black powder from the wick over the ground to the spot where they gathered.

Without hesitation, Baldwin dropped his torch into the dirt where the powder line began. It ignited, and the flame made its way to the jar. The men waited anxiously as the flame jumped from the powder to the wick.

The power of the explosion and brightness of the flash scattered even the bravest man in the group. Knowing what to expect, Baldwin and the bishop stood their ground looking at the small crater where the tree once stood.

As the men recovered and gathered around their leader, they were amazed at the sight of the explosion. If they had doubted the bishop, they were all believers now.

"Men, we must stay true to our plan," commanded the bishop.

Even going into battle, he wore his usual brown robe. Standing on a ledge, he had the height advantage on all of his subordinates as he addressed them.

"This will be our only chance of retaking our home," he said. "Despite what they say, this army will never leave. You can see the soldiers are already settling into our houses as if they have been living here for years. Will you let this stand?"

"No!" they all shouted.

Leaving his men, the bishop walked out onto the cliff overlooking the western edge of the city. There was now enough light from the rising sun to see the whole town. Baldwin approached his leader and stood next to him in silence.

"We may all die today," warned the bishop.

"It would be an honor to die saving our homeland," Baldwin answered, proudly.

"You are the closest we have to a professional soldier," praised the bishop, looking at the well-built man who had served him so well over the years.

Baldwin was a poor young man who had lost his entire family in a plague that swept through the population five years ago. Nineteen now, he was just the type of boy the bishop was looking for.

Baldwin was physically imposing and intelligent, and all hope seemed lost for him. Taking him under his wing, the bishop had molded him into the man who would help him take the city for himself. This had always been the bishop's goal. He just never expected to be given this opportunity by the invaders from another land.

"It begins," he commanded. "Take your men and unleash hell on the armored scourge. Kill them all. Leave none left to fight another day. It ends today. Wait for the first explosion before lighting yours."

"Yes, sir," he answered.

"Good luck Baldwin," offered the bishop.

"And you, sir," he said, and he left to fulfill his mission.

The men fell in line as Baldwin led them down the mountain. Each man had a sack flung over his shoulder filled with clay jars of black powder.

Each jar had a twelve-inch piece of cloth protruding from the top. This would give them time to light the fuse and get to safety before the explosion.

I would gladly see them all fall if it means winning the city, thought the bishop. *Control of Triopolis is the only thing that matters.* He watched until his makeshift army was out of sight before heading out.

The walk from the staging area to the city was about a mile. The western edge of the town ended very near the base of the mountain. This was precisely why the bishop decided to attack from the west. The cover of the forested mountain would help his men get into position without being spotted.

Reaching the city wall, he crawled through a section that had been broken away by his men, although not much of the wooden wall existed anymore. Most of it had rotted and fallen away years ago.

"When I recapture the city, I will rebuild this wall," he murmured to himself.

He was thinking about how easily the invaders had conquered them and how easily his men were entering the town. The way they had looked at everything in the past would have to change. They could never again live with the naïveté or arrogance that they were the only people in the world.

Triopolis under his leadership would have to build a defensive wall and a standing army.

The bishop immediately turned toward Town Hall. He did not take the most direct route due to his need for secrecy. The morning sun was now climbing higher in the sky, and he would be easily recognized.

His route took him through many back alleyways and away from the fronts of buildings and the main paths that cut through town. His brown robe with the hood pulled over his head was the best he could do to hide himself.

The men fanned out across the city heading for their first targets. Each rebel was given a list of specific objectives and a handful of jars to use randomly. The lists consisted mostly of homes and offices commandeered by the enemy soldiers.

It was thought that surprise attacks in comfortable surroundings would create the most unease among the enemy ranks. The bishop also hoped that he would catch them early enough in the day that they would still be sleeping in their beds. He thought it would be much easier to take them out individually using a scattershot type of strategy.

It was in front of the house that once belonged to Eric Feldstein, the owner of the market, where Baldwin now stood. He had never liked Eric. He considered him a deceitful, loathsome being, but even Eric did not deserve what the soldiers had done to him.

Eric performed the most heroic act that some would say he had ever done in his life. For the first time, he thought about someone other than himself.

Standing his ground, he attempted to push back the pillaging soldiers while his wife and daughter escaped out the back door. They made it to safety solely because of his heroism. Unfortunately, the soldiers were not kind to him. Like many others in Triopolis, he paid for his obstinance with his life.

Baldwin slipped around to the side of the house, hearing approaching soldiers. He was quick enough not to be seen.

Two soldiers chatted while walking up to the building unaware of the man standing just around the corner. When the men entered, he heard another man greet them.

Perfect, he thought.

His first objective was to take out three of the enemy. He couldn't have asked for a better target.

Digging a small hole, he inserted the bomb and nestled it against the foundation. Repeating the action so that each of the four corners of the house had a bomb against it, he cut the wicks to different lengths so they would ignite the explosive at the same time.

He had practiced running the distance to light each wick many times and felt comfortable with his estimation. In the mountains, it had only been a circle of trees, but he had run the perimeter of a large rectangular area and pretended to duck under windows to make it as real as possible.

The apprehension was building as he waited. He had seen many explosions during the testing of the black powder, but he had never planted them around a building before.

He wondered if he would get away in time, or if he had made the wicks long enough. What would he do if someone saw him? What if he tripped and fell as he was running away?

He was second-guessing himself, causing even more anxiety. His hand was shaking in anticipation. Then he saw the light.

An orange flash appeared in the western sky setting him into action. All of his doubts disappeared as he instinctively remembered his training.

Crouching so that he would not been seen through the windows, he ran around the building lighting each fuse. With all four now burning, he made his escape. It seemed to him that his legs were moving in slow motion as he exited the blast zone.

"Faster, farther," he repeated to himself. "I have to get farther away!"

It seemed every nerve in his body was on edge as he tingled with excitement and fear. Then he heard and felt the results of his work from behind him.

The peaceful morning erupted into chaos. The energy produced from the explosion hit Baldwin in the back with a force that he had never before felt. It engulfed him, and his body was thrown forward. Landing on his stomach, he gasped for air. He lay on the ground in a daze, teetering on the edge of consciousness.

At the same time that Baldwin's explosion pierced the morning sky, simultaneous blasts were heard and seen throughout the city. Flames were seen in all directions, and smoke and debris filled the air. The only thing the rebels regretted was that the whole population couldn't be warned.

Only those whose loyalties were known were told of the impending attack. The element of surprise was absolutely necessary for the plan to work, so only a select few had been warned. The collateral damage of buildings and innocent civilians was expected to be high. This was all deemed necessary to rid the city of the enemy.

Hearing was the first sense that returned to Baldwin, and his sight quickly followed. It didn't take long for him to realize where he was. Sitting up, he saw the results of his actions. The house had completely collapsed on itself and was engulfed in bright red flames.

Looking around, he saw other buildings burning and people running frantically through the streets. They were innocent people looking for a way out of the city. Taking all they could carry, they ran with children in tow. Screaming parents and crying children accompanied the flight.

Now able to feel all of his extremities, he sprang to his feet and on to the next target.

Carl sat in his home office and watched the burning skyline of his city from the window. The sadness he felt for his beloved Triopolis was overwhelming. A knock on the door interrupted his thoughts, and a man entered before Carl could answer. It was the bishop.

"Where have you been?" asked Carl, surprised to see him. "What is going on out there?"

"We are fighting back, which is what you should have done days ago!" yelled the bishop, his voice oozing contempt.

"How could you let this army take Triopolis without a fight?" he berated Carl. "You are pitiful!"

Carl looked on in amazement. *This is not the bishop I know. He has never spoken to me this way before.*

Standing nearly ten feet away, the bishop caught Carl's gaze. His eyes were locked on the former assembly leader's, leaving Carl unable to turn away. The bishop bore deep into Carl's mind in an effort to bring him under his control.

I can't turn away! panicked Carl to himself. *My body doesn't feel right. Oh, the pain!*

The headache that had disappeared was back. The throbbing in his head was becoming unbearable.

Why can I not finish it? wondered the bishop. *I can't get far enough into his mind. I must be too far away.*

Carl now knew there was a correlation between the bishop and his headaches..

As the bishop took steps toward his victim, Carl began to fight. The bishop was trying to correct his mistake. By entering Carl's mind from that distance, he could not go deep enough to gain complete control.

With the bishop closing in, Carl's anger took over. Fighting, he was finally able to wrench his eyes away from the attack.

"What have you done to me?" accused Carl, finding the internal strength to stand up to the man who had manipulated him for so long.

"Now, at our darkest hour, you finally want to fight?" asked the bishop, scornfully. "You are a pathetic excuse for a man!"

Carl was angry. He now knew that the army outside and the man standing in front of him were both his enemies.

"I have been in control of you for years!" taunted the bishop. "You were so weak after the death of your son. I saw this weakness and used it to my advantage."

Carl thought back to those difficult days. The day he lost Robert was the worst day of his life, and he remembered it as if it were yesterday.

Young Kelvin stood dripping wet and shivering in the doorway. "What happened to you?" asked his father.

Summoning the courage to tell his father what happened, Kelvin braced himself for the expected reaction.

Carl flew into a rage. "How could you let your brother drown?" he screamed.

Frightened by his father's uncontrollable rage, Kelvin just stood there shaking, but this time it wasn't from his wet clothes.

"I did everything I could," pleaded the son.

"If you had done everything, he would still be alive!" yelled Carl.

Carl rapidly approached his son, grabbing him by the shoulders and shaking him, thinking it would relieve his anger. He remembered the fear on Kelvin's face that day.

"I blamed Kelvin," admitted Carl, his eyes filling with tears. "Why did I blame him? The rocks were too heavy; there was nothing he could have done."

Sick of watching Carl's display of sobbing and feeling sorry for himself, the bishop changed the mood in the room.

"You blamed him because I told you to blame him," he said, laughing. "You were a mess, and I needed you to be stronger. I knew that transferring blame was the way you would quickly move past it, so I gave you a scapegoat."

The bishop had a smirk on his face showing his satisfaction at committing such a foul deed. Carl's sobbing stopped. Anger and revenge were his only thoughts now. He wanted to kill the man he had thought was his friend and ally. The sharp pain shooting through his head only motivated him more.

Looking to his right he noticed that he now stood only a few feet away from the magnificently decorated sword dangling on a single hook displayed for everyone to see. Meant to be an ornament, it still had all the qualities of a deadly weapon, including a sharp edge.

The bishop slowly walked toward Carl. When the distance was short enough to cover quickly, Carl sprang into action. Reaching up, he took the sword and in the same motion thrust it toward the bishop's mid-section.

The bishop lifted his hand, causing an unseen force to stop Carl's forward motion and fling the sword across the room.

The immense force of the unseen energy felt like a mountain crashing down on Carl, knocking him to the floor. A loud, evil, victorious laugh came from the bishop, who stood over his vanquished foe.

"I am all powerful!" he yelled. "You cannot kill me!" With that, he left the room and his former leader a broken man.

After a moment lying on the floor, Carl gathered his strength and got up. Seething with anger, revenge was his only thought. He picked up the sword that had been mysteriously torn from his hand. As he swung it back and forth, the adrenaline pumped throughout his body, needing release.

Soon the air was not enough of a challenge. With anger bubbling over, he screamed as he slashed a nearby curtain. The candle on his left felt the brunt of his recoil as it was sliced in two. Screaming and cursing filled the room, but it wasn't enough. This was more than just letting off steam. He needed cold, hard revenge.

"He turned me against my son!" yelled Carl, accompanied by more hacking and chopping with his elaborate blade. A loud crash brought him back to his senses. It was the front door of the house being smashed open by a group of enemy soldiers. He quickly opened the nearest window and climbed out with the sword in his hand.

Around him, the smell of burning wood filled the air. The majority of the townspeople had made it out of the city and to safety. The cries of men and boys fighting for their lives could be heard all around.

None of it mattered to Carl—not the burning, the smoke, or the death around him. His singular purpose now was revenge on the two men who had caused him the most despair. He would get revenge on the bishop later, but now he was after the man hunting his son. Town Hall was his destination.

From the look of the thick black smoke and ash filling the air above the city, it seemed as though every structure in town was ablaze. This was not the case, however, as the rebels were continuing their strategic bombings. Only targets that would kill the enemy and help them win were destroyed.

The closer he got to Town Hall, the more the debris piled up. Many of the surrounding buildings were on fire, but surprisingly, Town Hall stood tall like a phoenix among the ashes. Carl chose the back door, hoping it would be unguarded. His wish came true as he opened the door and stepped into an empty hallway.

Covering the distance of the short hallway, he quietly snuck around the corner and started up the stairway to his old office. He was sure that was where Terryn would be.

The anger he felt toward Terryn had not subsided on the walk from his home. He thought about the captain sending his soldiers out into the forest to catch his son.

He would probably kill Kelvin because he only wants to return the princess, he speculated. This enraged him even more.

Halfway up the stairs, he stopped in his tracks. The first soldier he had seen since entering the building appeared before him at the top of the stairs. Carl's passionate anger controlled him. Without hesitation, he lifted his sword and engaged the man clad in silver armor.

His first swing landed squarely on the plate guarding the man's right arm. A scream from the soldier satisfied Carl. He didn't realize that the man's only weapon was a small dagger. It was after his second slash made contact on the soldier's chest plate that he noticed the man didn't have his sword.

The soldier, remembering his training in this type of situation, knew he had to get close to his adversary's body to render his long sword ineffective. This was his only chance for victory.

Carl could see in the soldier's expression that he didn't respect him as a fighter. No one in the invading army did. They all assumed the people of Triopolis were simple people with no fighting experience.

It was true the people of Triopolis had never fought in a war, but they were very good hunters. Hunting wild animals in the forest is not so different from war, at times.

Carl remembered the incident with the wild boar when he was a younger man. The beast he was hunting suddenly turned on its pursuer and changed its role from prey to predator.

The young Carl was chasing the large boar through the forest when the beast realized it was much larger than the man chasing it. A quick stop and turn was all it took for the roles to be reversed.

It only seemed like a second before the wild pig was on him. He didn't have time to react as the large beast leapt. The boar's front hooves drove the boy into the ground. He could feel the animal's feet digging into his chest through the thick outer coat he wore.

A quick turn on his side under the animal was the only thing that saved his life. The pig's large tusks jutting out from its lower jaw slashed at his side, only missing because of his quick move. The animal didn't realize its precarious position with its underbelly exposed as it was only fueled by the anger and pain caused by the arrow stuck in its hindquarters.

Carl saw his dagger lying on the ground not a foot from his left hand. Instinct took over as he grabbed the knife and in the same motion drove the blade into the underside of the beast. He must have penetrated its heart, because the boar died instantly.

Like the boar, the overconfident soldier charged Carl. He led with his left arm trying to lock his enemy close to him so he could attack with the dagger in his other hand. Carl saw it coming and used his right arm to knock the soldier's groping hand away.

The momentum the soldier gained coming down the stairs combined with the force of Carl's blow knocked him severely off balance. Noticing this, Carl used it to his advantage and pushed him with all his might toward the rail. The soldier clad in heavy silver plate hit the rail with such force that it propelled him over the edge.

With his hands, he was just able to catch himself from falling, but it was already over for him. Carl continued his way up the stairs knowing that the weight of the soldier's armor would be too great. Turning around at the top, he saw the man's hands finally lose their grip, and he fell to the hard wooden floor never to move again.

Turning toward his old office, the hallway was eerily quiet. He could feel his heart beat faster and faster from the adrenaline that now controlled his body.

The door was cracked open so he peeked in to see how many people were in there. He was in luck. Terryn was alone. With a deep breath, he pushed the door open and approached the military commander.

Terryn was so surprised at the intrusion that he stood to his feet in silence, waiting for it to register. When it finally did, he asked, "What are you doing here?"

"I have come to take my city back," Carl proclaimed.

Laughing, Terryn replied, "All by yourself?"

When Carl didn't flinch, Terryn knew he was serious.

"Come, sit, have a drink with me," he said.

They both moved over to Carl's desk, but this time he was sitting on the opposite side. It felt strange for him to sit in front of the large desk, but putting things back in order was his purpose for being here.

A stout pour of the light brown liquor made from a combination of fermented grains was put down in front of him.

"From my own cupboard, no less," retorted Carl angrily.

"Yes, and what a collection you have," answered a jealous Terryn. "We don't have anything like this where I come from. It's all wine and ale. This is a drink made for kings."

As he said this, he took a sip of the potent beverage. Slightly shaking his head with a look on his face like he had just bitten into a sour apple, the liquid flowed down his throat. "Now, why are we here again?" said Terryn.

"You have taken everything from me," Carl stated, his gaze steady.

"Not everything. You still have your life."

The anger that had begun to dissipate from the liquor came rushing back. The arrogance with which his enemy reminded him that his life was in his hands was overwhelming.

Kicking his chair behind him, Carl sprang to his feet with sword at the ready. "I will have my city back!" he yelled.

"A fight it is then," replied Terryn, taking up his own sword.

The experienced Terryn fought defensively at first. He blocked each of Carl's swinging attacks with his blade. A swipe at the head was easily flung aside. A jab to his midsection was short.

This man has had no formal training with this weapon, realized Terryn. *He is leaving himself wide open.*

An unexpectedly powerful thrust landed squarely in the center of Terryn's chest plate. The armor was too thick to penetrate, but Terryn felt it. Thrown backward into the desk, he screamed in agony.

The surprise blow made Terryn realize that even though Carl was untrained, he was a man fighting for those he loves. He knew that was motivation enough for a man.

Seeing his adversary thrown back gave Carl a hint of optimism. He didn't know he had that kind of strength in him. He attacked again as Terryn lifted himself off the desk. He was quicker to defend himself this time getting his sword up just in time to stop Carl's attempt at his head.

Overpowering the smaller man, Terryn pushed him backward. Stumbling from the momentum of Terryn's push, Carl was able to catch himself before falling.

Terryn charged with his sword leading the way. The two long blades clashed, locked in heated friction. It was then that the soldier leaned on his experience in hand-to-hand combat and balled his fist just before planting it on the side of Carl's head.

Pain shot through his wounded skull, and blood poured from the gash above his ear. He stumbled, dazed and undefended. One more sword thrust from Terryn into his enemy's midsection sent him flailing to the floor.

Carl hit the floor with a thud, and he knew it was over. The immense pain he had felt was gone as his life slipped from his body. At this final moment, he only thought of Kelvin.

The loving father was somewhere between life and death as tears seeped from the corners of his eyes. Kelvin appeared before him in his mind. They were in a field on a bright sunny day.

"My son, I am proud of you," he muttered. "I know I have not said it enough, but I really do love you. I never meant to blame you for your brother's death. The bishop was controlling my mind. You didn't deserve what I put you through, and I am sorry."

They embraced in the field as the sun shone above and the tall grass blew in the light breeze. Satisfied that he was able to apologize to his son, he surrendered to death.

Pity stayed Terryn's hand after hearing the dying man's words. He vowed that if he ever had a son, he would not leave anything to regret.

"Your fate is now in the hands of your gods," Terryn said. "I am sorry it had to end this way."

His moment of pity was soon interrupted by the heavy footsteps of a soldier in the hallway. Roland soon appeared in the doorway screaming, "Sir, we must get out of here! The bishop's forces are converging on us, and we don't have much time."

Following his second in command, Terryn left the room and slipped out of Town Hall without being seen.

Baldwin and the bishop, with their backs to the statue of the founders in Town Hall Square, watched as the last remaining soldiers were in full retreat. Only a handful of the armored soldiers survived the surprising onslaught by the men of Triopolis.

Still holding their swords but carrying nothing else, they ran, fleeing for their lives.

"Let them go," yelled Baldwin to his men, who wanted to give chase. "Let them tell their king what happened here today so that they will never return."

The men stopped running, and coming back together, they let out a collective sigh of relief before breaking into cheering and laughter for their hard-fought victory.

"Come, Baldwin," summoned the bishop, walking toward the front door of Town Hall. "Let's see if the leader of the defeated army is still inside."

The door was ajar, so a slight push was all that was needed for them to enter. Upon entering, they were surprised at the state of disarray. The desk was overturned with a dead armored man draped over its side.

It looked as though the soldier had intentionally turned the desk on its side to use it as cover. The top of it had three arrows lodged in it.

The papers scattered about the room rustled ever so slightly as the breeze entered through the open door.

"Luckily this building is still here and didn't catch fire from the surrounding explosions," said the bishop. They made their way through the debris and up the stairs to Carl's office, which would now be his.

Entering the room, he immediately saw Carl's body on the floor. "It's a shame, I could still have found a use for you," he said, walking past.

Looking out the window, the bishop couldn't contain himself. "It's all mine!" he proclaimed. "I have waited for this moment for so long, and now it has come. We shall rebuild the city stronger that it's ever been!"

Chapter 25

Walking through the forest, Donovan wondered how he would find his long-time nemesis. After five hundred years of peace and quiet, with no one knowing his true identity, he was now out of time. Realizing that Luther would stop at nothing to exact his revenge, he had to find the man.

Thinking of the two he sent out into this forest without much help or advice, he wondered how Kelvin and Elizabeth fared. He wondered if she had figured out how to harness her powers. Would Kelvin understand and be able to cope with her growing knowledge?

Jealousy was the reason most Enlightened lived apart from the non-enlightened. In every story throughout history where a non-enlightened was in love with a partner who had the Blood of Alemon, it ended in disaster. He recalled the story of Cecilia and Petrus.

Many hundreds of years ago, in the days before the darkness, lived Cecilia and Petrus. They met one sunny day when Cecilia was walking down a country road. She was carrying a bag full of carrots that she had just purchased from a local farmer. The weak bag spilt at the bottom, spilling all of her carrots onto the ground. Seeing the accident, Petrus rushed to her aid.

He happened to be carrying a large rolled-up piece of cloth. Unraveling it, he collected all of the fallen vegetables on the cloth. He them scooped it up, lifting all four sides, and tied it tight at the top, creating a new and stronger bag.

When Petrus rose, their eyes met. It was love at first sight. He walked her home carrying the bag over his shoulder. Stimulating conversation and happy laughter consumed their entire journey. Neither could believe they had found someone with whom they had such similar interests.

Days turned into weeks and months, and still the two were inseparable. Finally, one day Petrus surprised Cecilia by falling to one knee and presenting her with a shiny golden ring. He asked her to be his wife. She answered yes without thinking about the secret she still held from him.

Her parents had always warned her not to tell her non-enlightened friends the secret of her powers. They always told her that they would not understand and would become jealous. She had followed these warnings all her life not telling anyone her secret, but she felt certain things were different with Petrus.

He loved her and was so kind and understanding; he wouldn't possibly be jealous. She decided to tell him. It would be impossible for her to marry a man and keep such a secret from him.

Her suspicion was correct. He said and did all the right things to make her feel like she was correct to tell him the truth. What she didn't know was that the anger and jealousy had already begun to grow inside of him.

He put on a smile and continued to show that he loved her, but he couldn't help the growing hatred. As the days went by, his envy grew until one day he caught himself staring at her, loathing everything in her being.

She used her powers around the house thinking it was all right since he knew, but it wasn't all right at all.

She healed cuts and scratches, combining the right mixture of herbs and minerals and her soothing words. Flowers seemingly grew at her command while animals came up to her just to say hello.

The resentment had completely overtaken Petrus on the day he admitted to himself that he wanted her powers. Why did she have them and not he? He could not have a wife who was stronger than he was.

She noticed the growing hostility in his words and actions, but refused to believe that she had fallen into the trap that her mother had warned about. She didn't realize the danger she was in until it was too late.

Under the guise of an apology, Petrus brought her a cup of tea. She accepted and lifted it to her lips, taking a drink.

It burned her throat as it made its way into her stomach. She knew what he had done from the minute the liquid touched her lips. The drink was poisoned. During the short time the liquid did its work, she could only think of the words her father had said over and over, "Don't trust the non-enlightened."

Watching his wife die by his own hand is what finally broke Petrus from his jealous spell. Looking into her expressionless face, he burst into tears. Distraught by his deed, he screamed and cried for her to come back to him, but it was too late.

With nothing left to live for, he took the cup and gulped down the rest of the tainted tea. His lifeless body fell to the floor settling to the side of his dead lover.

Donovan followed the trail left by the army. The path wasn't clear, as much of the undergrowth had filled back in, but the signs were still there for a well-trained eye.

Places existed where the grass had been torn away exposing the dirt, and tree branches had been hacked off allowing horses and riders to pass through.

Normally, he would pass through these lands quickly to get to the business he needed to attend to, but today was different. He rode at a gradual pace, enjoying the smell of the plant life and the sounds of the birds singing. The air was calm, without a whisper of wind, allowing the soothing music to carry for miles.

Later that afternoon, he came upon the final resting place of Lynessa. Allowing the memory of the place to enter his mind, he watched the scene unfold. This power came from his ability as an Enlightened to use the energy that surrounds all living things.

An emotionally charged action by any living being gives off an energy that stays with the location in which it occurred. The ability of the Enlightened to control their minds allowed them to harness this energy, giving them the power to visualize what occurred there.

People who possessed the Blood of Alemon, but who had never been trained to control the energy from certain events, often had visions of those events, but they did not understand where those visions came from. Because of their inability to control their mind, these visions usually came to them in the night while they were asleep.

He did not linger long at the murder site. He had a mission to complete, and time was of the essence. Seeing the fire pit used by Kelvin, he went straight to the river. He knew the way up the river and behind the waterfalls. Granite Lake was near.

Seeing the water rush over the edge of the falls and hearing it crash into the rocks below, he knew he had arrived.

Am I making the right decision coming here? Did Aaron receive my message?

After leaving Westville, Donovan had employed the services of a friendly young robin to solicit his friend's help. His only concern was that the bird could have befallen one of the many dangers in the forest on its journey.

He scanned the area not only looking for guards, but also for Aaron. He saw what looked like the usual number of sentries. This left him optimistic, because any more than usual might have signaled that they were alerted to his coming.

"There he is," he said to himself, watching his old friend come from around the waterfall.

Donovan was hiding behind a tree so that Aaron would not see him. He would wait until his friend got closer before making his appearance.

"Donovan," called Aaron watching his friend coming out from behind the spruce that was keeping him hidden.

"Ah, you received my message," he replied. "How have you been?"

"Much better for me than for you, I hear," said Aaron.

"I fear that is true," answered Donovan.

"Come, we can speak inside," said Aaron. "You never know who or what might be listening out here."

Walking closer to the entrance of the city, Donovan noticed that only two guards remained. Looking up at the placement of the sun in the sky, he realized it was suppertime. This left only a skeleton crew guarding the gate.

Aaron held out his arm in front of Donovan as a sign to stop behind a tree. A moment later, they heard what sounded like a deer scraping its antlers against a tree. The temptation of venison for supper was too great for the guards, and they left their post to search for the deer.

Donovan couldn't help but wonder if Aaron had solicited the help of the deer.

With the guards distracted, they sneaked behind the waterfall. Donovan stared up at the black granite walls that surrounded the city. It had been a long time since he had seen them, but he was equally amazed whenever he visited.

This place was called Granite Lake even though there was no lake. At one time long ago, the valley in which the town was built was filled with water. This body of water was called Granite Lake.

After the fall of his city, Hugh of Loran had the river that fed the lake diverted. It now flowed from the mountains above the city around the rim and over the edge, creating the falls that hid the entrance.

Hugh did not want to settle his people in another place that could be overrun by an army. In his mind, Granite Lake was impregnable.

Upon entering the library, Aaron took his guest directly to his basement workshop. He had put a CLOSED sign on the door and locked it when he left, so the building was empty.

As soon has he shut the door behind him, he warned, "Meric wants you dead."

"I know," Donovan answered. "Borin came to me and told me everything, but there is something that worries me more."

"What could possibly worry you more than your own death?" asked Aaron.

"The man in the cave is free."

A graven look came to Aaron's face. "We knew it would happen one day," he admitted after a moment of contemplation. "You just never want it to be this day. How did he escape?"

"I don't know," said Donovan. "I saw him in the Benzatine. He had approached the prince in the wilderness and was able to get a hair from his servant. The boy was in my presence when Luther looked into his own Benzatine. He saw me. He is coming for me."

"We should have killed him when we had the chance," said Aaron, concerned for his future as well. "He may now be more dangerous than ever. His need for revenge will drive him."

"I'm afraid you're right," said Donovan.

"Our Chasers say they have spotted an old man roaming about the forest of late," continued Aaron. "They say he has an odd way about him, but he is harmless."

"It must be Luther," replied Donovan. "The prince and his servant described the same old man."

"Yes, I have wondered since the first reports if the man was enlightened," said Aaron. "Not many old men go wandering in the forest without protection."

"Where was he spotted?" asked Donovan.

"Twice near Triopolis, but the one that concerned us the most was downriver from here."

"That must be how he came to Westville," said Donovan. "He must have picked up the remnants of the trail left by the army. The army was tracking two young people who escaped from the king."

"I met your two young people," replied Aaron.

"Kelvin and Elizabeth were here?" asked Donovan, surprised.

"Yes, over a month ago now. They escaped from here as well."

"I didn't know that was possible," replied Donovan, impressed.

"No one has ever done it before," said Aaron. "There is something about those two. I sense that they are in this world for a reason. The girl has the blood in her."

"Yes, she does," answered Donovan.

"Did you train her as Meric suspects?" he asked.

"I taught her the basics," answered Donovan. "I thought it was important for her to know who she really is."

"I understand why you did it," replied Aaron. "Those two have a part to play in the future of our world. Who were her parents?"

"Her father was a common man from Triopolis, but as to who her mother was, well that is a mystery," began Donovan. "She left Triopolis with Elizabeth soon after she gave birth. They were attacked in the forest, and the mother died. Elizabeth was rescued by a nobleman of Westville where he raised her as his own."

"This is very disturbing," contemplated Aaron. "A baby with the Blood hadn't been born in centuries."

"This is why I felt I had to mentor her," replied Donovan. "There were no known female Enlightened left to mother her. So, how did she come into the world, and more importantly, why?"

"I agree with you," said Aaron. "I think Meric is shortsighted in his decision. I will help you and her any way I can."

"Luther will be looking for her," warned Donovan. "She is the only other person known to have the Blood. He will want to train her in his way."

"I agree," answered Aaron. "He will want to mentor her just as Arnaud the Black mentored him."

"We cannot let that happen," said Donovan.

"Look around," offered Aaron. "Take anything you need from my armory."

This was not a gallery shown on the regular tour. It was the Enlightened Chasers' armory. Books lined the walls along with various gadgets with specific purposes. Every weapon or tool imaginable for hunting the Enlightened resided in this room.

A walk through the different sections was a walk through the history of the many theories of containing or eliminating the Enlightened. Some relied only on cunning while others were more physical. Each Chaser throughout history had his own way of completing his task.

For example, Dorin's freezing spell, which Donovan used when he first captured Luther, was written in one of these books.

Dorin hunted Enlightened a long time ago, when Chasers also had the Blood of Alemon, making fighting with spells possible. That time had long since vanished as the blood diminished within the ranks of the Chasers. The only Chasers left with the blood in them were Meric and Aaron, and they were no longer active.

Ribald the Red's infamous tools of torture were in a case in the back corner. Called the Red because of his blood lust, Ribald invoked the practice of bloodletting, which he argued weakened the Enlightened, making them easier to control. Most of his contemporaries believed he simply liked the sight of blood and causing physical pain in the Enlightened.

"What is it you need?" asked Aaron, as Donovan looked around the room.

"The freezing spell will not work," he answered. "He will be ready for it this time."

Grimacing as he passed by the case of torture tools, he commented, "I am not as crazy as Ribald!"

"Not many were," replied Aaron, with a smirk.

"I am not quite sure," pondered Donovan. "He is very cunning, and his anger will drive him. I fear my failure to kill him last time will come back to haunt us."

"His retribution will be swift and terrible," agreed Aaron.

"I need the Light of Florin," concluded Donovan. "That is the only weapon that will work on Luther."

"You also need someone to wield it," added Aaron.

"I have Kelvin," he answered. "There is only one place I know to find it. I must go to Luther's prison."

After being escorted through the tunnel and around the waterfall, he was ready to continue his journey. This time Donovan was given a robe to wear over his clothes. He pulled the hood over his head and never looked up at the guards. Because he was with Aaron, the guards did not question him.

Swiftly, he was able to move through the forest on the horse given to him by Aaron. Donovan had been through this forest hundreds of times in his life, so he knew what to avoid and which trails were safe.

He soon picked up a deer trail that began about a mile from the waterfall. Not having any paths that led directly to the city at Granite Lake was one way they kept it secret. Whenever more than a single person left the camp, they were required to take a boat downriver at least a mile to where the trail began. Even the horses had learned how to stand on one of the flat wooden river barges.

The Misty River flowed past Granite Lake and down the mountainside, and emptied into the sea where Midalo once stood. It was named for the thin layer of mist that always seemed to hover just above the water.

The Midaloans believed it was haunted because of the wispy wraith-like creatures they believed lived in the waters of the river. Their legends said that these wraiths were responsible for the disappearance of many riverboats.

There was some truth to their beliefs, as the protectors of Granite Lake would create these images when boats traveled too far up the river. The demonic apparitions were more than enough to cause anyone coming too close to turn back.

A guard post stood five miles from the falls, and that is where these ghostly diversions would begin. If the travelers continued past the wraiths, they would soon be ambushed and killed with all evidence being destroyed, thus creating the legend of the spirits of the Misty River.

The deer path led farther up the mountains, and that is where Donovan headed.

Richard jabbed with his pike, missing his opponent. This was one of the many matches entered into by the men of Westville during a tournament. The matches were based on feats of strength and agility, and were used to showcase one's fighting ability.

Fighting with swords on horseback, pikes on foot, and wrestling were all contested. It was thought that these were the three sports that most resembled battle. It was a requirement of any nobleman in his prime to participate, as Richard was doing today.

This tournament was staged during the ten days of feasting and celebration to honor the king's great victory at Triopolis. Unlike his past victories, the aging king did not take part in the fighting, but it was still considered his victory because it was won with his army.

Richard danced around Tristan, his childhood friend. It is true they were friends growing up, but Richard also hated him for the many defeats he had inflicted on him over the years. It didn't matter what the sport was; Tristan always bested him.

Richard often wished archery would be added to the tournament. Then he would surely beat Tristan in something.

A jab from Tristan landed on his breastplate knocking him backward, a feeler jab and nothing more, designed to see how your opponent would react.

Tristan had the unenviable task of fighting the prince. He had to win because everyone knew he was better, but he had to do it in a way that didn't embarrass the prince. Knowing Richard would one day be king, he wanted to stay in good favor.

It was Richard's turn to jab, and this time it landed on his opponent's left shoulder. Slightly stunned, Tristan backed away.

"Nice one," he said, and he applauded the prince. Proud that he had surprised his friend, Richard struck again, this time hitting him square in the chest.

Round and round they went, exchanging jabs as the crowd cheered each one. A jab from Tristan was off target, and Richard diverted it with his own pike. Driving his opponent's weapon into the ground, the prince slammed his metal armored foot down on top of it. Tristan tried to pull it away, but with Richard's full weight holding it down, the pike wouldn't budge.

An undefended jab with his pike landed on Tristan's shoulder. The sharp point hit directly at the seam of two metal plates piercing his skin and drawing blood. Tristan screamed in agony and the crowd cheered for their prince. Falling to the ground, he grabbed his injured shoulder. As he lay there recovering, he remembered his father's counsel. "Defeat him, but do not embarrass him," he coached.

Now that he had allowed the prince a few blows, he thought only of victory. Crouched over in pain, he waited for his opponent to come closer. As Richard stood over him to see if he had finally defeated his friend, Tristan sprang up like an attacking cat.

In one motion, he grabbed his pike and struck a blow so powerful into the prince's unguarded chest that it sent Richard reeling backward. Before the stumbling prince retreated far enough away, Tristan thrust another powerful jab that landed again on his opponent's chest. The blow sent Richard to the ground in defeat.

Stunned by the move, the crowd stood in silent amazement. Tristan threw down his weapon signaling the end of the match. Medical experts rushed to Richard's aide. It was soon announced to the still silent crowd that Richard was all right. He had merely had the wind knocked out of him.

After recovering from his loss, Richard joined the rest of the nobles in the Great Hall for their midday meal.

"My son," said the king, noticing his arrival. "Oh, my son, the imperfect warrior . . ."

A chuckle from the nobles was mandatory when the king made a joke, but they did not like laughing at the prince. After all, he would be king one day.

"I could never send you to the battlefield because you have never even won a fight in a tournament," joked the king. "It would be like sending you to your death."

Richard, now standing in front of his father, did the only thing he could. He stood there listening to all the ridicule dished out.

At this point, the nobles were no longer laughing and felt very uneasy watching Richard's temper rise. They were very aware, and many of them had witnessed that Richard had inherited his father's temper. He was almost at the breaking point when his father took notice.

Realizing he had taken enough, the king signaled for the music to commence and asked for a cup of wine. Richard didn't move as his temperature boiled and vengeful thoughts about what he would do to the man in front of him filled his head. It was Albert who saved him from an irrational reaction.

"Come on," he said, grabbing his arm and pulling him away.

Albert coaxed his prince and lover out of the Great Hall, knowing he needed some time away from all of the watching eyes. Albert was the only one Richard trusted and the only one who could have pulled him away as he did. If anyone else had tried it, they would have felt the Westville wrath.

They had retreated to the library where Richard stood at the window gazing out into the city, wondering what it would be like to be king. He found himself contemplating his future more and more lately.

It was obvious his father was getting older, and with his reckless style, an accident could happen at any time. He was always hunting or fighting in tournaments, and his body had many scars from his many battles.

"Earlier today, I spoke to the messenger from Triopolis," reported Albert. "Terryn's interrogations have turned up nothing. They do not know where Elizabeth and Kelvin are."

"That could be good or bad," replied Richard. "They could be dead in the forest. They could've been attacked by an animal or fallen off a cliff."

After a moment of reflection, Richard said, "I miss her. If she makes it back here alive, I will apologize for everything I put her through."

Albert listened in silence as his friend struggled with his thoughts. Richard's contemplation was interrupted by a commotion in the hallway.

"Get out of my way!" The king screamed at a servant girl, cleaning a dirty sconce.

Storming into the room, the king paused in surprise. He had expected the room to be empty. He looked at his son and then at Albert. "Of course," he muttered, with contempt. "You are always with him."

"Congratulations, Father, for another victory by your army," offered Richard.

"Yes, but Elizabeth was not there," complained the king.

"I am sure she will be there soon if she isn't already dead," replied Richard, horrified by the thought, but knowing it was what his father wanted to hear.

"You would like that, wouldn't you?" snarled the king, with contempt for his son. "Then you could spend more time with *him*." He jerked his head in Albert's direction. "Why is he here in my presence anyway?"

"Because he is my counselor," replied Richard defiantly.

Richard surprised himself with this bold retort. It was rare for him to take a stand against his father, and it only infuriated the king more.

"Your counselor? I am sick of this! I want to know if the rumors are true."

"What rumors?" asked Richard.

"You know what rumors!" screamed his father. "You and him!"

He was now standing right in front of them with crazed eyes.

Richard looked at Albert and said, "Yes, it is true."

He didn't know what had come over him. He was never this honest and direct with his father. It seemed as if he was becoming his own man at this very moment. The king might have been proud if it was a discussion on a different topic.

The king's temples pulsed and his face reddened with rage. "You are no son of mine!" he screamed.

His rage was uncontrollable, and it was whipping him into a frenzy. "It's your fault!" he accused Albert.

The king rushed toward him, wrapping both hands around his neck. Squeezing, he cursed and blamed the prince's counselor.

"Stop!" yelled Richard. "You're hurting him!"

Pushing Albert closer and closer to the window, the king tightened his grip. Albert was trying to speak, but all he could produce was a gurgling sound as he choked. Still screaming at his father, Richard reached out to pull him off his friend.

The king saw this attempt coming and swung his arm backward to fend off the attack. With one hand firmly around Albert's neck, his other landed on the side of his son's head. Knocked backward and off his feet, Richard fell into a nearby table.

Wiping the blood his father drew from the corner of his mouth, Richard got back to his feet. He was too late.

The king, with both hands again around Albert's neck, pushed him against the window ledge. Albert struggled and swung his arms in desperation, but it was no use. With life leaving his body, he had no energy left to fight. His eyes met Richard's as if to say good-bye.

With one last push, the king lifted his son's lover and pushed him out the window. He watched, wild-eyed and heaving for breath as Albert fell to the ground below.

"No!" yelled Richard.

Without thinking, Richard unsheathed his sword and lunged toward his unsuspecting father. The king turned, and his eyes grew large in surprise as his son thrust his blade into his chest. Richard stared defiantly into his father's eyes as his life faded.

He now felt vindicated for all of the cruelty his father had laid on him. All of the years of torment were finally over. He would never again have to listen to this man tell him he was useless and unworthy of his respect and love.

Richard finally let go of the sword and fell back into a nearby chair exhausted and emotionally tortured from the event.

A maid, having heard the commotion, entered the room and surveyed the scene. Looking at Richard, she bowed and said, "Your Majesty."

Chapter 26

It had been hundreds of years since Donovan looked upon this cave. Here he was, standing at the base of the cliff in which he had once held captive one of the most treacherous Enlightened ever to live.

Even though he had not been here in so many years, he still remembered exactly where every handhold was on the mountain.

Reaching the cave with ease, he entered. The cave did not seem as foul as he remembered, probably because its evil guest was no longer in residence.

Remembering what lay in wait to the right, he turned to the left. Quickly he walked through the turns and to the back wall of the chamber illuminated in green. Reaching the wall, he went straight through the portal to the other side.

He entered the former prison cell of his arch nemesis. Bristling, he looked at the White Lights thinking about the pain they caused. He immediately noticed that a stone was moved.

"That must be how he escaped," he concluded.

Slipping between the rays of white light, he entered the room that held Luther for so many years. The energy from Luther's torment was almost overwhelming. Like a hurricane within Donovan's brain, the memories fought for position.

Winning the battle in his head, he was able to corral the energy so that he could sift through the memories. He was looking for one in particular. "There it is," he said.

It was the energy that formed the memory of Luther's escape. He saw Kelvin, Elizabeth, and the old man in his mind.

"They fell for his deception," he said, disappointed. "I didn't prepare them for this. They wouldn't have been ready anyway."

Donovan was distraught. He didn't understand why he couldn't read this in their minds. "How could they have blocked their intent from me?" he questioned. "I taught Elizabeth how to control her mind, but how did I not see it in Kelvin?"

After thinking on this for a moment, he answered his own question. "Maybe it wasn't their intent to come here. It is unlikely but still possible that they accidentally found Luther."

Looking around the room, he saw nothing of importance—no clues as to what Luther might want to do. He searched for writings on the walls, on paper, and in books, but nothing appeared. Perplexed as to what to do next, he sat in Luther's old chair.

As he sat there, he could feel his enemy's torment—the long days and nights that Luther sat in this chair agonizing over the past. Finally, a strange shiver roused Donovan from his thoughts.

"Now you know the pain you caused me," accused Luther.

He came through the same portal in the wall that Donovan had used, but he would not take a step closer to his old cell. The mere sight of the tiny room made him want to run, but being able to finally confront his enemy kept him there.

"It's been a long time, Donovan," said Luther, spitefully.

"Luther!" spat Donovan. "I am surprised to see you back here. Do you miss it?" He said this with a smirk.

"I knew you would have to see for yourself how I escaped," answered Luther. "To see how I bested the great Donovan! All I needed was patience. I knew eventually some unsuspecting fools would come along and unknowingly help me."

"I only did what was necessary at the time," argued Donovan. "I am sure you agree now that you've had time to reflect."

"Agree with your treachery?" spat Luther. "I don't think so. You deceived me—one of your own kind. I was the only real friend you had in this cursed place!

Instead, you chose to put your faith in those weak, slow–witted, unintelligent men. How has that worked out for you? Have they been as loyal as you expected?"

"They have been good to me and treated me as an equal," answered Donovan, remaining calm.

"You lie!" yelled Luther. "You were shunned and forsaken much like me. You were forced to leave Triopolis and never allowed to return. You have become weak in your time with the unenlightened ones. I can see right into your mind and read every thought."

Donovan knew there was some truth to what he said. He was not as sharp as he once was, but he didn't let that stop him.

He made the first move. He knew he was trapped behind the Stones of Florin and needed to give himself enough room to get out of the cell.

He silently summoned the energy in the air just in front of his enemy. Spinning it, he slowly condensed his ball of invisible energy until it was so dense that it could do nothing but expand. In a matter of seconds, and without a motion from Donovan, the blast of air from this expansion sent Luther flying backward. He only realized what happened when he was lying on his back. The explosion had pushed him back through the portal and into the chamber illuminated in green.

Donovan quickly exited the cell and confidently walked through the portal to continue his attack. This time it was Luther's turn to manipulate the air around his foe.

Donovan's knees buckled under the pressure. He held his hands up trying to push the unseen force up toward the ceiling of the cave. The immense pressure of the air above him threatened to crush every bone in his body as it slowly descended upon him.

It felt as though the cave was crashing down on top of him. Fighting to stay on his feet, his strength finally failed, sending him to his knees. Still fighting, the pressure was now concentrated on his back.

His arms were useless now, as all strength had been sapped from them. He could feel the same thing happening in his back, and he knew that once it gave out, it would be over for him.

Luther watched as his adversary slowly succumbed to the growing invisible weight on top of him. "Your weakness is evident," taunted Luther. "If you had joined me instead of betraying me, this would not be happening. We could have ruled the world together."

On his knees and doubled over almost into a ball, Donovan summoned the last bit of strength in his body. "You will not defeat me!" he screamed.

Rising to his feet and launching his arms up as if throwing off a cloak, his inner strength threw off the great weight on top of him. The reaction from the collision of the colossal forces of the two Enlightened caused an explosion that shook the entire cave.

The energy created from the explosion slammed into the walls causing shards of rock to fly everywhere. In some places, larger pieces of stone broke free from the wall and crashed to the floor. A brief dust cloud filled the cave before disseminating.

The dust allowed Donovan to recover from his struggle, unseen by his enemy. The energy he exerted had drained him physically and mentally. Hunched over, he hoped the cloud would give him enough time to regain his strength.

Energy was precious to the Enlightened. Every time they used their power to control a substance or a living being, it drained them of vital energy. For this reason, they only used their abilities when absolutely necessary. In the case of Donovan, he utilized so much of the essential substance to stay alive that he had little left.

Luther did not rest as Donovan recovered from his fight. With the cloud of dust, he conjured a beast made of large pieces of fallen rock. One by one, the rocks came under his control. Stacked on top of each other, the stones soon resembled a large powerful man.

The rock man towered over both men. It let out a fearsome bellow as it started toward its prey. From his crouched position, Donovan looked on in horror.

The giant picked up a large stone and threw it at its enemy. Donovan easily ducked out of the way letting the rock fly past his head. Now standing, he was ready to do battle. He was able to regain a little energy, but he wondered if it was enough.

He took control of a nearby vine growing up the wall of the cave. It slithered down the wall and across the floor, doing its master's bidding. The stone man didn't see the attack coming. The vine quickly and silently wrapped itself around the beast's ankles.

From the ankles, it moved up its body wrapping it tight. Reaching its neck, Donovan commanded the vine to constrict. The pressure from the squeezing vine completely subdued the giant.

Luther was not deterred. A quick wave of his hand and the vine disintegrated.

Noticing the questioning look on his enemy's face, Luther replied, "I have been training. While you wasted your time with mortals, I was stuck in my cell with nothing to think about but my vengeance on you!"

The stone man gave him no more time to consider his enemy. A large stone arm was racing toward his head. Moving just in time, the stone hand met the rock floor causing the whole cave to tremble.

Drained from his struggle, Donovan didn't know how to defeat his nemesis. The stone man, being directed by Luther, was walking directly toward Donovan.

He picked up rocks with his mind and flung them at his attacker, but they just bounced off. He kept coming, and Donovan was becoming weaker with every attempt. Stumbling, he backed up, but there was nowhere to go.

The stone giant was near enough to grab him. It reached out its large hand groping for its prey. Donovan backpedaled with nowhere to go. A laugh came from Luther as his enemy fell backward through the portal in the wall, tripping on an unseen rock.

The momentum of his backward tumble took Donovan through the unseen doorway and into Luther's old prison cell. In a flash, Luther pressed his attack through the wall. Donovan, now lying flat on his back, had no energy to fight.

The stone man put the white rock back into its cavity, sealing the cell. "I've done it!" yelled Luther in euphoric victory. "No one can stop me now!"

The stone man followed as Luther rushed out of the chamber. As soon as they came through the portal, he waved his hand, and the stone giant crumbled into a heap of rocks on the ground.

***

"There it is!" exclaimed Kelvin, excitedly looking down at his home city of Triopolis.

"It's beautiful," replied Elizabeth, marveling at the bay and the town framed by the Red Mountains.

They stood on the mountaintop as the morning sun rose in the east. It was a glorious sight. For the first time since being washed ashore in a foreign land, Kelvin allowed himself to dream of a heroic return home.

Father will be so proud of me for surviving and finding my way home. Will he throw a feast in my honor?

Kelvin always wanted to make his father proud of him. He was always optimistic, even when faced with the usual uninterested and unimpressed responses from the man he looked up to. The disinterest his father showed never discouraged or defeated Kelvin. He just kept on trying.

Elizabeth had different thoughts as she gazed upon the city below. *What will this new chapter in my life hold? Will I be truly happy here? Will I be welcomed by the people, or will I always be seen as an outsider?*

Many questions would remain unanswered, but only a little while longer.

Seeing the city from a distance, Kelvin could just make out the buildings. They looked more like dark spots than anything else. From here, the destruction caused by the battling armies could not be seen.

"Let's not waste any time," said Elizabeth, and she began to descend the mountain.

Kelvin was glad to see that she was excited about the prospect of her new home. It was only now that he wondered how his father would react to Elizabeth. He wasn't concerned about him not liking her, but she was a foreigner. They had to figure out how to explain where she came from.

The sun was directly overhead as they reached the base of the mountain. "We are making good time," remarked Kelvin. "We have about a day's walk through the forest before reaching the fields that lie at the doorstep of Triopolis."

Biting into her jerky, Elizabeth complained, "I never want to see another piece of dried meat again." Laughing, Kelvin agreed.

"When we arrive, we will have a feast that could only be equaled by those in the Palace of Westville," replied Kelvin, trying to cheer her up and keep both of them positive. He didn't want either of them to think negative thoughts when they were so near the end of their long journey.

"There will be roast chicken and duck, venison with red wine sauce, and fresh vegetables from the gardens, but my favorite is the seafood soup," he explained, his mouth watering at the thought. "It has clams, shrimp, and crabmeat mixed with tomatoes and onions."

"The duck, chicken, and venison sound very good, but I have never eaten anything from the sea," replied Elizabeth. "River and lake fish are good, but I have never tasted clams, shrimp, or crab."

"That's right, I had forgotten that your people do not fish in the sea," said Kelvin. "You are in for a treat. Once you taste it, you will know why I love it so much."

Up and walking again, they trudged through the thick undergrowth of the forest floor. With twigs crunching underfoot, he was less concerned with the noise they made in this forest because he knew it well.

He knew there were no oversized killers like those they had experienced in the valley; just normal-sized animals that were used to living with people and would probably run away at the sound of their feet.

It wasn't until he had a spear inches from his nose that he realized he had miscalculated. Two men with wooden-handled spears appeared before them from behind a nearby tree. Elizabeth immediately recognized their uniforms. The bear claw on their silver breastplates told her they were from Westville. Her spirits sank as she expected death would soon come to her.

The soldiers did not look like she remembered. She was used to seeing them in shiny armor buffed to perfection without so much as a piece of cloth out of place. These men had a disheveled look about them.

Their armor was dirty and dented and smeared with bloodstains that looked like they might have come from their own wounds. Pieces of the metal from their protective skins were bent, and some were missing altogether. The men looked as though they had been to hell and back.

"Who are you?" one of them asked.

Knowing the soldiers were part of the army that was tracking them, they didn't want to tell them they were from Westville. They also weren't sure if Triopolis was the correct answer either. Finally, Kelvin said, "We are travelers."

"Travelers, eh?" one of the soldiers asked skeptically. "Why are you traveling alone this deep in the forest?"

Before they could answer, the armed man said, "It doesn't matter. We will take you to our captain."

"This is bad," whispered Elizabeth to Kelvin. "These soldiers are from Westville. Lord Rosser used to be the captain of the army. We are being taken to whoever replaced him."

Kelvin couldn't focus his mind on an escape. Thoughts of torture and death were the only images in his head now. *I can't believe we came all this way only to be captured so close to the end.*

Walking in front of the soldiers with their spears not a foot from their backs, they marched to their doom.

The army must not be far away, thought Elizabeth. *It has to be a sizable force to be this far from Westville. They would not have sent only a few soldiers all the way out here. Safety in large numbers is generally the thinking of the army's leadership.*

An army that large would surely be loud and difficult to hide. It seems odd that we do not hear any noise other than the birds chirping in the trees.

They walked through a small clearing and came to a grove of trees where they saw more men. The two captives were told to stop. Their captors moved in front of them as a stout man approached.

It's Roland! thought Elizabeth.

"Well, what have we here?" he asked, looking at his princess. Hearing this, Terryn approached.

These two men looked to be in as bad shape as the two who had captured Kelvin and Elizabeth. Roland had a heavy cloth wrapped around his left arm from his wrist to his elbow like a large bandage. Their armor was in disrepair and needed serious attention.

"Princess," Terryn greeted her, with a slight bow.

She returned the greeting thinking how funny it was that even this far out in the wilderness they still found it necessary to maintain court protocol.

"What happened to you?" she asked.

Terryn whispered something to Roland, and after a short conference with the soldiers who had captured them, the four of them were alone.

"Come, sit," Terryn said to Kelvin and Elizabeth, motioning to a log on the ground. They both thanked him and rested their legs, sitting on the not-so-uncomfortable fallen tree.

"You must be Kelvin," said Terryn.

Elizabeth was surprised to see that the arrogant man she once knew now seemed somber and demoralized. She had hated being around him when they were younger because he was such a braggart. Boasting, he would always make his achievements sound so much better than they really were just for attention. It worked with most people, as they talked him up and said he had so much potential, but she had never liked his company. Now he sat in front of her a broken man.

"Your city is in ruin," he said to Kelvin. "It has probably burned to the ground by now."

An astonished look came to Kelvin's face. "What happened?"

"We had taken the city, peacefully," Terryn began. "Controlling it for weeks, everything was calm and intact. The people were happy and content, and all was good. Then came the man they call the bishop."

Hearing his name made Kelvin cringe. It was strange hearing another man talk about him. For the many months he had been away, thoughts of revenge had filled Kelvin's head—revenge for what the bishop did to his father, revenge for what he did to Henry, and revenge for what he was doing to Triopolis.

"He and his men surprised us," continued Terryn. "We had no idea anyone in Triopolis had the ability to fight back like he did. They attacked us with explosions and fire like I have never seen."

As he spoke, Terryn stared off into the distance still in shock from his defeat. He relived every moment of the battle in his head, still surprised at the outcome.

"The bishop," spat Kelvin. "That sorcerer of evil."

"Sorcerer, indeed, for what he threw at us was not of this world," replied Terryn. "How can a black powder so easily turn into fire? How can such a small amount take down a whole building?"

"The bishop has always wanted control of Triopolis," said Kelvin. "Some say he ran the city through my father, the assembly chief. And now he has everything he wanted."

"Your father was Carl?" asked Terryn.

"Yes—do you know him?"

"Then I am sorry to tell you he is dead," answered Terryn bluntly.

It took a minute for the news to hit home with Kelvin. Once it did, he was surprised that he did not weep. The man he had looked up to his whole life was gone, and he felt nothing.

Elizabeth slid closer to comfort him.

"He was a good man, but he was not a very attentive father," said Kelvin. "We lived in the same house, and I idolized him as the leader of our people, but I am now able to admit that he did not love me the same way I loved him."

Elizabeth's first thought was that the daily life-and-death struggle since leaving Westville had hardened his emotions, but this couldn't be true because he was able to express his feelings for her. Knowing it wasn't easy for him to admit this about his father, she sat by him with her arm around his shoulders.

"You should know that your father understood his failures toward you before he died," said Terryn. "With his last words, he confessed to his gods his shortcomings as a father."

Terryn felt good about himself for sharing this information, and hoped that it would help Kelvin deal with his loss. It was one little bright spot in his otherwise bleak future.

"How did he die?" asked Kelvin.

"He died by my hand," answered Terryn truthfully. "He attacked me, and I had to defend myself. He did say something strange, though. He said the bishop was controlling his mind. I don't understand what he meant by that."

Kelvin looked at Elizabeth understanding what Terryn was saying but not wanting him to know what it meant. The quick glance went unnoticed by the now slow-witted captain.

"The king wants me to return you for your trial," said Terryn, changing the subject. "He blames you for my uncle's murder."

"And who do you blame?" Elizabeth asked.

"I don't know," he answered. "I believe when you are in a profession such as this, you have to understand that death can come any day."

Amazing how a lost battle can completely change a man, she mused with wry observation. *He was so arrogant and confident, and now he just seems worn out and weary.*

"If I brought you back to Westville, the king would be happy," he continued. "I will never be happy after the disaster at Triopolis. Who knows, I might be hanged when I return for the army I lost here."

Sadness and disappointment gripped him. "All those men, gone," he lamented. "I don't deserve to live."

Noticing the bottle he kept drinking from, they assumed the ale was probably making him more emotional than he usually was. Elizabeth decided to push her advantage.

"Terryn, please set us free," she begged. "I can tell you don't believe that we were involved in Lord Rosser's death, and we would only slow you down on your journey home."

"There is truth in what you say," he replied. "I already feel the wrath of the king. The army's entire mounted division is lost, and I am to blame. And blame me he will."

The tormented captain continued to lament his lost army while Elizabeth had other thoughts. She could hear the words in her mind before he spoke them. It was like two voices in her head, her own and another speaking his words.

Was I controlling his thoughts? she wondered. *Donovan spoke of this being an ability of the Enlightened. Is that what I just did?* Then she heard the words she wished for in her mind.

"You may go free, for I do not think we will survive the journey home anyway," commanded Terryn. "Now go and leave me to the wolves, for it is what I deserve."

The once formidable military commander didn't even rise as Kelvin and Elizabeth walked away from his presence.

Chapter 27

T he next morning came earlier than most. Sleep had been difficult to find during the night with the anticipation of what could happen that day. Kelvin was excited to be home, but his eagerness was tempered a little by the news from Terryn.

Could the bishop really have destroyed the whole town? Is it really true? If it is, how many people survived?

Elizabeth was still amazed that Terryn let them go. The humility of his lost battle had changed him, and for that she was grateful. His moment of charity had saved them from an unpleasant reunion with the king.

They ate and were on their feet, ready to go quickly this morning. Motivation was high with the end so near.

The first stop was the river to fill their water skins. With his knowledge of this land, Kelvin knew the river was only a short walk away.

Reaching it, he crouched down to the water and dunked the first leather container under the surface. Only a thin strip of sand bordered the river here. Roughly five feet of riverbank separated them from the forest.

Seeing the last of the air bubbles escape the container, he knew it was full and lifted it out. Putting the cork back in the top to seal it, he was ready for the next one.

Without looking, he handed the full skin to Elizabeth who was standing behind him. When she didn't take it and give him the empty one, he turned to see why. She was staring wide-eyed into the river.

"What is it?" he asked, not seeing anything.

Pointing, she said, "I thought I saw something move over there."

She was pointing at a large tree overhanging the river's edge not far downriver from where they stood. The tree hid whatever she saw, but they watched intently anyway. It wasn't long before the object showed itself.

"It's a boat!" whispered Kelvin loudly, trying to be as quiet as possible. "Run!"

Both stumbling, they made a hasty retreat to the forest.

They watched, camouflaged by a small pine tree that was just tall enough to hide their heads as they stood behind it. Peeking around the side of the tree, they could just see the tip of the bow of the boat bobbing on the water.

It hadn't moved farther down the river from the moment Elizabeth first spotted it, and now they saw why. The small narrow boat was being held in place by the tree. The long wooden tentacles of the tree had ahold of it as it fought to continue its voyage.

Kelvin noticed the breeze was stiffening causing the water to be choppy and the current swift. The boat undulated on top of the water fighting the tree for its freedom.

"I don't see anyone, yet," whispered Kelvin. "I would think we would hear them trying to get the boat out of the tree."

"It doesn't look like anyone is controlling the boat," she replied. "It might be empty."

With a strong gust of wind, the boat broke its bonds and floated into full view. They saw that Elizabeth was correct—the boat was empty. Jumping out from behind the tree, they ran toward the river and the boat that had beached itself on the riverbank.

Elizabeth was the first to reach it and confirm that it was empty. Looking in all directions, they realized they were indeed alone. The boat seemed to belong to no one.

"This would make the trip a lot faster," commented Kelvin. "And look, the oars are still in it! I can't believe it. We finally have some good luck!"

Not wasting any time, they hopped in and followed the river's current south toward Triopolis.

Traveling by water was a much easier task than trudging through the thick vegetation of the forest. Kelvin worked the oar in the back while Elizabeth sat in the front rowing on the opposite side.

Kelvin couldn't help but think of Henry. The last time he was in a boat, they were together. He thought it might be weird being on the water without his old friend, but having Elizabeth by his side kept him from getting emotional.

"There are rapids ahead," said Kelvin. "When we get there, I will switch spots with you so I can be in the front. That way I can steer us clear of any rocks."

His old fishing partner left his mind as he thought about the dangerous rapids fast approaching. Unfortunately, these rapids brought thoughts of his brother to his mind.

"I have not been this far up the river since my brother died," commented Kelvin. "It all happened in these rapids we are about to cross."

Noticing the scare he gave Elizabeth, he said, "Oh, don't worry, we will be fine. The accident happened because we were young and couldn't control the boat. It was the first time I had taken a boat through rough water, so I had no experience. I am confident that we will be fine."

Elizabeth wasn't completely convinced, but she had no choice but to trust his abilities. The choppy water was quickly approaching, and they were out of time to consider the danger.

Kelvin switched places with Elizabeth as they had discussed, and he was now in the bow of the boat. This was only the second time he had navigated through river rapids, and the first was the unsuccessful experience with his brother. He did, however, have a lot of experience steering a boat through rough seas, and he would need to draw on every bit of that experience now.

Holding his oar straight down in the water, the boat made a sharp turn avoiding the first large boulder they came to.

As they moved past it, Kelvin reached out his oar and gave a little shove against the rock to propel the boat away from it. By doing this, they missed the second big rock sticking out of the water.

Elizabeth sat and watched nervously as Kelvin steered through the danger. Holding on tight, she tried to think about less dangerous activities. The boat bouncing on the rough water and the occasional bump into a submerged rock made controlling her thoughts difficult. Then an overwhelming memory of this place overtook her.

She watched as the two young boys crashed against the rocks in their boat. Recognizing the position of the stone obstacles in the water, she knew she was seeing a flashback of an event that happened in this very spot.

"Kelvin!" screamed the younger boy, as the canoe veered off course. Elizabeth could see trouble coming in the form of a large dip in the river. She tried to yell but couldn't. She knew it was only a memory, but it seemed so real.

The young Kelvin tried to keep the canoe straight as they fumbled through the churning river. Using the oar in the water and trying to direct the boat by pushing off the rocks on either side was futile in the powerful current.

The boat continued to turn horizontally despite Kelvin's efforts to keep it straight. He wasn't strong enough to fight the raging water, but he tried to anyway. It was when his oar shattered against a rock that he lost all control.

The canoe spun sideways just as it reached the dip in the river. It went over the edge and careened down the slope. Reaching the bottom, it landed on its side, throwing its two passengers into the water.

In her mind, Elizabeth was then taken under the water to see what happened next. She watched as Kelvin fought to free his little brother. The boy's leg was stuck beneath a large rock that had fallen on him. It wasn't long before he stopped moving and Kelvin returned to the surface.

She broke from her vision just in time to see a large rock looming directly in their path.

"We're moving too fast!" Kelvin yelled.

Putting his oar straight down into the water, he tried to slow their descent down the river. He moved from one side of the boat to the other with the paddle trying to keep it from turning horizontal in the water. It was a long time ago, but he still remembered his fatal mistake.

"It's not working! We're still going too fast!" he yelled, as the boat slipped over the edge and down the slope—the same slope that bested him when he was younger.

He fought with the boat to keep it from turning as it had the last time he was here. This time, being much older and stronger, he was successful.

Crashing into the bottom, the bow went straight down into the water before popping back up. Kelvin was drenched and water now sloshed back and forth in the bottom of the boat. In the back, Elizabeth held on for her life.

Just as the bow of the boat emerged from the water, they slammed into a large rock. The raging water pushed the boat onto the side of the rock. They were now teetering on the steep slope of the boulder. Looking to their left, they saw nothing but water as it threatened to spill over the edge of the boat. Leaning to their right, they tried to keep from rolling over.

Not stopping, the current continued to do as it wished with the small wooden boat. It flung them from side to side with Kelvin using his oar to fight off the rocks. As they came close, he reached out with the oar, using it to push away from the oncoming boulders.

The fierce water seemed to win when they felt a bone-jarring crash that caused them both to lunge forward. Kelvin hadn't seen the submerged reef while he tangled with the rocks that were visible.

Luckily, they hit head on, and the rock struck the boat directly in the center of the bow where it was the strongest. Bouncing off, the boat and crew were disoriented. The submerged rock was the last guardian of the rapids, and the boat gently floated away from danger.

Kelvin sighed in relief. "We made it," he pronounced. Elizabeth gave him a watery smile, but for the moment, she was speechless.

They floated downriver on the much calmer water. For the next hour, they followed the current toward Triopolis. This time was a nice respite from their struggle through the rapids and allowed them to eat their last few pieces of jerky.

"We're getting close now," said Kelvin, excitedly. "Look, the forest is turning to fields. These fields border the town, and once we get around that bend up ahead, we will be able to see it."

As they approached the corner in the river, he steered the boat toward the left shore. "The Fletchers' house is close," he said. "We should stop there before getting too close to the city in case Terryn was telling the truth."

"Good idea," she agreed. "He sounded truthful, but you never know."

A wooden pier came into view as they floated around the corner. Kelvin steered the boat toward it and slowed their pace guiding it softly up to the dock. He secured it with a mooring rope that was already attached and wrapped around one of the support poles.

"This doesn't feel right," said Kelvin. "Something's wrong here."

They climbed out of the boat and onto the pier, and that's when he saw what was wrong. "The Fletchers' land is ruined!" he exclaimed.

The fields that Kelvin had picked cabbage and carrots and corn in as a child were destroyed. They looked as though they had been trampled by a thousand charging bulls.

He gasped upon seeing the house in full view. The structure had been ravaged. Half of the roof had collapsed, and there were holes in the section that remained. Wooden beams and remnants of the walls were strewn about, and the glass had been shattered in every remaining window.

"How could Terryn do such a thing to an innocent farmer?" commented Elizabeth, stunned by the devastation.

Kelvin now started to think the worst about his homeland after witnessing the wreckage of the house of a man who sat in the Assembly. Kevin Fletcher was the leader of the farmers, and now he had no crops.

This was the first time Kelvin had made this walk in silence. The sound of the Fletcher children laughing and singing usually greeted visitors, but not one peep was heard on this day.

The closer they got to what was left of the house, the worse it looked. It was nothing more than an uninhabitable pile of rubble.

"Kelvin?" said a familiar voice that he had not heard in a long time.

"Yes," he replied, looking around to see who was speaking.

Tristan Fletcher, Kevin's eldest son, emerged from the rubble. They exchanged pleasantries, and Kelvin introduced Elizabeth.

Tristan was a tall, skinny young man of roughly sixteen. He had long, brown hair and looked to be growing his first beard. Even though he was thin, he was deceptively strong. One fall, Kelvin helped the Fletchers with their harvest. Kelvin remembered how Tristan had carried and pulled more in a wagon than men five and ten years older than he was.

"Where is your father?" he asked.

"We should go inside," said Tristan. "Anyone could be listening out here, and it would be best for you not to be seen."

Kelvin wondered what they had gotten themselves into as he followed the young man into what used to be his house.

A path had been cleared through the fallen beams and broken furniture. They began where the front door once was and wound around mangled wood planks and debris, ending at the stairs to the cellar. Descending below ground, they saw where the Fletchers now lived.

The young ones were playing as if nothing had happened, and the sounds of children's frivolity filled the air. It was a much more pleasing sound than the deathly silence above. Seeing Tristan's mother, Beth, he asked, "Where is your husband?"

"He's gone," she replied. "They killed him and destroyed our home."

Mrs. Fletcher was surprisingly unemotional in her response. She had mourned her loss for days, but her tears dried when her youngest daughter was almost trampled by horses ridden by the bishop's men. She then realized that she had her children to live for.

"The army?" asked Elizabeth, feeling like it was her fault because the army had come here looking for her.

"The bishop," answered Tristan, with anger in his voice. "He controls everything now."

"Why would the bishop kill your father?" asked Kelvin.

"Things are much different here than when you left," answered Tristan. "The bishop is not the same man he once was. He came to us soon after the battle and gave my father an ultimatum. Vote for him or else. My father, of course, supported William Ward for assembly chief because he was the one who defeated the invading army."

"So, William Ward fought off the army?" asked Kelvin.

"Well, that's what the people thought," answered Tristan. "The bishop wanted to be voted in as leader so the people would know that he was the Assembly's choice. He knew if he didn't have the full support of the Assembly, his leadership would be questioned, and he could be the target of rebellion."

"My husband was so set in his beliefs," remarked Beth. "He could not be persuaded to change his mind, even when it meant death."

"When he gave his final answer after many threats, the bishop lost his patience," continued Tristan. "He nodded to his man Baldwin, who took over the negotiation. His action was swift. Right in front of the entire family, Baldwin ran him through with the long sword at his side."

Kelvin and Elizabeth gasped in shock.

"He didn't have to do it in front of the little ones and Mother," lamented Tristan. "They could have taken him outside instead of putting them through that. He said he wanted us to see what happened to those who weren't loyal to him. I knew it was directed toward me, since I was now the head of the family."

Elizabeth looked at Beth sympathetically, wondering how she could cope with such horror. The children continued with their games seemingly unaware of the conversation between the adults.

"After killing my father, he demanded that I give the family vote to him," explained Tristan. "I had no choice but to give him what he wanted. As they were leaving, the bishop said he was going to give me something to remember my promise. That's when they set the house on fire."

"I am sorry," said Kelvin. "I feel in some way responsible for the bishop since it was my father who allowed him to gain power."

"You cannot hold yourself responsible for the actions of your father," replied Beth. "It is the same thing I tell my son."

Changing the subject, she said, "It's getting late, and you must be hungry. I will prepare dinner."

While Mrs. Fletcher worked in her makeshift kitchen, Kelvin and Elizabeth stepped outside to survey the landscape. It was late in the day, but the sun had not yet set. In the devastated fields, they could see patches where Tristan had begun to plant new crops.

Off in the distance, Triopolis could be seen. It looked tranquil from here, and they could not see any damage. This was due to the distance and the fact that most of the fighting had occurred near the city center leaving many of the outer buildings undisturbed.

"What will we do once we get in?" asked Elizabeth, gazing upon the city.

"I don't know," he answered. "I have spent this whole time trying to get back here without a thought of what I would do once I returned."

"We have to do something about the bishop," she said. "He sounds like a loathsome creature. He has done horrible things to these people."

"I agree," he replied. "I want to free my people from him."

"But how can we defeat such a powerful man?" she asked. "After all we have learned about the Enlightened, I don't think I am ready to confront him."

"We have to get into the basement of Town Hall," he replied. "Maybe we will find something to use against him in Luther's hidden chamber."

Just then, Tristan arrived to inform them dinner was ready.

Sitting at an old table that was saved from the fire, they breathed in the wonderful smell of the stew Mrs. Fletcher prepared. It had a thick base and was loaded with large chunks of beef, carrots, and potatoes.

There was little conversation as the two guests scarfed down their bowls of the tasteful mixture of meat and vegetables. It was only after their hostess refilled their bowls that they slowed down.

"We must get into the city," declared Kelvin. "What is the best way?"

"You are unwise to go there," answered Mrs. Fletcher. "For your safety, I would turn around and leave this place. The bishop will not be happy to find out that Carl Drake's son is still alive."

"I have to do something," replied Kelvin. "I have many reasons to want revenge on the bishop."

With this comment, he looked at Elizabeth, and she knew what he meant. Not only did he want to save his people, but he also wanted to do it for his friend and father figure, Henry.

"If you must, the river is the safest way to enter the city," said Tristan. "All roads and gates are watched closely, but they have not yet blocked the river."

"Then that is the route we will take," said Kelvin.

Chapter 28

Untying the mooring rope, Kelvin flung it on the pier. He used the oar to push away from the wooden structure and propel the boat out into the river. They were on their way to Triopolis.

After dinner with the Fletchers, they found a quiet corner in the cellar to rest. It was only because of the lack of rest the night before that they were able to close their eyes and sleep. For Kelvin, the excitement of returning home was almost overwhelming, and for Elizabeth, it was the anxiety of a new home.

Without help, they woke in the very early hours of the morning and quietly left the Fletchers' home.

The half-moon in the clear night sky gave off just enough light to navigate the river. The current was strong enough that the use of oars was seldom needed. This fit in perfectly with the need for silence.

Approaching the city, Kelvin saw that Tristan was correct. There was nothing blocking them from floating right into town. They did not see any guards outside of the large wooden arch that spanned the width of the waterway, but Kelvin assumed they would be posted on the other side.

"We should hide," he suggested, and they both got on their hands and knees on the bottom of the boat.

With their heads just above the side rail of the boat, they slowly drifted under the arch. As Kelvin suspected, two guards were stationed on either side of the river inside the archway.

Unable to use the oars, they couldn't direct the boat. They were at the mercy of the river, and it was slowly taking them to the left. Nervously, they wondered what they would do if the guards saw them.

The two guards on the right had their backs to the water and looked and sounded as if they were playing a dice game. The two on the left were quiet. As the boat moved closer, they saw why. The two men were asleep.

They breathed a sigh of relief at their luck. Trusting the river, it continued to take them to the safer side. As they moved past the guards, the first signs of morning light appeared in the sky.

"I don't want to take any more chances," whispered Kelvin. "We have to get out of the boat." Elizabeth nodded her agreement, and Kelvin guided the boat to shore.

He brought the boat up to a wooden wharf that was used by the boat club. Racing small boats on the river was a very popular sport in Triopolis, and this was where the races usually began. The wharf was where club members left their boats, so it would be easy to hide their boat among the others.

They quickly exited the boat and crossed the wharf. With the sun coming up, Kelvin wanted to get away from the river. The waterway was used heavily in the transportation of goods within the city and from the fields and forests upstream. It would soon be teeming with watercraft, making it impossible for them to go unseen.

For the first time on their long journey, Kelvin knew exactly where he was going. The walk to Town Hall was only about five blocks, but today it would be ten. They couldn't walk directly there because those streets were too well traveled.

It was through back alleys and a less savory part of town that Kelvin took them. This was not what he had envisioned when he imagined showing Elizabeth what a great place Triopolis was.

The sun had risen high enough to fill the sky with morning light, but it did not reach into these alleys. This was the reason Kelvin came this way. They would have to endure the smell of a disgusting mixture of rotting trash and night soil, both of which were tossed into these alleys.

Kelvin was admittedly relieved when they finally came through the run-down neighborhood. It is not somewhere he would have taken Elizabeth at any other time. Most of the vagrants were still sleeping off the previous night's drink at this early hour, so he thought they would get through unscathed.

Coming out of the alley, they could see Town Hall. A quick walk through the market and they would reach their destination. Most of the shops were not yet open, making this part of the journey much easier than Kelvin originally anticipated.

Empty tables lined the street waiting to be filled with the fruits, vegetables, meats, and other wares that would be sold today. The morning sun had not yet dried the dew that had accumulated on the canvas canopies covering the tables.

The few merchants who had arrived early to set up their shops were easy to avoid. Their main concern was preparing for the day's business and not two people walking down the street. Most didn't even look up as they walked by.

Reaching the end of the market, they saw the full impact of the battle on Triopolis. Town Hall still stood, but many of the surrounding structures were destroyed. Fire had gutted them, leaving portions of walls still standing as the only remnants of the once proud city center.

"It's an eerie feeling seeing this," lamented Kelvin, looking at the hollowed-out buildings. "It used to be so beautiful here."

"It will be again," consoled Elizabeth, holding onto his arm for comfort.

They walked through what used to be a garden that lay between the market and Town Hall. It no longer resembled a garden, though. There was nothing green and nothing growing in what had been a lovely green space where people would sit and have a picnic.

It was not an easy walk in the garden for Kelvin and Elizabeth either. Debris was everywhere. Bricks and chunks of charred wood littered the area. The landscape looked bleak and desolate from the thick layer of ash that covered everything.

They entered Town Hall through the back doorway where a door no longer hung. Two large holes in the frame where the hinges were once attached showed them that the door was removed in anger.

Town Hall was no longer a majestic sight. Even though it still stood, it was far from unscathed. Burn marks and battle scars covered the exterior of the building.

The interior was no better as they slowly made their way into the once impressive structure. Wallpaper was torn and singed. Places where axes and swords missed their targets, instead landing on the walls, dotted the hallway. Paintings were slashed, and there were holes where light fixtures had once been attached. This was no longer a welcoming place of government.

Kelvin remembered the awe he experienced the first time his father brought him into the hall. He must have been six years old. The magnificent paintings of the founders and other heroes from Triopolis's past hung in majestic glory high on the walls. The beautiful depiction of the founding of the city captured on the ceiling of the lobby amazed him. All of these were now tainted by the signs of war.

"It looks deserted," commented Elizabeth.

"That will make it a lot easier to get into the basement and begin our search," replied Kelvin.

The floor was littered with debris from broken furniture, mangled candles, bent metal from the light fixtures, and papers. Sword, pike, and axe wounds covered what was left of the furniture, and there were even some on the floor.

As they made their way across the lobby toward the corridor, the occasional obstacle had to be removed with a slight kick or shove. The larger obstructions couldn't be moved, such as the large oak table turned on its side.

"Used as a shield by the looks of it," commented Kelvin, walking past.

Opening the door to the archives, Kelvin reached for the oil lamp he knew was on the small shelf immediately inside. Not worried about being seen because they were alone, he left the door open.

Rubbing his flint and metal together, he lit the lamp and they descended the unusually long staircase. Quickly and quietly, they moved through the room and behind the secondary wall.

Kelvin noted that the pile of books that guarded the entrance last time he was here was now moved to the left leaving a clear path. This fact told him he was in the right spot. The bishop was still using the room.

Between the two walls, they inched forward with only the lamp to lead the way. Anxiously, they wondered what or whom they would encounter in the chamber.

Elizabeth hadn't been here before and had never met the bishop, but she could feel Kelvin's nervous energy and it put her on edge as well.

Kelvin peeked around the corner into Luther's chamber and was happy to see it empty. Remembering the mistake he made last time, he decided not to light any candles. He might not get away with leaving them burning again if the bishop arrived.

Not having any idea of where to start, they headed for the large table at the back of the room. Reaching it, Kelvin lifted the lamp higher to illuminate the large portrait of Luther.

"Look familiar?" he asked.

"It's Luther," gasped Elizabeth. "He looks much more sinister in this picture than the old man we met in the cave."

"I won't fall for that trick again if an old man shows up," said Kelvin.

"What are we looking for?" she asked, turning away from the painting.

"I don't know," he admitted. "We need something we can use to fight the bishop, whether it's a substance or a spell or a weapon. I thought we could look on the shelves and through his papers, and hopefully we will find something."

They both started by sifting through the documents on the desk. The old papers had obviously been read recently because there wasn't a bit of dust upon them. Not seeing anything on the table, they moved out into the chamber to see what else they could find.

Elizabeth marveled at the vaulted ceiling, but was repulsed by the stone heads of ogres and dragons carved into the walls. The blood dripping from the fangs of the dragons made her cringe in fear.

Walking the length of the room, Kelvin looked at shelves filled with books and papers, as well as small animals and parts of animals preserved in glass jars. As he made his way closer to the entrance, he saw the wooden coffin that he once hid behind. This time the lid was closed and the body hidden.

"That's a relief," commented Kelvin. "I didn't want to see you again."

"There's nothing here that will help us," said Elizabeth, frustrated.

She had taken a candle off a stand near the table and was searching the other side of the room. They both investigated every inch of the chamber, looking for something to aid their cause. Two small flames guided them through the room in the darkness.

The side of the room she searched was cluttered with astronomical gadgets and mineral samples. A few of the ground substances looked to have been used recently.

"Someone has definitely been using what's in these jars, but I don't see any weapons," she said.

It was at that moment a chill ran down her spine. Someone was in the hallway leading to this room. Putting out their flames, they waited silently in the dark. With all nerves and senses on edge, they stood quiet and still.

As the man entered the chamber, his footsteps echoed through the silence. She could just make out his outline, and saw that he was wearing a robe. He walked toward the center of the room and stopped. Smelling the fumes from the recently extinguished flames, he knew he wasn't alone.

In an instant, they were blinded. Every torch and candle in the hall was ablaze. They lined the walls, hung from the ceiling, and stood on pedestals throughout the chamber. The room was now alight as if the ceiling had opened up allowing the sun's rays to fill the cavernous hall.

Elizabeth stumbled backward and fell to the floor. Kelvin was frozen with fear. There was nowhere for him to go, and he was spotted immediately.

"Well, well, if it isn't the prodigal son returned," announced the bishop.

"Bishop." Kelvin practically spat the word in disgust.

"Yes, that's right," he answered. "I took you for dead, Kelvin. I didn't think it possible that you would actually make it back here."

"Well, here I am," he replied obstinately.

Elizabeth sat watching from across the room wondering what she could do to help. Many thoughts were whipping around inside her head, but none of them seemed plausible in her frightened state.

"You are as stubborn as your father was," the bishop replied, with a maniacal laugh. "That is, before I took control of his mind."

The confirmation that his father was being manipulated angered Kelvin even more. He had always thought it was true, but actually hearing it from the bishop's own mouth affected him more than he had expected. His face reddened and his eyes narrowed. Glaring at his enemy, he flexed his fists.

"I see you're angry," taunted the bishop. "Come on, you must have known. You must have seen a difference in your father when it began."

"It was soon after Robert died," remembered Kelvin. "My father used to play games with me and take me fishing and hunting. We were always together laughing and having a good time. He was my best friend. Then he changed toward me. He avoided me and was always too busy to spend time with me."

"When I discovered this chamber, I learned my true powers," explained the bishop. "You and your father were so close that I knew I had to break that bond before I could ever control him. Even as a boy, I could see you were intelligent; you would've caught on to what I was doing to him.

"The person it's happening to never knows. It's always those close to the victim who see. That's why I had to turn him against you first. The accident with your brother was not my doing, but it was perfect timing.

"I used the loss of his youngest son against you. I made him believe it was your fault, that you killed Robert. He never fully believed it, but the seeds of doubt planted in his mind were all I needed."

Kelvin's anger was now boiling over. He wanted to kill the man tormenting him. Veins pulsing and still clenching his fists, he let loose his anger. He lifted his arm as he charged the bishop, but something grabbed his leg.

His enemy had noticed his rage and prepared for his attack. The bishop had summoned the dead man in the coffin to rise, and that was what was holding Kelvin's right ankle.

Looking behind, he couldn't believe his eyes. The half-decayed arm of the dead man gripped his leg and wouldn't let go no matter how much he squirmed.

Crawling out of its box and onto its feet, the dead man released its grip on Kelvin's leg and wrapped both arms around his chest. This held Kelvin in place as the bishop slowly approached with a victorious smirk.

Elizabeth looked on in horror at the possessed cadaver. Her mind was racing as she tried to figure out the best way to help. "Wait!" she yelled, unintentionally.

The bishop, surprised at the second voice, turned and saw Elizabeth across the room. "Ah, you must be the princess everyone is looking for," he concluded, as he advanced toward her.

She scooted backward, searching for an escape, but was stopped by the wall.

"You have nowhere to go!" he exclaimed.

Raising his hand toward a vine peeking through the wall between two bricks, the bishop commanded the plant. Doing its master's bidding, it shot out of the wall and wrapped itself around Elizabeth. She was stuck, unable to move her arms.

The bishop looked into her eyes. Deeper and deeper he tried to penetrate her mind. She wasn't sure how, but she fought him mentally. It was as if her mind was instinctively fighting against the attack.

This is odd, thought the bishop. *Why can't I see inside her head? This has never happened before.*

Elizabeth's eyes grew suddenly foggy, and then they cleared again. The bishop's eyes focused on the scene playing out in hers.

"What is happening?" he said as he looked at her eyes, perplexed. He could see a man lying on the ground. As his view moved closer to the man, he realized the man appeared dead.

The bishop couldn't figure out why, but he was terror-stricken. Just then, the view was directly over the man's face. "It's me," he gasped. "No, no, it's not possible!" he shouted, stumbling backward.

"Who are you?" he screamed. "How did you kill me?"

As she watched the bishop panic, she remembered something the high priest told her when she was a child.

It was at a large gathering of nobles in the Castle Garden. She was around nine years old and had just been pushed down in the dirt by a much larger girl. She screamed, kicked, and scratched at the older girl but was only pushed back to the ground.

In tears, she ran away and bumped into the high priest. He took her aside and used it as a teaching opportunity for his new pupil. "The one who remains calm will always win the fight," he said.

Using this advice now, Elizabeth closed her eyes and breathed deeply. After a few moments, she opened them and her mind had cleared. Looking around the room, she only saw one thing that could defeat the bishop. It was Luther.

Having witnessed the bishop use the dead man to fight for him, she wondered if she could summon the Luther in the painting to fight for her.

Watching the bishop's reaction to Elizabeth, Kelvin squirmed, trying to break free of the dead man's grip. Freeing one arm, he swung back toward his opponent with his elbow. It landed on its stomach, sending it to the floor.

The corpse grabbed Kelvin's leg as he tried to run away. Kelvin retaliated with a kick to its head, but it didn't let go. The second kick had the same result, so Kelvin used all of the force he could muster for his third attempt.

The skull was dislodged from the body, and it flew into the wall behind them. The hand released Kelvin's leg, and he stepped back. Elated, he thought the fight was over, but he was wrong.

The headless body rose and lunged at Kelvin, knocking him to the ground. Rolling around, the two men wrestled for control of the other. First, Kelvin was on top trying to tear the cadaver's arms from their sockets.

The dead man quickly reversed the position and was now on top trying to gouge Kelvin's eyes. The skinless fingers aimed for his eyes as his hands pushed back with all his might.

Occasionally turning back to watch Kelvin's fight with the corpse, Elizabeth stared at the painting of Luther unsure if this was the right thing to do. Looking into his eyes, she concentrated on what she wanted, but her thoughts wavered. Her uncertainty was her undoing.

The skeletal fingers were getting closer to Kelvin's eyes. He fought using every bit of energy he had left. Finally, the dead man relented, but its quick motion caught Kelvin by surprise. It was a trick. The cadaver abandoned its attempt at Kelvin's eyes but now had its bony hands around his neck.

The bishop laughed hysterically at his certain victory. "You will soon be with your father again!" he taunted.

Kelvin was still filled with anger and wanted revenge more than anything, but his strength was failing him. He tried to pry the dead man's fingers from his neck but they wouldn't budge.

Seeing this, Elizabeth knew she was his only hope. If she didn't do something now, he would die. Turning back toward the painting, she tried again. Focusing with extreme determination, she blocked out everything else around her. Her head cleared, and everything went silent except for a light whisper in her mind calling out to Luther.

After what seemed like only a second, she came back to reality. She thought all was lost, watching Kelvin suffer. Turning back to the painting, she saw the most amazing thing happen. Luther had come alive and stepped out of the frame as if it were a doorway.

Elizabeth's mouth hung open in shock, but the bishop was more surprised than she was.

"How is this possible?" he sputtered.

With the bishop's change in focus to Luther, the cadaver's grip on Kelvin's neck loosened. The dead man returned to its lifeless state and lay limp on top of him. For some reason, the body seemed a little more repulsive now than when it was alive. Kelvin quickly rolled it off him.

"Who is controlling you?" the bishop asked Luther. He watched as Kelvin got to his feet, wiping the dust from his clothes.

It can't be him, he thought. *He doesn't have the Blood of Alemon.*

"No one will ever control me again," bellowed Luther.

Luther noticed Elizabeth tied against the wall to his right. "What have you done to my friend?"

"She is my prisoner," answered the bishop, defiantly. "What are you going to do about it? You're a man in a painting."

"You fool!" exclaimed Luther. "I am much more than that!"

He then walked directly to Elizabeth. Running his finger in a line over the coiled vine as if it were a knife, he sliced the restraints in two.

"And now I will deal with you," he spat at the bishop.

He raised his hand to the sculpture of a dragon's head carved into the wall that flanked the painting he came from. After a moment of concentration, the head trembled and its eyes opened. From its position on the wall, a streak of fire shot from its mouth just missing the bishop.

Trying to match his unknowing mentor, the bishop raised his hand to the dragonhead on the other side of the painting. Locked in concentration he tried to make the beast come alive, but nothing happened.

"You may have read my writings and learned some tricks, but you are not enlightened!" Luther laughed in derision.

The bishop, now realizing he was in over his head, headed for the exit. Luther raised his hand and turned the air in front of his fleeing opponent into a solid wall of air. Stunned by the collision with the unseen wall, the bishop fell to the floor.

The heat of another flame from the mouth of the stone dragon brought him back. It hit the floor just to the right of him sending him rolling to his left.

Quickly back on his feet, the bishop scampered toward the side of the room containing the medical specimens and instruments. He knew there was no other way out, but he was looking for something to protect him from the fire-breathing dragon.

Before he reached the table he was running to, he froze in his tracks. Luther had manipulated the air around him to form an invisible cocoon. He was paralyzed from the neck down.

Luther was laughing again. Kelvin and Elizabeth, feeling comfortable that Luther was there to help them, stood behind him.

The bishop tried to look into his eyes. It only took a moment for Luther to realize what his opponent was trying to do. "You cannot control the mind of an Enlightened!" he spat.

Luther entered the bishop's mind. At close range, their eyes were focused on each other.

The bishop was remembering that he could not control Elizabeth's mind either. "Yes, the girl does have the Blood!" Luther confirmed, reading the bishop's thoughts before he could ask the question.

The bishop was growing weaker in his battle with his more powerful opponent. It was too late by the time he realized that Luther was right. His body became tingly all over, and it felt like a tornado was churning in his stomach.

It was in his midsection that Kelvin and Elizabeth first saw the spinning light. A blur of various colors, it spun wildly. Spreading, it soon consumed his entire body. Luther kept his eyes focused on his enemy as the funnel of spinning light devoured the bishop.

Kelvin and Elizabeth looked on with mixed feelings. They were happy that the bishop was gone but worried about the power of the man they had let escape from the cave.

As Luther broke his gaze, the spinning light came to a halt. Only the bishop's brown robe remained as it fluttered into a heap on the floor.

Turning toward his two scared guests, Luther said to Kelvin, "I have helped you, and now we are even."

"Thank you," he answered, but then he was thrown to the floor. Luther had caused the air in front of him to expand at such a speed that it created a small explosion with the concussion knocking Kelvin off his feet. He lay flat on his back, unconscious.

Luther grabbed Elizabeth by the arm and whisked her off into the painting with him. As soon as they were through, the picture returned to normal.

The room was silent while Kelvin was sprawled out on the floor unconscious. Moments later, his eyes flickered. Staring at the ceiling, he took a moment to remember the events leading up to his loss of consciousness.

Sitting up and looking around the room, he called for Elizabeth. With no answer, he turned and looked at the painting on the wall. It was nothing but an empty black canvas. Luther was gone, and Kelvin knew instinctively what had happened to Elizabeth when he saw a piece of her shirt clinging to the frame.

"He tricked us again!" he said, feeling foolish.

Gathering his strength and standing to his feet, Kelvin raised his fist and proclaimed, "I will do everything in my power to find you, Elizabeth!"

About the Author

Greg Johnson finds inspiration for his writing through his love for travel, history, and adventure stories. He is currently continuing the saga of Kelvin and Elizabeth as they discover the world beyond the red mountains. Greg lives in Chicago with his wife, stepson, and their cat.

CPSIA information can be obtained at www.ICGtesting.com
Printed in the USA
LVOW10s1907030615

441064LV00001B/1/P